KISS AND SPELL

T0383978

ALSO BY CELESTINE MARTIN

Witchful Thinking

KISS AND SPELL

Celestine Martin

FOREVER

New York   Boston

This book is a work of fiction. Names, characters, places, and incidents are the product of the author's imagination or are used fictitiously. Any resemblance to actual events, locales, or persons, living or dead, is coincidental.

Copyright © 2023 by Sharae Allen

Cover design and illustration by Selina Saldívar. Cover copyright © 2023 by Hachette Book Group, Inc.

Hachette Book Group supports the right to free expression and the value of copyright. The purpose of copyright is to encourage writers and artists to produce the creative works that enrich our culture.

The scanning, uploading, and distribution of this book without permission is a theft of the author's intellectual property. If you would like permission to use material from the book (other than for review purposes), please contact permissions@hbgusa.com. Thank you for your support of the author's rights.

Forever
Hachette Book Group
1290 Avenue of the Americas, New York, NY 10104
read-forever.com
twitter.com/readforeverpub

First Edition: September 2023

Forever is an imprint of Grand Central Publishing. The Forever name and logo are trademarks of Hachette Book Group, Inc.

The publisher is not responsible for websites (or their content) that are not owned by the publisher.

Forever books may be purchased in bulk for business, educational, or promotional use. For information, please contact your local bookseller or the Hachette Book Group Special Markets Department at special.markets@hbgusa.com.

Library of Congress Cataloging-in-Publication Data

Names: Martin, Celestine, author.
Title: Kiss and spell / Celestine Martin.
Description: First edition. | New York ; Boston : Forever, 2023. | Series: Elemental love
Identifiers: LCCN 2023012597 | ISBN 9781538738085 (trade paperback) | ISBN 9781538738092 (ebook)
Subjects: LCGFT: Fantasy fiction. | Romance fiction. | Novels.
Classification: LCC PS3613.A77779 K57 2023 | DDC 813/.6—dc23
eng/20230316
LC record available at https://lccn.loc.gov/2023012597

ISBNs: 9781538738085 (trade paperback), 9781538738092 (ebook)

Printed in the United States of America

LSC-C

Printing 1, 2023

For Trish
I'll always remember you with faery wings on Halloween

Acknowledgments

This book took a tiny part of my soul in the best way.

I'm extremely grateful to my agent, Lauren Bieker, who encouraged me through many phone calls and texts. You've got the heart of a lion and the sweetest soul.

To my editor, Madeleine Colavita, thank you for being kind and honest with my work. You trusted me to find my path even when this book was a glitter-filled tangled ball. You are gifted at what you do and deserve every wonderful thing.

I'm sending a huge special thanks to the production team at Forever, with a special shoutout to Anjuli Johnson and copy editor Carrie Andrews. You are the sprinkles on the cupcake that is this book.

Words cannot express my gratitude to the readers, bloggers, reviewers, booksellers, and librarians who shared, retweeted, and celebrated my debut novel. I'm fortunate to share my stories with you and I don't take this honor lightly.

This book would not exist without the love and support of my family, friends, and writing community. Real talk, it took a while to find this story, but because I'm so lucky to be surrounded by people who believed in me wholeheartedly, I found the story I wanted to tell. Thank you to those who cheered me on all this time. Mama, Brother, and Papa, thank you for nurturing me all these years.

Love to my husband, Matthew, one of the best people in the solar system, partner to me, and father to our Poppyseed. To my Poppyseed, thank you for being a bundle of giggles, kisses, and giving me the best sticky hugs in the world. You will always have my heart and love.

I'm deeply indebted to Emily, my beta reader and best friend, who continually humored my random texts and ideas in the middle of the day and night. I can't believe a friend like you exists and I'm lucky that I found you. One day we will get that spa weekend and order room service.

Thank you to Frankie, Meredith, and Susan, my fabulous working Mamas who checked in and helped me navigate the first years of motherhood. I'm blessed to have you all in my life.

To Soraia, my friend. Thank you for being a source of joy, happy mail, and crochet gifts. You are glitter in human form.

Thank you to Chris for being a pleasant and good-natured person and being welcome support. I owe you dinner and a big old hug!

Finally, to Patricia "Trish," my poetry-quoting, karaoke-singing, faerie-loving best friend, whose last text to me was about this book. I finished it. I miss you something awful and I love you. Thank you for giving me wings so that I can soar. This story is for you.

KISS AND SPELL

Freya Grove Press.com
Jilted Bride Turns Heartache to Hope
By Minerva Shaw
Staff Writer

August 30

A Freya Grove bride was recently stood up by her groom this past weekend. Once it became clear to Ursula Caraway, age 30, that she couldn't get her money refunded for the lavish reception, she decided to invite members of the local community center Hopeful Heart to enjoy the food and live entertainment.

Ursula was quick to explain her reasoning: "I've volunteered with Hopeful Heart in the past. It was no question that I'd donate the reception to them. They host important programs and events for the Grove."

Ursula, who works as a consultant at the local mystic shop Light as a Feather in downtown Freya Grove, was set to marry Lincoln Walker, a technology entrepreneur and Mayor Des'ree Walker's son. When Mr. Walker called off their wedding the day of the ceremony, Ms. Caraway didn't hesitate to turn her heartache into a moment of hope. She donated the wedding flowers to a local nursing home and invited current members and staff of Hopeful Heart Community Center to the reception at the world-famous Berkeley Hotel. Children danced with their parents to the live band, enjoyed a gourmet meal, and ate cake, all courtesy of the bride. Gifts were scheduled to be returned after the event took place. The *Press* reached out to the groom repeatedly for comment but received no response.

Guests were grateful to Ms. Caraway and spoke kindly about the former bride-to-be. "I hope that young lady gets her happy ending one day," said one guest, who wished to remain anonymous. Ms. Caraway requests that any readers who feel moved by her actions consider supporting Hopeful Heart with a monetary donation or volunteer their time. Volunteers are always needed for serving food, chaperoning dances, and running the monthly Bingo Night. When asked about her next steps, Ms. Caraway told us: "I lost my crystal ball recently, so I don't know what the future holds. Maybe there's room for a little magic in my life."

March

THIS MONTH'S BIRTHSTONE: AQUAMARINE

Aquamarine, from the Latin for "seawater," is believed to protect seafarers and seafolk. This stone is thought to bring intellect and personal happiness.

Chapter One

Today had the potential to be a stressful adventure.

First, Ursula slept through both her alarms. Some-how, she set her phone to silent and then forgot to turn the sound back on.

Second, as she rushed to finish breakfast, she spilled her peanut butter and chia oats all over her work clothes. Then, Ursula ended up splashing coffee mixed with flavored creamer on her backup outfit.

"Why?" she squeaked.

No one wanted to have their future read by someone who smelled of dried coffee and holiday cookies. But the only clean clothes she had available were her pajamas or the special events costume. Ursula shuddered. It was reserved for Renaissance fairs or moon markets when she was hired to read fortunes during the summer. No matter how many times she stuffed the pockets with cleansing parsley and lavender, it still had this odd vibe attached.

Like a pack a duffel bag and run away with a traveling carnival type of vibe.

She checked the time on her phone and groaned. The shop opened in less than five minutes. It was either wear the costume and be a little late or take the day off and wash all her dirty clothes, and she needed money to hit her checking account, like yesterday. She had plants to feed and weekly groceries to buy. There was only one choice. Ursula dug out the costume from her closet and changed quickly. It smelled of stale roses and was covered in chunky glitter. She gave the outfit a quick, generous spray of homemade fabric freshener in the bathroom. Now, it smelled like old flowers with a hint of lemon and eucalyptus. *Fantastic.*

She popped in her contacts and left her glasses by her bed-side table. Ursula gave her reflection in the mirror one last look and let out a huff. All she saw was a hot, yet cute mess draped in a paisley print headband, too-tight peasant blouse, and floral print maxi skirt.

"Mirror, mirror on the wall, who's the foxiest of them all?" she muttered.

Ursula fought the urge to yank off the outfit and get back into bed.

Instead, she went all the way and completed the look with a faux leather brown bootie.

Boho vibes all day.

Even though she was in a hurry, Ursula couldn't forget about tending to her plants. She went out the bedroom and over to the window that looked out on the street. Sunshine flittered down upon the row of overgrown plants and raw crystals that were set up on the sill.

Ursula quickly watered them and did a quick twirl. "How do I look, y'all?"

The plants' leaves seemed to swivel away from her general direction.

"Well, at least I think I look cute," she said with a smirk.

She grabbed her keys, purse, and phone and ran out of the apartment. Thankfully, Ursula only had to report downstairs for work since she lived right above the shop. Despite the convenient location, she found herself running late at least once a week. Maybe it was time for a career change. Ursula wouldn't mind being stuck in an office making copies or typing in data if it meant she'd be left alone to wallow in her grumpiness.

She quit her consultancy job last fall because she couldn't trust herself to make good choices anymore. The nonwedding didn't merely damage her confidence; it crushed it into fine dust. During one memorable office lunch, Ursula's co-worker had innocently asked her whether she wanted guacamole or salsa on her taco salad. Unable to pick a topping after five minutes, Ursula quietly took her salad, went to her desk, and wrote a letter of resignation.

She had messed up her own life; she didn't want to hurt her clients with her indecision.

It was ridiculously difficult to get a new job, especially after future employers could search her name and discover the entire wedding drama. She had an online footprint the size of an asteroid crater. The *Freya Grove Press* article was the first thing that popped up when anyone searched her online. Search the phrases *big-hearted bride* or *bad luck bride* and a picture of her frowning in that bohemian antique lace dress popped up like a relentless horror movie villain haunting her. Jobs dried up faster than cotton underwear in a hot dryer once people learned the whole story.

So, for six to eight hours a day, Ursula sat in the front window of Mama's psychic shop perched over Great-Aunt Lulu's rediscovered crystal ball. She was on full display for the entire town and felt like a circus sideshow, a carnival barker's brassy, drawling voice ringing in her brain. *Step right up, step right up! Come view the psychic who couldn't predict her own future! Her groom jilted her with a text! Marvel at her gullibility! Bring your funnel cake!*

At this point, Ursula just existed in a constant state of embarrassment that kept her off balance, like she was wearing her shoes on the wrong feet. She thought about leaving town and starting over, but she only ever got as far as Toms River before she turned and went back.

Caraways didn't run. Ever. The Grove was home, and she wasn't going to leave in shame.

Enough with the past. Her present waited for her to show up and work.

The door chime jangled as Ursula entered Light as a Feather. Deep purple curtains hung from the high ceiling to the floor, giving the shop the intended mystic vibes. Bone-white shelves were filled with various items—large books, sparkly amethyst geodes, and tall pillar candles—used to aid customers in tapping into their natural intuition. There were wooden bowls filled with different types of tumbled crystals from amazonite to rose quartz in the glass display. A reading table tucked under the front window was decorated with a printed cloth and artfully set divination tools. A purple beaded curtain led to a storage space/back room and office. The music that played overhead was a blend of lyrical humming and bouncing flutes. Cone incense burned on the wood counter, filling the space with the distinctive smell of fresh earth. One sniff instantly eased any frantic energy Ursula felt from this morning's chaos.

Mama, the one and only Ms. Niesha Caraway, former soap opera star and current shop owner, stood at the counter ready to sell orange blossom soap to forthcoming customers. She wore her usual ensemble, a dark blue and white star-covered belted kaftan that displayed her buxom shape. Turquoise jewelry and silver statement rings adorned her body and stood out against her tawny skin. Her gray hair was clipped close to her head, showing off the elegant curve of her scalp.

Ursula approached the counter. "Morning, Mama. Sorry I'm late again. I overslept."

Mama's wide brown eyes brightened. "No worries. Good morning, my darling."

She embraced Ursula in a tight hug, smothering her in lavender oil and affection. Mama always wore this special oil to open her mind and body to the universe, and the scent lingered on Ursula's clothes for hours after they'd worked together.

She leaned back and gave Ursula a long scan. "You look very... festive today. What happened to your work shirt?"

Ursula placed her purse behind the counter in a small alcove. She went to the back room, clocked in on her time-card, then rejoined Mama out front. "It's a long story."

For once, she wanted to have a short and sweet tale for her life, not an epic poem of woe.

"It's been a rough morning," Mama offered.

Ursula groaned. "It's been a rough year. I feel like Lady Luck took me out for drinks, stole my wallet, and stopped answering my texts."

"Lady Luck can be raggedy like that," Mama said. "You said you overslept. Did you try putting an amethyst stone under your pillow? It helps with dreams and rest."

Lately, Ursula was wary of using any enchantments to solve any of her issues. Last year, she fooled around with magic and quickly found out how a single spell could mess up her whole life. If she was having trouble sleeping, she'd drink chamomile and watch reruns of *Living Single* and *Bob's Burgers* on her laptop until she fell asleep. No magic needed.

"No thank you, Mama. Not everyone wants to sleep on rocks," Ursula said drily.

"Try it tonight and see what happens," Mama said with a smile. "I do have good news."

"What? Has NASA perfected time travel?" If they had, Ursula wanted a one-way ticket to her childhood, so she could knock the fairy tale book from her little sticky hands. She'd wipe the stardust from her young eyes and just…stop believing in happily-ever-after. Save herself the future heartache. Ursula refocused on Mama, who bounced with excitement.

She could hold a secret as well as a pasta strainer held water.

"No, it's something better." Mama shook her head. "The Chamber of Commerce just dropped a new poster for our window."

"Are we having a spring ghost crawl?" Ursula cringed. She didn't do haunted houses or buildings, having watched enough paranormal reality shows to know better than to deal with that drama. Not all ghosts were friendly. Ursula held her breath, waiting to see what scheme the town had come up with. The Chamber of Commerce of Freya Grove was always dreaming up creative and odd events and activities to help boost interest in local businesses. They were always trying to repeat the success of the Historical Society's Founders' Day Festival, which was one of the most popular events at the Jersey Shore.

"Nope, it's better than that!" Mama reached underneath the counter and pulled out a poster with a show woman's flourish. *Oh no.* Ursula read the delicate, cutesy font on the poster.

Smitten By the Shore
Music-Food-Fun

Find your fairy tale in
Freya Grove this spring!

March 20–June 23

"Look what's coming back this year!" Mama did a little shimmy. "Smitten is back, baby girl!"

Ursula studied the poster with a critical squint. The graphic designer went ham with the artwork and used their imagination to fill up the entire 11 x 17 sheet. A cartoon couple with matching goofy smiles steered a hot-air balloon over a town landscape while sprinkling huge hearts to the waiting crowd. A website address and social media icons were included underneath the illustration.

What were the odds that a lovey-dovey festival was coming back at the same moment she was ridiculously, hopelessly single?

Ursula folded her arms. No way. Her witchy senses were on high alert.

"I thought it was on indefinite hiatus," Ursula said slowly. "How can our town suddenly afford this festival after all this time?"

She remembered the final email from the organizers announcing that the festival was taking a break. Everyone in the Grove knew indefinite hiatus was code for "we don't have the funds to host this event." Smitten hadn't been held in three years and she assumed it wasn't coming back. Ursula wasn't going to celebrate until she knew if her once cherished event was back for good.

"That's a good question," Mama said. "I heard from my hairdresser's sister that an anonymous donor decided to bring back the festival. They provided enough money to fund Smitten for the next five years."

"We already have Founders' Day," Ursula said. "We don't need another party."

"So what? There's nothing wrong with having a little fun," Mama countered. "If you have enough confetti, life can be a party."

Ursula sighed. "That sentence should be our town motto."

Mama affixed tape to the poster's four corners. "Hang that up for me."

Ursula took the poster and placed it in the corner of the front window.

She watched the morning light filter through the paper

hearts, making them sparkle through the poster. Was she seeing things? Of course. Magic, love, and high pollen count were in the air this spring. Years ago, Freya Grove went completely gaga over Smitten by the Shore and all the romantic lore connected to the event. Shops made specialty items, eateries created limited-edition treats, and romantic comedy movies were played at the local theater for a discounted price. Massive flower chains, balloon arches, and public proposals would be shared and reshared all over social media. There was even the Smitten Sweetheart Contest in which the town nominated locals looking for love and had a fancy ball to celebrate the end of the spring season.

"I thought it was gone for good," Ursula said over her shoulder to Mama.

"So did I. I guess we were mistaken," Mama said. "You know Grampa James used to say, 'Anything can happen during Smitten Season, baby doll.' He had his first leap and met your nana all in the same week."

"I didn't know that." Ursula faced Mama. Those family members who had the gift of second sight sometimes were able to leap or project themselves into the future and experience it firsthand. She'd heard about the leap but had yet to have one yet. It was probably like jumping to the end of a book or fast-forwarding through a movie. Ursula often yearned for a remote to skip to the good parts of her life.

Mama gave a wistful sigh. "You knew your grandparents met at Smitten by the Shore."

"Really, you've never told me," Ursula said in an *I've heard this story five hundred times* tone.

"Don't sass me." Mama clucked. "Your grampa knew they

were soul mates from the moment they kissed on the dance floor. They just clicked."

Ah, yes. Here was yet another piece of family lore. The mystical click that every Caraway experienced when they met their soul mate. Since she was tiny, Ursula had loved the story of how James and Ruth Caraway found each other. They, according to family legend, fell in love over the course of an unforgettable evening at a Hopeful Heart Dance Marathon. Once upon a time, Ursula imagined she would feel the same way when she finally met her soul mate. But when she didn't click with Lincoln, she convinced herself she'd feel it once she got to know him. In retrospect, she didn't know him as well as she thought she did. Ugh. Lincoln hadn't spoken or even texted Ursula since he sent her that final message in the hotel ballroom. She never learned why he ditched her; all texts and emails went unanswered. It was too early in the day to think about her ex.

Mama squinted. "I thought you'd be happier to hear the news. You used to love Smitten."

Ursula shrugged. "I used to . . . before."

Neither of them talked, and the sound of emotional pan-pipes playing on the overhead speaker filled the tense silence. Ursula studied the tops of her scuffed boots so she wouldn't have to see Mama's face crease with worry. She didn't like bringing up the past, so she did her best to forget what it was like when she believed in true love and fairy tales. There was a time when all she dreamed about was being surrounded by faithful woodland creatures, put under a powerful spell, and rescued from a hundred-year curse with an enchanted kiss. Ursula once yearned for a love that would be told and shared by her descendants to come. It would be a love that would be legendary. That time was long gone. She'd gotten a rude awakening once her supposed Prince Charming ditched her at the altar and left her to deal with returning wedding gifts and huge catering bills.

It was time to wake up and deal with real life.

Mama's warm voice broke into her reverie. "You'll find a reason to love it again."

It was the note of optimism that made Ursula lift her eyes and look at Mama. There was a little worry on her face, but a glimmer of knowledge that eased the tension in her heart. *Say something, Sula. Make her feel better.*

"Stranger things have happened," Ursula said. She mentally put this conversation in the For Later folder in her mind. *Change the subject.*

She pointed to the crystal clock on the wall. "Look at the time. We should get started."

Mama nodded. It was showtime.

Ursula took her place at the reading table. It was outfitted with a handful of divination tools that she used during the day. She favored raw crystals and stones whenever she had to work. Touching those items made her feel grounded. Once in this seat, she transformed into Madame Caraway, the premiere psychic consultant to the Grove. Head witch in charge. Confident in life and love. Ursula pulled the crystal ball closer to the edge of the table. Her mere presence would beckon people from the sidewalk to come in and seek advice.

Ursula put up a placard sign in the window next to the poster. It read, *Free reading with any store purchase.* If a customer paid for any item, they were offered a reading at no extra charge. This policy had kept them in business for years and kept a roof over their heads during the lean times, when Mama was between acting jobs.

Ursula sat perched in the chair, watching the foot traffic. With every passing minute without a client, her confidence ebbed as the entire world passed by. No one gave her even a first glance. For a moment, Ursula yearned for everything she had wished away—her old life, her friendships, her reputation. She could divine everyone else's future, but she couldn't see her path forward. Ursula willed herself to stay in the mystical zone. *Be Madame. Be still.*

Eventually, customers wandered in, bought an item or two, and came over to her table for a reading. Many times, people wanted someone to share their secrets with, so Ursula gratefully obliged. She wiggled her hands over the crystal ball, read the images that appeared to her, then offered guidance. Ursula was in the zone, and clients sat up straighter and gained a twinkle of happiness in their eyes once their readings ended. During a brief lull, Ursula texted Gwen, her half-sister, to let her know that she was working through lunch and wouldn't be by the bistro today. Six hours of wind chimes and ethereal lyrics playing overhead left Ursula feeling loose and calm.

Today was actually turning out to be a good shift.

It was a few minutes after five when he appeared in the front window. She knew that midnight-black designer peacoat, pressed khaki pants, and fresh sneakers anywhere. An odd blend of surprise and irritation spun through her, causing her to ache.

Lincoln Walker was back in the Grove.

He looked slimmer, lighter from when she'd last seen him in August. A small part of her wanted to know why he ghosted her, but the larger part wanted to throw his smartphone into the Atlantic. Questions popped up in her brain like phone notifications.

When did he get back in town? Does Marcus know? Should I say something to him?

Then Ursula noticed the pink cloud of a lady by his side. Her head was covered by a bubblegum-colored crocheted hat, a puffy jacket fitted over her solid curves. Her face was done up with flawless makeup. He gave her ass a tender squeeze, and she leaned back and chortled. Lincoln brightened and...blushed. He never blushed with Ursula. Something dreadful and painful twisted inside of her at this sight of domestic bliss.

Well, at least he got his happy ending.

Ursula let out a noisy, sharp breath—that somehow in this universe, Lincoln must've heard through the glass. He turned toward the window and stiffened when he recognized her.

Shame rushed through her and heated every inch of her skin. She jerked back, and her arm connected with the crystal ball, knocking it off its base. Customers shouted as it tumbled over the table's edge, and Ursula dove from her seat, barely saving the precious item from shattering on the floor. Panic raced through her, and she sat immobile on the floor until her heart rate settled down. The crystal ball had belonged to Great-Aunt Lulu, and it had been passed to Ursula. She cradled the heirloom against her chest. Lately, all she seemed to be talented at was breaking things. *When will you stop being so careless?*

"Sula, beloved," Mama said. Ursula glanced up. Mama's eyes were gentle as she approached. "Take a break. Get something to eat. I'll watch the table."

Mama carefully took the crystal ball from Ursula's hands and pressed a quick kiss to her forehead. The shop was eerily silent. Ursula nodded. She stood, grabbed her purse from behind the counter, and left the shop, avoiding their customers' worried stares.

A quick glance down the street confirmed that Lincoln had hurried away from the shop with his boo-thang. Ursula walked in the opposite direction. A few people gave her curious looks as they passed her on the sidewalk. She was, for lack of a better phrase, internet famous and there wasn't a ghoul, ghost, or enchanter in the Grove who didn't know her cautionary tale. Ursula knew what question everyone asked themselves when they saw her around town.

How much of a psychic could she be if she didn't know? She must've had a feeling!

Of course, she had a *feeling*. Everyone had feelings, but she couldn't just follow them because things felt off between her and Lincoln. On paper they were the storybook couple, the town prince falling in love with the local witch. How sweet! But when it came to her magic, Lincoln had questioned whether she needed it. He had raised a silent brow whenever Ursula dabbed her honeysuckle and sunflower oil perfume on her wrists. He had given her an earful when she'd suggested growing an herb garden in the kitchen, claiming that she was being held back by outdated superstition. Ursula bit her lip until it ached. His words reminded her of the conversations she overheard between her parents. Dad's urgent words echoed in her memory: *Niesha, if you love me, don't do your witchy thing with my family. Leave the crystal beads at home. Don't wear all that lavender. You've got to love me more. Be stronger than the magic.*

Rather than be forced to choose between her craft or their relationship, Ursula chose Lincoln before he even asked her to make a choice. However, the magic still called to her, and the very last spell she cast was the one that ruined her life.

In the end, Ursula learned the hard way that happy endings were never meant for witches.

Chapter Two

P eople were coming home to the Grove. Downtown, with its antique lampposts and bare trees, was filled with the early evening traffic. Shoppers cradled crocheted totes heavy with fresh produce and foodstuffs. Commuters ambled from the transportation center, their clothes wrinkled from their travels. By this time, the golden hour was on its way, giving buildings a shiny metallic glow that filled Ursula with a muted feeling of anticipation—it was time to treat herself to something cheesy and delicious. Ursula went to Mimi's Diner and ordered the Shore Nachos, avoiding eye contact with curious diners and trying to ignore their not-so-hushed conversations.

"Is the Ren fair in town?"

"No, that's Ms. Niesha's daughter who works down at that feather shop."

"Oh, that *is* her. Tsk. It's terrible what happened to her..."

Ursula tuned out the rest of their talk, but fatigue had already settled in. *I don't want to be the main attraction in this spooky town anymore.* Once her order was called and her to-go bag arrived, Ursula hustled out of the diner.

She walked until she reached the waterfront. Gulls squawked

and coasted overhead. The sand was bare, absent of colorful towels and beach chairs. It was the off-season, so the Grove's boardwalk was sparsely populated with a few people walking around bundled up in their light spring coats. A few storefronts were closed with blue and white SEE YOU IN THE SUMMER! signs dangling above their doors. A chilly breeze came over Ursula and gave her goose bumps.

The wood bench was cold underneath her when she sat down.

She'd once hated going to the beach, haunted by the memories of carefree days, but now this place comforted her. Nana Ruth, rest her soul, always called Ursula her beach baby when she was small. While the cousins splashed and played in the waves, Ursula scooped up sand in her purple bucket and pail. She made sandcastles, decorating them with broken seashells and driftwood. On those summer days, she imagined that she ruled a kingdom where witches could become queens of the night. As she grew older, Ursula lied to everyone and said that she couldn't be bothered with the beach. The sand had once given shape to her childhood dreams that intimately crumbled under the weight of adult responsibility. Now the sand reminded her of the innate magic that flowed in her veins, the same magic that she ignored in an effort to be someone normal. Someone who could be loved by a man like Lincoln.

She shook off those melancholy thoughts. It was time for Jersey-style nachos.

Ursula ate her dinner while watching the waves crash against the sand. The spring equinox was upon them. The earth was waking up from its slumber, but Ursula felt confined in a dreamless sleep. She worked so hard at her job and maintaining her life that she didn't even have the energy to dream anymore. It was time to wake up and make plans. Every time she went to make a new life list, Ursula froze, the cold dread of indecision keeping her from doing anything meaningful.

But this time that same dreadful feeling had lessened greatly, and she felt eager.

A voice inside asked the million-dollar question, *So, what's different this time?*

Seeing Lincoln outside her window living free of their past made her feel angry and a little jealous. Why couldn't she just move on? The memory of her not-wedding day lay heavy around her neck like a massive statement necklace made with uncut ruby crystals. She couldn't take it off, and it was on display for the world to see. For years, Ursula molded herself into the woman she thought was perfect. Flawless. Respectable. She'd transformed herself into the partner she figured Lincoln needed by his side.

He still left.

Ursula cringed at the woman she had been last summer. She couldn't forget the worst version of herself, the pastels and pearl-wearing menace of Freya Grove. The Ursula who heartlessly threatened loved ones with hexes. The Ursula who swallowed her true feelings and smiled until her face burned. The Ursula who gave up her magic as easily as strangers dropped well-loved clothes into donation bins just for the sake of being normal. She didn't want to be the person she once was; she needed to be better. The same way a hermit crab moved from shell to shell, Ursula needed a new role to inhabit. One that would be hers alone. Not the perfect wife. Not the ideal woman. Someone special.

I want to feel magical again.

Ursula picked at the soggy chips at the bottom of the container, thinking of her next steps. No more daydreaming about hermit crabs. It was time to plan.

She finished eating and folded up the container. The lingering gulls gobbled up what crumbs she left behind on the planks. Ursula took her phone from her purse and opened the digital planner app Planner Bae. The screen glowed in the dark of the impending evening. She clicked through the digital pages of the last several weeks, each day filled with the same routine. *Wake up. Work at the shop. Eat. Sleep. Repeat.* Was this routine the rest of her life?

Last winter, she switched from a massive paper planner to a digital app to jump-start her hunger for life. It didn't work. Irritation bubbled up in her throat and stayed there. She had made perfect plans—but what did she have to show for it now? An empty heart, a near-empty bank account, and barely enough magic to get her out of bed in the morning.

Ursula looked out to the ocean, the sea foam curling and swelling around the jetty rocks. The ocean didn't fear going to the shore. Fear couldn't keep her from going forward. She popped her earbuds in and pressed shuffle on her Plan on It playlist. While Jill Scott sang melodically about living a golden life, Ursula opened a new note and labeled it **Boss Witch List**. It was time for her to step up. Her fingers quickly moved over the keyboard. She wanted to go back in time and snatch her wish from the fire. To get a redo. To start over. Once she finished writing, Ursula reread the list.

1. Reclaim your magic.
2. Find more wishes.
3. Change your life.

This was the plan. Ursula's powers were tied to her emotions, so in the last several months it had been difficult for her to cast solo spells. She had enough magic to snap her fingers and light a candle. Even so, she needed three or more of her Caraway kin to complete the Wish Spell. She frowned. Ursula still felt so ashamed by her behavior last year that she didn't feel like she had the right to ask her family for a cup of tea, let alone a new wish.

She was, as Patti LaBelle sang, on her own once again.

Think on it. There had to be a way to find another wish without having to cast a spell. Didn't she know any leprechauns who owed her any favors? Maybe she could convince a gnome to help her out. She quickly abandoned that idea. Grove gnomes were too unpredictable for her liking. Once she completed the first two items on her list, then number three would take care of itself. But if she was going to complete her Boss Witch List, then she needed to add a rule. Ursula hit enter a few times and added another line and put it in bold:

No more fairy tales

Been there. Listened to that playlist, and she wasn't going to repeat it again. She had been so focused on the promise of a prince coming to sweep her off her feet that she didn't pay attention to the warning signs. Rather than deal with her rising doubt in her life, she tried to wish her problems away.

From now on, she was living in an epic fantasy. It was settled. She was no longer an abandoned princess; she was now a fierce enchantress ready to strike like a sexy bejeweled cobra. Smitten was going to be her personal wine-soaked quest. The Grove wasn't ready for her. There wasn't going to be a rosé bottle that she wasn't going to drain. Feast on food until she couldn't see straight. Ride a unicorn. Have a torrid affair. True love or lust was going to be on her terms.

Ursula wasn't going to let life surprise her anymore.

"Suddenly Cinderella?"

Ack! The booming voice caused her to snap her head up. A pair of smoky dark topaz eyes stared down at her. She'd been so caught in up in her daydream she hadn't heard this stranger approach the bench. Well, she wasn't going to be surprised—starting now. Ursula slammed the pause button on her music, studying him.

His profile stood out against the yellow-orange sky. The bold outlines of his large body seemed to strain against the fabric of his tailored waistcoat, dress shirt, and black dress pants, which ended at his polished shoes. There was a flower—a cherry red rosebud—pinned to his lapel. She blinked at him; a quick, pulsating glow seemed to emanate from his body like a firefly. Was he really glowing? The shadow of his black beard gave him a playful aura, as if he strolled out of the woods after frolicking there for an afternoon.

He held out a small bouquet of yellow sunflowers, artfully wrapped in butcher paper. Suspicion skittered through her brain. The last time she'd been given flowers, Jupiter was aligning with Saturn nearly two years ago. The glow faded away. It was probably just her eyes playing tricks on her. He was too beautiful to be anywhere in her personal space.

She yanked her earbuds out to hear him better. "Um, hello."

"Suddenly Cinderella?" he repeated, a little softer. "I'm Xavier. It's nice to meet you."

Ursula shook her head. "I'm sorry. I'm not anyone's Cinderella."

Not anymore, not again if she could help it.

A sheepish look crossed his handsome face. "My apologies." Xavier tucked the flowers into the crook of his arm. "It seems that I'm lost. My phone stopped working. I can't get a signal." He peered at her for a long moment, curiosity in his gaze. Ursula peered back at him. Did he expect her to sprout wings, grow a bill, and start stealing French fries from strangers? She chuckled to herself at that bizarre image.

"Don't worry," she said. "I won't turn into a bird and fly away."

He laughed sheepishly. "Sorry. I've heard if you pay attention, you'll see strange things in Freya Grove."

Ursula raised her chin in his direction. "Do I look strange to you?"

"No," he said softly. He regarded her with the same careful interest a scholar might study a handwritten illuminated manuscript. This man tilted his head to the side, as if seeking to know what secrets she possessed. Ursula shivered, stunned by the poetry of her thoughts.

What was going on with her tonight?

He glanced down at the flowers he held, breaking off his stare. "I didn't mean to bother you."

"You're not bothering me." Ursula stood from the bench and assessed him further. There was something about this stranger that held her attention.

His jet-black hair was styled with a sheen of gel that made him look as though he was going to get onstage and give a lecture about ancient kingdoms lost to sand and time. The tops of his ears were pointed and angled slightly away from his head. Awe filled her chest. *He's fae.* No wonder she was feeling a bit twitterpated. According to her old storybooks, humans often found themselves affected just by being in their presence. No wonder she was conjuring her inner slam poetess.

Say something, Sula. You've been staring at him for like an hour.

She cleared her mind and focused on him. "Tell me where you were supposed to meet your Cinderella."

He glanced around, looking for a sign. Ursula knew there were none by the waterfront. Gnomes were always stealing them.

"We agreed to meet on the boardwalk. This is Ocean Avenue, right?"

Ursula rocked back on her heels. "Yes, but probably not the one you're looking for."

Xavier looked at her, his forehead wrinkling in surprise. "There's more than one?"

She looked at the landmarks that dotted the Grove beachfront. "Well, this is Ocean Avenue North, and Ocean Avenue South is the other way."

It was a common mistake for out-of-towners to make. Springtime usually attracted visitors to the Grove who were looking for enchanted mischief. Ursula had dealt with plenty of lost folks who came into the shop asking for directions. She motioned to the twinkling low building in the near distance, aglow with lights and shadows of suspended galloping horses.

"Walk toward the carousel, look to the left, and you'll be there in five minutes."

He nodded. "Thank you for your help."

Xavier gave her another once-over and started heading south. His attention was pulled toward the crash of the waves and a possible siren's song, and concern washed over Ursula. There were so many lovely diversions in the Grove. He'd probably end up walking right into the ocean and having dinner with a mermaid or three. She sighed. It wouldn't be the first time. Right now, Lucy was probably living her best life with the merman of her dreams. Ursula couldn't leave this bright-eyed stranger to a watery fate.

There was another part of her that didn't want to let him go just yet. This fae, like a piece of old jade, radiated an unspoken vitality that drew her to him. She didn't want to think any deeper about why she was suddenly drawn to Xavier. There wasn't any harm in walking him over to the carousel.

"Hold up," Ursula called out. "I'll walk you over there. I'm headed in that direction."

He nodded. "That's very kind of you."

If only he knew. After all the hurtful things Ursula had done last year, she was relearning how to be kind to everyone, herself included. Xavier waited for her to join him, and when she did, he offered her a grateful smile.

"Let me properly introduce myself. I'm Prince Xavier Alder of the Alder Fae and you are...?"

Hold up. Did he just say "prince"? Ursula blinked slowly. She glanced around for any cameras in case she was secretly being recorded for an online prank show. Nope. They were alone.

Ursula tried and failed to hide the disbelief in her voice. "Seriously?"

His smile broadened as he held out his hand. "I assure you I am."

She looked down at his hand, not moving to take it. Ruth's warnings played in her mind. "Well, Your Highness, I've got to be honest with you. My nana warned me about giving my name to the fae."

Amusement lit up Xavier's handsome features. "Tell me why."

Ursula lowered her voice. "You might bewitch me and whisk me away to your castle."

He stepped closer so that there was only half a foot between them. His cologne, a sweet mix of pepper and fresh flowers, made her lean in a little closer. He peered down into her eyes and didn't look away. "I might, but only if you wanted to come with me."

Well, damn. When was the last time anyone asked her what she wanted? Mayor Walker told Ursula what to do for the wedding. Lincoln left all the decision-making to her and didn't ask. Even Dad, busy with his perfect life in Meadowdale, told her what steps she needed to take to get her life together. Lucy cared enough to ask her, but it was too late for Ursula to do anything to break the spell. She'd given up her voice to be accepted by the people she wanted to impress. What did she want? She blinked up at His Highness.

Well, against common sense, she wanted him to know her name.

She took his hand. "I'm Ursula. Ursula Caraway."

His gaze roved over her and quickly appraised her outfit. "I assume you go by the title Madame Caraway."

"Ah, yes." Ursula ran her free hand over the fortune-telling costume. After today's nonsense, she wanted to shove it underneath her bed with her unicorn slippers when she got home. However, with Xavier studying her with that interested gaze, she might consider keeping it out for another day.

"It's a pleasure to meet you, Madame." His hand held hers gently, and small green sparks emitted from their connection. A hot shiver ran through her as the sparks bounced between their joined hands. Ursula inhaled sharply. It was like holding a sunbaked limestone in her palm. She hadn't realized how cold she was until she touched Xavier, his magic warming her skin.

A voice rattled in her brain, interrupting this feeling.

This man is not your date. Ursula took her hand back quickly. Had he felt it too? Xavier cleared his throat and looked away from her. His throat seemed to tighten. The paper wrapped around the flowers crinkled as he clutched them tightly to his side. Without another word, they started strolling, their footsteps echoing along the boardwalk. The wind picked up, causing a chill in the air. Ursula shook her hand out by her side to rid herself of the electricity of his touch. No luck. Her body was buzzing more than a neon sign left on all night long. He stood so close she could extend her hand and touch his arm to see if he was real.

Stop it. Her inner voice snapped. *He's meeting someone else for dinner. Ask him about that.*

"Where were you meeting your date?" she inquired.

"We agreed to meet on the boardwalk and dine at a place called Lighthouse," Xavier said. He lifted an eyebrow at her. "Are you familiar with it?"

Ursula made a low sound in her throat. "They have good cake."

Xavier grinned, seemingly satisfied with her response. Oh, she knew the Lighthouse restaurant very well. A heavy feeling hit her stomach as she recalled her last dinner there. Lincoln had proposed to her over the super-expensive ganache chocolate cake with golden flakes. She'd been so shocked by the pricey dessert that she almost missed Lincoln down on one knee holding out a huge sparkling ring. Her throat had dried up when she saw it. The diamond ring with its square cut and platinum band looked perfect, as if it had been taken straight from a jewelry ad.

You didn't say no with a ring like that.

Ursula, too caught off guard to question whether she wanted to even get married right then, had automatically said yes.

You didn't say no to a Walker.

A sense of foolishness stirred inside her chest. If only she'd known what the future held for them. She would've left the ring on the table and taken the cake instead. She would've saved them the trouble that loomed on the horizon. Ursula brought her attention back to the boardwalk. She stole a glance at Xavier's profile. His firm mouth curled at the corner as if he was bemused by the world around him.

What a plot twist. The instant she'd declared to the universe that she was giving up on the fairy tale, fate threw a full-grown prince in her path. He hadn't rolled up in a horse-drawn carriage, but he had managed to captivate her with a few lingering looks.

Once they reached the carousel, Xavier glanced over to the fancy eatery covered in twinkle lights next to it and nodded. "There it is."

He turned to Ursula and pressed his free hand to his chest. "I would've been lost without you, my heroine."

No way. A smartphone with a good GPS system could've rescued him from his dilemma.

"I'm only a humble boardwalk psychic on her dinner break," she said, gesturing at her outfit.

By the carousel lights, his eyes seemed to shine with a humorous glint. "Give yourself more credit, Madame Caraway. I could've been swept up by a fae-eating dragon."

"I gave you directions. I didn't slay any dragons for you," she said with a dry chuckle. "You would've found your way eventually."

"Yes, but you made all the difference." Xavier looked to the rose on his lapel. He unpinned it and offered it to her.

Ursula stiffened, unsure of what to do. Anguish filled her. A handsome fae prince was offering his rose. Wasn't this how all the fairy tales started? She'd envisioned a romantic moment like this since she first read the story of the beauty who loved a beast. He gave her a small grin, the rose still outstretched in his hand.

Ursula pressed her fingers into her palm to keep from reaching for it. Accepting his rose would've taken her back to a place where she wanted to be worthy of such chivalrous, yet ultimately empty gestures. Ursula straightened and looked him right in the eye. Xavier was not her Prince Charming. He was here to meet a Cinderella, not a witch like her.

She set her chin in a stubborn line. "Thanks, but no thanks."

His brow creased and a flash of surprise crossed his face. Xavier returned the rose back to his lapel and he licked his lips in thought. It was clear from his expression that the prince wasn't used to anyone turning him down. She needed to leave before she explained what was going on with her. It wasn't him; it was that she was taking a break from all princes. Then again, she probably wasn't going to see him after tonight. He'd tell this story to Suddenly Cinderella over their appetizers and forget about Ursula by the time dessert came out. Tonight was the start of his fairy tale and the end of hers. In her heart, she wished him well.

Ursula stepped back. "Enjoy your date, Your Highness."

"Good evening, Madame," he murmured.

Ursula turned and went in the opposite direction, back toward downtown Freya Grove. She repeated the words in her head, like a chant: *Remember the rule. No more fairy tales.* The glowing carousel lights faded away as she strolled back to the shop. If this was the start of her journey, then she had to start on the right step. She and Xavier weren't on the same page—they weren't even in the same book.

Chapter Three

An hour and a half into his mystery date with Cindy Mendoza—the real Suddenly Cinderella—Prince Xavier Alder realized that he would've been better off lost on the boardwalk with his flowers. The longer he listened to her talk about life goals, the clearer it became that they were not compatible. Cindy had a zeal for life. She reminded him of a hummingbird zipping from flower to flower looking for a taste of nectar. He, on the other hand, had to recharge every day like a five-year-old laptop battery just to have regular interactions with most people. Everything about this date, from the food to the low lighting, was perfect, but he knew this match wasn't going to work out.

It wasn't her; it was definitely him.

Cindy, with her bubbly personality and beauty influencer, ring-light-ready looks, was lovely. She taught theater to freshmen students at Meadowdale College. Pride shone in her eyes when she spoke about helping others explore the stage and express themselves. As she talked about the importance of finding the perfect monologue for your voice, Xavier's spirits sank.

Had he ever loved anything as much as she did?

He enjoyed his plants. Xavier tended to the royal green-house and worked with his mediation clients in the Faerie Realm, but his true passion eluded him. His search for bliss was on hold until he could sort out his magically inclined problem. Xavier studied Cindy over the crisp linen-clothed table and sparkling water glasses. Her earrings were dangling smiling suns. Next to the ray of sunshine that was Cindy, he felt like the world's biggest rain cloud.

What made Whitney believe that they'd be compatible?

"How do you know my godmother?" he asked.

Cindy played with her water glass. "We're part of the same Crass and Crafty group online. My username's Suddenly Cinderella because I crocheted my own dress for my brother's wedding."

"That's impressive," he said. "I wouldn't know how to cro-chet a hat."

Cindy brightened. "It was a fun challenge. I didn't have any mice or birds to help me make it. Honestly, I'm more of a Sleeping Beauty person because I love to sleep in."

Xavier nodded. "I see."

The conversation came to a jerky halt. They sipped from their drinks in companionable silence. He ordered them des-sert, but Cindy politely declined to share the order.

"Can I be real with you, Your Highness?" Cindy asked carefully after a few minutes.

Xavier watched as she cradled her glass between her pol-ished nails.

"You can be real with me." He was trying to use more human slang to fit in, but the words always felt a little odd in his mouth. He'd been trained in the ways of royalty and manners since he had a silver rattle in his hand. Once an Alder prince, always an Alder prince.

She tilted her head, her brown hair falling around her oval face in waves. "You seem like a great guy, but I don't see us going on a second date. Whitney told me all about your...problem." His stomach dipped. Cindy glanced around and lowered her voice so only he could hear. "I like fairy tales, but I'm not interested in starring in one, you know?"

His heart thumped in disappointment. Yet another date gone bust. He gave a soft smile. "I understand your hesitancy."

Cindy smiled back; her dimples winked at him. "Besides, I don't think I can help you with your situation."

Xavier said nothing. Cindy continued talking. "I'm a terrible Grove resident. I leave pennies on the ground. I spill salt everywhere. I wouldn't know how to break a curse."

Cindy sipped her water with a grin, clearly relieved to have made her confession.

There it was. The real reason why he'd been on twelve first dates in the last two weeks and why he found himself stuck to the Garden State. How could the universe ever let him forget that he was hopelessly, impossibly cursed to find his perfect kiss?

Xavier looked down at the remnants of his dark chocolate cake. *Madame Caraway told me they had good cake.* He shoved that thought back down and touched his pendant, the last gift from his sister Primrose. If he had any chance of seeing her or the kingdom again, he couldn't get distracted. Focus.

"If you need help with an audition or staging a play, then I'm your person," Cindy said gently.

"I'll keep that in mind." He was being polite. Once he

dealt with this pesky setback, he would be running through the closest fae door back to the Realm as soon as possible.

"The Grove is filled with plenty of qualified people who can help you," Cindy pointed out. "This town is a magnet for strange, nice people."

Xavier made a sound of agreement. His mind recalled one not-so-strange person. The one who helped him when he was completely lost. An image of Ursula standing on the board-walk appeared before him. A cream-white blouse hinted at her shapely body. The gathered printed skirt matched the headband that held her lush, curly hair out of her eyes. Those dark chocolate eyes held his attention. Her teasing question echoed in his memory.

Do I look strange to you?

He blinked away that image. A rush of guilt filled him when Cindy peered at him from across the table. Her attention quickly dropped to the phone in her hand. The lady was possibly texting an SOS to a friend to save her from this extremely uncomfortable evening. What was wrong with him? Thinking about another woman before he'd had a chance to properly talk to the one in front of him.

Had his eagerness to break his horrid curse made him so thoughtless?

A waiter approached, arms folded behind his back. "Can I get you anything else tonight?"

Xavier glanced over at Cindy. From where he was sitting, he could see she'd had her finger lingering over a rideshare app button. Right. This date was officially over. They split the bill, finished their drinks, then left the restaurant. By this time, the stars were coming out and night sounds played in the near distance. A well-lit car parked across the street flashed its lights. Cindy waved to the driver, then jerked her chin toward it. "That's my ride."

Xavier extended his hand to her. "Thank you for a wonderful evening."

Cindy quickly shook it and let go. "I wish you nothing but the best."

Xavier watched as Cindy departed in her ride; the taillights glowed in the darkness. The night was still young, but disenchantment had settled over him like a layer of fog hovering above the ground. Once again, he failed to be the charismatic prince he needed to be to break the curse and get back to his real life. He looked toward the streetlamps and headed downtown. Xavier wanted to be anywhere but here, but he didn't know where to go.

Ursula, in her loose tank top and bubbling cauldron–patterned pajamas, stared at the half-wilted, gray Swiss cheese plant on her windowsill. She held back a warrior princess scream. She'd just gotten her new leafy pal two weeks ago and the leaves looked terrible, as if moths had devoured it for a midnight snack. A leaf broke off and fluttered down onto the sill.

She took a deep breath and tried to relax, but hot frustration seared in her gut. Why couldn't the universe just leave her and her plant alone? After Ursula finished out her shift, she climbed up the stairs to her apartment, changed into her pajamas and watched her favorite episodes of *Living Single* on her laptop. After watching Maxine and Kyle flirtishly spar with each other for an hour, Ursula still couldn't get to sleep and decided to clean up the apartment and brew herself some tea. She had just finished drinking her second cup when she noticed the dire state of her plant.

Ursula pressed two fingers to the bridge of her nose. Breathe in, breathe out.

Earth spirits, aid me in my quest.

She drew a small thread of earth energy from the floor through the bottom of her soles up until it reached her chest. The frustration eased and she refocused on the plant. She ran a finger over the leaves, a small vibration of terra magic tingling her skin. He was a fighter, just like her.

"Don't worry, Sir Duke," Ursula said. "I'll figure out what's going on. I got you."

Ursula would have to wait until next payday before she could visit the plant nursery and buy whatever she needed to save it. Until then she'd try and self-diagnosis what was going on with Sir Duke.

"When did life get so expensive?" Ursula muttered.

She went from bougie to broke in the matter of a single weekend. Lincoln skipped town after their non-wedding, leaving her to deal with the fallout of overdue bills and loose ties. Her savings dwindled within a matter of months, forcing Ursula to make a few hard choices about her lifestyle. She couldn't have champagne taste when she had a strawberry soda budget. So she'd swallowed her pride and sold off her designer bags and couture clothes to a local consignment store in Meadowdale, giving her enough money to move out of their condo apartment. She clipped digital coupons, learned how to make enough soup to last a week, and shopped in bulk.

No more getting her weekly dry cleaning done, but now she had an embarrassingly huge stack of laundry in the bedroom closet. Goodbye tasting menu with her fancy girlfriends; hello scarfing down leftover garlic spaghetti out of a pot on the couch after working an eight-hour shift at the shop. Even more upsetting, the bond with her witchy Caraway family had changed from gleeful Friday night get-togethers to trading awkward texts about moon phases and impending retrogrades. Cousin Sirena had forwarded her slow-cooker recipes, but recently those emails had ceased. If Ursula couldn't rescue her relationship with her kin just yet, she was at least going to try to have a good night's sleep.

She moved away from her plant and went over to her bookshelf. Maybe there was a soothing book that would help calm her thoughts. Instead, Ursula found a flat amethyst crystal tucked between her spell books and laughed softly. *You said you wanted to reclaim your magic, and the universe answered with a crystal.* She had to start with small acts of magic if she was ever going to get her natural intuition back.

Ursula went into her bedroom and slipped the stone underneath her pillow. Maybe tonight would bring her good dreams. Her stomach grumbled. It wouldn't hurt to have a late-night snack. She went back into the kitchen and pulled out Gwen's latest food experiment from the fridge. Gwen, who owned the Night Sky Bistro downtown, was always feeding Ursula possible additions to the menu. In turn, Ursula made sure Gwen never ran out of her favorite smoky quartz.

Ursula peered at the item in her hand. It looked as if someone smushed an entire cupcake into a small mason jar. Gwen even included a portable spoon taped with the treat. Ursula closed the door with an impressed laugh. She read the top, curious to know what type of cake she was sampling this week.

The handwritten label said *Faery Sprinkle Cake.*

Ursula froze for a moment, then she sat down at the kitchen table. She cradled the jar in her palm. Her heart throbbed.

Mama used to make them faery cake to cheer them up on gloomy days.

Nana might have been wary of fae, but Mama loved them. When Ursula was younger, Mama would brew chamomile and lemon tea, make sprinkle cake, and dance around their gossamer capes. They rented books on faery lore from the library and read stories about terrifying queens and alluring princes. She tended to the honeysuckle and thyme that grew in Nana's garden and hid crystals for the fae to find all over their apartment.

When Mama lost out on an audition or Ursula had a long day at school, they would dress up in glitter, have tea on the living room floor, and invite the fae to drink with them. Dad humored Ursula's sparkly activities, but he politely declined to wear anything with bows and ribbons. He claimed all those frills messed with his business suit.

Mama understood Ursula's crystal-loving ways, and for a moment Dad had understood as well. Until his family, the Ellises, insisted that he take a firmer hand with a teenaged Ursula. She overheard their concerns by the cooler at the family cookout. Too lazy. Unfocused. Head in the clouds. Dad, feeling pressured to please his family, chased the dreams from her head and insisted that she make realistic, serious goals. So, she dressed in polo shirts, khaki skirts, and preppy shoes.

She got her first student planner and made lists. She typed her full name—*Ursula Rebecca Caraway Ellis*—on every assignment and paper she handed in to make sure everyone knew that she was serious about her future.

For a brief time, Ursula was the perfect Ellis child, and she was embraced by her aunts, uncles, and cousins on that side of the family. She turned down faery cake and never wore anything covered in glitter or rhinestones. But then her dreams returned and started coming true. Soon, Ursula realized these images were intense visions of the past and future. With a touch of a hand or a kiss on the cheek, she saw all the Ellises' hopes and fears in living color. It wasn't that Ursula was too much of a dreamer; it was the Ellises' kin who lacked courage to follow their dreams. She grieved the fact that her Ellis family seemed too afraid to follow their hearts. Gwen was the exception, but Ursula knew that Dad would work hard to make sure her little sister followed the typical Ellis path to a successful life.

Ursula knew she needed to cut her own path.

So, on her sixteenth birthday, Ursula decided that she was going by Mama's maiden name from then on. She was an Ellis by birth, but she was a Caraway by good luck.

When she told Dad her decision, he hugged her tightly and looked into her eyes. "I guess can't deny the magic in you," he said reluctantly.

Dad gave her his support and even to this day addressed her birthday cards to Ursula Caraway. The Ellises weren't so forgiving and still gave her major attitude whenever they saw her around town. They seemed to envy her and Mama for embracing their dreams instead of keeping their eyes down on the ground.

Caraways looked to the stars.

Ursula blinked. It was time to reclaim this forgotten magic.

She twisted open the cake jar, grabbed the spoon, and scooped herself a huge bite. The mix of creamy vanilla frosting, sprinkles, and tender cake hit her tongue. Ursula closed her eyes, and she could practically hear the jolly fae laughter and smell pungent tea roses.

A vision of His Royal Highness Xavier Alder standing on the boardwalk flashed in her mind. He looked, with his mysterious eyes and secret smile, like he'd been conjured from the sea mist and sand. No matter what happened on his date tonight, Ursula hoped that he ordered dessert. Everyone deserved a little sweetness in their life.

Chapter Four

One lesson Xavier learned when he was very, very young was never keep a faery godmother waiting. He'd heard of fae children who had been turned into mice because they dared to be late to afternoon tea. Whitney wouldn't turn him into a mouse, but she wasn't above shrinking his ears just to teach him some manners. She'd want to hear all about his night, so he made his way back to her house shortly before midnight. The rideshare driver let out an impressed whistle as they drove up to the Gilded Age mansion.

"Are you a celebrity or something?" she asked.

"I'm something," Xavier responded simply.

He left the driver a huge tip and the highest rating on the app before exiting the car. Xavier entered the house, walked through the foyer, and went into the parlor.

There he found Whitney sitting on the full couch, her head bent down in thought. She looked like a sparkly cat playing with a massive ball of bright yellow yarn jumbled in her hands and most of her lap. He studied her for a quiet moment. Whitney's thick, curly, graying hair was worn in a practical style that showed off her heart-shaped face and prominent cheekbones. Her black skin shimmered as if glitter was fixed to her. She wore a magenta set of pajamas, and her feet were encased in fluffy slippers. Her wings, as delicate and transparent as gossamer, peeked from behind her back. A mixture of adoration and sadness churned within him. Everyone he cared for and knew was back in the Realm, waiting for Xavier to come home.

That meant Whitney was the only family he had in this world.

She looked up from her task. Her face brightened. "You're back. How was it?"

"It was okay. I had a nice time. You didn't have to stay up for me."

"It's fine. I was finishing a project." Whitney held up the tangle of yarn, her metallic hook looped in one of the stitches. She made a face. "It was going to be a scarf, but I think I dropped a loop or five."

Xavier sat next to Whitney. "I see you're enjoying your retirement."

Whitney snorted. "I'm semiretired, thank you very much. Besides, you never really stop granting wishes, but it's about time I slowed down. My wand isn't as fast as it used to be."

Xavier observed while Whitney fiddled with the crochet hook as she silently counted the stitches. Their relationship was simple, yet complicated. Whitney Blackthorne, a faery godmother who had been granting wishes to humans over the last four hundred years, was Xavier's real godmother. The instant he gave his first smile, she was there covering him with kisses and baby-friendly glitter. Whitney took the role seriously, helping raise him when his parents were away on diplomatic trips in the Realm, sending him care packages filled with homemade baked goods when he was away at boarding school. When he was a teenager, she didn't grant his wishes, much to his heart's dismay, but she gave him endless advice. It was Whitney who took Xavier into her home here in Freya Grove when the curse had grown unmanageable and threatened to destroy his family's reputation. A sudden thought filled his chest with icy fright.

How long will it be until the curse ends up hurting her too?

Whitney's hiss of anger interrupted his musings.

"This yarn isn't going anywhere." Whitney dropped the project and regarded Xavier. "So, tell me about your date. How was Suddenly Cinderella?"

He hated to disappoint Whitney, but—to borrow a phrase—he had to be real with her.

"Cindy is a wonderful woman," he said gently. "If I ever want to perform a romantic monologue, then she's the first person I'll call. We didn't connect."

"I was sure she'd be perfect for you." Whitney clicked her teeth and sighed sadly. She must have gone through a lot of trouble convincing Cindy to meet with him, and he'd been a disappointing date. A twinge of displeasure rose in his throat.

He swallowed it down and gave Whitney a gracious grin. "Her happily-ever-after is waiting for her, but she won't end up with me."

"Oh well." Whitney glanced over at the wall clock over the mantel. She made a clucking noise. "You left seven hours ago. Where have you been?"

"I went for a long walk."

Whitney rubbed her hands together in eagerness. She'd

encouraged him to explore the town more, but he'd been busy going on dates. "So, how do you like the Grove?"

He hesitated for a heartbeat, trying to decide on the right words. Whitney might have adored the Grove, but this town was his unfortunate way station.

"It's charming...but it's not home," he said finally. Silence enveloped the room.

Freya Grove was nothing like the Faerie Realm, where anything a fae desired would be delivered to their hand by magic. Xavier had possessed the ability to get whatever he wanted at a moment's notice. He'd be in bed reading, snap his fingers, and a steaming cup of sweetened coffee appeared right on his nightstand. No small talk. No awkward interactions. Just wonderful caffeine. Here, in the human world, he had to go outside the house and meet people. Discuss the weather. Have his name misspelled on a paper cup by a chatty barista. This place was...interesting to say the least. His magic was greatly weakened in the human world, forcing him to work a little harder than he was used to. He could rouse weak houseplants and conjure small flowers, but he couldn't revive an oak tree or a dying vine. Bitterness stormed through his blood.

He was hardly pleased with his sudden change in circumstances. Things were so easy within the Faerie Realm, and he craved to go back once he got rid of this irksome problem. To break free of this curse, Xavier had to gain the one thing he'd never been interested in keeping—love. It was as if the Faerie Queen had asked him to find the rarest gemstone on Earth by digging with his bare hands.

He frowned deeply.

"What's going on?" Whitney leaned forward, her attention solely on him. "You got that someone-stole-my-fae-dust look on your face."

In the Faerie Realm, Xavier didn't worry about things like dating, courting, and wooing. As a fae prince of the esteemed House of Alder, his story was already written. It was assumed Xavier would court a princess from a neighboring kingdom. She'd be biddable, make an agreeable marriage partner, have an heir or two. They'd live out the rest of their lives in a castle overlooking a garden landscape. Easy. Simple. Now he had to make up a whole new story.

What were the chances that he was going to find his perfect kiss? A billion chances? How long would he have to go on random dates, hoping to find the one who could release him from this romantic drivel? Uncertainty made his hands shake with barely controlled irritation.

"There has to be another way to end this nonsense."

Whitney shoved the yarn away. Weariness clouded her eyes. "Please, Xavier. Enough."

Enough was never enough for him. He was an Alder fae descended from kings and queens, blessed by stardust and morning dew. There had to be something else he could do without having to resort to finding his so-called true love. "I could write a letter to the court, or personally plead my case." His mind raced. "Maybe if I spoke to the Queen again and...apologized for my behavior, she might—"

"Stop!" Whitney held up her hand, effectively quieting him. When she spoke, her voice was firm and had an air of chill. "Remember what's at stake. Do you really want your father making the final choice for you?"

His stomach tightened and the knot didn't go away. He reached up and ran his finger over the stone pendant hanging from his neck. It warmed under his touch. *Protect the House of Alder.* This extended visit to Freya Grove, New Jersey, had knocked him off balance, but he needed to regroup. If he was ever going to get a chance to return to his plush life, he had to think like a main character in a fairy tale. *What would Prince Charming do? Find the princess and get to the end of the story. Get to the happy ending so you can go home.*

"I won't do anything else. I promise not to get cursed again," he said.

Her mouth twitched in annoyance at his teasing.

"I don't like it when you joke like that," Whitney said in a soft tone. "Besides, you're not under a curse—it's more of an enchantment."

His mind floundered. "What's the difference?"

"Your situation is not as dire," Whitney said. "You have everything within your power to break the curse."

"I can't kiss myself," Xavier pointed out.

"Details, details," she murmured.

"You are aware I need to bestow a perfect kiss or have it bestowed upon me." He gritted his teeth, feeling ridiculous even saying such a silly thing. What made a kiss perfect? Flowers? Chocolates? Music playing overhead?

"You're overthinking things," Whitney said. She leaned over and lovingly tapped his forehead. "Turn off that beautiful brain of yours and just fall in love."

Xavier grumbled. Love. He had no place in his life for the merciless emotion that made rulers thoughtless and drove kingdoms to the brink of disaster. Love wouldn't render him powerless. Plain and simple, love couldn't hurt him because he didn't believe in it.

His reputation for being cold about love earned him a not-so-kind nickname in the fae court—the Tin Prince. The one without a heart.

Whitney dropped her hand away and cleared her throat. "Besides, you can't hurry love. I don't know why you're in such a rush to get back there. I understand you wanting to break the enchantment, but you don't have to rush off once you've found your kiss."

"The Realm's my home," he said automatically.

"It's where you started," she said sagely. Xavier had a feeling that there was a hidden meaning behind her comment, but it wasn't clear to him. The Realm was where he started and where he belonged.

Xavier swiveled to Whitney. "You don't know any more eligible ladies interested in meeting an enchanted prince?"

"Well, there's always the party," Whitney said brightly. "I'm hosting a little get-together for a few friends. I'm inviting people from around the Grove. Feel free to bring a guest."

"I don't know anyone here." Xavier scratched his beard thoughtfully. "A little get-together means that you've invited at least a hundred people to the house."

"I have space," she said.

He couldn't argue. When he couldn't sleep last night, Xavier read about the history of Freya Grove on his phone. The town, being a natural threshold of elemental magic, had some supernatural advantages to it but it was nothing compared to the Realm. The Grove, as the locals called it, had a mix of historical and modern buildings that gave the place a distinct, mystic feel. Whitney had purchased one of the largest properties in the area, a huge mansion built during the height of the Gilded Age. The mansion was nestled near Grove Lake and boasted a beautiful view of the tonier houses of Freya Grove. This fact meant Whitney's party was probably going to be well attended by all.

"Maybe you'll meet someone at the party." The sheer optimism in Whitney's voice made the tips of his ears hurt.

"I'd rather take the night off," he countered.

"Listen, Xav, you don't have much time. Before you know it, midsummer will be here and then—" Whitney's wings lowered. His stomach churned.

Father had been crystal clear when he gave Xavier that ultimatum. Either break the curse—or rather, enchantment—by midsummer or Father would be forced to intervene and get the job done for Xavier.

King Roman Alder wouldn't let anything silly like a love curse interrupt the plans for his children. Everything, from Xavier's schooling to his royal duties, had been meticulously structured by Father's hand. He wasn't fascinating like his brother Royce or commanding like Primrose, but he was an Alder heir, which mean that he had to act the charming role. At least when he was in Freya Grove, he could pick his perfect kiss himself. That thought weighed on him heavily.

Xavier tented his fingers. "I'm aware, Whitney. I should do more research and figure out... the best strategy."

She eyed him. "Strategy? Beloved, you're talking about love, not winning a game show!"

"Maybe I should go on the dating show with the roses," he said crisply.

Whitney waved him away, dismissing his suggestions. "Find your perfect kiss, and then, voilà, the enchantment is lifted."

Xavier let the disdain bleed into his voice. "When you say it like that, it sounds super easy. Who decided that fairy tales must end with a kiss? Why can't they end with a hug or a friendly handshake?"

Whitney lightly smacked his arm. "Hush. I'm talking about true love. Do I need to remind you of a plucky young woman, an overgrown pumpkin, and the perfect glass slipper?"

"I've read the book and I've seen the movie," he muttered.

She shook her head. "You're not going to find your kiss sitting up in your room moping. Get out, get into the Grove, and be you. Dazzle. Be friendly. Remember, sometimes the fairy tale we're living in has a different ending. Be open to how your story unfolds."

"I'll try," Xavier said. On his walk tonight, he had found a star-themed bistro that served coffee and pastries. No doubt there was probably a local bookstore that could help him research fairy tales and happy endings. He strolled past a community garden; his heart dropped to his shoes. Xavier missed his little corner of the world.

He'd been content reading in the royal greenhouse, away from the gossips of the Fae Court. He faithfully attended family dinners and showed up for special occasions, but for the most part he was left to his own devices. Since he was a second son and an earthbound fae who lacked wings, Xavier was granted a degree of freedom that his older siblings lacked. He could just be himself—no expectations, just show up and smile. He'd been fine with his life until that fateful night he accidentally insulted the Faerie Queen and ended up with this enchantment on his head.

He'd mocked love, and now love was going to make a mockery of him.

Mother was oddly quiet about his twist of fate, but Father saw this moment as an opportunity to make a strategic marriage. Once news spread about his quest, princesses and well-off ladies from every corner of the Faerie Realm arrived by carriage to their castle with flirtatious smiles. Father forced him to smile and play host to their eager guests in hopes of making a good match. They spoke love with their lips, but Xavier saw the calculating glint in their eyes. To them, he was not a prince to be courted, but an alliance to be won.

An Alder prince followed through no matter the task, but he couldn't find his perfect kiss in the Faerie Realm. One heated moment with the wrong fae princess could lead to an unexpected commitment to wed a woman he didn't know. What if he found his perfect kiss with a titled lady his parents didn't approve of? What if he became honor bound to wed an innocent princess he probably wouldn't know how to love? His blood went cold.

Xavier swore he would break this curse, before it broke him.

Each Grove date had been pleasant with him, but there hadn't been a spark. He'd look into their eyes and . . . feel disappointment about the evening. He never got a second date.

When Xavier thought about what his perfect happy ending looked like, he came up with a blank page. No castle. No princess. No kiss. Time was of the essence, especially with every passing midnight bringing him closer to his midsummer deadline. He'd wished that tonight would bring him one step closer to solving his pesky curse.

If wishes were pennies, he'd have enough money to take him back to his royal gardens.

Whitney's voice broke into his thoughts.

"The caterer's going to be here all day, so feel free to go into town and have some fun," Whitney said. She rewrapped the yarn ball and put it in a basket next to the couch.

Right. Fun. In the Realm, he'd been so consumed with his job settling disputes between local royals that he often declined party invites. How did one have fun again?

"What does one do for fun here in Freya Grove?" he asked.

Her face brightened with merriment. Xavier's ears tingled once he saw that expression. The last time he saw that look, he and Whitney ended up feeding her birthday cake to the unicorns in the stables at home. Mother made him clean off the rainbow frosting from their horns.

"I heard there might be a festival of some sort," she said coyly.

"What type of festival, Whitney?" he asked in a warning tone.

She rose from the couch quickly, as if she were running away from his question. Whitney gave a big, showy yawn and blinked sluggishly as if the Sandman had dosed her with some of his shiny dust. "Oh dear. It's late. I should retire for the night."

Xavier grumbled. She could run, but she couldn't hide forever. This conversation wasn't over, and he'd speak to her in the morning about this mysterious festival.

"Good night, Whitney." Xavier pressed a kiss to her cheek.

"Sleep well, beloved," she said, her eyes kind.

He went up to the guest bedroom on the second floor. Xavier turned on the overhead light and adjusted it using the dimmer switch. The bedroom was bathed in a low light that seemed to invite him to rest. Once Whitney learned he was staying with her, she'd redesigned the room with his favorite colors, shades of green and gray. She wanted him to have a home away from home. Fresh daisies in a vase on the bedside table brightened the room. The walls were painted sea green that matched the curtains of his four-poster bed, with its lush sheets. With a very undignified grunt, Xavier flopped onto the bed, letting the blankets swallow him whole. He was so tired that he didn't even bother to undress. This was not his life. He'd slipped into this borrowed life the way that someone slipped into a coat left over at a party. This was not his bed. As sleep called to him, Xavier let memories of past evenings wash over him.

When he was a child, Mama read him and his siblings bedtime stories about enchantresses who were as powerful as they were beautiful. Enchantresses who controlled the elements with a snap of their fingers. The one who could divine the future in a glass of water. Maybe a visit with a local fortune teller would help shake him out of this foul mood. His mind replayed his interlude with Ursula. Ah, yes. Madame Caraway. The crystal-gazer.

His blood still hummed from their handshake. It only lasted a few seconds, but it stayed on his mind for hours and seared his skin. He'd been briefly taken aback when she declined his rose. Xavier was used to fae folk fighting over a single petal from an Alder family member, let alone a rosebud. He once saw two royals brawl over who was going to claim his brother's discarded lapel rose. But Xavier understood Ursula's reasons for turning his gesture down.

He was a stranger, and he was on his way to meet his actual date. She probably thought he was a princely rogue, careless with his affections and intentions. That was not a good look for him. But he wanted to thank her for seeing him to the boardwalk. For making him truly smile for the first time in what seemed like months. For being a friend to a stranger. If he ever saw her again, he'd properly thank her and apologize for his arrogance. She might have been dressed like the typical fortune teller but something more was there behind her costume.

Xavier had peered into Madame Caraway's eyes and saw a light that was absolutely spellbinding. He saw a light that made a dreary part of his spirit glow.

—

Chapter Five

It was the flickering candlelight that caught Ursula's attention in the glittering ballroom. The flame burned neon green, giving the space an otherworldly glow. Wall-length mirrors in gilded frames reflected the beauty around her. She caught her reflection in the mirror and stood stunned. *Is that me?* Her bone-white gown was embroidered with crystals that caught the green light and made her shimmer. Ursula glanced around. Guests wore designer tuxedos and fine twinkling dresses. Dancers twirled on the floor like spinning flowers falling from a tree. Everyone danced and swayed except for one person, a man dressed in regal clothes. From his wide sash and the crown on his head, she knew that he was a prince. Her prince.

He was masked, but recognition echoed in her bones. Even though she hadn't seen his face, she knew his soul. She called out to him, but once she spoke, the dream faded away into darkness. Ursula woke up, rolled over on her back, and looked up at the ceiling. She let out an annoyed grumble and reached underneath the pillow. Ursula pulled out the flat amethyst crystal and sighed. It seemed her subconscious hadn't gotten the memo that she was done with fairy tales. She dropped the crystal on the bedside table next to her phone.

Everything was super quiet in the apartment. Sunlight streamed into the window, but the clock on the oven was dark. Ursula didn't hear the familiar hum of the fridge that usually lulled her to sleep. She checked her phone, plugged in on the nightstand. It was only charged halfway. Oh, that wasn't good. Ursula called Mama.

She answered with a pleasant trill. "Good morning, my darling. Happy equinox."

There was a rustling of pans on the other end of the line. Ursula returned the greeting, then addressed the situation. "Is something going on with the power? Nothing's working in the apartment."

"Did you get my text?"

Ursula arched and stretched, trying to shake off any lingering sleep. "I just woke up. I forgot my alarm."

There was more banging of pots from Mama's end. "I meant to tell you. The light company called. The power is out in the whole building," she said. "We're closed."

Ursula rubbed her eyelids and bit back a curse. "When did that happen?"

Mama let out an annoyed breath. "It was in the middle of the night, but they're working on it now. It's going to take a while. Take the day off. I'm going to be busy prepping for the house party. You're welcome to come over and hang out. Your cousins are here."

"Oh, really?"

"Come over to the house. Ask if Sirena or Callie are doing

anything fun today. Maybe you can join them. It's been so long since you've been together."

Nope. Ursula's gut clenched at just the idea of being in the same room as Sirena, Callie... or even Lucy. *Don't go there.* She wasn't ready to even think about seeing Lucy again.

"Thanks, but I'm good. I'll probably stay here."

Mama made another annoyed sound but didn't push the issue any further.

Ursula hadn't been to the Caraway house since she demanded Lucy recast the Wish Spell and was rightfully refused. The memory of her acting so selfishly and cruelly at that fateful dinner filled her with shame. No, she wasn't ready to see them or the house yet. The ancestral Caraway home had been passed from Caraway to Caraway witch since the turn of the century. The Victorian manor was the safe space for all the witches and casters in their family. Ursula wasn't going to step over the threshold until she'd completed her list. Nana Ruth once said the worst thing you could do with your natural magic was to misuse it, refute it, or waste it. In her quest to reach that happily-ever-after, Ursula had refuted everything about being a Caraway. For her, completing this list would allow her to celebrate and honor the familial magic she disrespected.

She'd revisit the Boss Witch List once she got hot coffee and breakfast in her system. Her eyes darted to the fridge, thinking of all the food that might spoil due to the lack of power. If she kept the door closed, she might be able to save the milk. *Why couldn't I see this problem coming?* Ever since she cast the Wish Spell, it was like she was wearing blinders and stumbling into the uncertain future.

The universe apparently wasn't done with knocking her down.

Mama's soft voice interrupted her thoughts, making Ursula refocus on her words.

"Sula, don't sit in the dark," Mama said. "Get yourself something to eat. I'll Zemo you."

Ursula covered her face, charmed at Mama mistaking two separate cash-sharing apps for one. "That's...not a thing. That doesn't exist."

"Go and treat yo' self," Mama sang. "Go visit Gwen. I'm sure she'd love to see you."

"I don't know." Ursula rocked back and forth.

"Doesn't she make her chocolate croissants today?" Mama asked in a not-so-innocent tone. Ursula perked up. That question kicked her tastebuds and her butt into gear. Gwen's handmade pastries made gargoyles weep with bliss and sold out every day. If she left now, she might manage to get a chocolatey puffy treat in her hands.

Fifteen minutes later and using a fierce power walk that would make Olympian competitors proud, Ursula made it to Gwen's bistro. She paused for a second before she went inside, studying her reflection in the front door. *Please let me look gorgeous just in case I run into my ex and his new woman today.* Long-sleeve graphic T-shirt with a bohemian image of a celestial moon. Cute dark-wash jeans. Ankle boots. Messy bun, whole lotta fun. Her quartz crystal pendant swinging from her neck. Tote bag slung over her shoulder.

Eh. It was a step down from her previous bougie witch style, but it would do.

Ursula took one last calming breath and repeated her brand-new mantra.

Be the enchantress.

She entered the Night Sky Bistro; the bell jangled at the corner. Framed antique postcards of Saturn and constellations lined the back navy-blue wall. Artisan sandwiches and bowls were arranged in a window display next to the stainless-steel counter and sleek cash register. Tall glass cases were almost empty save for a few leftover items: glazed doughnuts, paper-wrapped muffins, and croissants. Daily specials named after heavenly bodies were written in elegant white script on the black chalkboard by the cashier.

The sitting area consisted of small tables, where students from the local colleges had their laptops open and coffee cups half empty. Ursula approached the counter. Gwen was finishing making a fancy-looking drink in a big porcelain cup. Her microbraids were pulled away from her heart-shaped face, showing off her light silver eyeshadow and glossy lips. She wore the employee outfit—a Bistro T-shirt and black jeggings with high-top sneakers.

"Something wicked this way comes," Gwen said in a sing-song voice.

"You can only use that joke when it's October or Halloween," Ursula playfully countered.

"Haven't you heard? Halloween is a state of mind," Gwen said. Ursula pointed to the glass case, but Gwen waved her hand. "Don't worry. Ms. Niesha called ahead and put in your order. Your croissants are being warmed up."

"You're an angel." Ursula sauntered up to the counter,

noticing the heart-covered laminated menu. Smitten wasn't coming; it was already here. "Oh, this looks fancy."

Gwen gestured with her chin. "Check out the Smitten menu."

Ursula studied the offerings. It was a pastry paradise. Her inner baking competition judge shouted with glee.

"Éclairs. Cream puffs. Smoothies. Oh my. What should I order today?" Ursula said. What drink would an enchantress want? She looked over the menu and tapped the top drink option. "I'll have a Love Potion Number Ten, please."

Gwen pouted. "Order that next time. I made you something special. Voilà!"

She placed the finished treat on the counter and slid it over to Ursula. Her senses tingled. The lovely tan drink smelled like autumn spices, heavy with a mixture of cinnamon, nutmeg, and cloves. It was topped with a dollop of whipped cream and a generous sprinkle of dark orange pumpkin spice. This drink would be pinned on a kitchen witch's Pinterest page. Ursula licked her lips, then remembered what month it was. It was March. Her senses went into high alert. She looked at her younger half-sister with a raised brow. *What's up with this?*

Gwen answered the unasked question. "I was feeling like autumn."

"Did you even have pumpkin spice seasoning in the pantry?" Ursula asked.

Gwen's eyes lowered to the countertop. "I picked it up. I wanted to make your favorite drink. It's made with love."

Oh no. She said "favorite" as if she was trying to distract her from something else. Ursula grabbed the drink, and a vision shimmered in her mind. *Gwen in her pink and green froggy pajamas hustling through the aisles of a fancy grocery store, dropping jars of cinnamon and pumpkin spice into her basket, her hair wrapped under a silk headscarf. "Just tell her straight. Don't waffle. Be the boss like Dad said. Be kind. Be clear," she mumbled to herself. "Bad news goes down better with pumpkin spice."*

Ursula blinked back to see Gwen now giving her a big, wide smile. It seemed forced.

"This latte was made with lies!" Ursula hissed.

A nearby patron glanced over to the counter, a smirk on their face. Ursula studied Gwen. Something serious was going down in the Grove. She whispered the words from the vision. "Don't you remember? Bad news goes down better with pumpkin spice. Also, I didn't know you still have those froggy pajamas."

Ursula scooped up the drink.

Gwen's lips parted in surprise. "Beckett!" she trilled. "Watch the counter."

Beckett, one of the college workers busing tables, gave a thumbs-up. She dragged Ursula into the manager's office and shut the door. The office was spacious, with a desk and a bulletin board filled with a collection of payment invoices, scheduling sheets, and possible menu ideas. It was controlled chaos.

"Give me the bad news," Ursula said.

Her face fell a fraction. "I wasn't expecting to do it like this, but... Lincoln Walker asked me to cater for him. He wants to rent out the entire bistro for his birthday party."

"Oh, okay." That wasn't the news she was expecting, but

fine. She clutched the pumpkin spice latte with both hands. Lincoln's birthday was next month, but Ursula had completely pushed that date out of her mind, doing her best to move forward.

Ursula's phone buzzed repeatedly in her purse, but she ignored it. With her luck, that call would be the universe letting her know that an asteroid was coming to destroy her apartment. The hits kept coming.

"So, this is a latte spiced with guilt." Ursula took a sip of the drink, and her taste buds rejoiced at being transported to a pumpkin paradise. "That *is* good."

Gwen pressed her hands together. "I haven't responded to his email. I wanted to break the news to you before I... decided."

She worked her bottom lip between her teeth. Ursula shook her head. *My sweet Gwendolyn.* She had the same tell since she was in first grade, once conflicted between which costume to wear for Halloween. She didn't know whether she wanted to be an astronaut or a cheerleader, so she dressed up as a cheerleading astronaut.

"Business is business. Family is family. I can't assume that family will understand business," Gwen said a little stiffly.

Ursula narrowed her eyes at that all-too-familiar phrase. Her stomach tensed. "Dad called you, didn't he."

Gwen looked away. "I might have asked for his advice."

Ursula rolled her tongue in her mouth. Dad just couldn't leave things alone. He thought he knew best for everyone in the family, and he wasn't shy about telling them his opinions. The man gave her a subscription to JobMeetsHunter, a career and business website, as a holiday gift. He was always buzzing in Gwen's ear, saying that the bistro business was just something "she needed to get out of her system so she can start her real life." Now that the bistro was showing a profit, he expected Gwen to grow it into the next major fast-casual chain. He wanted a Night Sky on every corner in every town, but Gwen seemed more interested in nurturing her work-space than in replicating her business.

Dad was well meaning, but at some point, his advice was...too much. The expectations were too much. Gwen gave off major kitchen-witch energy, but Dad already had one caster for a daughter and he probably couldn't handle having another witchy woman in the family.

Gwen played with a pen on the desk. "Dad says I should take the job, despite everything that happened last year."

Ursula's lips thinned with irritation. It wasn't like Lincoln was her absent prom date; he didn't show up to their wedding! Memories of that night returned to her. Even as Ursula had stood in her wedding dress, Dad had peppered her with questions. *Did you scare him away? What did you do? People don't just leave for no good reason.* Mama stepped in and warned Dad to back off and give her space. Even Violet, Dad's wife, and Gwen's mom, took him outside and told him to take several breaths and calm down. Couldn't Dad take her side for once? A sense of bitterness went through her. Gwen had made sure that her champagne flute was full, and she had an endless supply of cake on her plate. She'd even led the crowd in an impromptu Wobble dance that had Ursula laughing through her tears.

Her little sister didn't leave her side.

Ursula pushed that night from her mind and refocused

on Gwen. There she sat in the swivel chair, her shoulders slumped and face creased sadly, as if she were the last kid to be picked up from school waiting for someone to claim her. To help her find her way. Protectiveness overshadowed any lingering feeling of bitterness.

Gwen's big sister needed to step up.

"Forget about what Dad wants. What do you want to do?"

Ursula noticed the sparkle of irritation in Gwen's eyes. "I want to serve Lincoln stale cake and warm pineapple juice, but... I really, really need the money."

"Then do it," Ursula said. "I'll be fine. Just promise me you'll misspell his name on whatever delicious cake you make him."

Gwen laughed. "I'll do what I can."

"I'm joking, of course. Make them your divine food and make their mouths water." Ursula pulled her in for a long, tight hug. Many times, the best part of Ursula's week was hanging out with Gwen and baking treats. The Walkers could be very demanding with their high expectations for low-stakes events. One word from the respected Walkers could make or break a business in Freya Grove. Gwen was going to need patience and a little touch of magic on her side.

She sent up a silent prayer to the new and old gods. *Keep her calm.*

"I'm drinking that pumpkin spice latte," Ursula said with a smile.

"It's on the house." Gwen kissed her cheek and pulled away. She opened the office door for Ursula, who carried the now-free drink. Beckett, who overheard everything, handed her lukewarm croissants on a plate. The bistro dining room was full, so Ursula sat at one of the tables outside. It was warm enough today that she'd be able to take in the sunshine without feeling like a Popsicle.

Ursula sipped from her drink, letting the flavors calm her mind. She pulled out her phone and saw a missed call from an unknown number. Probably a scam call. She noticed that she had a voice mail, but she'd check it later. If Gwen was hired to cater Lincoln's birthday party in mid-April, then it was only a matter of time before she'd run into him again. She'd be forced to make small talk. Her ears rang with what that horror show of a conversation could sound like.

How are you, Linc? I'm good. Just working at Mama's shop, reading fortunes, and struggling to keep my plants alive. No, I'm not dating anyone. I don't even have a cat, I have plants. Your new lady seems nice. You made the right decision to ditch me. I'm just going to dive headfirst into a bag of chocolate sprinkle doughnuts. I'll see you later.

Her body went into a full cringe. No. She needed to get into full enchantress mode.

She opened the Boss Witch List. The second item stood out to her like a stop sign. It was time to double down on her list. Ursula typed rapidly in between taking sips of the latte.

Ways to Get a Wish
Throw a coin in a fountain
Wish on the first star in the sky
Wish on a new pair of shoes before you wear them
[Grandpa James]

<u>Things that You Can Wish On</u>
Eyelashes
Ladybugs
Double numbers

Ursula took the last sip of her drink, letting the spices linger once she finished. Many of these ways to wish were mundane compared to her previous acts of magic, but they were doable—aka, cheap. It didn't cost much to wish, but she needed a fearless heart and a desire to change her fate. The stars knew that she had both in her possession and was ready to work.

Chapter Six

To pumpkin spice or not to pumpkin spice, that is the question? Ursula sat at the table scrolling through her screen, debating whether to order another latte. Right then, a broad shadow fell over the table. "Is this seat taken?"

She peered up from her phone and saw Xavier standing on the sidewalk in front of her.

His deep brown eyes widened a fraction once their eyes met. "Madame Caraway."

Ursula perked up in her seat once she heard her name on his lips.

"Your Highness," she said. "Is your superpower sneaking up on people?"

Xavier's mouth curled upward in a smile. "Fae *can* turn invisible, but I couldn't grasp that ability in boarding school."

Ursula let her eyes fall over Xavier. With his forest-green cardigan, open shirt, and pressed slacks with loafers, he was giving off a serious professor's-day-off vibe. Like he'd just finished his lecture about the best herbs for faery gardens and how to care for your enchanted plants. He held a cup of some tasty-looking coffee brew and a flaky croissant on a plate. The open collar of his shirt revealed a stone pendant on hemp thread. It immediately caught Ursula's attention. Why hadn't she seen it before? There wasn't a gem or crystal that she didn't stop to admire no matter what she was doing. She didn't pick the gemstone life; it picked her. The stone, the size of a half-dollar and light green with black stripes, gave off a delicate light, like a glow stick. Ursula blinked and the light disappeared.

Well, that was odd. Things were getting stranger in the Grove.

"May I join you?" He gestured to the open seat at her table.

She clicked off her phone and set it down by her mug. "Please sit, Your Highness."

"I insist that you call me Xavier." He sat down, put his items on the table, and rolled up his sleeves. Ursula's brow lifted in interest as she studied him quietly. The man had forearms for days and weeks.

She pumped the brakes on that thought.

Don't get too excited. He just went out with another woman last night.

"How was your date, Xavier?"

He blew out a soft breath and scratched the back of his neck. The look on his face was unreadable. "It was fine."

Ursula played with her mug. "So, you're going on a second date."

His face pinched as if she suggested that he eat chocolate-covered sardines. "No, but it was still an enjoyable evening, despite how it ended."

Her stomach dropped. She breathed deeply, rallying herself for what she was going to say.

"I want to apologize about last night," she said. "I turned down your rose because I'm not looking for anything serious."

Xavier tilted his head and remained quiet.

She continued. "I didn't mean to offend you. I should've explained how I felt." Ursula didn't want to share her sad tale again. She didn't want to see the flash of pity cross his face, the same pity that she constantly saw whenever someone learned about her abandonment. Ursula watched Xavier, noticing the faint shadow of discomfort in his eyes.

Did she say something wrong?

Xavier touched the bridge of his glasses and cleared his throat.

"Madame. You have nothing to apologize for. You don't know me or my intentions. I should clarify. We Alder Fae offer our lapel flowers to those who have aided us. It's a sign of friendship, nothing more."

Oh, okay. Ursula dropped her eyes downward, unable to look at him. Embarrassment coated her skin uncomfortably like spilled sugar that she couldn't brush off. Here she thought that he was considering courting her and the prince was being nice. She'd read more into the moment, because...well...she'd seen the sparks between them and thought there was more between them. Foolish Sula.

It would take longer for her to let the fairy tale go. But until then, she could use a friend or at least someone to talk to outside of Gwen and Mama. Her plants weren't going to tell her when she was going too hard on the orange blossom oil.

Ursula caught Xavier's eye. "Is it too late to accept that rose?"

He brightened and tapped her empty coffee mug. The dregs of the latte sparkled and twirled until it transformed into a bright orange rosebud. A soft gasp left her lips at the open display of magic. Her heart lifted in awe.

Xavier picked it up and held it out for her. "It's not much but it's yours."

Ursula plucked the rose from his fingers, accidentally brushing up against him. There weren't sparks this time around, but there was an invisible pulse of electricity that made her skin pop. He pulled back and rubbed the spot where they touched. Oh, he felt it too. She brought the bud to her nose. It smelled earthy and raw like a crushed pumpkin. The magic hummed against her skin.

Ursula tucked it behind her right ear.

"Do you come to this place often?" he asked.

"I practically live here," she said. "I inherited the family sweet tooth. If I could put sprinkles on bacon, I would."

There was a trace of laughter in his voice. "My godmother's the same way. I caught her pouring rainbow sprinkles in her tea."

"That sounds like an adventure," Ursula said with a grin.

Xavier wrinkled his nose in disgust. "I wouldn't use the word adventure to describe that drink."

"Maybe I can convince Gwen to put it in on the menu," Ursula offered. "She owns this place, and it's only going to get more crowded once Smitten by the Shore starts."

Xavier scratched his beard. "Tell me about Smitten by the Shore."

Ursula slapped a hand to her forehead. That's right. He had no clue what was coming this spring. As she went over the ins and outs of the festival, Xavier finished his food and drink, listening with his face scrunched. Once she was done telling him about the upcoming occasion, he crossed his arms.

"So basically the town becomes a huge matchmaking festival," Xavier said slowly. There was a sharp edge to his voice, as if someone played an elaborate trick on him. Maybe he was looking forward to a quiet stay in the Grove. You didn't come to the Grove to rest; you came here to let off steam. To revel by the Shore. Ursula pushed on, wanting to explain to Xavier what the return of Smitten meant to Freya Grove.

"Other than Halloween and the Founders' Day Festival, Smitten was one of the biggest and sparkliest events in town. It was so popular that even the goblins wore sequin capes and danced around."

"Was Smitten canceled because of a love spell gone wrong?" Xavier leaned forward, seemingly interested in her response. Everyone who came to the Grove assumed that magic was the root of all trouble, but it wasn't when it came to Smitten.

Ursula waved her hand. "It had nothing to do with charms or spells. The festival organizers spent more money than they were making and went out of business. The town took it hard."

Xavier nodded slowly but said nothing. She hoped that her answer calmed his concerns.

Ursula took a deep breath to keep down the swell of emotion. Secretly Ursula had been completely crushed when she received the email that her beloved festival wasn't coming back. She saved every souvenir T-shirt in her closet and kept all the tickets and pictures she collected over the years in her scrapbook. She believed in her heart of hearts that she'd meet her soulmate during Smitten season, just as her grandparents had, and finally start her love story. Once the festival was gone, Ursula felt silly for being so romantic. She put her memories in a box and stored them in Mama's storage unit. Soon after Smitten's demise, she and Lincoln met, and she forgot how joyful she had been about the festival until now.

Smitten was back, and she would take full advantage of this moment. Eat, drink, and be absolutely sexy.

"Everyone's excited it's back. The full schedule's already online." Ursula tapped her phone. "Freya Grove loves to help locals find for their own happily-ever-after. Don't worry, you won't notice the event that much. No one's going to sneak a love potion in your latte."

Xavier gave her a guarded look. "I should hope not."

"You might run into a few matchmakers and Cupids, but no one's going to make you fall in love," Ursula said gently.

Something uncertain flashed across his face. "Are you looking to be smitten this spring?"

There was a hint of hesitancy in his voice that gave her pause. She once was love's most passionate defender, but love had let her down when she needed it the most. Ursula needed to find her way back to celebrating love, but for now she was taking a break from the emotion.

"Ask me on another day," she said. "You don't want to hear my answer."

He lifted a brow. "Forgive me, Madame. Your words earlier piqued my curiosity."

"I said a lot of things," Ursula joked.

"You're not looking for something serious. May I ask why?"

All her reasons bubbled up in her head. Fun nights in the local tavern. Torrid love affairs. Freedom to make magic. Those reasons, while perfectly fine, weren't the true heart of the matter. When she fell in love again, she wanted it to stick for good. She wanted forever.

"I want to get it right next time," she said finally.

He made a small, empathetic sound. Maybe His Highness

had his own troubles with love. A tony-looking couple on the sidewalk holding their drinks glared at them. Gwen, cleaning off a nearby table, caught Ursula's attention and signaled to the time limit sign by the door.

It was time to head out.

"I think we're being rousted from our table," she said.

Xavier glanced at the hovering couple. He gave Ursula a sheepish grin. "I didn't even notice. Where are my manners?"

"I guess you were really enjoying yourself."

He held Ursula's eyes for a long second. Sincerity entered his voice. "Yes, I was."

His words made her feel seen after feeling invisible for so long. This fae man was too charming. Ursula rose from her seat. Xavier followed her lead, and they cleaned up after themselves before conceding their table. They dropped their cups and plates in the plastic dish bin left at the server's station, then strolled down the sidewalk away from the bistro.

"May I escort you to your next stop?" he asked.

"I'm only walking back to where I work."

"I'd love to see where the magic happens." He extended his bent arm to her.

Ursula took it and tucked herself into his side. Xavier slowed his pace and matched his stride with hers. With their arms intertwined, she felt a little giddy about being escorted by a prince to her day job. The little Sula inside of her heart, the one who would always believe in charming princes, cheered with glee. Tall trees with their bare limbs lined the sidewalk. Joyful birdsong played overhead. Streets were slick from what must have been a late-night rainstorm.

Xavier glanced down at the lingering wet patches.

"If we come across any large puddles, I regretfully left my cape in the Realm," he mused.

Ursula chuckled at his comment. "Don't worry, Your Highness. Despite what you've heard, witches aren't scared of water. We find swimming to be great cardio."

He leaned back in amusement. "Is that so?"

"Yes, it is. I thought that fair folk were fond of the water," she said.

"Only if the element calls to us," he said. "I find myself earthbound. I draw my power from crystals. Rocks. Being around plants revives me."

"Same here," Ursula admitted. "After a bad day at school or work, I'd spend an hour in my nana's garden and feel recharged. She planted daisies and zinnias to invite the fae to dance. I thought it was my own secret corner of the Grove."

"Tell me more," he insisted.

"I...adored it." Her voice broke as a vision flashed in her mind. She could see the wild honeysuckle-green vines climbing up the back trellis and thriving flowers in their beds. Butterflies fluttered around finding nectar and insects buzzed in the space. Weathered statues of gnomes and elves were dotted in random spots. The seashells and stones Ursula collected from the beach lined the narrow stone path to the house. Nana stood on the path wearing her blue house dress and a wide gardening hat covered with fake cherries, clearing out the old growth to make room for new life. The garden had been Ursula's playground, where she searched for leaping fae and learned the language of flowers. She missed that feeling of taking joy in magic. A swift wave of sorrow went through Ursula, forcing her to stop walking. She let out a shuddering exhale as the vision faded. Tears gathered in her eyes, and she shook her head, unable to speak about it anymore. Xavier, seeming to sense her change, took her hand and squeezed.

"I'm sorry," she said. She hadn't cried like this in months, but now she was leaking like a broken garden hose that couldn't be fixed. Lincoln had hated seeing her cry and often left the room to let her deal with her emotions. Ursula stepped back from Xavier and tried to wipe the tears before they fell. It was too late, and she felt them run down her cheeks. *Lock it up, Sula. He's probably looking for an escape plan.* The tears came steadily and didn't stop.

Xavier didn't flinch. He reached into his pocket and offered her his handkerchief.

Ursula took it and pressed it to her cheek.

"I usually hold back the tears until I know someone better," she joked.

He graced her with a kind smile that lifted her heart. "You don't have to hold back with me. I can handle it."

Ursula dabbed her face and returned the handkerchief to Xavier. They continued walking down the sidewalk, but she didn't take his arm again. She'd leaned on him enough for the day. Soon they reached the lavender storefront of Light as a Feather. Ursula peered through the main window to see the store was empty. The lights remained off and Mama's handwritten CLOSED DUE TO NO POWER sign was taped to the front door.

Ursula gestured to the sign. "We can't have customers inside the store now."

Xavier studied the shop with wide eyes. "I'd be happy to

come back another day for a reading," he said. "I'd like to know what the future holds."

Surprise skittered through her at his words. She assumed that a prince like Xavier wouldn't have to worry about his future. Woo a princess. Find a castle. Live happily ever after. His story was already lined up for him; all he needed to do was follow the plan.

If only I had that problem. Her path was unwritten. Blank. Empty. That emptiness scared the Hades out of her, but at least she had the list to guide her. She'd start working on it tonight.

Ursula fished her keys out of her purse. "Please visit. We'd be happy to have you."

She'd probably go upstairs and do a little light cleaning. For an instant, she thought about inviting Xavier up to the apartment for tea. But he'd already seen her cry; she wasn't ready for him to see her crystal collection just yet.

"Thank you for walking me back," she said.

"My godmother's having a party tonight," Xavier blurted out in a quick rush. There was a faint tremor in his words, as if he was nervous about telling her. No, she didn't believe that he'd be anxious about anything. Who wouldn't want to party with a prince? He probably had a dozen people waiting to hang out with him. Ursula waited for Xavier to speak again.

He stuffed his hands in his pockets. "I don't know if you have any plans for the equinox. I'd like to formally invite you to join us."

Ursula toyed with her keys, twisting them between her fingers. A fae prince was personally inviting her to a party. Old Ursula would've texted her cousins to enlist them in helping her find the perfect outfit to impress Xavier. This year's Ursula was grumpier and a whole lot wiser. Why invite her? Xavier probably snapped his fingers and people came running to entertain this royal fae. He probably invited all the Grove to keep him company and amuse him for the evening. Guests would be clamoring for his attention, and he'd forget about her when someone more interesting would come along. She'd be just another guest. It was on the tip of her tongue to turn Xavier down, but then she looked into his eyes and saw it— a flash of vulnerability that was so quick she might have missed it. Ursula recognized that emotion because she'd seen it in herself whenever she looked in the mirror.

"I don't have many friends in the Grove," he said in a low steady voice. "It'd be nice to know someone else at the party."

His eyes went down to his shoes as he studied the cracks in the sidewalk. A slight frown played on his lips. Her heart ached for him. She knew from firsthand experience what it was like to scroll through your phone and feel like there was no one you could call. To share your troubles with. Ursula wanted to chase that frown away and make him feel better. To make him feel seen.

"Well, wait until you meet the gnomes. They don't quit." Ursula gave a full-body shudder. She'd spent countless hours helping Nana clean up the herb garden after the gnomes got a little buck wild after a full moon.

Xavier looked up from the ground and laughed. He had an enjoyable laugh—it sounded like melodic summer rain on the roof and made her feel warm and light.

"I'd be honored to have you there," he said in a lower, huskier tone.

She stared wordlessly at Xavier, her heart pounding in her ears. From his tone, it was becoming clear that he wasn't handing out party invites like restaurants handed out take-out menus. This invite was meant just for her. It was the equinox, and she didn't want to be alone tonight.

It was time to dry her tears and welcome the spring.

"I have to watch the shop until the power's fixed. I might be late," she said.

"I'll wait for you," he said. "We should exchange numbers." Ursula nodded, took out her phone, and pointed to the camera lens. "May I? I get so many spam calls, I take pictures of my contacts," she explained.

A look of confusion crossed his face. "There's so much I don't know about this world."

"Well, I'm here to help."

Xavier posed, one hand in his pocket and one hand to his chest as she snapped a photo of him for his contact page. She studied his picture, her throat itching with thirst. If you searched the words "sexy whimsy professor aesthetic" online, you'd end up with an image that would closely match Xavier. He was effortlessly photogenic, while Ursula believed the last time she looked great in a picture was back in grade school. The jazzy blue and green laser backdrop made her look adorable, in her opinion.

"May I?" Xavier held up his phone. She nodded. He snapped a picture of her, stared at it for a long moment, then smiled. "Lovely."

She bit her lip to keep smiling.

They exchanged numbers and chatted for a moment about the weather. She didn't want him to leave yet, but she didn't have a reason for him to stay. Just when she was going to ask him in for tea, his phone buzzed. Xavier made a concerned face.

"I'm being summoned back to the house. There was a mix-up. Apparently, one of the caterers accidentally brought an iron grill."

Ursula winced. "Oh, that's bad." Those folks who knew their fae lore were aware that iron items were toxic to these beings.

Xavier bowed slightly at the waist. "Until tonight, Madame."

Charmed, Ursula gave him her biggest smile. He watched her, seemingly dazed for an instant, then turned away and walked down the sidewalk. Her fingers touched the rose tucked behind her ear. She felt the enduring fae magic, soft like dew water, on its petals. Her brain raced to recall what an orange rose symbolized. Ursula uttered a breathy laugh of wonder once she remembered its meaning. This flower represented bright energy and strength, two things that she desperately needed. She pressed a hand to her chest to quell her racing heart.

Slow down, Sula.

Princes like Xavier didn't exist except in pages of her storybooks and in her late-night dreams. She'd convinced herself that a man like him simply didn't exist. She'd told herself this story so she could swallow her doubts and finally commit to Lincoln. But Xavier was as real as the bare trees above her head and the morning sunlight falling on her hair. Even though her brain whooped and warned her about falling for the fairy tale again, she let herself indulge in this moment.

Chapter Seven

☾

"*We've arrived at your destination.*"

Ursula's phone chirped as she drove up to the residence in question. She looked out her car window and whistled loudly. *Come through, Gilded Age realness.* The manicured grass stretched out into the darkness, and down in the near distance was the wide Grove Lake. The water sparkled in the moonlight. Sleek luxury cars were parked neatly in the driveway, illuminated by path lighting. The house was at least two stories, and the wide doorway was filled with party guests clutching snack plates and half-empty glasses. Ursula parked down the street and made her way on foot back to the house. Under her breath, she whispered the mantra to keep herself from turning back, going home, and changing into her pajamas.

Be the enchantress.

She walked into the foyer and made her way into the main ballroom. The space was decorated with pastel ribbons and bunches of gardenias in tall vases. Her pulse kicked up with every step. Guests wore flowers pinned in their hair, draped around their necks, and woven in thick bushy beards. *Oh no.* Ursula shoved down the rising sense of alarm that she was seriously underdressed for the night. She'd let her gemstones be her decoration for the evening rather than spend money on flowers. Money was tight since she had to replace all the spoiled food in her apartment. Tonight was the first time she'd been to a party without a date by her side in years, so she needed to make a statement. *Come at me, universe.*

Only a color as fierce and bold as the sea would give her the confidence she needed.

A color like aquamarine. Ursula knew the stone with the same name gave the wearer a calm heart for difficult times. Right now, as she faced various expressions of surprise or pity from partygoers who either knew who she was or had heard her story, she drew strength from the color.

Everyone else wore the traditional pastel pinks, yellows, and greens of the spring season, while Ursula stood out in the oceanic shade. It was a bold move, but she wanted to start off the spring season strong. Enchantresses didn't wear muted shades; they were seen and admired like a precious stone.

This dress was Gwen's, who'd let Ursula borrow it only if she texted her from the party.

"Text me when you get there," Gwen had demanded. "Text me throughout the evening."

"I'll text you. I promise."

Ursula focused on the moment at hand. She took her phone from her clutch and sent a message: Got here safe. Thanks for everything. XOXO

Gwen's response came almost instantly: Go, do everything I wish I could. Then do it again.

Ursula sent a text to Xavier letting him know she arrived.

He responded: Thrilled to have you here. Will find you in a moment. Handling a flower emergency. Be with you soon.

She tucked her phone back into her clutch. Ursula walked around the party while beings and creatures chatted and gossiped. A considerable hush went over the room when they saw her. It seemed that she was magically infamous, the psychic who couldn't see her own downfall. Humans gave her the side-eye and wary looks, while supernatural beings gave a low hiss of interest.

Every time Ursula spoke to a guest, they gave her a stiff smile, listened for a moment, and walked away with a wave. Even the crushed-velvet-wearing vampires didn't make eye contact. She was starting to feel like a party foul in human form, as if she stunk up the place. Ursula went to the drink table, scanning the selection of water bottles and soda cans in a bin of ice.

A random horned partygoer bumped into her arm.

"Don't get too close," a deep voice hissed behind Ursula. "I hear bad luck is contagious."

Cold fury roiled in her gut. She turned to see a few guests peering at her over the top of their drinks. The one guest, with his all-black clothes, ghoulish facial features, sunken cheeks, and bug eyes, gave her a stare full of mockery. Of course, he'd been the one with the snide comment. Ghouls were notorious in the Grove for feasting on other folks' misfortune. She'd dealt with them since she was a baby witch and usually didn't let them rattle her nerves. But when Ursula felt so unsteady in her own skin, she couldn't let that comment slide. She'd already dealt with enough high school drama in her life, and she wasn't going to do it again when she was on the other side of thirty. Ursula faced him fully.

The best way to deal with a ghoul was to put them in their place.

"I'm sorry to hear the news," she said, injecting her voice with sympathy.

"What news?" the ghoul snapped. Folks were crowding around watching their exchange. If they wanted to see the sideshow act in person, then Ursula was going to give them a show to remember.

"I heard the local haunted house didn't hire you back last year," Ursula said.

"I...Don't...How dare you." His pale face became mottled with anger.

She waved a hand in his direction. "That's why you're dressed like a Halloween decoration in March, right? So you don't have to shop at Party Zone year-round."

Shocked gasps and laughs went through the crowd once they heard her comeback. Ursula wouldn't lift her pinky finger to hex him, but she wasn't above reading him like a library book. Mr. Ghoul breathed deeply and fixed a brittle smile on his face. He walked forward, stopping in front of her. He stood close enough to Ursula that she could make out the half-moon shadows underneath his gray eyes.

"I'm surprised you still have a sense of humor," he said softly, yet coldly. Ursula stilled at his icy tone. From his gaunt features and sullen expression, he looked like he needed a year's sleep and wouldn't hesitate to steal it from her. Maybe she should have ignored him, but it was too late for regrets. She reached up and touched her aquamarine necklace, drawing power from the gem.

Calm your heart.

"I like to laugh," she said in a small but steady voice.

"Well, I have a joke for you," he said. "What do you call a bride without a groom?"

Ursula shrugged.

"You call her a never wed," he said, his words dripping with ridicule. "A never wed. Isn't that funny?" Those gray eyes clawed into her skin like talons, causing a ripple of pain to vibrate over her body. She'd have to check to see if he'd drawn blood with those razor-sharp words.

"Hilarious," she whispered roughly.

His expression became openly amused as he seemed to think of something else to say. "Enjoy the party. Who knows? You might get lucky and find the next man who's going to ditch you."

She bit back a curse, recalling a key fact about these beings that she blocked out. Ghouls had the nasty ability to see your secret shame and lay it bare for the world to see. When she was young, they teased her mercilessly about Dad moving off to Meadowdale with his brand-new family. She'd managed to bury that hurt under her polished, prim exterior so that the ghouls would leave her alone.

Now she was laid bare, and her fresh pain made her a moving target.

Mr. Ghoul sauntered out of the room with his entourage following him. Guests who saw the whole conversation avoided looking in her direction. Suddenly she didn't feel thirsty anymore, wanting to get away from this area and be alone. Her hands shook and she couldn't catch her breath. This house was big enough that she could get lost for an hour. She'd find Xavier when she was steady enough to face him.

Ursula wandered the house until she found a reading nook filled with mystic items. She texted Xavier where she was and went about scanning book spines, running her fingertips over the embossed titles. The nook, outfitted with fluffy pillows and leather cushions, was next to a wide window looking out over the neighborhood and onto Freya Grove. The town from this view, with its crooked houses and dimly lit windows, looked like a hand-painted miniature of a spooky village. The scene before her was, for lack of a better word, enchanting.

Ursula took out her phone and opened her wish list. Tonight wasn't going to go to waste. What was one thing she could do now? **Wish on a star in the sky** caught her eye. The stars were out. Ursula scanned the sky outside the window, trying to find the brightest one.

"Star light, star bright," she sang. She settled on one that seemed to twinkle just for her. She heard someone approach the nook. From the corner of her eye, she saw his profile and knew Xavier had found her. Ursula quietly wished for a sign. She needed a sign that the magic, no matter how small or tiny, was still on her side. She'd felt it, but she hadn't seen it.

"The first star I see tonight, I wish I may, I wish I might—"

"Have this wish I wish tonight," Xavier finished.

A sudden thread of night magic, as delicate as a cobweb, shimmered in the air around her. She gasped softly at the sight. Ursula didn't move, not wanting to disturb it. The thread disappeared. Hope lifted her spirits. She thanked the star and turned toward the waiting prince.

Xavier stood by the tall lamp by the doorway, which gave

the room moody lighting. His bright eyes blinked at her from behind wire-rimmed glasses. His beard was a bit wild. He wore a light-green button-down shirt that was slightly open and showed off a V-shaped slice of skin. The stone pendant shined bright against his collarbone.

"I apologize for being delayed." Xavier held out a white gardenia. "Happy equinox."

"Thank you." She studied it for a heartbeat. Gardenias symbolized tenderness. Joy lit up within her. Ursula took the flower and tucked it behind her ear. She moved over in the nook and patted the spot next to her. Xavier sat down near Ursula, the leather cushion squeaking underneath him.

"I interrupted you."

Ursula shook her head. "It was nothing. I was just looking at the stars."

"I haven't seen natural magic like that in a while," he said.

"You saw that," Ursula said carefully. Practicing her craft in front of another person always made her feel as if she were caught cooking buck naked. It was private. Intimate. She looked at Xavier warily, worried about what she'd see in his face. Lincoln had treated her craft with disdain. Dad ignored it.

But right now, Xavier peered at her with nothing but curiosity. She relaxed.

"You picked a good spot to cast a spell," Xavier said. "I think Whitney bought this place just for this room."

"This home is lovely." Ursula chuckled. "Did your godmother win the lotto?"

"No, but plenty of people have asked her if they could win. I think that's her most requested wish," Xavier admitted.

She was quiet for a moment, putting all the pieces together. Her face burned as the realization hit. "Wait, your actual godmother is the Faery Godmother."

Xavier nodded; a small smile crossed his face. "She's one of them. Whitney inherited the job title from the previous fae when they retired."

"I can only imagine the retirement plan for faery godmothers," she said with a hint of awe. "I hope they get to keep their wands when they leave the office."

His smile widened at her comment. "Well, Whitney used to grant wishes full-time, but she's semiretired now."

Ursula made an impressed sound. "Does she only grant wishes on the weekend?"

"That's a good question." Xavier's brow lifted in thought. "I'll have to ask."

"My godmother's a soap opera actress," Ursula said teasingly. "How did you end up with a whole Faery Godmother to yourself?"

He wrinkled his nose in recollection for a second, then said, "Whitney grew up with my mother in the Realm. They attended boarding school together. When I was born, she insisted that she be my godmother."

"I wonder why."

His voice grew wistful. "We were both born on a blue moon. She took it as a sign to look after me."

"I like that story." She leaned in slightly toward Xavier, tilting her face to his.

He was close enough that she caught a whiff of his cologne. Fresh-squeezed grapefruit, newly cut grass, and hot-syrup-drenched pancakes on the table. *Stars above.* How did he smell like the perfect weekend? He pushed his glasses up the bridge of his nose and peered at Ursula. An invisible arrow of desire worked its way past her ribs and landed right in the base of her spine. When was the last time she was attracted to someone like this? Heat rose inside Ursula, causing her skin to flush all over. The arrow dug in deeper and twisted.

"Have you ever wanted to just skip right to your happy ending?" he whispered.

"I wish," she said earnestly. Her voice broke on the second word.

That was the *freaking* problem. She did wish with every ounce of magic in her bones. Lincoln ditched her. She messed up her closest friendships. Ursula lost everything—her career, her life, and her relationships with one single spell. The truth was right there. *You don't deserve a happy ending.* Her wish wasn't good enough to be granted. She looked down at her open-toed sandals, trying to remember the name of her nail polish so that the tears wouldn't fall from her eyes. Maybe it was the equinox, maybe it was the ghoul's words, but it was too much right now. *Don't cry. Don't cry. Do not cry.* No, not again. This had to be a record. The last time she cried twice in one day, she'd missed out on Comic-Con and Beyoncé tickets in one afternoon. Ursula looked up at him through her tears. His face softened. He took his handkerchief from his chest pocket, then handed it to her.

His voice was soothing, kind. "I didn't mean to...upset you again."

She took it and brushed away her tears. "It's not you. I've had terrible luck with wishes."

Would she ever forgive herself for casting her charmed life

away? Ursula clutched the handkerchief tightly against her palm.

"What did you wish for?" he asked.

Ursula gave him a side-eye. Reluctance held her tongue. It was bad enough that she didn't get what she wanted. She wasn't going to tell him or anyone. Caraways didn't share wishes. The only person who ever asked her was Lucy, and even then, Ursula hadn't had the nerve to tell her cousin. Now this gentlemanly fae wanted to know her secret. Even crazier, a tiny part of her wanted to tell him everything. To unburden her heart. To let him in. She opened, then closed her mouth.

The wish hadn't come true, but it was still hers to keep safe.

Ursula thrust the handkerchief back at him. "You don't randomly ask people what they wish for."

He took it back. "Why not?"

She fumbled for an answer. "It's like you asking me what color underwear I'm wearing."

He scanned her over thoughtfully, as if he was trying to imagine her in just her panties. Her skin tingled as he met her eyes.

"I bet it matches your dress." He tucked his cloth in his pocket, flexing a little bit, showing off his strength. "I've always liked teal."

"It's aquamarine," Ursula corrected.

Xavier straightened and adjusted his glasses again. "Hmm. Even better."

Hmm. That syllable sent her dormant imagination spinning. She envisioned his steady hand reaching over, slowly pulling her dress up her thighs to see her panties. His eyes would flash as he studied what lay underneath that aquamarine lace. A shiver of lust went through her as that image stayed in her mind. She pressed a hand to her stomach. Was there something in the air? Maybe they were pumping pheromones into the ventilation system.

She'd only known this fae prince for twenty-four hours, and she was already fantasizing about him. It'd been too long since anyone had looked at her as he did. Even Lincoln in the last six months of their relationship hadn't glanced at her like that. She wasn't searching for anything serious yet, but she was seriously liking Xavier. *You promised yourself no more fairy tales.*

The last thing she needed was to like a whole fae prince.

Ursula let out a sharp breath. "You wouldn't like it if I asked you about your wishes."

A defiant look crossed his face. "I'll gladly tell you, Madame."

Xavier lifted his hand and held up three fingers. He casually counted out his wishes. "One, I want to break this curse. Two, I want to go home to the Faerie Realm. Three, I'd like to know you better."

Ursula opened and closed her mouth, taken aback by his bluntness. That was a lot of information to take in all at once. She decided to start with the first wish.

"You're cursed." The words felt odd on her lips. She'd only read about cursed princes and princesses transformed into reptiles and birds as a child.

He spread his hands in a gesture of apology. "Yeah, it's kind of a big deal."

Xavier let out a heavy sigh. He motioned to the pillows

tucked behind Ursula. He reached over and fluffed them quickly for her. "If I'm going to burden you with my problems, I'd like you to be comfortable."

His hands briefly brushed her back, causing a little thrill to go through her body.

Ursula watched him lean against the nook wall. "How long have you been...cursed?"

His face paled. "It's been about a month. Whitney says it's more of an enchantment, but I've come to the Grove to try and break it."

Ursula tucked her legs under her butt. "A curse is meant to harm a person or being, but an enchantment is usually used to delight the person."

He snorted. "I don't feel delighted. The Faerie Queen thought I needed to learn a lesson."

"Do you need to learn a lesson?" Ursula asked subtly. She didn't get a beastly vibe from him, but he seemed to give off a sense of innate authority. That wasn't a surprise considering he was born a prince.

Xavier moved his shoulders in a shrug of anger. "I learned not to drink lilac wine ever again—I put my whole foot in my mouth, Madame. The Queen decided to enchant me for my rudeness."

What did he say to end up on the bad end of a wand? She held on to that question for later, worried that her fae prince was really a frog in disguise. *Wait. He's not yours. Pump your brakes.* Ursula knew enough about fairy tales to realize he'd probably have to complete a task to unburden him of this magic. "How can you break it?"

He frowned. "I have to find my perfect kiss."

"Oh, okay," she said. Ursula licked her lips. Awareness sparked her nerves. Well, that was new. It was usually the princess waiting for a kiss to free her from a wicked spell. She wanted to push for more details, but she held back and truly looked at him. His lively eyes shone with weariness. In all the stories she had read, those who were enchanted often had the power to set themselves free from their spell.

A growl of frustration left his mouth. "I don't even know what that is, a perfect kiss." He glanced at her mouth. "Have you ever had one?" he asked.

Oh. Ursula touched her lips, trying to remember kisses from previous romances. They all blended into a mental scrapbook of intimate caresses and smooches. She'd had some great kisses in her time, but not a single perfect one.

He lifted a brow in curiosity, but she shook her head. "I don't kiss and tell."

Xavier gave her a grin. "Does there have to be fireworks or rose petals thrown from the rooftops to make it perfect?"

"It doesn't have to be perfect; it has to feel perfect," Ursula said.

He gave her a questioning look, as if asking her to go on. She continued. "Think about the last perfect day you had. A day when you felt like anything was possible if you believed it could be. A good kiss should hint at the possibility of love. A perfect kiss should make you believe in a lifetime of love."

Xavier watched her for a second. "Whoa."

There was a world of wonder in that single word.

She shrugged sheepishly. "I know a little bit about story-book kisses. I have an unofficial degree in fairy tales, folklore, and mischief."

His jaw moved side to side, as if considering her. "I could use your knowledge in my quest. Will you aid me, my lady?"

Ursula smothered an uncertain groan. She was good at breaking budgets, but not enchantments. Xavier smiled again, but this time there was light behind it. It reminded her of the morning sun rising and setting the world aglow with the promise of a new day. Thoughts skittered to a halt. Ursula knew that smile would be the end of her sanity if she allowed it. Fae, in all their vicious beauty, could drive humans to distraction with the promise of satisfaction. He stared at her long enough that she saw the flecks of gold in his eyes, tempting her to tell him yes. A voice in her head whispered a dire warning. *If you start saying yes to him, you probably won't be able to stop.* A ripple of excitement went through her at that possibility.

Keep yourself safe. Yet her whole being filled with want.

She had her own problems to solve and didn't know if she could take his enchantment on right now. Besides, she'd sworn off fairy tales, and he was a whole storybook prince. Then again, he'd shown her kindness today on the sidewalk. Ursula wasn't saying no, but she was saying not now. Her phone buzzed in her clutch, but she didn't reach to answer it. She wanted to give Xavier the same time and attention he'd given her earlier.

Finally, she spoke. "I have to think about it."

"I respect that," Xavier said. "Would you like to discuss this offer over a drink?"

"My nana warned me about taking a drink from a fae."

"Is there anything you can do with me?" he joked.

There are about fifty things I'd like to do with you or to you.

She mentally shoved that aroused thought in a broom closet and locked that door.

"I'm sure we can think of something." Ursula glanced over his shoulder to the wall clock. She clicked her teeth together once she noticed the time. It was way past her bedtime. "It's getting late. I'm opening the shop tomorrow."

The power had been fixed shortly before she came to the party.

Ursula stood up, holding her clutch. Xavier rose with her. His lips dropped into an endearing pout. Oh, he was dangerous.

"Stay a little longer. Celebrate the equinox," he said. "I promise to have you back before midnight. I'll order you a ride."

Why was she racing home? Her plants were probably having a great time without her. It wouldn't hurt to stay out a little longer.

"Sure. I can stay for a little while."

His pout disappeared and that smile of his returned in full force. Her knees weakened, but she held strong. Ursula's phone buzzed rapidly. Someone left her a voice mail, so it must be important.

"I've got to check this message. Give me a moment, then I'm all yours."

The words sounded strange leaving her mouth. She hadn't been anyone's anything for a while, but she liked being here with Xavier. He nodded; his eyes twinkled with anticipation.

"I'll go get us a bottle," he said with a bow. "The space is yours, Madame."

She waited until he left the nook space, then took her phone out. The voice mail icon in the corner stood out.

Ursula typed in her code, then pressed the speaker button. Mama's voice came on the line. *"Hey, darling! Someone wanted to say hi!"*

There was a rustling on the line as if the phone was being traded from person to person.

"Hey, cuz. It's Sirena. I called before, but it was from a new number. I don't blame you for not answering, those robocalls are a hot mess. I wanted to say hey. My email got hacked, but Auntie gave me your contact info. A few cousins are getting together for drinks at the next full moon to celebrate. You know how we do. Text me. Don't be a stranger. Love you. Bye."

Ursula played it again. One phrase stood out to her. *You know how we do.* Yes. She did. Once, when Mama was on location for a Lifetime TV movie, Ursula had stayed with her cousins Lucy, Sirena, and Callie at their house. They stayed up late watching SNICK, eating cheesy snacks, and brewing beauty potions for the next morning. Ursula brought her crystals, Lucy read their tea leaves, Callie read their palms, and Sirena made chocolate milk.

They'd snuck into the kitchen to get the good syrup from the fridge and the full-fat milk. Sirena stirred the chocolate and whipped it up exactly seven times, until it was nice and frothy. They'd stood in the light of the fridge, being quiet so they wouldn't wake the adults.

"Look at the bubbles," Sirena had ordered them. "They'll form into a letter. Whatever letter appears in the milk will be the first letter of the name of your true love."

"No way!" Ursula peered at the bubbles in her cup. "I don't see anything."

"I can see it! It's an *L* or it might be a *Y*," Callie chirped.

"No," Lucy said. She glanced into the glass and grinned. "It's the letter—"

They all jumped when the kitchen light snapped on, and Auntie Vanessa stood, sleepy-eyed and in her nightgown. They were busted.

Auntie rubbed her forehead and gave them a stare. "Please tell me you weren't making a mess in this kitchen."

They guiltily looked around at the syrup stains, spilled milk, and chocolate-covered spoons on the counter.

"We were just having fun. Ma, you know how we do," Sirena said. She wiggled her fingers as though she was trying to coax her mama back to bed. From the you-really-think-I-was-born-yesterday look on her face, Auntie wasn't falling for it.

"I know," Auntie Vanessa said affectionately but firmly. "Y'all can do what you do tomorrow. Clean up this mess, then go back to bed. Now."

The party was over. They cleaned up and shuffled off to bed, falling asleep once their heads hit the pillows. Ursula never got to ask Lucy what letter she saw in the kitchen and forgot all about it when she woke up. Mama picked Ursula up the next night and she didn't sleep over at their house for a long time afterward.

What if fate had given her a hint all those years ago?

Suddenly, she was overcome with the desire to know the letter. That meant she'd have to screw up her courage to talk to the same cousin she'd threatened to hex. Yeah. The only way Ursula could face Lucy and her cousins was if she properly honored their magic. To do that, she needed to sincerely transform herself from the inside out, starting with her heart.

Ursula needed to make it strong enough to not only love another, but also herself. She'd ignored it like a plant she'd abandoned, left to wither on the windowsill.

That meant she had to give it light and space to grow. She couldn't hide in her upstairs apartment and lock herself away with her crystals. Ursula pressed her palm to her chest.

She looked toward the doorway where Xavier had departed from mere minutes ago. He had this glowing light he carried within him, a light that drew her close. Maybe it was truly fate that brought Xavier into her life. Maybe she was destined to use her charms and spells to aid this sweet, awkward prince his perfect kiss. If she couldn't get her happily-ever-after yet, then she was going to help him find his.

Maybe once she did complete this act, then her heart would find the courage to bloom into something magnificent.

Chapter Eight

"*C*an someone please turn down the sun?" Xavier hunched over in his seat, pressed his head against the coolness of the table, and wished for a bathtub filled with caffeine. Everything from his hairline to his fingernails pounded and ached. How much pink wine did he have to drink last night? Where were his glasses? Why was he covered in thick rose gold glitter? Outside on the patio this morning, birds chirped in nearby trees; the sky was a shade of baby blue with fluffy clouds. Insects buzzed overhead and flew down toward the sparkling lake in the close distance. He groaned. It was a true shame that he felt so terrible on a lovely day.

"Why does it all hurt?" he whined.

Whitney's voice came out crystalline and bemused. "Beloved, I believe you're hungover. Where did you put your glasses?"

"I don't recall. This is awful," Xavier said painfully. "I never got this hungover in the Realm."

He raised his head sluggishly and propped himself up on his arms, cradling his chin in his hands. Back home, he drank cases of the finest spirits and never had a single headache.

Here, he drank a few glasses of fancy grape juice they called wine and it felt like a tiny unicorn was tap dancing on his head.

"It's a mystery to me," Whitney murmured sympathetically. "Eat something, it'll make you feel better. I ordered breakfast!"

Xavier perused the feast before him. An assortment of sugar-crusted pastries, fresh-squeezed juices, and wrapped breakfast items labeled with Little Red Hen stickers was arranged on silver platters. Low vases filled with crayon-bright gerbera daisies decorated the table. Leftover party guests lingered around, grabbing a few items before blowing kisses to Whitney and departing the house. It seemed that people literally partied until dawn or at least until the food arrived. Xavier checked for the telltale silver container that held the brew his body literally ached to consume.

"Is there any coffee?" he asked, his voice croaky like he ate three frogs.

"I'm brewing some now," Whitney said. "It should be done soon."

Xavier sighed. "You know you could wave your wand and—*poof!*—you'd have a full spread."

Whitney clicked her teeth together. "It's not the same. I like the anticipation, which reminds me." She snapped her fingers and a thin smartphone appeared in her hand. Whitney turned the screen toward him. "I signed you up for a Smitten event at the tavern tomorrow! How whimsical!"

He didn't even bother to read the email. "I really don't feel like it. I'm still annoyed with you."

"Oh, you'll get over it," Whitney said with a confident

grin. "I saw Smitten as a chance to invest and give back to the community. Nothing more, nothing less."

During their floral emergency, he'd spoken to Whitney last night about Smitten by the Shore. Apparently, she completely "forgot" that he'd be staying with her during a matchmaking festival that she'd secretly paid for. Xavier grumbled irritably at her confession, but he loved her generous heart. Whitney was a patron of happily-ever-after and happy-for-now endings and loved seeing people live their best lives. From what details Ursula shared with him at the bistro, the entire Smitten event meant a lot to the Grove. A nagging thought came to him through his haze.

"Does Father know about this event?"

Xavier's head pounded. He found it difficult to make a genuine connection with anyone at such a chaotic mass dating event, but his father relished this type of rapid-fire matchmaking, believing that wooing as many ladies as possible was an effective strategy to finding a mate. He joked many times how he could manipulate situations with a snap of his fingers. He thought it would be hilarious to get Xavier caught in a compromising position in Rose Garden with a willing lady.

Whitney let out a shocked squeak. "Of course not! What His Royal Highness doesn't know won't hurt him. Now, back to the event. It's being held at a place named Two Princes! It's a sign from the universe."

Xavier would've rolled his eyes if it didn't hurt to blink. Whitney would take the name of the pub as a sign since Royce and Xavier were the only two princes in the immediate family. They also had Primrose, an outspoken princess who wasn't afraid to speak her mind about diplomatic matters. His chest ached. His missed his siblings terribly.

Xavier mumbled, "Not everything is a sign. I'm taking the week off to recover."

Whitney placed her phone on the table with a grin. "It seems you had a memorable equinox."

That was an understatement. Yes, it was so memorable he could barely lift his head. He'd been so excited that Ursula decided to stay that he indulged in wine and her company. They got a bottle of the finest wine from the caterer, borrowed two long-stemmed glasses, and talked in the nook for hours. As the evening progressed, he found himself becoming sprung on Ursula.

She spoke of herbs and charms with a vibrancy that made him sit up and pay attention. He'd never met anyone who spoke about the importance of black pepper like she did.

A snarky voice entered his head. *You like her. You like like her.*

This night wasn't part of the plan. He'd drunk more wine to keep himself from holding her hand. He'd had another drink to keep himself from cupping her cheek. The wine hit him hard, making him get bold with his thoughts and actions. *Ask her out.* As the alcohol flowed through his bloodstream, he was compelled to move and celebrate this moment. If he was moving on the dance floor, he was safe from asking her out for dinner. From asking her out on a real date.

She'd told him clearly that she was looking to get things right next time. She was holding out for real love. A witchy woman like Ursula deserved to keep her options open, not to be tied down to an enchanted prince.

He'd asked for her help, but he refrained from asking for her kiss.

They'd left the nook and went out to the dance floor, among the writhing bodies and flashing Technicolor lights. Music reverberated over his skin and through his bones, giving him the ability to let go and enjoy. With every note that blasted from the speaker, his concerns about the curse that clouded his mind cleared and gave way to movement. Dancers found the beat and moved together. Ursula mouthed the words, slinking her hips hypnotically back and forth. Xavier paused and just watched. Dance lights overhead made her hair shine like polished obsidian. Her turquoise necklace glowed against her lovely skin. The shimmery fabric of her dress—that *dress*—showed off her generous curves and she looked like an enchantress.

The sight of her in motion stole his breath and his sanity. He wanted her. Now.

He'd reached out for her hand, but she seemed to blend into the crowd, and after that, the night blurred into a glitter-filled memory. He'd woken up in a random bathtub still in last night's clothes, clutching a loofah to his chest. It was a little after nine o'clock. He'd changed into clean clothes and searched the common areas for Ursula, but he couldn't find her. His spirits dropped. She didn't come to the house to be his nursemaid; she'd come here to have a good time.

You fool, she probably left after your shameful display last night.

The thought tore at his insides. Whitney had called him down to eat breakfast, which he dutifully attended.

Once he drank a jug of coffee and got food in his stomach,

he would set about finding Ursula and apologizing for whatever he did.

"Did you tell your guest that breakfast's here?"

"Wait." Xavier stared at Whitney. "She's here."

"Yes, beloved. She stayed the night."

She did? He swiveled his head to look for her among the remaining guests. Wrong move. The world spun wildly, forcing him to lean back in his chair. He was sprawled out like a beached starfish with his arms and legs akimbo. For a long moment, he watched the clouds float in the vivid morning sky. *Hmm, that cloud looks like a cat eating ice cream.* He heard approaching footsteps on the patio; then Ursula appeared above him like a daydream. He sat up. Instead of the body-hugging aquamarine outfit from last night, she wore an oversized dress shirt that hit right below her knees. Wait. *She's wearing your shirt.* As long as he lived in this world or the next, he'd never forget how pretty she looked in his clothes. The mint-green shirt molded nicely to her form and brought out the natural glow of her skin. Her hair was swept up, away from her face, showing off those big brown eyes. She shifted underneath his attention, holding her clutch to her side.

"You look good in my shirt," he blurted out.

"Thanks," she said. A cautious grin spread across her face. It was splendid, like watching a morning glory open its petals to the dawn. His chest tightened. Did she somehow get prettier overnight?

"You've got glitter on you, Your Highness," she said.

"Uh...yes." Xavier stood to greet her, even though every muscle in his body shrieked for rest. Manners won out over pain. He rose to his feet for Ursula because she'd stayed. Whitney cleared her throat, reminding him of her presence, which prompted him to make a proper introduction. He heard an excited squeak escape Ursula's lips once she saw his godmother.

"Whitney Blackthorne, I'd like for you to meet Madame Ursula Caraway."

"It's an honor." Whitney extended her hand to Ursula, who shook it.

Her grin grew confident and widened a fraction. "It's a pleasure to meet you."

Whitney held her hand for a beat, then let it go. "Forgive me for being nosy, but by any chance are you related to Ruth Caraway?"

Xavier looked between them. He noticed Ursula's eyes dimmed a bit. "Yes, she was my grandmother."

Whitney pressed a hand to her chest and smiled. "I knew you looked familiar. You have her eyes and that cute button nose. Oh! I was heartbroken to hear about her passing. You have my condolences. Please sit."

Xavier pulled out Ursula's chair for her. As she sat down, she gave him a glance over her shoulder. "How are you feeling? I thought you'd still be in the bathtub."

Pardon me? Apparently she knew more about what happened last night than he did. They'd have to speak later without Whitney listening in.

"I'm good. I managed to get out on my own," he quipped.

She gifted him with a small laugh. He was close enough to Ursula that he caught a hint of her scent. It was rich, flowery like a warm breeze through a blooming garden.

There was another base note beneath there that reminded him of fresh earth in the summer. He inhaled. A fae could get hooked on that scent. He pushed away from her chair to give his nose breathing room. He quietly chided himself. *Mind your manners. Don't sniff your guest.* Xavier returned to his seat.

Whitney turned to him. "Why didn't you tell me you knew a Caraway?"

"I didn't know I knew someone so exceptional." Xavier looked to Ursula.

Whitney cooed. "Absolutely! Tell me how you met each other."

"Prince Xavier thought I was his mystery date," Ursula explained.

"Get out of here," Whitney said. She clapped her hands excitedly like a little child who was allowed to eat candy for breakfast. "What a cute meeting!"

He was going to down an entire pot of coffee as soon as possible. "It was embarrassing, but Madame Caraway was kind enough to point me in the right direction."

What if she hadn't corrected him? What if they'd just pretended even for a night that they were fated to meet? *What if...* Xavier reined in those fantasies.

It made no sense to dwell on the past. They were here now. Together.

Whitney held up her phone to Ursula and Xavier. The screen was open to the Two Princes Tavern website. There were hearts dancing all over the screen. His head spun. *My crown for a cup of coffee.*

"Please convince Prince Xavier to go," Whitney insisted.

"I'm not that magical." Ursula beamed a bright smile at Whitney. "I have a feeling His Highness can be hardheaded."

His face ached. Why wasn't she calling him Xavier? Did he do or say something wrong last night?

"I think that he'd have a good time," Whitney said with a sigh. "He's always been so shy. On his first day of school, he hid behind the teacher's desk. He'd only go back to school if he could bring his stuffed dragon in his backpack. What did you name it?"

"His name was Herb." Xavier's cheeks burned, and he scrubbed a hand over his face. It was too early for the dragon stories. "Whitney, please can we wait until I have coffee before you embarrass me?"

"That's right! I almost forgot!" Whiney jumped from her seat and came over to Ursula. She squeezed her shoulder gently. "You must come back over for tea! I'm so thrilled he found a friend like you."

Whitney cooed at him like a proud parent whose pre-schooler found a playmate by the swing. He ducked his head down, feeling the tips of his ears prickle. She planted a quick kiss on his head, then hustled back into the house. Xavier glanced around the patio area. Apparently, only he and Ursula were left alone with the breakfast spread.

"How did you sleep?" he asked.

"I slept well. Thank you for asking, Your Highness," Ursula said.

She looked down at her hands. Disappointment flickered through him. He liked when she called him by his name. He wanted to hear it again.

"Madame, is there a reason you're not calling me Xavier?

Did I offend you somehow? I don't remember what happened." He gave his head a slow shake. "I probably ruined your dress. It looked nice on you."

Her head snapped up. "No. You earned your title last night. You were an absolute prince. Literally. There *was* an accident," Ursula said. She frowned deeply. "I'm sure the stain will come out. I hope."

He suddenly felt ill. "I'll make it up to you. I apologize for ruining your night."

"Oh no, Your Highness. You didn't ruin it. It's just..." Ursula sighed. Her words came out in a rush. "Whenever I hear the song 'Finally' by Ms. CeCe Peniston, I can't help it. I go into trance. I start dancing like a drunk octopus." She winced. "We were having a great time; I went too big. I knocked into a satyr and spilled his drink all over me. I made a scene. It was humiliating. You spent your party cleaning me up." Her face flushed. "You even insisted I take your bed."

She...was in...your bed. He rubbed his eyes with the heels of his hands. Xavier usually didn't let anyone who wasn't related to him by blood or honor this close to him. Even back in the Realm, Xavier made his own bed and washed his own clothes, much to Father's horror. It wasn't about being humble; it was about protecting his privacy. Court gossips weren't above paying off their servants to search through his brother's dresser for secrets or spy on his sister for evidence of a scandal. His ears burned at the mere thought of a stranger being in his personal space.

But the idea of Ursula, supine and sleepy, in his bed didn't sound so bad.

Xavier blinked that thought away. He dropped his hands on the table.

"I agree with Whitney," Ursula said. "You'd have a good time at the tavern."

"We could have a good time together," he suggested.

She regarded him for a long second, then nodded. "Be careful, Xavier. We might accidentally become friends," she teased. "You're going to get sick of me."

If I got sick of you, I'd just take medicine.

"I've decided, after much thought, to help you with your enchantment," Ursula said. "I can be your wingwoman."

Gratitude gripped his throat. She was on his side. He swallowed to clear a knot of emotion.

"You have wings," he said. "You didn't tell me you were an angel."

Xavier bit his lip. Even he knew that line was cheesy. Ursula winced at his attempt at flirting. "We've got to work on your game. Don't worry, Xavier. I got you. You're going to get that kiss and fall in love."

Discomfort spiked within his head at her seemingly hopeful words. He'd told her about his curse last night but had omitted the one key detail. He didn't believe in love. Even though her words on perfect kisses and love last night had stirred longing within him, he shut it down. Alders didn't really do love. In fact, when it came to the subject of love, Father's personal motto was *First comes marriage, then companionship, and if you're lucky, love will arrive in time.* Over time, that motto transformed into a prophecy as Xavier watched his closest relatives make good matches but affectionless marriages. Love was meant for other folks, but it wasn't meant for him. Xavier didn't want to tell Ursula this because she was the real deal—she was a true romantic. His heart twisted. It didn't feel right to lie by omission. He didn't want to see the disappointment flicker in her eyes when she learned the truth about him. His brain set his heart straight. *You don't need love to break the curse; you just need the kiss. Toughen up.*

Whitney returned to the patio table, cradling a cup of steaming coffee. "Apparently you can make coffee too hot. Be careful."

"Bless the glimmer on your wings." Xavier clutched the cup for dear life. Just smelling the brew made him perk up.

"Don't drink too much," Whitney warned. "I'm ordering lunch. It's almost noon."

Ursula stilled. She reached into her clutch and looked at her phone. Her eyebrows popped up to her hairline. "It's—What?!" She leapt quickly from her seat like it was covered in angry spiders. "Where did the time go?!"

"Time flies when you're having fun," Whitney said with a wink.

"I'm super late for work! I've got to go."

"I'll walk you out." Xavier went to stand despite his lingering aches, but Ursula placed a gentle hand on his chest. He'd push through the pain if it allowed him to be near her an extra moment.

"No, stay," she insisted. "Finish your coffee. Rest. Um... I'll text you later."

Later. There was a hint of a promise in her voice that eased his headache. Xavier sat down again. Ursula hovered for a second, then hugged him. He pressed his head into her side, relishing in her softness. Blood rushed to the tops of his ears. The hug was over as quickly as it began. She let go of him, brushed a few flakes of stray glitter from his shoulder, and left. Xavier stood still for a long moment, then faced Whitney.

Her hazel eyes were kind, open and shining with a wild mischief usually reserved for circus entertainers.

"You look good without your glasses. You should lose them more often." Whitney flicked a quick glance at him. "If you need any new clothes, I know a fabulous outlet mall nearby we can go shopping."

He nodded. Whitney would use any occasion—a barbecue, a rainstorm, a parade—to go shopping. "Thanks, but I'll make do with my wardrobe."

"I know a good barbershop downtown. Get yourself shaped up before the event tomorrow." Whitney winked at him and reached for her teacup. Xavier blinked, his mind turning with options. He rubbed his beard, which was overdue for a cut. *What are you going to wear?* Excitement went through his chest as he thought about going out with Ursula.

Is this what having fun felt like? He was really starting to enjoy it.

Chapter Nine

*I*s that minotaur flirting with me?

Xavier's mouth dried up. He held on to his pint of ice water as the horned creature in question gave a finger wave in his general direction. *Okay. Be cool. Be friendly.* How would he flirt with a minotaur? What would he make small talk about? Mazes? Mythology? Now he wished he'd paid more attention in Professor Lavoe's art history class. He emptied his water in one gulp and clutched the glass to his chest. The minotaur was now waving frantically as if trying to get his attention. Xavier looked over his shoulder, to see another minotaur coming into the tavern. Relief flooded through him. He leaned against the dartboard and let out a sigh. That interaction would've been an absolute disaster on his part. He could barely flirt with humans let alone mythical creatures. Ursula had insisted that they go off in separate directions in the bar, then come back together later in the evening. She didn't want to "mess up his vibe" or "send the wrong message" by staying together.

"People might think we're a couple," she said jokingly. Xavier bit the inside of his cheek to keep from commenting.

He should be so lucky to have a woman as gorgeous as her by his side.

Exactly thirty-two minutes into the event, he wanted to hide under his bed and eat kale chips. Xavier hadn't managed to make a successful conversation with anyone in the bar, which only made him miss her company even more.

A stray thought floated through his mind like a lost balloon. *I wish I'd stayed with Ursula.*

Smitten by the Shore was increasingly becoming his personal gauntlet. Every flirty smile or innuendo-laced comment from a stranger hit him like a body blow and he froze. This was the same way he felt whenever he was required to attend a ball or dance back in the Realm.

He didn't know what to say, so he resorted to his default mode.

Shut up and smile. Look the princely part. Don't shame the family.

At least he wasn't alone. Xavier scanned the bar and found Ursula cradling her half-empty glass while talking to the woman on the neighboring stool. He breathed a little easier. She arrived at the tavern literally wearing hugs and kisses— her bubblegum pink dress was covered in Xs and Os in a cute design. He couldn't stop staring at how the dress showed off her shapely calves and the small heels made her sway like a bluebell flower on the vine.

Stop it. He snapped his attention away from Ursula.

From where he stood, he had a good view of the tavern space. Flags with dueling unicorns and roaring lions hung from the exposed beams. A garland of paper hearts decorated over the bar and doorways. A huge sign read NOMINATE YOUR

Smitten Sweetheart today! Details on the Smitten by the Shore website. Waiters switched between delivering steaming plates of appetizers and cleaning off tables with a damp cloth. The Two Princes Tavern was becoming increasingly crowded as more customers flowed in through the front door, but there were a few empty two-seater booths in the back, away from the bulk of the action.

He went over to the long wooden bar and eased next to Ursula. She was still chatting excitedly with the same woman with blackish hair and silver jewelry. Xavier just watched Ursula without saying a word. A rose quartz necklace dangled between her lush cleavage. Her black hair was artfully tousled around her face. From his angle, he could see the pale shimmer on her eyelids and slick gloss on her lips. Underneath the dim tavern lights, her skin looked smooth. He'd bet all the money in his pockets that her skin was smoother than fresh rose petals.

She turned to Xavier and her smile widened. His pulse kicked up.

"Your ears must be burning; I was just talking about you," she said.

Ursula moved so he could clearly see her friend. Oh. His face burned.

Where were his manners? He'd been so busy stumbling to get over to Ursula that he hadn't properly introduced himself to her companion.

Ursula gestured between the two of them. "Diane Dearworth, meet Xavier Alder. You're a magician, he's a fae prince. He's visiting the Grove and looking for love. She's open to new experiences."

"Thanks for being subtle," Diane joked in a velvety voice. She held out her hand to him. Xavier shook it. Her silver skull bracelet jangled as she moved. "Pleased to meet you."

He dipped his head in greeting. "Likewise. How do you know Madame Caraway?"

"Well, we went to high school together," Diane said fondly. "We played faeries in *A Midsummer Night's Dream*."

"Moth and Cobweb," Ursula supplied.

Diane pushed Ursula's arm with a friendly nudge. "We were also baby goths, until someone decided to go all country-club style on me."

"I couldn't pull off the vamp look," Ursula said sweetly. "Not all of us can rock black velvet and lace."

"You won't know until you try," Xavier said to her in a low, encouraging murmur.

He studied both ladies trying to imagine having their teenage witch escapades all over the Grove.

Diane was draped in complete onyx. The dyed ombré locks sitting on her wide shoulders popped against her black velvet dress and complemented her rich brown skin. Her lips were painted black and matched her pointy boots. Heavy eyeliner rimmed a pair of dark brown eyes that scanned him. Xavier wouldn't be surprised if she had a skull, bat, or spider hidden in her pocket. Where Diane was dressed in the colors of midnight, Ursula was wrapped in the pale pink colors of dawn. Whitney would have a field day dressing this witchy woman in the finest clothes she could find at the mall.

She caught him looking at her but said nothing. Ursula tucked a loose curl behind her ear. His heart skipped a beat.

He bet she could wear every color in the rainbow and look fabulous. His brain knocked some sense into him.

Hey, Prince Charming. She's not your possible date. Focus on Ms. Dearworth.

He looked over to Diane, who swirled the dregs of her drink against her wineglass. She gave him a piercing glance.

"Ursula's been singing your praises," Diane said. "I almost thought that you didn't exist, that she made you up from a storybook."

He eyed Ursula again. Why couldn't he stop looking at her? "She's too kind."

Xavier let something warm and gentle ease into his comment. She flushed lightly but remained silent. Suddenly, Ursula stood up from the stool as if she forgot a super important meeting she had to attend.

She positioned Xavier closer to Diane. "I'll be right back. I have a lip gloss emergency."

"Okay." Xavier peered at her lips, which had a shiny gleam. There was nothing she needed to fix; everything about her looked great.

Ursula winked at Diane, then moved to whisper in Xavier's ear, "I told you I got you."

Her breath tickled his skin, sending shivers up his spine. Her floral perfume floated in his nose. Made him think of secret gardens and parted tulips. He allowed himself to lean forward for a moment to capture a hint of her essence. She turned and left them alone. Xavier watched her saunter away, then faced Diane. They stared at each other across the sudden ring of silence between them. She gave him an intense, penetrating glare that made him feel like he was under a spotlight auditioning for the role of boyfriend. Ursula had gone through all this trouble to talk him up to her friend, so he was going to be a gentleman. He was going to be charming, damn it.

He sat up. "So, Ursula told you—"

Diane held up a hand, effectively cutting him off. "It's fine, Your Highness. I'm only talking to you so Ursula doesn't get too suspicious. I was raised in the art of distraction."

"Um—" Xavier let his mouth hang open.

"Pretend you're talking to me," Diane insisted.

Xavier cocked his head to the side. "We're talking now, right?"

Diane stroked her chin. "Honestly, I'm looking for a hookup, not a happily-ever-after. Ursula was so determined for me to meet you. I didn't want to hurt her feelings, especially after everything she'd been through, so I said yes to meeting you. We've met. We're not a match. I'm not your type."

"You're not?" Xavier asked.

Diane wagged her brow. "Magicians notice everything, Your Highness. I noticed you really, really like pink. You seem to like the shade of rose."

An image of Ursula's rose quartz flashed in his mind. Xavier remained silent, but he felt his ear tips turn red. Stupid fae ears were always telling on him.

Diane chuckled under her breath. "Life's so funny. I was hoping to set her up with Gus but…you…finally arrived. Timing is everything and you're super late, but at least you showed up."

She sipped her drink until it was completely empty. The

conversation had more twists and turns than a two-story water slide. Questions flew around his brain like fireflies buzzing around an open field. Why would she think that Ursula was waiting for him? What had she been through? Who was Gus? Judging from her silent glare, Diane didn't seem eager to answer any questions, so he wasn't going to ask her. Who knew magicians were this cryptic?

Xavier folded his arms. "So, you're not interested in me."

"Oh, no." Diane tilted her head, a twinkle of secret knowledge shining in her eyes. "I don't flirt with other people's dates."

He shrugged to hide the alarm that went through him. Was it that obvious that he favored Ursula?

"With all due respect, she's not my date. We're friends."

Diane snorted. "Just thank me in your wedding toast."

Xavier opened and closed his mouth, unable to come up with a response. Instead, he imagined himself dressed in a tailored tuxedo surrounded by wedding guests, looking at Ursula standing by his side in a white gown that made her sparkle like a treasured crystal. She probably would wear flowers in her hair on that day. His heart hoped. *Shut it down.* His brain stopped that fantasy. He wasn't here in the Grove to dream; he was here to break the spell. Besides, Ursula had plans for her life that didn't include him. Plans that had everything to do with falling in love and nothing to do with his enchantment. Diane nodded, seemingly pleased with his non-comeback.

She stood up, patting Xavier on the arm like they were old friends.

"She's been waiting for a long time, so don't let her down," she said in a warning tone.

Xavier sat upright. He couldn't let Diane leave yet. "Ursula's going to ask what happened. What should I tell her?"

Diane sighed and threw up her hands. "Tell her I had to pick up my top hat from the cleaners. Good night, Your Highness. Have fun."

She wiggled her fingers at him and swept out of the bar. Xavier rubbed his forehead. What a mess. He tanked a pre-date in record time, and it wasn't even his fault. Maybe he should have stayed in bed and recovered from his hangover. There was still a dull ache in his head, but he didn't want to read flora books and sulk about his situation. He let his attention drift around the tavern. This event seemed to be more popular than Whitney had led him to believe. Creatures and humans intermingled with each other, effortlessly laughing and flirting with ease.

It was so easy for everyone else, but not him. Xavier ordered another glass of water with extra ice, trying to decide what his next move should be. Ursula returned after ten minutes.

She stood before Xavier with a hopeful look on her face.

"Where's Diane? Are you guys going somewhere for dinner?"

Sweet Mab, he hated to disappoint her. Xavier delivered Diane's message. Crestfallen, her smile quickly faded.

"I'm going to get that Dearworth chick," she mumbled, seemingly more exasperated than angry. "I'm sorry, Xavier. I thought you'd be a good match." She leaned in next to him at the bar, close enough that their shoulders touched.

"It's not anyone's fault," he said.

Ursula stood in front of him. "Did she say anything else to you?"

Xavier shook his head, trying to remove Diane's words from his brain. A passing customer rudely pushed Ursula, forcing her to stumble and hop-step into him. Xavier caught her by the waist, holding her close to him to steady herself. They fit together, nice and snug. A rush of blood flowed through Xavier as she moved against him, her arms pressed against his chest.

Ursula murmured an apology, but Xavier didn't hear it. He heard the faint strain of someone singing a jubilant melody, but he didn't know where it was coming from. No, it wasn't music. It was his blood. He halted. Holding her in his arms made his blood sing.

What spell is she casting on me?

"It's getting crowded in here." She shifted, looking around to get a better view and accidentally rubbing up on him. In that moment, his soul leapt from his body. Where was here? Here was nowhere. Here was everywhere. Touching her felt like he escaped Earth's gravity, and everything felt weightless. He held her tightly so that he wouldn't float off into outer space. His hands held her tighter against him. Ursula faced Xavier, and her eyes softened, turning glossy.

He felt himself start to swell and grow excited.

Prince Xavier Henrie George Alder, get control of your hormones and act right. Smothering a groan, he blinked rapidly to force himself to calm down. He had to let go of Ursula— her soft, round curves—before he didn't have the strength to release her.

"Outside," he blurted, forcing his soul and reason back into his body.

She blinked. "Okay."

He eased up from the stool and took her by the wrist. Xavier motioned with his chin to the back entrance. Ursula nodded and they made their way through the crowd. People were going out to the back garden, and he'd spied some tables outside earlier in the evening. He pulled her along behind him until they found an empty table near the white trellis.

As they sat down, Ursula watched him closely. "I wish you were having a good time."

Xavier shook his head. "You're not responsible for that. Besides, I'm enjoying myself."

She perked up at his comment, but she seemed a little resigned. That pesky inner voice whined in his head. *Yes, you're enjoying yourself now because she's here. Alone with you.* Xavier turned that voice down until it was nothing but static.

"I'm supposed to be your wingwoman!" Ursula chirped. "We've got to get your perfect kiss." She narrowed her eyes, then gave him a curt nod. "That's it. We're attending as many Smitten events as possible. We're making you available to the eligible women of the Grove. There's even a dating app we can have you join. I'll help you with your profile."

He stared at Ursula; her eyes were now filled with what could only be seen as sheer defiance in the face of his enchantment. He sat back in awe. He was in the presence of a woman who would defy the will of the stars if she didn't like what she read in them.

"Someone has to live happily ever after," she said fiercely.

Ursula was working so hard to help him out, but he hadn't been honest with her. A strange mixture of gratitude and guilt churned in his chest. If she knew the truth about how he sincerely felt about love and all its trappings, she probably wouldn't lift a finger to help him. Here she was draped in love, and he had long shucked it off like a discarded scarf.

"I don't deserve your help," he said. "I haven't been honest with you about everything."

"What? You're not really a prince," she said quietly. She added a smile.

He folded his hands. "I am, but I never told you what I said to the Queen."

Xavier knew he wasn't perfect or charming as the fairy tales have promised.

"Let me guess. Did you tell the Queen her shoes were gaudy? Insult her throne? Tell her the tea was terrible?" Ursula asked, amusing herself.

He hated to be the one to end the fun she was having. The truth felt rough on his tongue, like sandpaper.

"I said something thoughtless." Xavier licked his lips but was unable to bring himself to speak again. As if sensing his mood shift, Ursula lowered her voice so only he could hear.

"We all have flaws," she said. Her fingers nervously toyed with the prism of rose quartz that hung from her necklace chain. He met her eyes as she spoke carefully. "If my life were being written by Shakespeare, believing in love would be my tragic flaw. I adored being in my last relationship so much. I wanted to be his perfect everything—girlfriend, partner, and even his perfect kiss. I acted horribly and hurt people trying to be what I thought he wanted. I understand being thoughtless, trying to be perfect and failing."

Ursula met his gaze and didn't back down. He'd seen that fierce look before when Mother awarded the knights of the Realm. Ursula was a fighter just like the knights who served the Alder House, the ones who secured their lands and watched over the people. They protected the lands with the same fierceness and strength that she had fought for love. She fought, failed but she still believed in love.

"Tell me what you said when you're ready." Ursula dropped the prism and placed her hands over his. Indeed, her skin was as smooth as it looked, as if she bathed with rose petals and milk bath lotion. Her touch was a balm his soul craved. He let out a relaxed sigh and stared down at their connected hands. A thread of fuzziness twirled inside Xavier. He never understood why holding hands was such a big deal when he was younger. It was so innocent. Now, having her hands on him felt so personal, as if she reached inside and tapped on his heart. His mind drifted, allowing him to wish for a precious second. He wished to feel her hands on his face, his chest, and his body. To feel her touch on the parts of him that yearned to be free from solitude.

Chapter Ten

Xavier didn't know how long they sat there holding hands at the wooden table, but he knew he didn't want to let her go just yet. He studied her hands, remembering reading a special book in the Royal Library that described how one could predict a person's traits just by studying their fingers, nails, and palms. Xavier smiled to himself. He liked the history he saw on her skin.

"What?" Ursula asked. "Did I mess up my manicure?"

"You have Earth hands," Xavier said merrily. He looked to Ursula, knowing that he was talking to a professional fortune teller, trained in various mystic arts. A small part of him wanted to impress her with what little knowledge he had. "I'm sure you know this fact."

Ursula grinned. "I do, but I like hearing it from you. Tell me what you see."

Xavier flipped his hands over so that they were palm to palm.

He cleared his throat, then spoke in a low tone. "Square palms. Short fingers. Strong headed and hearted. You can be grounded, but sometimes you find yourself looking to the stars."

Ursula said nothing but pressed her hands into his. They fit so right inside of his that it was nearly perfect. Her skin was soft and warm. Xavier wanted nothing more than to bow his head forward and kiss those hands.

"Excuse me?" a soft voice interrupted.

The spell was broken. They weren't alone anymore. Xavier reluctantly moved away from Ursula, shutting down his imagination before turning to the questioning voice. A statuesque woman in a pink puffer jacket and leggings stood nearby, clutching a laminated menu. She motioned to their empty chairs.

"Hiya! Would you mind if my boyfriend and I shared your table?"

"Please, be our guest. There's enough room." Xavier looked to Ursula for her agreement. It was her table too.

"Um, sure," she said. "Please join us."

"Hey, babe," the pink-shrouded woman called out, and a man wearing a polo shirt and khakis who had been hovering near the bar's patio entrance came over. "I found us a spot."

Xavier turned to Ursula. There was a stricken expression in her eyes as the man approached. The glow in her face dulled.

"I'm Zoe! This is Lincoln."

Xavier waved. "I'm Xavier. This is Ursula."

The couple sat down next to them. Xavier noted Ursula's set face and tight lips. He glanced at Lincoln, whose dark eyes appeared to hold a secret. Zoe placed the menu between them.

"Hello, Sula. You look good." The surprise in Lincoln's words sent a twinge of discomfort through Xavier's chest. He spoke as if he expected her to look different and was shocked to find her looking as she did. As if he expected to see her broken. Xavier slid closer to Ursula.

She didn't speak for a long, tense moment, then said, "Hi, Linc. You're doing well."

Zoe glanced from Lincoln to Ursula. "You know each other?"

Their eyes locked over the table. "We're friends," Lincoln said.

"We're old acquaintances," Ursula said in a tone that meant the opposite. Xavier knew that tone. It conveyed they had a hidden history, the same way that vampires didn't get along with werewolves. "It's been a while since we've last seen each other. Right, Linc?"

"So, this is a mini reunion!" Zoe trilled. "You'll have to come to Linc's birthday party. We're having it at Night Sky."

"We know that place," Ursula said. "Right, Xavier?"

He nodded. "Great coffee."

Zoe reached over and pinched Lincoln's cheek. "His birthday's coming up!"

"Oh, I remember," Ursula said with a clever smile. "It's April twenty-third. He's the best and worst of a Taurus. Strong, but stubborn." Zoe chuckled and they shared a quick laugh. Lincoln looked between the two women and frowned sightly. It seemed that he didn't like Ursula and Zoe getting along. He wrapped an arm around Zoe and held her close.

Lincoln's voice was cool when he spoke. "You sure there isn't a full moon that night? We don't want to interrupt any of your spell work."

"No, I checked my lunar almanac," Ursula said brightly.

"The full moon falls on the sixth. I don't know if you're aware, Zoe, but I'm a witch."

"Really?" Zoe's eyes widened. Her mouth dropped slightly.

Xavier glared at Lincoln, who watched the scene unfold with an uncomfortable grimace. *Why was he uncomfortable?* He'd been the one to stir up the punch bowl and didn't like the flavor. *I barely know you, sir, but I don't like you.*

Zoe clapped her hands. "That's so cool. My brother swears he can see ghosts. I can't, but I think it's awesome." She bounced in her seat.

"You do?" Lincoln said flatly.

She shot him a glance. "I never missed an episode of *Charmed*! You must join us."

Lincoln scowled. "We hope you can fit us in your schedule. You and your boyfriend are absolutely invited."

He said the word "boyfriend" with the same energy one said "unicorn poop." Even though he was mistaken about their relationship, Lincoln had had an attitude with Ursula since he sat down with them. What was his problem? Xavier seethed with fury. That was no way to speak to a lady.

"We'll be there, but he's not my boyfriend," Ursula countered. "He's my friend."

Her declaration wrapped around him with an invisible tenderness.

Lincoln glared at Ursula but stayed quiet.

Zoe, seemingly eager to move on from the awkward moment, held up the menu.

"Now, who wants to order some pretzel bites?"

Ursula raised her hand. The two ladies started chatting over appetizers and complimented each other's jewelry.

Lincoln watched them with a puckered brow. There was a thread of trust in those three words *He's my friend*, as delicate and beautiful as handblown glass. He didn't want to break it by being careless or let her down by holding back a simple truth about his enchantment. No one knew what he said to the Queen, because he'd been so ashamed to say those words out loud.

What would she think of him if he told her how he truly felt about love? The way she wholeheartedly believed in love humbled him. As a fae prince, he was expected to not only believe in love, but also effortlessly deliver a happily-ever-after to the lady he selected as his intended.

How was that possible? So, he didn't find his perfect kiss tonight. He glanced over to Ursula laughing at something Zoe said. Once Xavier heard her sweet laugh, in his soul he knew he'd found someone special.

Yarn flower garlands hung from budding trees. People staggered around clutching coffees in wrinkled clothes and dresses. Sidewalks were covered in wilting flower petals scattered from a previous night's celebration.

Put on your cutest underwear and open your heart. It was Smitten season.

Ursula sat near the gargoyles sleeping on the Gothic façade of the Freya Grove Public Library. She wasn't due back to the shop until the afternoon shift, so she decided to return a few books to the library. Ursula did a little research on spring charms and slow-cooker recipes at the computer center. There was nothing like late March weather with the light breeze, crystal blue sky, and fluffy clouds greeting her. She even saw a ladybug as she walked out of the building—the red and black spotted beauty flew right past her.

The wish left her lips before she could stop it: *Send me something sweet.*

Ursula hadn't found her groove yet almost three days into Smitten. She hadn't even gotten a chance to partake of Gwen's specialty menu yet. Mama's shop had been slammed with customers eager to find the perfect candle or oil that would give them a confidence boost. Xavier's perfect kiss avoided him, but he faithfully attended regular events with Ursula.

She checked her phone for any unread messages. She had three waiting for her.

One was from an unknown number.

Hi! This is Zoe! I enjoyed meeting you and Xavier. We've got to go shopping. I need to know where you got that necklace. Rose quartz is my jam.

Uncertainty stirred within Ursula. Zoe, who must have gotten her number from Lincoln, had sent her a text. What were the rules of befriending your ex-fiancé's new girlfriend? Maybe she needed to rewatch old episodes of Mama's soap opera for tips on how to handle this sticky situation. Zoe was so sweet to Ursula, her teeth were starting to ache, but her current relationship with Lincoln just made Ursula feel weird for responding. The man didn't do conflict and wanted everyone to get along. Eventually the truth would come out, but until then Ursula would be kind to her. She pushed through the oddness of texting her and responded.

> I enjoyed meeting you too! Of course, I'm a HUGE gemstone fan. I bought the necklace at my family's shop. Swing by sometime and I'll hook you up.

Zoe reacted with an excited emoji. All evening, she'd asked a dozen questions about Ursula's magic and listened closely. They'd shared a plate of pretzel bites with ground mustard while discussing the best way to wear birthstones. Lincoln watched them with a frown, sipping his drink and eyeing her. It was super clear that Zoe had no clue that she was talking to her boyfriend's ex-fiancée. If he hadn't told his new lady about their mutual past, then Ursula wasn't going to do it. Lincoln could do his own dirty work.

Ursula checked the next text. It was from Gwen. Her stomach tightened.

> Hey sis! I'm gonna need my dress soon! Got a 🔥 date this weekend.

Ugh. The dry cleaner couldn't completely fix the dress, and the stain looked like a shadow. She'd tell Gwen what happened, but she'd tell her in person.

The last outstanding message was from Diane. Annoyance splintered through her gut when she saw her name. Ursula figured Diane wasn't like her vagabond brother Gus, the local heartbreaker of the Jersey Shore, but Dearworths were all a little odd. Nana was right. Magicians could be so strange sometimes. If Diane wasn't interested in Xavier, then why did she let Ursula blather on about him for twenty minutes? She read the message hoping that maybe Diane would clarify why she didn't click with Xavier. Behind his professor-chic attire beat a big, chivalrous heart that was looking for a perfect kiss. Diane's text was only a hyperlink.

"I hope this isn't a scam or a Rickroll," Ursula said to the slumbering gargoyle. She clicked the link and was brought to a Shakespeare website. There on the page were three high-lighted lines from *Midsummer Night's Dream*: *"For aught that I could ever read, could ever hear by tale or history, The course of true love never did run smooth."*

Ursula scoffed. Yeah, okay. Leave it to Diane to put a cap-ital *D* in "drama." She always had a play quote or a comment that could relate to any situation. In another universe, Diane was either an award-winning actress or a theater reference guide with everything she knew about the theater world and plays. Maybe Ursula was coming on a little strong when it came to finding Xavier his kiss. She didn't want to consider a world in which a fae prince couldn't find a love that would break a spell. If he couldn't find his happy ending, then what chance did anyone else have? Even though the Two Princes Tavern evening was a bust in finding Xavier a date, they were going to meet up to get his online dating profile together. She would not fail him.

Ursula returned to Light as a Feather and relieved Mama from shop duty.

The afternoon was quiet, and she only had a handful of customers in two hours. Maybe everyone was taking the day off to sleep off the love magic. She sent a quick text to Gwen telling her to come over to the shop for her break.

Ursula settled in the front window chair eyeing Aunt Lulu's crystal ball. She couldn't recall the last time she'd read for herself or wanted to look into her future.

She touched the polished ball with a fingertip. *Slow your breath. Calm your mind. Seek the shadows.* Her mind sank into the crystal's center, trying to find the future inside that might come forth. Minutes burned away, but the crystal remained empty. It was clear. Open. Vast. She focused and went lower. Still nothing. Ursula lifted her mind out of the trance state. She blinked out and slumped back into the reading chair.

Great, she was being ghosted by a crystal ball.

The door swung open, and the shop bell jingled.

"Hey, soul sister!" Gwen came in wearing high-waisted jeans, ballet flats, and a T-shirt boldly stating GIVE ME SPACE with an astronaut dancing with a rogue planet. Waves of exhaustion and latent magic practically radiated from Gwen. Maybe little sister was brewing up more than just cookies in the kitchen and decided to dabble in a few potions. She held a coffee holder containing two drinks and a folded treat bag.

"Happy Smitten," Ursula sang. She stood from the chair to greet her.

Gwen studied her with a squint. "I'm loving the look. Hold on."

She plucked something small from Ursula's shoulder. It was an eyelash.

Gwen held it out on her fingertip. "Make a wish."

Ursula closed her eyes, made a silent request to have a

nice dinner and released a breath. She opened them to see Gwen scanning her with a critical eye. "I hope you wished for another shirt. You're giving me a Jersey country club vibe."

Ursula touched the shirt. Oh, right. This wasn't hers. Xavier's dress shirt was the only clean one she had in her closet, and she threw it on this morning. The cotton fabric was well-loved under her fingertips and against her skin. Despite being drunk that night, Xavier had been so gentle helping her out of the soaked dress and into dry clothes. She remembered the unspoken want that shimmered in his eyes when he accidentally caught a glimpse of Ursula in her underwear.

He'd turned too soon and seen her standing there in his unbuttoned shirt.

He'd flicked a quick glance over her body and inhaled sharply.

Xavier had buttoned up the shirt delicately as if he were covering a valuable statue, his hand lingering a beat too long on the last button. His finger grazed her chin. She'd closed her hand over his and grasped him. He leaned down and pressed his lips against her knuckles, his curly beard tickling her skin. Need zinged through her. Xavier whispered good night and left her to sleep. She'd lowered herself onto the bed's edge and stared at the closed door, wanting him to stay.

It had taken fifteen minutes until the need eased away.

"Earth to Sula!" Gwen stood in front of her with her brow raised.

Ursula blinked the memory away. "How's your Smitten going so far?"

"It was terrific." A deep blush came over Gwen's face.

"There was a cute centaur who just had to sing me a love ballad on the sidewalk—and you know how I feel about horses and...I lost track of time. I'm glad my dress helped you. Where is Oceana?"

Ursula winced. "You name your dresses."

"People name their wigs, why wouldn't I name my dresses?" Gwen pointed out. "So, where's my darling?"

Ursula let out a breath and told Gwen the bad news. "I was dancing with this cute fae. I got carried away and spilled wine all over Oceana. Xavier helped me soak it, but the stain didn't come out all the way, but I'll get it professionally cleaned. I ruined it. I'm sorry."

Gwen gasped sharply. "Wait, you were dancing with a cute fae named Xavier?"

"But I ruined your dress," Ursula repeated.

Her sister waved her hand in the air. "I'll consider it a sacrifice to the love gods if it means you're getting out. You haven't danced since..." Gwen's voice faded away.

Ursula made a noise. She knew. She hadn't danced since the wedding reception.

Gwen shook her head. "When was the last time you went out?"

"I picked up dinner last night. I had a large swamp soup from Magic Bone and Broth."

"Okay, Ms. Fancy." She peered at Ursula. "You know what I mean. When's the last time you went out with a friend? On a date?"

Ursula studied her chipped nails, not wanting to answer Gwen's well-meaning question.

It seemed that Lincoln inherited all their mutual buddies

in the aftermath of the jilting. No one wanted to lose the power that came with being near the mayor's son. She texted a few contacts, but no one responded—all her messages were left unread. Even Marcus, once her best friend, wanted nothing to do with Ursula. Loneliness felt like an itchy sweater she couldn't take off and wore underneath her clothes. She even created a dating profile and went out to dinner with a kindhearted Cupid who was a good listener.

She met Gwen's waiting stare. A sly look entered her sister's eyes. "Tell me more about this fae Xavier. Have you seen him again?"

"We went out the other night," Ursula said. "It was nice."

Despite running into Lincoln and dealing with his snide comments, the evening at the Two Princes Tavern ended up nicer than it started. Zoe bought her a glass of rosé and bent her ear about the next Mercury retrograde. She and Xavier shared plates of grilled cauliflower, baked cheese dip with sliced bread, and stuffed mushrooms. When they were almost done with their plates, he left her the last bite. His thoughtfulness always made her feel seen and cherished.

Gwen's excited squeaks brought Ursula back to the shop. She placed the drink holder and goodies on the counter and grabbed Ursula by the arm. A humorous gleam sparkled in her eyes. "Did the sun come out or was that a smile?"

"It was more of a grin, but yes, I had a nice time," Ursula admitted.

Gwen squealed. "It's about damn time."

Her stomach dropped. She didn't invite Gwen over here to giggle over Xavier. This conversation was getting a little off topic and she needed to get back on track. Maybe if Ursula brought up the dress again, Gwen would forget about Xavier. Then she could stop thinking and smiling about him.

"I'm so sorry about your dress. I promise I'll replace it," Ursula said.

Gwen waved her words away with a dismissive hand. "Buy me two dresses for my birthday. When can I meet your secret fae man?"

Nope. Her sister wasn't going to be distracted.

"You've kind of already met him," Ursula said slowly.

Gwen's eyes widened. "Was it that cute nerdy fae guy you were having coffee with? Oh, sis, he's gorgeous."

Ursula shook her head. "Um . . . he's just a friend."

Yes, her gorgeous friend who held her hands and read her history. Her friend who made her pumpkin-smelling roses. Who made her body pulse with need when he held her in his arms.

Gwen gave her a side-eye. "You're blushing a lot over a guy who you say is just a friend."

"You know what? I need to cleanse my thoughts." Ursula relit the incense holder. No matter how much incense she burned, his natural scent of fresh grass and sweetness refused to leave her alone. She like-liked Xavier like a middle schooler writing her crush's name all over her journal. No wonder it was called a crush; Ursula felt pressed like she was on a packed NJ Transit train on Memorial Day weekend.

The firm press of his body against hers at the bar haunted her waking hours.

Chapter Eleven

By two o'clock, the shop was as empty as a free plate of food samples at the local supermarket. After they finished their drinks and snacks, Gwen decided to hang out with Ursula and kept opening and twisting candle tins. Ursula reorganized the candles on the display for the third time, making sure that all their labels were facing out. Now that Light as a Feather was becoming known more for their specialty candles than their mystic offerings, she had to restock them every day.

Gwen studied the labels. "Which one of these candles will bring me money?"

Ursula playfully rolled her eyes. "You can buy a lotto ticket. These candles are for giving good vibes."

"Okay, so which one has 'give me money' vibes?" Gwen asked.

The doorbell jingled, effectively interrupting their conversation. Ursula's stomach dropped when she saw Quentin Jacobsen, current head of the Freya Grove Alumni Association, cross the threshold. His mouth was thin with a probing twist to it, and his inky black eyes were assessing. He was of medium height and build but carried himself with a commanding air of confidence. Hide your secrets and lies. There wasn't a rumor that he couldn't hunt down or a scandal he didn't spread.

If knowledge was power, then Quentin was an earl or at least a duke.

"Welcome to Light as a Feather, Quentin. How can I help you?" Ursula said in her most professional voice. A nosy customer was still a customer.

He gave them a polite smirk. "Good morning, ladies. I'm here for a little sandalwood and a chat," Quentin said. "You know Lincoln's back in town."

He went over to the essential oils and bath section. Ursula cut a quick look to Gwen, who took a protective step toward her. It was only a matter of time before someone scurried over here to tell her about Lincoln's return. Quentin picked up a bar of soap wrapped in paper and held it in his palm.

"I know. I saw him," Ursula said. She walked over to the counter, wanting to get some space. Quentin had Terminator vision and with one quick scan could determine a person's background, weaknesses, and possible actions.

He peered at the soap label. "So, you've spoken to Mr. Walker."

"We've talked," she repeated a bit more forcefully.

He looked up from the label and watched her. "So, you know he's not alone."

Oh, come on. The Hubble Telescope could see that Lincoln wasn't alone. Quentin knew this, but he wanted to know Ursula's opinion about this development.

"I'm aware and it's none of my business," Ursula said. She wanted to be left alone about this topic, but he was still a customer. "Do you want to pay now, or are you still browsing?"

"I'm still looking." Quentin, item in hand, moved over to the crystal shelf, his attention focused on an amethyst geode. "You know I'm running Smitten by the Shore."

Gwen congratulated him.

He nodded as if the job was a forgone conclusion. "I figured they'd ask for my help. Since the last alumni reunion was so successful, the Chamber of Commerce hired me. I noticed that you didn't attend the reunion last year."

"I was busy." Yes, Ursula had been busy trying to drag her way to the altar.

"I remember." He approached the counter with his item. "Well, I must come clean. I didn't come in to just shop and chat. We need to talk business."

"Okay." Ursula stiffened. She was ready to throw glitter in his face and run upstairs. He might be fast, but she was crafty.

Quentin stood tall and placed his item by the register. "I'm pleased to tell you that you are an official Smitten Sweetheart nominee. Over two hundred people personally named you."

She clutched her rose quartz necklace, trying to come up with the right response.

"The ballot's only been open two days!" Ursula said.

Well, she wasn't expecting this news. She expected Quentin had come in ready to tell her that Lincoln was going to propose to Zoe via skywriting or something that would make her feel even more haplessly single.

"I know. You broke a voting record." Quentin lifted his hands in surprise.

Gwen clapped and bounced on her toes. "You're a winner, baby!"

"Why did you ask all those questions about Lincoln?" Ursula asked.

"I wanted to know if you were over him," Quentin said with a clever smirk. Was he gleeful? "You can't waste this Smitten bait on your old guy. You're catching a new fish."

"Bait?" Reluctance squeezed her belly.

Quentin gave Ursula a sideways look. "Once we announce that you're the first nominee and your personal preferences, folks are going to be knocking down your door to woo you."

Gwen grasped her hands together. "You can only accept the nomination if you're single."

Ursula glanced from Gwen to Quentin. "I'm single, but why does it matter?"

"Don't you remember the Sweetheart legend?" Gwen pressed. "You taught it to me."

Ursula rolled her hand impatiently. "It's been a long year, sis. I forgot what I had for breakfast. Please remind me."

"Make the Sweetheart your wife, have a blissful life!" Gwen sang the rhyme with gusto.

Quentin gave her a thumbs-up. "The Committee wanted to recognize this milestone even though the official dinner and ceremony isn't until June. We're offering you and every nominee a complimentary gift basket stuffed with sweet goodies and a fancy dinner. Your picture's going to be in the paper and online. We're thinking about having a masquerade theme."

"That sounds like fun," Gwen said. "You'll be famous rather than infamous."

Ursula flinched inwardly. *You just had to ask for something sweet.* Over the last six months, she'd dealt with the story going viral and having strangers offer to marry her. Random people online quoting wedding songs at her and asking to meet them at the altar in her white dress. Ursula changed her work email and locked down her social media accounts. She wasn't looking forward to receiving any more public attention, no matter how well meaning it all was.

"Thank you but no," she said automatically.

"Hear him out," Gwen said.

Ursula slid her a sharp look. "I heard him out. The answer's still no."

She had her list; she was getting back to making wishes.

"I can make it worth your while." Quentin took out his phone and started typing on the keyboard. In an instant he went from friendly-ish customer to laser-focused manager.

"Are you going to pay me?" Ursula asked. "I take cash only."

"We can make a donation," Quentin said. "Our anonymous Smitten benefactor basically gave us a blank check to do anything we want. If you help us out with a few Sweetheart appearances, then we'd be happy to donate to Hopeful Heart in your name."

"Aw! Think of the kids! Think of the bingo-loving seniors!" Gwen pleaded. "How can you say no?"

Ursula rubbed her chin. Even though her sudden wedding reception and the media coverage brought in much needed attention, Hopeful Heart was always in dire need of donations to get through the next year. Quentin was making it hard to say no, but she still hesitated.

"I don't know," she said.

Was she ready to relive the jilted bride narrative in the media again?

"Listen. I'll be real with you." Quentin faced Ursula, rooting her to the spot with a firm stare. A glint of desperation shone in his eyes. "The previous Smitten Sweetheart Contest was a total disaster. There was a ballot-stuffing scandal that nearly tanked the entire thing. Your story is exactly what the contest needs. An almost-bride getting her second chance at happily-ever-after. You couldn't write that story!"

I didn't want the story in the first place.

"Real talk," Ursula said. "I'm moving on from all that botched wedding stuff. The online algorithm is messing up my flow. When you search my name, the first thing that pops up is me in that awful vintage dress."

"You didn't look bad in lace," Gwen said gently.

"We'll change the algorithm," Quentin said, slapping his hands together with each word. "Be our Sweetheart. Go out. Dress up. Find a handsome date to show you off to the Grove. Break the internet with how lovely, blessed, and hydrated you'll look. Change what people search and find about you. You're doing the Grove and me a favor." Quentin's heart was in the right place. Hopeful Heart absolutely needed the money and she wanted to help them out as much as possible.

Ursula scrubbed a hand over her face. "Maybe I'll accept the nomination."

Quentin held up his hands. "Say no more. Call me when you decide."

He thanked her again, then left, the shop bell jingling as the door closed behind him. Ursula went over to the door and flipped the sign to CLOSED.

She turned to Gwen, her face wrinkled in confusion.

"You've always said yes," Gwen said. "I don't think I've heard you say no—or maybe—before."

"That's the problem," Ursula said.

In the past, she'd busied herself with so many responsibilities so she wouldn't have time to stop. She filled her planner with meetings and events so she wouldn't have time to truly feel the deepening doubt she had about the life she'd artfully created. She'd thought that if she gave up pieces of herself for her and Lincoln's relationship that she'd gain something greater—a life worthy of a fairy-tale ending. She wanted it all back. Her courage to love. Her trust in magic. The only way she was going to get her life back was to complete her list.

If she'd paid attention, then maybe she wouldn't have got caught off guard and ended up jilted. Now she had the space to consider what she truly wanted from her life.

"Being a Smitten Sweetheart means you get pampered! Focus on you," Gwen said.

"What if I get caught up in all the romance? What if I meet a guy?"

She didn't want to get it wrong again.

Gwen folded her arms. "Okay, let's say you meet a guy, and you like him, and he likes you." She gave Ursula a questioning look. "What's the worst thing that could happen?"

The problem was she had met a guy. He was the prince who stayed by her side at the tavern. The one who offered his handkerchief and his arm when she needed it. His gentle touch kept her grounded. She closed her eyes and imagined his hand resting on the small of her back. His lips touching hers—Ursula closed her eyes, shutting down that runaway thought.

No, ma'am. Not today. His kiss was meant for someone else. His Highness was not allowed in her fantasy file. That honor was reserved for her internet boyfriends and handsome singers who serenaded her in her daydreams. She reconsidered Gwen's question. The worst thing that could happen was that she could lose herself.

Ursula could lose herself to the fairy tale again.

<u>Ways to Get a Wish</u>
Throw a coin in a fountain
~~Wish on the first star in the sky~~
Wish on a new pair of shoes before you wear
them [Grandpa Jay]

<u>Things that You Can Wish On</u>
~~Eyelashes~~
~~Ladybugs~~
Double numbers

April

THIS MONTH'S BIRTHSTONE: DIAMOND

*Diamonds when worn are thought to bring
courage to the wearer.*

Chapter Twelve

Xavier stared at his phone on the wooden coffee table, willing it to buzz. Was there a signal? It had a charged battery, and the cell signal was at full bars. Maybe he should sit closer to the door in case the coffee machine was messing with it. He glanced at his fellow Night Sky customers, many of whom were on their phones, texting and watching what sounded to be cat videos at high volume. At least the Wi-Fi was working.

Xavier stared at his phone, silently demanding it to heed him. *Buzz. Buzz now.*

It seemed to glare back at him on the table as if to say, *I don't know you.*

Last night, unable to sleep, he'd borrowed Whitney's laptop and logged onto EnChant, the premiere dating website for the weird, sexy, and supernatural, to update his bio. He thought this morning he'd get at least one notification, but it was nothing but crickets. No DMs. No chats. Not even a like. Yes, he was battling against Cupids, werewolves, and at least one superhero for dates, but was he not interesting? Was he not clickable? Was he not thirst worthy? He should've waited until he had Ursula's opinion, but…his saving grace was also his temptation.

The night at Two Princes Tavern had changed something within him. Sitting close to her at the table, brushing up against her in light touches, and laughing with her flipped on a switch within his chest. Why search for someone else when the woman who appealed to him was by his side?

They'd fallen into a nice routine over the last two weeks. From Wednesday to Saturday nights, Xavier and Ursula attended as many Smitten events as possible, trying to find him a date that would lead to his perfect kiss.

Wednesdays were game night at Two Princes Tavern. He'd watched in amusement as Ursula did a fist pump victory dance when she managed to win top score for trivia. They won a food and drink gift card and treated themselves to a platter of salt and pepper fries with extra seasoning.

Thursday nights were the art walk, where he and Ursula went to the Grove Emporium and browsed the various paintings and photographs on display. Afterward, they went to Mimi's Diner, shared a plate of mushroom nachos, and discussed their favorite pieces. Not surprisingly, Ursula was drawn to the art pieces that were picturesque. She'd been charmed by a photograph of a little child clutching a handful of dandelions in the middle of a field. Fascination hummed through him as he listened to the joy in her voice when she told him about how she tried to collect all the dandelions in her nana's garden in hopes of getting a hundred wishes.

"I didn't get those wishes, but I learned how to make dandelion tea," she said with a wink.

Friday nights were for rom-com double features at the

Jewel Box Theater, where they watched two romantic films for the price of one. He held back a grin when he caught Ursula mouthing the romantic declarations of one of the leads and cheering when the two lovers finally, predictably reunited. When the big movie screen kiss moment arrived, Ursula grabbed his arm and pressed. Her innocent touch froze his heartbeat mid-thump.

"Take notes, Your Highness," she insisted.

He stared at the screen, the swell of the romantic music, the dynamic lighting, and the frantic, passionate lip-lock searing this moment into his brain. Meanwhile, he felt her touch through the layers of clothing and willed his heart to start beating again. Once the kiss ended, Ursula pulled away from him. His heart picked up its rhythm, but he yearned for her touch.

Saturdays were a surprise. Last week they'd gone to the farmers' market, but the week before they'd managed to find a handmade-art festival being hosted by the local hardware store, Home and Hearth. He spent hours discussing wood-working and carpentry with the friendly shop owner, Mr. Giddings, and picked up a brochure for the local woodcraft group. Ursula introduced him to a few lady friends of hers whenever they went out on the town, but he wasn't inter-ested in talking to anyone else when Ursula was around. Even though she was his self-proclaimed wingwoman, he didn't feel right talking to anyone else when she was by his side.

When they were together, he wasn't just the second son or an Alder heir, but a man discovering new things every day. He liked salt and pepper fries with ketchup, enjoyed talking about the beauty of bronze sculptures, and knew the difference between walnut and oak wood. It was as if he was digging for and discovering new parts about himself he'd hidden away from the Realm. Despite all these outings, Xavier hadn't scored a date, but he found himself becoming increasing bewitched by Ursula.

One question kept turning in his brain. *Why not her?*

Those three words had kept him up past midnight for weeks. It had kept him from opening EnChant and starting his profile until last night. He didn't want to test the fragile, precious connection that they had for the possibility of a kiss that may or may not be perfect.

To kiss Ursula would be like cracking an opal—the action wouldn't change its beauty, but it would alter a precious thing almost behind repair.

He didn't want to alter someone so beautiful.

For that reason, he ignored how a simple brush against her hand sent a jolt through him whenever they touched. He pretended not to notice how her perfume lingered on his clothes and made him think of her smile hours later.

Xavier scrubbed a rough hand over his beard to try to reset his brain.

Enough daydreaming. It was time to get to work.

He opened EnChant on his phone, liking profiles and messaging any pixie or elf that looked interesting. Xavier kept waiting for a swipe, a text, or a like. Nothing. Happened. Soon, the screen blurred before him, and his eyes felt like they were being rubbed with sandpaper. The more he searched the site, the more doubt bubbled within him. There were so many other choices. So many interesting beings.

Who would pick an enchanted fae prince over a hipster zombie?

A voluptuous woman in a Night Sky shirt, an apron, and jeans approached his table. She held a strawberry drink and two muffins on a plate.

"I'm Gwen, Ursula's sister." She put the treats down on the table.

"I'm pleased to meet you." Xavier creased his brow. "I'm afraid I didn't order anything."

"Ursula texted. She told me to take care of you."

He stared at the items as if she'd delivered edible gold. It was a small act of kindness that lifted his gloomy mood. It seemed that Ursula was indeed a true lady.

He spoke through the lump in his throat. "Thank you very much."

Gwen strolled away. So far, his inbox was empty. His plate and heart, however, were not. He ate but saved Ursula the bigger muffin for when she arrived. Xavier was in the middle of changing his avatar picture when he heard the front bell jingle.

He looked up from the screen, and time slowed to a crawl.

Ursula walked into Night Sky, clutching an empty iced tea in her hand and a tote bag slung over her shoulder. She waved to Gwen at the counter, then glanced around the bistro sitting area searching for him. Xavier took her in. That lump in his throat now felt like he swallowed a whole sunflower. She wore a bright yellow dress, a strawberry-patterned sweater, and ballet flats with a pair of sunglasses that made her look like a glamourous movie star. He perked up when she spotted him, as light-headed as a teenager waiting for his cute lab partner to sit with him. Her loose curls bounced around her face as she approached, giving her an impish appearance.

How would she look twirling in the forest with flowers in her hair?

Xavier blinked rapidly. He reined in his thoughts. They were acting like free-range unicorns whenever it came to Ursula, running wild and free all over his sanity.

"Good morning," she said as she sat down across from him at the table. Her fingers played with the empty cup, rattling the ice around.

His nerves felt just as jumbled whenever she was around him.

He cleared his throat and returned the greeting. "I saved you a muffin."

Ursula lifted her sunglasses on top of her head and smiled. Her eyes looked a little tired, as if she didn't get much sleep last night. Concern fluttered his chest. "Thanks! I'm glad you got your food. I can't believe it's mid-April. Time's flying. We've got to get your kiss soon."

"That's old news." Xavier leaned back in his seat. "Is there anything new with you? How's the local Sweetheart?"

She slid the muffin plate over to her. "We had the Sweetheart Mixer last night. It was going great until someone suggested we go to Atlantic City. Suddenly, I find myself on a party bus speeding down the Garden State Parkway with Quentin and my fellow nominees."

Xavier blinked. Well, he didn't expect that answer. He'd read about the coastal resort town nicknamed the World's Famous Playground, but he'd never been there before.

"What happened next?" he asked.

He listened raptly as Ursula explained how she ended up

next to a roulette table drinking rose lemonade and playing something called the penny slots.

"So, listen to this," Ursula said in a low voice. "I'm on my last dollar and a cute demigod comes up my machine. He says he likes my smile and gives me the rest of his pennies."

"Okay." His mouth turned downward. Envy, deep and fiery, bubbled within him. He wished he could've been there to compliment her and make her blush.

She placed her cup on the table. "The moment I play Hecuba's—that's the demigod's name—pennies, I hit the jackpot! I never win, but I did. I tried to give him half but turned it down. I treated Hec and everyone with me out for late dinner instead. I forgot how good buffet food could be, but it was delicious." Ursula clapped her hands excitedly. "We just got back a few hours ago."

He let his gaze roam over Ursula, taking in her seemingly effortless beauty. Hecuba must have been spellbound by her presence. Did he really expect no one to notice this gem of a human being? It was only a matter of time before another man or fae would see how lovely she is, but Xavier didn't expect it to happen so soon.

"Are you going to see Hecuba again?" he asked.

Ursula wrinkled her nose. "I don't think so. Quentin invited him to the Sweetheart Ball in June, but he didn't seem interested. Demigods are fine as hell, but they don't really do commitment."

Xavier knew that Hecuba was indeed a fool for letting Ursula go. Xavier spied the lingering stares from interested men and supernatural beings whenever he and Ursula attended Smitten events. They studied her with open interest, while Xavier had to steal glances of her when she wasn't looking. He couldn't let himself like her too much. He had an enchantment to break and didn't want to make promises he couldn't keep. He couldn't stay.

Her face creased. "Is everything all right?"

No. I couldn't get you off my mind.

"I'm just feeling anxious about putting myself out there online," he said.

Ursula nodded. "I hear you. Dating is hard enough without adding block buttons and emojis. I can give you some feedback if you like."

"Absolutely, Madame." Xavier handed the phone to her. She scrolled through it, making some indecipherable sounds. Did she like it? Was he too cringe? Maybe he shouldn't look up slang on the internet anymore.

Ursula read aloud. "'Ill-fated prince looking for perfect spell-breaking kiss. Be the one who breaks the spell.'" She gave a pained look. "Oh, Xavier."

"I should change it from 'spell' to 'enchantment.' Is there too much repetition?"

She scoffed. "Yes, and are you trying to scare off dates?" Ursula pointed to his phone as if it insulted her shoes. "If I saw that profile, I'd say thank you, next. I'd burn frankincense to ward off bad energy. I'd cleanse my browser history."

"You've made your point, Madame." He lifted his chin. "My dates need to know what to expect with me."

She narrowed her eyes. "Has anyone clicked on your profile yet?"

He worked his jaw into a circle. "No, but give it time."

"Forgive me for being rude, but is time on your side?" she asked gently.

His chest burned at her blunt question. He shook his head.

"Give them a reason to click on you," she said. "Hint at the fairy tale."

His gut burned. Everyone loved the fairy-tale kiss, but no one ever asked what happened after. He'd witnessed how something that started sweet could quickly sour over time. Xavier counted the chocolate chips that dotted his muffin to keep from letting out a very ungentlemanly yell. He believed in being as honest as possible, not wanting to mislead anyone about his magical status.

He forced himself to look back at her. "Do you suggest I lie?"

If he had to mislead an innocent lady to get this so-called perfect kiss, he didn't want it.

"Wait until the first date or coffee date to talk," Ursula said. "Give her a chance to decide whether she wants to try to help you break the enchantment. I mean, you told me."

"Yes, but...you're magic," he said smoothly.

She smiled at him again, then looked back at his profile. "All is not lost, Xavier. Let's see what we can do to jazz up this profile."

He held back a smile. "Jazz up? Is that an official magical term?"

Ursula smirked but kept her eyes on his screen.

She was right, as usual. If he wanted to get home by mid-summer, then he needed to find his perfect kiss soon. Xavier loathed feeling the slow crawl of desperation up his back the longer he went without finding it.

She scanned his profile silently for a moment, but then made a surprised squeak. He grinned. The woman was a walking sound machine, her laughs and little sounds giving him a trill of amusement whenever she was near.

"Here's the problem!" she said. "Your profile's incomplete. Ladies probably think you're a bot! You didn't answer the last three questions about love and dating. Let's do that right now."

His chest hollowed out. "It's not necessary, is it?"

"It's a love and dating site." Ursula gave him an *Are you kidding me?* stare, complete with a lifted brow. "I'm sure future romantic interests want to know what you think about—well—romance."

From his experience, princesses and ladies in the Realm didn't think to ask what Xavier thought. They were only asked and instructed to care about his title and his crown by the matchmakers. They played the love match game as much as he did. Asking serious questions caused problems, so everyone smiled and asked about the weather and the latest juicy gossip.

Xavier took a fortifying breath. *You'll be fine.*

Like a fanged monster under a bed, love couldn't hurt him if he didn't believe in it. He didn't believe, but she did. What would Ursula think about him when she found out?

His stomach twisted. He clutched his chair's armrests to quell the rising nerves.

Ursula read off the screen. "'What's your ideal date? Be as specific as possible.'"

"I love to have lunch in a local park or garden," he admitted. "We'd look at the blooming flowers and plants while eating as much bread and mushrooms as possible. Then we'd stroll through and talk until the stars came out. What about you, Madame?"

"I like eating snacks and watching movies at home," she said. "It's not exciting, but I'd want to spend as much time alone with my date as possible."

"You wouldn't want to go to Lighthouse for a nice dinner?" he suggested.

Xavier pictured Ursula at the table dressed in pink, glowing under the candlelight, sharing a slice of chocolate cake. It was a pretty image.

"I've been there," Ursula said coolly. "I've eaten at the best places in town, but I had a terrible time. I want to enjoy the company. Give me turkey and Swiss sandwiches from Wawa with a bottled iced tea and a good conversation at the beach. That sounds ideal to me."

Xavier quietly filed that information away. Once he found his perfect kiss, he'd take Ursula out to say thank you for all her help.

She read off the screen again. "'Describe yourself in three words to your potential date.'"

"Loyal. Direct. Humorous."

"I didn't hear charming," she sang.

He shook his head. "I'm definitely not that."

"Okay. If you're not charming, then what are you?"

He thought for a second, then answered. "Awkward. Really into plants and rocks. Terrible sense of direction."

"Determined. Passionate. Unique," Ursula countered. "You're a literal prince. Fairy tales are the ideal, not the rule. We all want a shot at the castle in the sky, but what we get if we're lucky is a warm place to lay our head. Maybe we find a man who cares enough to kiss us good night."

Who did she want to kiss?

"Have you found that guy?" he asked.

"I thought I did." There was a tart note in her voice that didn't invite any follow-up questions. Sometimes, like back in the tavern, she was open about her past relationship. Other times she was vague about certain details. It was like slowly gathering pieces of a puzzle and he was seeing the full picture before him take shape. She didn't share specific names and places; he got the sense that Ursula fought for and lost love before. This lady-knight had battle scars on her heart.

Ursula looked to him expectantly. "Do you believe in true love?"

He paused. Blood rushed to the tips of his ears, and he opened his mouth. Nothing, no sound came out. The pause went on too long.

He licked his bottom lip and forced the words out. "I...do?"

Ursula's face scrunched in confusion. "Are you asking me or telling me?"

Xavier held back an unprincely curse. His breath grew thin. "Yes."

Her eyes narrowed. He felt pinned to the chair, unable to move under her glare. "Your Highness, do you believe in true love or not?"

"No." He lowered his head, unable to bear seeing the disappointment in her eyes. A sarcastic voice inside sniped at him. *Great job, Prince Charming.*

"Um...wow."

Xavier forced himself to look at Ursula. There was something about her soft tone that bothered him. She looked at Xavier sideways rather than straight on like she usually did. An uncomfortable feeling that felt close to humiliation grew in his belly when she finally gave him a pained grin. The truth hit Xavier square in the chest and stole his breath.

She wasn't disappointed. It was worse. Ursula pitied him.

Xavier sat with that knowledge. *She* felt sorry for *him*. The humiliation quickly turned into pure defiance. He raised his chin and stared back at her. Xavier Henrie George was the second son of King Roman and Queen Hazel, an honored member of the House of Alder, one of the finest and strongest families in the Realm. Pride threaded within his body as he pushed away that feeling in his belly. He didn't need or want her pity or her sympathy, no matter how those big brown eyes secretly made his heart soften or how her smile lifted his spirit. No one in this world would ever feel badly for him.

"If a fae prince doesn't believe in true love, then—" Ursula bit off the rest of the sentence.

He stroked his beard, trying to ignore his emotions. "Don't feel sorry for me, Madame. I've managed fine without love."

She leveled a curious look at Xavier. "I know it's none of my business, but…what or who made you stop believing in love?"

He wanted to make her understand, to chase away the obvious pity in her eyes, but how could he? How could she ever know? It was clear, from the way she spoke and acted, that she was surrounded by love. For years, he overheard the callous words his parents exchanged when they thought they were alone and promised that he'd never allow love in his life. To love someone was to invite future pain. To grant them absolute power to wreck you with a single sentence. He didn't have that luxury. No, Ursula's parents were probably happily celebrating their thirty-fifth anniversary and showering their daughter with love she then shared with the world.

"No one broke my heart," he said. "I've never been in love. I just learned that happily-ever-after isn't real and life can't be fixed with a storybook kiss. There's mess, pain and...it doesn't seem worth it."

"Is that what you told the Queen?" Ursula asked. She stared at him head-on, as if daring him to lie. No more omissions. He wanted her to know what he truly believed. His friend deserved to know the truth about him.

Xavier met her stare. "I said, 'Love's a trap meant to catch wishing fools and desperate hearts. I don't need love to get the perfect kiss.'"

He flinched inwardly. It sounded worse than he remembered. Her mouth fell open in surprise, but she quickly recovered. It pained him to be blunt, but he had to be realistic. Love was a means to an end and nothing else.

Ursula touched her throat. "I mean, you love your family and your godmother?"

"That love won't help me break the enchantment," he said stiffly. "I wish I told you sooner how I felt."

"I believe in love," Ursula said. Her words were strong and final.

Xavier met her eyes. "I haven't seen it, and I haven't felt it."

Right at that moment, it felt like a line was drawn between them. Even though they sat at the same table and shared food from a single plate, they might as well have been separated by a tower wall. He could lean over and touch Ursula, but he didn't know if he could reach her.

She gave him a sidelong glance of complete disbelief. "I haven't seen the center of Earth, but I know it's there because it's under my feet. It's solid."

"That's different," he said. "One can feel the Earth with your bare hands." He could reach down and grasp the dirt between his fingers. Love was nebulous, like mist evaporating under the heat of the sun. It could go away in an instant.

"Yes, but it's the same idea," Ursula said. There was clear passion in her voice. "You trust the ground will be underneath your feet as you walk. A person trusts that love will be there when they need it. Just because you haven't seen or felt it doesn't mean it isn't there."

After those words, Xavier was completely convinced she earned her nomination. There Ursula sat with her heart on her sleeve, looking ready to charge forward into battle for everything and everyone she loved. How could she walk around so openhearted? She was going to be hurt horribly one day, bad enough that she wouldn't want to ever love again. He wasn't going to be around to comfort her. To protect her from such terrible pain. His face contracted into tight lines. No, that hurt couldn't happen if he had breath in his body. He had to beseech her to guard that big heart of hers from this world that treated beautiful things with cruelty.

The words left his mouth before he could take it back. "Please, Madame, don't be naïve." Fire flashed in her eyes. He swallowed as it dawned on him that he clearly messed up.

When she spoke, her voice was cold and flinty.

"You may not need love to get your perfect kiss, but you'll need trust. Kisses don't have to promise forever, but they do require care and tenderness. If you can't trust, how can a woman rely on your words...or...your kiss?"

Her question rendered him silent. No one had ever questioned his honor before, but she just called him out right then and there. He didn't move. A few customers turned in the direction of their table.

"I'm an honorable prince," he said primly.

"But are you a brave one?" she demanded.

He stared at her, speechless. Xavier could see it now. Madame Ursula Caraway dressed in armor, sword drawn ready to protect everything she loved from harm. From danger. A heroine willing to rush into an unwinnable situation. She wouldn't run away from an enchantment of a perfect kiss; she'd charge through it. The woman had more courage in her pinky than he had in his entire body. If he was truly brave, he would've asked her out on the equinox. He would've wooed and romanced her weeks ago. He would've kissed the beauty mark by her mouth and enjoyed her sweet sighs.

But he was a whole coward.

"My enchantment doesn't need me to be brave," he said.

He kept his mouth shut, not wanting to say anything further. It seemed that that wasn't the right answer.

Disappointment clouded her eyes. She let out a shaky breath. "Okay, then. Well, I should get going. I've stayed long enough."

He didn't want their meeting to end on an uneasy note. Xavier stood. "Madame, wait."

Ursula got up from their table. "Good luck with the online dating and everything, Your Highness."

She hustled out the front without a backward glance. Gwen tried to get her attention, but Ursula was outside on the sidewalk and running way from the bistro. No, she was running away from him. Anger shredded at his skin. He shouldn't have been so rude with her. He was wrong to call her naïve, but…he didn't want to see her hurt. Ursula couldn't know what he was thinking or what was in his heart. Xavier also didn't want to make promises with his kisses that he couldn't keep. It wasn't too late to tell her how he felt. To make amends. Maybe it wasn't too late to be a little brave with her.

He texted Whitney. Which flowers are best for an apology?

She responded immediately. Purple hyacinths and don't forget the chocolate.

Ursula: Hey cuz. I'm sorry I couldn't make it to this month's gathering.

Sirena: I get it. Auntie told me you were working. Make that money, but we miss you. 😞 Tell me more about that fine fae man. Auntie told me about him too. 😊

Ursula: He's a just friend.

Sirena: Listen, the best relationships start off as friendships. All it takes is an upgrade and the removal of clothes.

Ursula: It's complicated.

Sirena: Oh, that sounds juicy. Let's talk later. I need all the details. And photos.

Ursula: You play too much.

Chapter Thirteen

*W*here *was Mr. Sandman when you needed him?*

Ursula tossed and turned in her bed, trying to get back to Dreamland, but of course it was no good. She glanced at the digital clock on the nightstand and released a frustrated groan.

The dream god was sleeping on the job because Ursula couldn't get to sleep. Not a single wink.

Every time her phone buzzed, she jumped up and checked it.

The subject heading for the first email was **FWD: Dine Ravenous: Sautéed Mushrooms with Cheese Polenta and Spinach.**

Ursula grinned. Apparently, Sirena was back online and sending her recipes. Even though they didn't see each other much, they started texting and keeping in contact. She starred the email for later.

The next email was from Quentin. He wanted to know about how many tickets he needed to reserve for the Smitten Ball for her. His message was on brand for him—polite, yet nosy. **As a nominee, you are given two free tickets to the ball and dinner. Do you have a plus-one or are you riding** solo? Let me know when you know! Xavier's confession spurred her to embrace whatever the universe was sending her way. She emailed Quentin that she would be bringing a date.

Ursula didn't know who her date was yet, but she knew she had to find one soon. She didn't mind going alone to the ball, but it would be nice to have someone by her side. The other Sweetheart nominees had started a text thread about what they were wearing and when they were shopping for the ball. Ursula responded to their texts with likes and emoji hearts but didn't talk about possible outfits. The last time she wore a fancy dress it didn't go so well.

Ursula turned off her phone and stared up at the ceiling.

What was it about the darkness of the night that made a person recall their regrets? She'd been saddened to hear that someone like Xavier with such a kind, thoughtful nature didn't believe in love.

It was like finding out the Tooth Faery hates teeth, or the Sandman prefers to use potting soil instead of sprinkling sand in dreamers' eyes.

Her stomach ached as this afternoon's events played and replayed in her mind.

She'd pushed Xavier with her comments, made him uneasy, and asked for answers that she had no right to know. She wasn't his wife or even his girlfriend. Even so, Ursula was concerned about what would happen if he allowed his heart to wither and fossilize. It would cease to exist and become buried deep within him without ever knowing true love.

A heart like his shouldn't be forgotten.

Xavier in turn had called her naïve. A familiar brew of

anger, hurt, and disappointment stirred within her chest. How many times had Lincoln said something like that to her at a Walker family gathering or party? His low, smooth voice droned in her head.

Don't be so naïve, Sula. You don't really believe a few words can change your fate. Sweeping your feet with a broom doesn't chase away your luck! Don't be silly, honey! Of course I'll see you at the altar tomorrow. I'll be in a tux. Don't be so nervous.

She wasn't a fool, but she was naturally inclined to imagine the best and sometimes the worst of life.

Ursula could envision Xavier—sitting in his castle, the light in him faded and nearly snuffed out. A ripple of grief went through her. Ursula was saddened for all his desires that would fade away into painful regret.

Ursula didn't want that life for Xavier, but she couldn't bully him into believing.

She kicked off the covers, got out of bed, and went into the kitchen. It was time for sleepy-time tea. Ursula was searching through her cabinet when a noise at her window caught her attention. It sounded like pebbles plinking against the glass. Wait. Someone *was* throwing pebbles at the front window. She went over and threw it open, ready to yell at whoever it was, but her mouth dropped when she saw Xavier. He peered up at her, holding an upright box with a crooked bow. His striking profile was brightened by the streetlamp, which illuminated his beard.

"Your Highness?" She yanked her robe closed.

"Madame!" He visibly relaxed. "Thank goodness. I've been throwing pebbles at random windows all night. There's a very angry gargoyle down the street who doesn't like me."

"Baltazar's always mad. He deals with pigeons perching on him all day," Ursula said.

Even so, the grumpy but kindhearted gargoyle had kept an eye out for her when she moved into the neighborhood. She made a mental note to leave Baltazar a sweet roll the next time she saw him. Ursula stared down at Xavier. He was in his usual professorial attire, but he looked wrinkled, slightly undone.

Her heart jumped at the mere sight of him. Apparently, it didn't get the message that she was currently angry with the prince.

"You could've texted." Was there a tremble in her voice? *Lock it down, Caraway. He hurt you. Don't let him see it.*

"I needed to talk to you face-to-face." He sounded insistent.

She wrinkled her brow. Really, now? "Why did you come over so late?"

"I had to pick something up from Meadowdale. I got lost. I took . . . a taxi." He said the word "taxi" in the same mystified tone a person would use if they took a spaceship. Xavier lifted and dropped his shoulders. "They got the address wrong and left me in the West Grove. There are a lot of mystic shops in town."

"You could've asked Gwen!"

"I did ask, Madame! She said I had to, and I quote, 'work for it.'"

Gwen must have seen her leave abruptly from the bistro without saying goodbye. Ursula exhaled. She was lucky His Highness hadn't accidentally ended up three towns over in Belmar or Point Pleasant. Did princes have a terrible sense of direction? Rapunzel didn't have to deal with this nonsense up in her tower. Which reminded her: She couldn't yell down at him all night. Gargoyles were nosy and would tell the ravens her business.

"Don't wake up the neighborhood with our foolishness. I'll be right down."

He pressed his free hand to his chest. "Thank you."

Ursula belted her robe, looked quickly in the mirror, and went downstairs to the front door. If she was going to entertain royalty for a little while, she could at least look a little put together. She opened the door and ushered him inside.

The stairs squeaked as they ascended to her apartment. Once Ursula closed the door behind Xavier, she held on to the knob. Why did her place seem so small around him? Her place was a spacious studio with one bedroom with a pale pink accent wall, but with him standing tall, it felt like a kindergartener's closet. There was a quiet authority about Xavier that demanded she pay attention. Ursula shook herself. She wasn't going to let herself get caught staring at the prince. Being angry with him was safer than feeling any other emotion—hurt and disappointment right now. At least she could offer him a warm cup of tea before she showed him out once he delivered his message.

"I was going to brew tea. Would you like some?"

"I'm good, but thank you." He scanned the apartment quickly, holding the upright box to his side. "Your place is very cozy. I like it."

She rolled her shoulders as she filled the kettle at the sink. "You don't have to be polite. I'm aware it's small."

"I like it," he repeated, warmth bleeding into his voice.

She smiled to herself. Yes, it was small, but it was hers. She worked hard to make this place into a home, and she liked climbing those stairs every day to her private space. Mama had helped her out by letting her rent the apartment, but she didn't want to take advantage of her generosity, so Ursula made sure to be the best tenant. No loud noises. No parties. No overnight guests. *Until now.*

She pushed that thought out of her head. "What's in the box?"

Xavier placed it on the table. "It's for you."

Ursula went over to the stovetop, quelling the curiosity inside her. No, she wasn't going to give in so easily. He wasn't going to win her over with some fancy gift. He probably got her a brass statue or handmade sculpture. She'd had enough of that from her old relationship. Lincoln didn't do plants but loved buying her lifeless objects. He thought plants were too messy, not worth the trouble and cleaning. She wanted to be surrounded by life.

Ursula turned on the burner to low, put the kettle on the stove, then faced Xavier.

His eyes kept darting nervously to the box. "You might want to open it soon."

"Why? Is there a troll in there?"

Ursula knew trolls loved to gift wrap themselves and pop out of boxes to scare people.

"I don't know how much soil shifted," he said.

Her senses tingled. *Soil?* Ursula went over to the gift in question and yanked at the bow. The box fell apart, revealing a flower held in a teal green flowerpot. The apartment immediately filled with the spicy, fragrant scent of hyacinth. She pressed a hand to her mouth to hide her smile. Purple hyacinths. In times of sorrow, these flowers offered mourners empathy and well wishes. But after a disagreement, they symbolized a real desire for forgiveness.

Xavier stood off to the side. "The florist in town didn't have it, so I had to go to a nursery in Meadowdale. They didn't have an aquamarine pot, so I thought teal would work."

Ursula touched the pot. It was love at first sight. She fought desperately to hold on to the anger, but it started to slip away in the face of his gift.

"If you don't like it, I can take it back," he said.

She shook her head. He wasn't taking her plant—Raspberry Beret—anywhere.

Ursula took a step toward Xavier and stared at him. "Why are you here?"

He didn't look away. "I'm sorry. I said thoughtless things to you, and I wanted to apologize. You didn't deserve my anger. It was uncalled for."

Her chest swelled when she heard the sincerity in his words. She took a cleansing breath.

"I accept, and I offer my own apology. I shouldn't have pushed you. It's none of my business why you feel the way you do," Ursula said.

Xavier gave her an accepting nod. She retreated into the kitchenette. He'd lived a whole life in the Realm before she met him and she had no right to inquire about his past. Besides, she hadn't told him about her experience and how she really gained her nomination.

Xavier went over to the windowsill. In a fit of passion, Ursula had bought a trio of herb plants—mint, rosemary, and basil—from Home and Hearth so she'd have something else to care for in her loneliness. She'd also been drawn to the Swiss plant, which she loved and named after the Stevie Wonder song "Sir Duke." Their earthy presence gave her much needed comfort in her self-imposed solitude and gave the apartment a little life.

He examined Sir Duke with an interested glance. "Hello, there."

Xavier looked to Ursula, his hand hovering over the plant. "May I?"

She got a mug and put a chamomile tea bag inside it. "Please. Sir Duke's been under the weather."

Xavier caressed the leaves with a light touch. He waved a hand over Sir Duke, which perked up as if seeking attention from his palm. Small green sparks trickled from his hand and landed in the soil.

She smiled. "Thank you."

"I gave him a little boost," he said. "You've done a great job caring for them. The Swiss plant—Sir Duke—doesn't need so much water, but he loves it when you talk to him."

"I thought he was annoyed with me."

Xavier grinned a little. "No, he enjoys hearing you talk, but he misses the singing."

A flicker of sadness went through her, but she let it pass. Ursula hadn't gone to karaoke in months, but she missed the music and performing. One day she'd find her song again.

Xavier gave her a caring glance. "They're flourishing. Sunlight, water, soil, and love. The last ingredient tends to be the most difficult one to source."

He moved away from the plants and came into the kitchen. "I'm sorry to come over so late."

She stayed by the stove. The water wasn't even boiling yet, so she had time. "It's okay. I was already up."

"I would've gotten you chocolates, but I didn't know which ones you like."

"Caramel," Ursula said. "I like the ones with caramel."

"I'll remember for next time." He said this very studiously, as if he would be quizzed about her likes and dislikes later.

"Would you like the grand tour?" she asked.

"Lead the way, Madame."

Ursula brought Xavier over to the main living area. It was odd having him over. She hadn't had much company since she moved in last fall with the few items she'd taken from her former life. But this apartment was filled with touches of witchy goodness that she'd reclaimed in the aftermath of her disastrous engagement. Apothecary vases from the Winter Market were arranged among half-melted candles. Crystals lined her bookshelf, which held everything from anime fairy-tale collections to zodiac lore. He examined the small grouping of stones with wide eyes.

"Excuse me, Your Highness." Ursula wiggled her fingers at him. "Don't ogle my crystals too much. I have to charge them soon."

He angled himself toward her and quirked a brow. "It's in my nature to be dazzled by pretty things. I can't help it."

There was a playfulness in his voice that unnerved her a bit. When he mentioned pretty things, Ursula had a sneaking suspicion that he was also talking about her. The teakettle whistled loudly. She went over to the kitchen, shut off the burner, and poured the hot water into the mug. Ursula grabbed the squeezable honey bear bottle, popped the top, and drizzled honey into her cup.

"Your necklace is malachite, right?" she asked.

Xavier reached up and touched the pendant. "You're good. It is. My sister Prim told me it would help me be successful in my goals."

She capped the bottle, getting honey on her fingers. "It's a good stone. It gives you insight so you can grow into the person you need to be."

"Can you tell me anything else about it?" he asked.

Ursula moved to stand next to him, leaving her tea to cool on the counter. "Some legends say malachite is a traveler's stone. You can use it to locate the wearer no matter where they are."

Xavier pointed to the row of gilded books. "I see you like stories and legends, especially fairy tales. The spines are cracked and worn from repeated reading. You have a few ones missing."

Ursula nodded. There were a few books she couldn't bear to keep once she realized her wish wasn't coming true. She gave them away along with her wedding dress and all her plans.

"I was an English minor in college. I loved studying folklore and folktales."

"I didn't think you'd like fairy tales," Xavier said. "Witches get a bad reputation in those stories."

Ursula laughed as Nana's words echoed in her mind. *Don't feel bad for the witch, beach baby. Everyone fears and respects the witch because of what she can do with just her words. She's in charge of her fate. How about that?*

"Reputation can't make up for character, Your Highness." Ursula faced him. "Besides, what's wrong with being bad?"

She held up her hand and distractedly licked the honey from her fingertips.

He watched her closely, as if eager to answer the question she posed.

Xavier was here. Alone. With her. Suddenly she became super aware of the situation. This wasn't right. She shouldn't flirt with him. He was desperate for a spell-breaking kiss, and if Ursula wasn't careful, she might offer him hers. Even after she'd sworn off fairy tales. Even after she knew the truth about how he felt about love. The longer she stayed around Xavier, the more she put her heart in danger of truly falling for him. The prince was looking to break his curse and return to the Realm. Nothing else. Nothing more.

She cleared her throat. "Is there anything else you want to discuss, Your Highness?"

He put his hands behind his back and stood to his full height. "It's none of my business, but I wanted to know—what or who made you believe in love?"

Ursula picked up her teacup and sat down at the small table. She extended her hand and wordlessly invited Xavier to join her. His long legs stretched out before him when he took a seat.

"I learned how to love from my mama's family," Ursula said finally, after an extended moment. "My Caraway grand-parents and my mother's family treated love like air. It's given freely and without conditions. It's passed from generation to generation, and it's in our blood. I mean, I'm loved and cared for by people whose names I don't know but whose magic flows in my veins."

There was a long pause. Xavier made a small sound of understanding.

"So, I guess you've never had your heart broken or been disappointed by love," he said.

Tell him. She sighed in exasperation, resigned to revealing all. He'd been honest with her; it was only right that she did the same with him. Let the internet tell the story. "Search me."

He scanned her lazily from top to bottom. A thrill of heat went through her. "Um, where do you want me to start?"

Ursula huffed. "No, search me online."

Xavier took his phone from his pocket. She watched as he typed her name into a search engine and clicked on the *Freya Grove Press* article about her. A wave of nausea went through her.

After five minutes, he said, "Sweet cosmos." That phrase was filled with disbelief and a hint of something else. Was it horror?

Ursula winced. "Keep reading. It's not done yet."

Xavier read quietly for another few minutes before turning off his phone and returning it to his pocket. Now he knew she was the Big-Hearted Bride. Jilted. Leftover. Unloved. Ursula watched the steam curl skyward from her mug. Maybe Xavier had a point. She'd been a wishing fool, one who'd ignored all the signs that she was making a huge mistake. Her heartbeat pounded in her ears; her entire body grew cold with humiliation. She pressed her hand to the mug to try to warm herself.

"Is this why you got nominated for the Sweetheart award?" he asked.

She only nodded, unable to look up from her tea.

"Sula, love. Look at me."

She blinked and looked up, stunned. *He called me Sula.* The shadow of fury that swept over his features stole her breath.

"I'm going to say this once." His voice hardened. "He's a whole fool. He should be on his knees begging your forgiveness. If you asked me to marry you—" He took a steadying breath as if trying to tamp down his anger. "I'd crawl through broken glass just to be there on time."

His words hit and echoed within her soul. She knew he'd move heaven and earth to stand there with her. *I believe you.*

He watched her carefully. "Did you know he was going to run?"

"No," Ursula said. "If I had seen him run in my visions, I would have tried to convince him to...I don't know. Stay. I would've done everything within my power to make...my wish come true. Instead, I ended up having the town's biggest block party."

"You helped those people without a second thought," he said.

Ursula ducked her head. "It seemed like the best thing to do."

There was awe in his voice when he spoke. "Even after everything that's happened, you still believe in love."

"I believe," she whispered. She let go of the mug and shrugged. "I guess that makes me the real fool."

Xavier jumped up suddenly. "No, never. It makes you... brave." He went over to the kitchen. His attention darted all over as he scanned the space.

"Madame, where are your knives?" There was an urgency in his movements that gave Ursula pause.

"Um, they're in the second drawer. Are you making a sandwich?"

Xavier laughed. "I'll make you one next time."

He found the correct drawer, opened it, and took out one of the dull butter knives. Ursula used them to spread hazelnut topping on her toast. The handle was decorated with a faded green vine design. Nana bought her that cutlery set for her birthday. Her eyebrows lifted when he turned to her with a wide, excited grin.

Ursula sat up in her seat. Was he hungry? "If you want some peanut butter, it's in the cabinet."

"No, Madame." The butter knife remained in his hand. "Since I don't have a sword, I thought this might be a suitable replacement."

She rubbed her forehead, leaning a little away to gather her thoughts. Was he feeling all right? *Maybe I should call Whitney.* Xavier stood before Ursula, holding the butter knife blade away from her but close enough that he could touch her shoulder. She dropped her hand to her lap.

"I'll stand so you don't have to kneel," he said.

Excuse me, sir. Her brow lifted in surprise. "Kneel for what?"

"I'm knighting you," Xavier said in a regal tone.

"Can you do that?" Ursula asked. She didn't want him to get into trouble for doing anything unofficial. "Is it allowed?"

"They can't enchant me again. I'm doing this." Xavier gave an impish grin. Her stomach fluttered. She blinked rapidly and a feeling of amazement began building in her chest.

Ursula gave a slow, disbelieving head shake. This was really happening.

"Good evening." Xavier addressed the plants and Ursula. She pulled back her shoulders and straightened in her chair as if she were at a glamourous awards ceremony.

"To all here currently, know that Ursula…" He waited for her to supply her middle name.

"Rebecca," she said.

His face lit up. "Know that Ursula Rebecca Caraway, having been recognized for the following achievements, her tireless service to the community of Freya Grove and for acts in the name of love and for a courageous heart. She is hereby being admitted as a Distinguished Knight in the Esteemed House of Alder. I, Prince Xavier Henrie George Alder, confer this knighthood upon Madame Caraway in the name and in honor of Queen Hazel Alder."

For a moment she forgot everything else, and all she could see was Xavier with a charming gleam in his eye. He gave her a half-grin that made her feel as if this night would always belong to them and no one else.

"Please, kneel and receive your knighthood."

Ursula bowed her head, emotion constricting her throat. Xavier gently touched the butter knife to each shoulder as he spoke in a hushed voice. "Ursula Rebecca Caraway, I hereby knight thee into the Esteemed House of Alder. Arise, Knight, and be recognized."

She heard the knife fall on the table. He briefly stroked her cheek, moved to cradle her chin. His touch was careful and measured. Her skin hummed under his hand. He lifted her face so that she could meet his stare. Her heart filled to the top with bliss.

"Arise, my lady-knight," he whispered.

Ursula stood and met his stare. This so-called ceremony was silly, and a little foolish, but he'd acted a fool just for her.

She had given up on the fairy tale, but it hadn't given up on her. It was here in front of her in full flesh and magic. Maybe she didn't have to give it up, but rather reimagine what it meant to live happily ever after. Ursula bit her lip and willed herself not to cry, again. Tears remained at bay and instead, she felt her heart burst. The fairy tale wasn't going to leave her alone, no matter how far she ran away or tried to give it up. For a heartbeat, she believed again.

Fate delivered a prince who brought her potted flowers and bestowed upon her lovely words and respect. He studied her, but it was different now. There was clear affection in his eyes. *You're his knight.* Stars above. If he kept watching her like this, she might do something stupid like ask him to stay and talk with her all night. If he stayed, she might get used to having him here with her. If he stayed, she might offer him the one thing that would break her all over again. Her love. She took a mental step back. Like that, the moment was broken between them.

A wave of tiredness swept through her. *What time is it?* She glanced at the oven clock and groaned. It was almost midnight. "I didn't know it was this late."

He moved away. "I've taken up enough of your time. I'll text you in the morning."

Ursula walked Xavier out of the apartment and downstairs to the landing. She remained on the stairs while he put on his coat in the vestibule. He peered up at Ursula, concern on his face.

"How sleepy do I look?" she asked.

One corner of his mouth lifted. "Madame, you should be counting sheep."

Ursula stifled a yawn against her hand and shook off the second wave of sleepiness. She swayed a bit, and Xavier stepped up to steady her. He placed his hands on her shoulders, their bodies less than a foot apart.

She felt his strong touch through the robe's fabric. "I think I can sleep now."

Xavier playfully rolled his eyes while trying to hide a grin. "You're saying that I've bored you to sleep."

"No," Ursula said through another big yawn.

He looked up at her. Right then, the atmosphere shimmered, and it felt like she was looking at the world through frosted glass. Midnight brought with it the magic of possibility. All Caraways knew that midnight was the time for mischief.

A brief shiver rippled through Ursula as a fuzzy vision took shape before her eyes. His steady gaze bore into her with silent, potent anticipation. She drank in his nearness and his alluring scent of earthy wildflowers and musk, which threatened to dull her sanity and reason. He beckoned her forth like mountains on the horizon, inviting her to explore him. To learn his peaks and valleys, and the hidden glory of him underneath those clothes.

She pulled him roughly, desperately against her. He

opened his mouth to ask something, but his last words were smothered against her lips. This was a kiss that she could sink herself into and not come to the surface for hours. Delight spun inside her like falling flowers as she kissed him. His soft beard tickled her face; his mouth was inviting on hers. She parted her lips and licked him, taking in the taste of him—a mixture of coffee and natural sweetness.

All she wanted right then was to have him in her hands and inside of her.

She kissed him with the hunger of a forlorn castaway finally seeing land.

Xavier gathered her into his arms as Ursula arched her body against him. His hand traveled up the length of her body, outlining her curves through her thin nightclothes. He cupped her breast in his hand and teased her nipple with his fingers until she whimpered for more. Their heavy breathing echoed in the stairwell as she whipped off her nightclothes.

When she gripped his shoulders and held on to him, she knew that she'd never let him go.

Ursula drew in a breath and blinked out of the vision. Xavier was still dressed, but...she saw it. The glimmer of attraction was there. Her body shook from the phantom touch of his lips brushing kisses against the sensitive skin of her nipples. *Back away.* She moved away from Xavier and held out her hand. It was all she could offer him.

He leaned in, took her hand in his, and pressed a light kiss to her palm. Oh.

"Sweet dreams, my lady."

"Good night, Xavier."

Ursula watched him walk out the door, not moving from

the stairs for a long moment. Her skin tingled from the brush of his beard against her hand. She was going to do something stupid. She was going to fall for Xavier. He was that type— the dream man who you'd run away with to a beach house for a weekend, drink bottles of expensive wine in long-stemmed glasses and play strip poker until you ended up sweaty and naked, shivering in pleasure on the floor. He was also the type of man who would kiss the gray hairs on your head and watch you from across the room with complete affection in his eyes.

He was dangerous. He was fae.

Ursula let herself truly, honestly wish for the first time in nearly a year.

I wish I found you before my heart was crushed.

EnChant Profile:
Xavier Alder

A fae prince hoping that his fairy tale ends happily.
I don't believe in true love, but I'm open to
discussing the possibility.

You have three messages:

A New Paige
Would you like to discuss this idea over coffee? 😉

Marie All Day
I love your honesty. Let's go out for dinner and see if I
can convince you to open your mind.

Amelia_Okay
Are you still single? Tell me I'm not too late and you're
still free for lunch.

Chapter Fourteen

Ursula loved making up reasons to get her hands on a book.

It's Tuesday. Get a book. It's raining. Rent a book. Pluto's in retrograde. Buy an audiobook. When Xavier texted her last night and agreed to go to the Smitten with the Shelves bookstore event, she held back a scream of bookish joy. She'd always wanted to go to this specific event, but there was a Walker dinner or volunteer meeting that she had to attend.

But this was her year not to have shelf-control.

Ursula hovered outside Rain or Shine Bookstore, peeking in the front window at the crowd inside the shop. She was already running late due to some candle drama, so she decided to take a second to herself. Xavier milled around the shelves. She noticed him sipping from a clear plastic cup filled with what appeared to be wine. His attention darted over to the door every time it opened, and his face fell when he saw she hadn't arrived. *He's looking for you. Go to him.*

She forced herself to stay where she was and keep her distance.

Just when she thought she was done with fairy tales, the magic and Xavier pulled her right back in. She got swept away by those gorgeous eyes staring at her. He'd knighted her right in her robe! It was becoming increasingly clear that being in Xavier's orbit was going to test her in more ways than one. Hmm, maybe she shouldn't fall asleep listening to an astronomy podcast.

Ursula opened her note app and scrolled down to her one rule. **No more fairy tales.**

It was time to rethink her rule. She put away her phone and went into the store.

The walls were painted a bright peach, and waist-high bookshelves gave the space an open feeling. Shelves were a deep cherrywood color and filled with new and used books.

An altar by the front door was filled with silver-plated hearts, glitter-dipped roses, and half-cut dimes—leftover offerings from the spring equinox. The long table at the front of the bookstore was filled with finger foods, cups, and drinks.

A decent-sized crowd mingled around the couches and seats. Classical music played at a low volume overhead. There was a massive table in the middle of the floor filled with three levels of books that were wrapped in plain brown paper and red and white twine. Booksellers had written one-sentence descriptions on each of the books. Ursula rubbed her hands together in silent glee.

She found Xavier in the arts and crafts section. Gravity tugged her forward until she was right in front of him. He wore a light blue shirt that showed off his collarbones and gem pendant. How could she even find his collarbones sexy? She had it bad for him. His dress pants and plaid socks clashed, as if he'd gotten dressed in the dark. Of course, he wore his dress shoes, but these ones were scuffed and well loved. His beard looked springy and well oiled. His drink was gone but he still carried the aroma of earthy fruit. Ripe apples and squeezed oranges. He appeared carefully mismatched, and she was living for this whole vibe. Click, download, and save another image for the fantasy folder.

"Sorry I'm late," she said, a little bit breathless.

"You're right on time." Xavier leaned in and gave her a quick hug. Oh. Okay. They were hugging hello now. She ignored the little jump of joy in her chest when he held her close, then let go.

"I hope everything's okay."

"We got a huge delivery of elemental candles, and I couldn't leave until they were organized," she explained.

The dozen boxes had been delivered minutes after she came back from coffee with Xavier. So many new items were dropped off that they had to close for an impromptu inventory day. Ursula had never seen so many wax-coated seashells and quartz crystals in her life.

Xavier's face creased. "If you need to go, we can reschedule."

"No, it's fine. Mama and I literally just finished. Forgive me, I probably smell like pine."

Xavier, without a second thought, leaned into her space. He was close enough that she could see the flecks of hazel in his eyes.

"You smell like a garden."

"What, like fresh dirt?" Ursula joked, trying to ignore how her skin buzzed when he got close.

He caught her eye. "No, like jasmine," he said with quiet emphasis.

Her heartbeat kicked up a notch. Jasmine flowers were

small, but their scents were powerful, even mesmerizing. They were often used in spells to attract true love. Ursula mumbled a thanks and turned to the bookshelf to collect herself.

Be cool. She faced him again. "So, did you find anything to read?"

Xavier gestured to a thick book spine on the shelf above her head. "I'm curious about woodworking. I've already read this manual, so I'm looking for a new one."

Ursula watched him for a beat. "You like making cabinets and carving wood."

"I'm interested in the craft," he said carefully. "I haven't made anything in years, but I've enjoyed reading about it."

An unreadable expression settled on his face. "You must think it's an odd hobby for a prince. I should probably stick to raising unicorns, tending gardens, or cataloguing the armory."

She heard a bitter edge of frustration in his voice. "Do you like doing any of those things?" Ursula didn't want to even imagine how much unicorn poop Xavier had cleaned up over the years.

"I do what is required of me, Madame." His lips twisted into a resigned smile, as if his future was already planned and set in stone. His story was already written.

Ursula met his eyes and held his attention. "Do what gives you joy."

His face changed and became almost wistful. "I wish I could."

They moved to another section of the bookstore. Xavier

stopped next to a spindle of zines and graphic novels. "I revised my profile. I've gotten three messages."

"I don't want to say I told you so, but...I was right," Ursula said.

He graced her with an excited smile.

"I have a possible date. I'm just waiting for my date to confirm." Her stomach twisted a bit. It was only a matter of time before ladies noticed Xavier. There was no reason for her feel jealous, but her stomach twisted again.

She cleared her throat. "Well, give me details."

Ursula hadn't dated anyone since she was jilted, but she liked hearing dating stories from Gwen, who still had the courage to try.

"Her name's Paige. We're going out this weekend."

From the wide way he smiled, he seemed pleased with this outcome. A bubble of melancholy expanded in her chest. It wouldn't take long before Paige graced Xavier with that perfect kiss and unbound him from the enchantment. He'd probably be back home before the end of the month. A flutter of sadness went through her at that idea.

Xavier nodded. "Now I've got to figure out where to take Paige. I still don't...know my way around the Grove."

"You said you like long walks in gardens and being outside. I have the perfect place," Ursula said. "I hope you have clothes you don't mind getting a little dirty."

"I like getting dirty," he said with all seriousness. Somehow, his serious tone made his words unexpectedly sexy. She imagined him whispering those words against her mouth in the darkness of her bedroom, leaning her up against the wall and slowly stroking his hand between her thighs until she collapsed in pleasure.

Welp. Her throat went dry. Another phrase uploaded to her fantasy folder. By the end of the night, it was going to be completely full, and she was going to have to open another one.

Focus up, Caraway. You have no right to fantasize about him. He has a real date.

"You should take her to the Grove Garden." Ursula took out her phone and pulled up a picture gallery of Grove Garden from the website. "I used to go there all the time with my nana. We used to watch the bugs and butterflies."

She held up the photo for him. "I'll text you the address. We can go there tomorrow."

"I'd like that. Enlighten me, Madame," Xavier said. "I'd love to hear a few first date topics."

"I haven't been on a real date since Jupiter and Saturn aligned," Ursula said.

He tipped his chin at her. "I respect your opinion."

She popped her lip, then spoke. "Start with the basics. Ask about her job, interests, and who she is as a person. If there's a connection between the two of you, then you might want to take things further. Be your charming self and you'll be puckering up in no time."

She noticed his throat lurched with a hard swallow. "You're worried about your kiss?"

Xavier touched his necklace in a self-soothing gesture. "How will I know if it's perfect?"

Ursula sized him up, thinking of how he might look once he was disenchanted.

"Maybe you'll feel like you did before, but just different. Like how the air feels recharged after a rain shower. Renewed. Alive."

He bobbed his head as if he took her words to heart. "You've been invaluable. Let me help you with your wish list."

Ursula thought back to the spring party, where they'd chatted for hours in that hidden nook. That night seemed so far away from her mind. "I forgot I told you."

"I didn't forget. We'll make it happen. You'll get what you desire." He turned to study the gold leaf on a book cover on the sale table in front of them.

The sheer confidence in his voice made her pause. That single word stole all the air from her lungs and made her feel unsteady. *Desire.* What did she truly desire? A job that made a difference in her hometown. A true purpose in her life. To feel not only happiness but also sincere joy. She let eyes drift over Xavier, taking him inch by inch while his attention was elsewhere. *Let yourself have him for just this second.* Here he was, the storybook prince she'd dreamed about when she was young, shrouded in melancholy, yet still regal.

The enchantment on his head may have dampened his spirit but she saw him. Despite her best attempts, she was very much a part of his fairy tale. It was up to her what role she was going to play. Witch. Enchantress. Lady-knight.

A lanky woman with shaggy brown hair wearing a faded Fleetwood Mac shirt standing at the front of the store waved her hands and called out, "Good evening! Let's get started."

Only a few people were paying attention to her; the rest kept talking to each other. Empathy moved through Ursula. Through her committee work, she'd hosted enough events to know it was a pain in the butt to get the undivided attention of a roomful of strangers.

"Hello, hello!" the woman shouted. Finally, the room quieted down. Ursula gave her a mental fist bump. *Show them what's up.*

"Welcome to Smitten with the Shelves. I'm Edwina, Eddie for short. I'm the night manager and your host. Poe and Theo, the owners, thank you for coming out tonight! We invite you all to thumb through our shelves. We hope you might find your next late-night read. Maybe you can find a book you can bring to bed."

Eddie gave the crowd a big stage wink. A knowing rumble went through the crowd. Ursula looked to Xavier. Wait. Were the tops of his ears turning red? She held back an amused smile and focused back on their hostess.

"We have our popular Book a Date table!" Eddie cheered. "We've wrapped our favorite romance novels and written clues and prices on the covers. These books are buy two, get one free, so please don't be afraid to treat yourself. Remember, you don't need a library card to check these books out!"

A few people groaned at the pun, but Eddie flashed them all a big grin.

"But seriously! Thank you for coming out. Eat, drink, and be bookish!"

Everyone returned to their conversations and went for the snack table. Ursula approached the Book a Date pile with Xavier by her side. She rubbed her fingertips together and picked up a stack of wrapped books.

"Are you looking for anything special?" Xavier asked.

"I'll know what I want when I see it," Ursula said.

She read the book descriptions to herself while Xavier peeked over her shoulder.

A thief for hire accidentally steals the one thing that might end her career—the heart of a billionaire's son who stands to inherit his father's empire.

Ursula pursed her lips. She did like a good romantic caper. "Let me think about it."

She tucked the book under her arm and read another cover: *A lady-knight, looking for a lost treasure, meets a wayward prince hoping to outrun his past.*

A scoff escaped her lips. Okay, that description was a little too on the nose for her. She couldn't look at her butter knife without her stomach jumping in memory. Even more, her dreams were taunting her with the prospect of Xavier's touch.

"That sounds interesting," he murmured.

Ursula handed it to him. "That's all yours, Xavier."

He took it from her. Ursula helped herself to a quick snack of Swiss cheese and crackers while scanning the table. She read a few more descriptions until she had a tall stack of possible reads in the crook of her arm. Ursula juggled her unread books with the others she wanted to hold on to for safekeeping. They threatened to spill out of her arms, but Xavier was by her side catching any strays that fell. She picked up another book, the description making her heart race.

An imaginative woman wakes up one morning to find herself inside the storybook life she's always wanted. Talking frogs, bad kisses, and brave knights, oh my!

The cheese in her mouth went sour. It was a copy of her favorite book. The first book she gave away the day after the wedding. She rid it from her life, and here it was haunting her. Ursula dropped it on the table as if it were a lit match. No way. She had no intention of letting herself get pulled back into that story. But her hand hovered over the book.

Maybe fate was trying to tell her to pay attention to the past.

"Do you see something you like?" Xavier asked.

Ursula showed him the book in question. "Maybe." He quickly read the description written on the paper cover and made a sound of agreeance.

"I don't know what that book is but it sounds perfect for you," Xavier said.

This book reminded her that she tried to make her life into a storybook but failed miserably.

She gently placed it back on the pile. "Well, it'll go home with someone else." Ursula collected her final selections in her hands. "I've got everything that I need."

Those familiar words felt bad in her mouth, like she swallowed sour cherry candies. The last time she said that sentence, she was less than twenty-four hours from getting jilted. From becoming estranged from her family. From weakening her magic. Xavier picked up a few books from the table and followed Ursula. Eddie stood behind the front counter and cashier area. She waggled her brow at the large stock.

"Looks like someone's not going home alone tonight," she said happily.

As Eddie rang up the books, Ursula glanced at Xavier. He blinked slowly as if trying to collect his thoughts. As if he was mentally trying to choose the right words.

"You have something to say, Your Highness," she said.

Eddie hummed loudly to herself, as if she was getting ready to drown out the conversation.

He licked his lips and straightened. "Forgive me for speaking out of turn, but you shouldn't give up on something that makes you happy."

"What makes you say that?"

"Your face lit up when you talked about stories the other night."

Ursula licked her lips in thought. Why did he have to do that? Notice things about her. Eddie hummed a bit louder and off key. Ursula listened for a moment. Was that the *Jeopardy!* theme?

"I get happy around books. It happens to a lot of people."

"You get—to quote Whitney—diamonds in your eyes. It's clear that you love them, even if you don't like them right now."

He knows what makes you happy. Your former fiancé didn't even know that.

"Yes," Ursula said in a high-pitched voice. "Who wouldn't want to live in a castle?"

Eddie paused her song. "I've heard that they're really drafty."

Ursula gave her a polite smile. Eddie finished ringing up Ursula's purchases and handed her a book-filled tote bag. "Happy reading."

Ursula thanked her and took her items. Xavier paid for his three books and then they left the bookstore. They sat down on a bench on the sidewalk outside the store, examining their purchases.

Xavier handed her one of his books. "Consider it an early Beltane gift."

It was her lost book. She held up a hand. "I can't accept it."

He extended it out to her. "It's yours."

Ursula took it and unwrapped the book feverishly, like a child receiving an extra-large candy bar. She reached out and ran a finger over the illustrated cover of an Afro haired princess leaning over to bestow a kiss on a crowned frog with a hopeful look.

Xavier studied the cover and frowned. "*Until the Morning Breaks.*"

She nodded. "It's a retelling of the Frog Prince. It's my second favorite fairy tale after 'Cinderella.'"

"It should be called *The Frog Prince: A Horror Story*," he quipped.

She scrunched her face in thought. "What's wrong with the 'Frog Prince'? It's innocent. A frog finds a princess willing to give him a kiss and transform him back into his true form. You should be inspired by it. You're much cuter and you don't eat flies."

She noticed his ears blushed a bit. He rubbed his forehead as if trying to remove the image from his mind. "Yes, but how long was he a frog? Two days? Two months? Two years?"

"It takes as long as it takes." Her tone was apologetic but firm. "You can't hurry love; you can only create the conditions for love to flourish."

He let out a childish grunt. Ursula laughed.

"Princes don't date where I'm from. We court and figure out the rest later. First comes courtship and marriage, then comes love. What about your family?"

Ursula twisted her mouth to the side. "My parents fell in

love after two weeks. It was a whirlwind romance. They got married after six weeks."

"Wow," Xavier said. "Are they still together?"

She wished the story ended with her parents riding off into the sunset, but it didn't.

"They had me a year later and were happy for a while, but Dad's family kept telling Mama that she needed to give up her magic. They said she wasn't committing to her family the way she should."

Xavier blinked in annoyance. "How can you give up magic if you are magic?"

Ursula shook her head sadly. "Well, the Ellis family expected her to give it up. Mama tried but couldn't do it. They got divorced when I was in fourth grade. Mama and I moved to the Grove. Dad got remarried and moved to Meadowdale with his new family."

Ursula knew happy endings existed. Even though her parents didn't have theirs, she held on to the hope that she'd find hers if she worked and wished for it enough. However, she didn't know how to have a happily-ever-after without changing some part of herself to be accepted and loved. All the fairy tales required some type of transformation. Servants became princesses. Frogs and beasts turned into princes. She faced Xavier, wanting to hear a happy story.

"Was it love at first sight for the King and Queen?" she said in a small voice.

"It was something like that," he said quietly. She figured he didn't want to talk about the family he missed. There was no need to push Xavier. Ursula held up her gift, so Xavier could see the cover better.

"I bought this book the summer Dad got remarried," she said. "I wore out my old copy."

"What is it about?"

Ursula thumbed through the pages. "A young woman who gets tired of her ordinary life wishes to live in a fairy tale. One day she wakes up and she's a princess who fights dragons, kisses frogs, and insults knights. She has a horrible time and decides her old life was better. By the end of the story, she wakes up and the entire adventure was a bad dream."

Ursula looked at Xavier.

His eyes searched her face, as if trying to read her thoughts. "Do you want to wake up?"

She breathed deeply. "I don't want to wake up. I made a bad wish. I pushed people away because of what I wanted. The worst thing about all of it was it never came true. I lost everything, and I don't know what I gained."

He surveyed her kindly.

"A wise godmother once told me no matter what happens, you can always wish again." His voice held a note of hope. This charming prince was too sweet and tempting. He was everything that she could ever wish for but she couldn't have. She tossed her book into her tote bag. Frustration rolled through her. Ursula couldn't let herself truly want Xavier because she didn't want to get hurt again.

"Don't do that, Xavier." He tilted his head to the side, obviously confused by her words. She worked her jaw. "Don't make me want to be selfish with my wishes. I'd wish for something I don't deserve."

Xavier hunched over, his arms resting on his thighs. "What don't you deserve, Madame?"

His words held a challenge, as if he was daring her to admit what was on her mind. Ursula looked down at her lap. They were thigh to thigh on the bench; his closeness made the atoms inside of her vibrate with need. *Stars above.* She recalled the deck of tarot cards she used to own as a teenage witch. Xavier embodied the Knight of Cups—all romance and charm. He invited her imagination and her body to come play with him. He'd ride in on his horse and carry her away from student loans and overdue bills. No, she couldn't and wouldn't ask him to rescue her from the mess she made. Only she could save herself.

Ursula leapt from the bench, separating her body from his. She flashed him a small grin and grabbed her book haul bag. "Thanks for the book. I'll text you the details about the garden. Good night, Xavier."

She didn't wait for him to respond, worried that if she turned around, she might be tempted to stay and wish for him.

Chapter Fifteen

☾

It was a day filled with fresh sunshine and blooming trees. It was made for fae and humans alike to go outside, drink lilac wine, and be merry. It was a day that Xavier decided to wear jeans. When he asked Whitney where he could purchase a pair of skinny jeans for his upcoming date, she jumped off the couch and cheered. "Let's go to the outlet mall."

Over the course of the morning, Xavier drank three large cups of coffee and ate honey buns to keep up with Whitney. His godmother could outlast a box of batteries with all the extra energy she had when she shopped.

She bought him denim in every shade of blue available and brought them back to the mansion. While she was distracted with a pair of acid-wash shorts, Xavier checked his email on his phone to see if his order had been completed yet. Last night, he'd ordered a collection of woodworking books from a local bookstore. He even signed up for an evening woodcraft class at Shark River Community College for next month. Ursula had a point.

While he was in the Grove, he might as well discover what gave him joy.

Whitney took the phone from his hand and shoved a pair of jeans at him. "Less phone, more fashion."

Xavier tried on every pair but settled on the dark-wash jeans that matched well with his forest-green shirt and open vest. He even allowed Whitney to conjure him a pair of contact lenses to replace his missing glasses. He, despite her imploring, kept his shoes. There was only so much of a makeover he could take in one afternoon. When he finally looked in his bedroom mirror to check out the completed outfit, he did a double take.

Who is this charming brother staring back at you?

There was a light of confidence in his eyes that he didn't recognize, and he stood with a certain swagger that he'd only seen in movie stars on the red carpet. He walked downstairs feeling like he had gold flakes on the soles of his shoes.

Xavier showed off the outfit to Whitney in the salon, and she gave him a snap of appreciation.

"You're not coming to play today, are you," she said. The pride in her words bolstered his confidence. Finally, he was doing something right. It was about time he found his stride.

She picked off a few random threads from his shirt. "I think Paige will find it difficult not to be charmed by you."

Xavier gently corrected her, explaining that he was going to spend the day with Ursula at Grove Garden. Once Whitney heard this news, she halted. Her eyes pinned him to where he stood.

"You have a date with Ursula?" she asked lightly.

His chest jumped. He hated how much he liked hearing that sentence from Whitney. But he shook his head. "No, she's helping me plan this date."

Whitney twisted her lips to the side in thought. "But you're dressing up now, not for tomorrow. Hmm. Doesn't that seem odd?"

Xavier blinked. "It's not a date. Today's a practice run."

He focused his attention on the salon's mantel, studying his reflection in the looking glass on the wall. He didn't want to think too hard about the question she was asking him, but her words took root in his brain.

Why was he trying so hard for some who wasn't his actual date? He was breaking in the clothes in case he split his pants. What if he made a fool of himself in his new jeans—that was completely reasonable, right? Xavier was just hanging out with Ursula so he wouldn't mess things up with Paige. That idea sounded like a perfect explanation.

You're such a terrible liar, you can't even lie to yourself.

Even his reflection looked dubious. Xavier flexed his jaw and tore his eyes away from the mirror. This wasn't a date with Ursula. It couldn't be a date because she wanted to fall in love, and he couldn't allow himself to love her. He just couldn't.

As if sensing his discomfort, Whitney held up her hands in surrender. "Forget I said anything," she said.

Xavier merely nodded. Whitney continued fussing over him. "Since you're seeing Ursula, tell her that I loved the article about the nominees in the *Press*. I forwarded it to my crocheting circle, and they thought it was so romantic. We're rooting for all of them, especially her to find love. Have you read it?"

Xavier made a low sound. Oh, he read the article.

He'd read the article five times, listened to the audio

recording, and studied the picture of her posed by the carousel along with her fellow Sweetheart nominees. Everyone looked great in the group photo, but his attention stayed on Ursula. The photographer was truly gifted because he managed to capture Ursula's bubbly personality in a series of candid photos. In it, she was perched on a bucking painted unicorn in an ombre purple dress, looking fierce like a lady-knight riding off to battle a dragon or rescue a prince.

His phone buzzed. His chest lightened when he checked the screen.

"She's waiting outside for me. Thanks for your help, Whit," Xavier said.

Whitney squeezed his shoulder. He left the mansion and went to Ursula's car. She gave him a wave from the driver's seat, unlocking the door for him. He climbed inside and settled next to her. The space smelled of fresh-cut tulips and pressed jasmine, of rolling in flowerbeds. Ursula angled her body toward him and grinned.

"You look nice," she said. "I'd hate to get you all messy."

"Please, Madame. Make a mess of me," he teased.

Ursula's grin turned into a full smile. She looked away. "Let's go."

She eased the car from the house and drove off. As they made their way to the Grove Garden, Xavier shared Whitney's compliments.

Ursula grimaced. "I have to get used to all this attention. My inbox is a mess, and I haven't answered an email in days. The article title didn't help."

"A Shore Sweetheart is a great title," he said.

Ursula playfully stuck out her tongue. "My family wouldn't

agree with you. I haven't been sweet in a long time. I've already gotten asked out on like ten dates this morning. A goblin left me a diamond—or a really big paperweight—at the shop. The *Press* wants to do a follow-up interview at the end of June to see if I've found a forever love."

Oh. Xavier pressed a hand to his stomach to quell the sudden burn that fired up in his gut. All that coffee was coming back to haunt him. He had been fine until Ursula mentioned a forever love. Did Whitney see something he couldn't? Paige probably wanted a forever love, but he'd been clear with her that he was only looking to get his kiss, break the enchantment, and leave the Grove.

What would it be like to love someone like Ursula forever? His mind couldn't think that far ahead. Instead, he thought about what it meant to love Ursula right now.

No. He couldn't love her, but he could want her. Yearn for her. Cherish her.

She eased the car to a stop at the traffic light.

He peered up at it. "How long does a traffic light stay red?"

Ursula chuckled. "I asked my Grandpa James the same question. He repaired all the lights in the Grove when he was alive. He told me the light cycle lasts for one and a half to two minutes, or about a hundred twenty seconds."

"Okay," he said. He'd want her until the light turned green. Xavier was only strong enough to allow himself to want Ursula for that brief time. For those blessed seconds, Xavier let himself relish in her closeness. Let himself honestly desire her. Emotion flowed into him like he was a thirsty plant finally being given water after months of waiting for rain.

Ursula looked at him. One corner of her mouth lifted. "Are you good, Xavier?"

Warmth filled his heart down to the roots of his soul. Yes, he was more than good, he felt wonderful. A car horn blared behind them. His eyes snapped up to the traffic light. It had turned green. Time was up. Xavier swallowed and nodded. *You're done. Stop.*

The warmth ebbed out of him, leaving him chilly. It was lovely while it lasted.

Ursula gave him a once-over then refocused on the road. She cruised the car smoothly through the green light and into a tree-lined neighborhood. Traces of that warmth remained within him, but he tried to push the feeling away.

Xavier took a moment to collect himself before requesting softly, "Tell me what's next on your to-do list."

"I still have to find a date for the ball," she said.

He swiveled his head in her direction. "There's a ball."

Sweat beaded on his neck. Just the thought of hearing the words "pencil me into your dance card" made his beard itch badly.

"It's more of a dance party, but with poofy dresses and tuxedos," she said. "It marks the official end of the Smitten season and the crowning of the Sweetheart."

"Are you going?" he asked carefully then held his breath waiting for her incoming request. He assumed since they attended all the Smitten events together that they'd go to the ball together. In the Realm, balls were opportunities for the wealthy and titled to trade information, gossip, and flirt. Fae danced in the gardens, on flowers and even raindrops. They never frolicked at balls.

He'd grit his teeth and bear it but remain by her side all night if she needed him. It wouldn't be too difficult to fake his way through a waltz. Then again, he'd get another opportunity to dance with her. His body hummed at that idea.

Ursula focused on the road. "Gwen said if I don't go, then she'll slap on a wig and pretend to be me."

"Ah," Xavier said, a grin coming to his face. "So, you'll be in attendance."

She shrugged as if accepting her fate. "It seems so."

Here it comes. He braced himself for the request. He waited, but she said nothing else. She hummed to a little tune, but she didn't ask him to be her date. His brain celebrated. *You're off the hook. You don't have to attend another ball.* But his heart yearned. He wanted to go with her.

Xavier cleared his throat. "Madame, if you're in need of an escort, I humbly offer my services."

She didn't look at him. Her hands gripped the steering wheel. "The ball's on midsummer."

He shut his mouth as icy realization washed over him. If he got his perfect kiss, then he'd be home by then.

"We're here," she said.

Pristine blue skies and sunshine greeted them as they arrived at Grove Garden. She had texted him this morning that this space would be the perfect backdrop to help Xavier get his kiss. He didn't need to be convinced. If she believed it was perfect, he trusted her. With every fiber of his being.

They parked in the lot, got out of the car, and walked down a short path lined with black antique lampposts. Xavier studied one warily, feeling drawn to it for some reason. Ursula stood by him.

"Don't worry," she said. "It's not made of iron. It's safe. I checked."

"There must be a story here." Xavier eyed it. "If you rub the base, does a ghost jump out and tell you the future?"

Ursula laughed. "No, but Grampa James believed that if you were feeling lost, the lampposts would guide you in the right direction."

He nodded, pleased with her family legend. Xavier faced her and let his attention roam over Ursula. Her light pink daisy-print dress boldly displayed the curves he'd been thinking of for days. Her face was framed by her curly black hair. Those same curls brushed the top of her cheekbones and briefly brushed against her mouth as she watched him.

Ursula gestured down the path. "Shall we, Your Highness?"

"Lead the way, Madame."

They left the lamppost and walked down to what seemed to be the garden's main gate. A large sign by the garden's entrance warned visitors and their animal guests not to eat any of the herbs or flowers.

"Close your eyes," she whispered. He did as she requested. Xavier reached out and he felt her hand pull him forward through the garden's gates. His shoes crunched on dead leaves. Dangling vines tickled his ears. Curiosity kept his steps steady. From what he could guess, they were walking down the pathway to the garden.

"I couldn't bring you home to the Realm, but I wanted to bring you here." She let go of his hand. He felt inviting sunshine on his face. Birdsong, vibrant and spirted, played above his head. Cool air brought the natural scent of flowers to his nose. He inhaled and exhaled the air into his lungs, feeling at ease.

"Open your eyes, Xavier," she whispered.

What greeted him rendered him speechless. Bell-shaped flowers, purple tube blossoms hanging from long stalks, and blooming plants crawled over tall fences. This hidden garden, filled with flourishing buds, was a place where fae dwelled. There wasn't an inch of this space that didn't immediately hold his attention and bring him a sense of peace. A sense of power. His chest expanded. He'd claimed his true name, the one bestowed upon himself and that gave him his power with plants, in a space just like this one. That name, the one he'd buried deep within his mind, cracked to the surface. He hadn't thought about it in so long that merely remembering it gave him a feeling of lightness.

Appreciation, like a cozy blanket, enfolded Xavier's body and made him feel grounded. He turned to Ursula, affection gripping his throat. She said nothing but gave Xavier a kind, understanding smile. "Thank you" wasn't enough. Her hair caught the wind and kicked up. He breathed in, her delicious floral scent tickling his nose and making him focus on her and the flowers surrounding them. She faced him.

"Which one is the prettiest?" she asked.

You. He bit his tongue to keep from blurting out that single word.

"Tell me yours," he said instead.

"I like this one here." Ursula's fingers brushed the petals of the highest honeysuckle dangling from the vine. The flower shivered under her touch. He'd never envied a living thing more.

"We fae love its nectar. It thrives in the shade."

Xavier reached up, plucked the flower, and delivered it to

her. Their fingers brushed, sending a vibration through his body. He pulled away from her to gather himself.

Ursula pressed it to her nose, then tucked it behind her ear.

"The clinging vines are said to symbolize seduction," Ursula said. "It might help you get your kiss."

"Yes, but from who?"

Ursula blushed. A thread of guilt went through him. He shouldn't flirt with her, but being with Ursula made him forget about being enchanted. Made him remember when he felt powerful and capable of magic. The conversation with Whitney and being here with Ursula was making him question everything. *Do you even want to go out with Paige anymore?*

He was still a gentleman and a royal of his word. He'd meet with Paige out of respect for her, but he was rethinking being on EnChant altogether. It was becoming clearer that what he was looking for was closer than he expected. They sat down on the stone bench underneath the wooden trellis. Sunlight trickled through the lattice overhead.

"We used to let honeysuckle grow wild in the family garden. Nana said that it needed to grow free, so it could thrive."

"She sounds wise."

Ursula nodded; a light smile appeared on her lips. "She taught me to respect, but be wary of, all magical beings. She had a rhyme for everything. 'Gnomes and fae make the garden flourish every day,'" Ursula said. Xavier let out a soft laugh. Her smile fell. Sadness dulled her eyes. He moved closer to her. "They didn't bloom the spring she passed away. I haven't been to the garden in a while. I don't know if the honeysuckle returned this year."

He hated to see her so upset. All he could offer were words, but they were hers to have. "They'll return. Give it time."

Ursula nodded. She blinked and the dullness eased a bit. "Tell me about the fair folk."

"What would you like to know, Madame?"

She paused and met his eyes. "How do you attract a fae?"

Xavier ran his tongue over his lower lip. When he spoke, his voice was softer than he expected. "Tempt them with something they want. Flowers. Trinkets. Coins. Leave them offerings in plain sight. The fae can find treasure anywhere. They can fit anywhere an ant can."

"I once saw a fae who was as big as a mouse," Ursula said.

He pinned her with an interested stare. "How big was he?"

She held up her thumb and forefinger and spread them three inches apart. "There."

He wrinkled his nose. She was giving his brethren too much credit. Fae shrunk smaller than humans could ever imagine or see. Xavier reached out without thinking and adjusted her fingers, down by two and half inches. His flesh prickled at her touch.

"That's about right."

She raised an eyebrow. "Really? That small?"

"You have to be able to squeeze through a keyhole. To get into a locked room or tower."

"A tower?" she asked, a little breathless.

"That's where the treasure is," he said. He imagined her as a bejeweled princess up in a high tower, not awaiting rescue, but waiting for something or someone worth leaving her space for.

Xavier studied their intertwined hands. How was her skin

so soft—as delicate as a flower's petal? The vibration inside of him turned up and it felt like everything down to his atoms were celebrating. He folded her hand into his, gently grazing her knuckles with his thumb.

He heard her small inhale of breath.

"Is it all right?" he asked. His parents raised him to always respect another's space and ask every time before he took a lady's hand. Before he asked for a dance.

"Yeah, it's all right," she said in a low voice.

There was a time when he wanted to pluck out his heart and bury it in the ground. Maybe then the loneliness would ease, and he could just be at rest. No pain. No yearning. No need for companionship. Now, holding hands with Ursula, he was so thankful to have an anxious heart pounding against his rib cage. Making him feel like every closed part of him was blooming.

Like a flower opening its face to the rising sun. He leaned in close.

Ursula stilled. "Shouldn't you be saving your kisses, Xavier?"

His chest expanded as if it were going to burst.

"Why are you saving yours, Sula?" he countered. She'd been named one of the Smitten Sweethearts but hadn't gone on any dates with any other men or beings. He'd quietly seethed in envy of all the men who openly wanted her. He envied those who weren't bound by magic and were free to desire her. All Xavier allowed himself was a few seconds to cherish her and he already knew it wasn't enough.

A daring look flashed in her eyes. "I know my worth."

Tell me the price. I will pay twice it just to taste you once.

The thought of her kiss sent a jolt of pure desire through him that nearly sent him to his knees. She leaned into him; they stood chest to chest. Body to body.

Xavier cupped her cheek. Ursula pressed her lips to his palm, then to the inside of his wrist, brushing his skin with her flower-soft touch. She shut her eyes and burrowed close to him. He studied her, the witch who could easily be mistaken for a sleeping beauty. Her face, so delicate and lovely, bathed in sunbeams and bright sky. Those full lips. Apple cheeks. Round chin. Deep eyes. He breathed in her scent; the top notes came to him immediately. Overgrown honeysuckle. Raw sugar. The unique spicy hint of natural magic that emanated from her center. He hovered right there, inches away from those lush lips, so close that her panting sweet breath brushed his beard.

With his finger, he traced a slow trail down her bare shoulder to her hand. She shivered under his attention. A rosy blush covered her exposed skin. Xavier envisioned that blush painted over her bare body in his bed. He imagined her legs spread wide, his mouth drinking every inch of her desire, and his hands caressing her core—making her body taut with pleasure. To see those eyes flutter with ecstasy and hear her trembling breath sound off in his ear.

To cry out his name and ask him for more.

That simple truth stilled his hand on her skin. Ursula deserved more. She'd want beyond the fairy tale he could spin for her. She'd want beyond the kiss that was his escape from this world. Her world. He reached up and brushed his thumb over Ursula's lips and moved away. Her eyes snapped open, unfocused with craving. She swayed slightly, her eyes considering but unseeing. He'd done something, whether with his innate magic or his touch, to change something within her. Did remembering his name give him the power to bewitch her? Was this the enchantment at work?

No, he wasn't going get a kiss from her.

She hugged her arms to her body. "It's getting late. We should go."

Xavier took her by the hand and led them out of the garden.

Once they returned to the car and drove away, a single question repeated in his brain. *What would you give to possess her kiss?* He'd drain the ocean and give her all the sunken treasures. He'd pick every flower in the royal gardens for her.

But he couldn't give her forever.

The best thing Xavier could do for Ursula was to get his perfect kiss, return to the Realm, and leave her alone.

Chapter Sixteen

$$\smile$$

Saturdays were always Ursula's favorite time to make a magical brew because she liked to start fun trouble during the weekend. Back in college, she'd always have her Sunday Funday brew ready to drink so she could recharge after turning it up at the frat parties. She wouldn't have passed her senior art history final if she hadn't chugged a Berry Brain Power smoothie to help her stay awake for an all-night study session. Now, ten years later, Ursula flipped through her pocket-sized spell book, trying to find one entry to help her with her current...frequent problem. The bistro was half empty, so Ursula was able to get a booth inside. She wanted to hide out for a bit from a certain prince who occupied her thoughts and—unfortunately—her dreams.

"One iced Love Potion Number Ten to go," Gwen said cheerfully. She dropped off the reusable cup on the table in front of Ursula.

Gwen noticed the aged book in her lap. "Oooh, what are you cooking up in the kitchen?"

"I'm making up a special brew." Ursula covered her mouth as she gave a big yawn and shook off the drowsiness.

"You look sleepy," Gwen said. "Should I upgrade your drink to an extra-large?"

Ursula flipped another page. "No, I just need to get more rest."

Gwen lifted a brow. "Something keeping you up at night? Or maybe someone?"

Ursula ignored her questions and took a deep sip from her drink to avoid talking too much. The intense, vibrant raspberry and lemon flavor gave her a much-needed energy boost. Every night for the last three days, whenever she went to sleep, Xavier was there to greet her with that big smile that knocked her off kilter. The dreams started out innocent enough with them doing couple-ish things like cuddling on the couch under a blanket, watching a movie, and even completing a crossword over breakfast. It was completely harmless. Then in an instant, she found herself being pulled into his arms, stripped naked and underneath him while he eased inside her with gentle, urgent movements. His curly, thick beard brushed against her thighs as he pleasured her leisurely with his mouth and hands.

Every dream ended the same way. Xavier took her face in his hands, pulled her close, and kissed her deeply. His lips brushed against hers as he spoke low with words of devotion and reverence. She shuddered as her mind replayed the dream, taunting her with its vividness.

"Is the drink too cold?" Gwen asked. "You got this strange look on your face."

Ursula refocused on the tea-stained page in front of her. "No, it's great. I just zoned out for a second."

Gwen eased into the booth. "Tell me everything about your Sweetheart experience. I need details. Have you gotten your dress?"

She held back a scream. "Add another item to my never-ending to-do list. I'll hit up Circe's Closet and pick something out."

Circe's Closet was the local clothing shop where you could find everything from an extra-large JERSEY GIRL 4 LIFE T-shirt to a zebra-print dress that was great for a beach night out.

Gwen made an outraged squeak at her announcement. "Not on my watch. You're getting a real gown. I need this in my life. Have you found a date yet?"

Ursula shrugged. "Well, it's been interesting trying to find one."

"Hmm, how interesting? Is it like sexy werewolf or sexy goblin king?"

"It's like a gnome gave me a bouquet of mushrooms in the store type of interesting," Ursula said. "That whole situation happened yesterday."

Gwen giggled. "So, I guess you're not going with Mr. Gnome?"

Ursula shuddered in disgust. "No way. I got a very angry email from Mrs. Gnome telling me her boyfriend is a player."

"Why don't you ask Xavier?" Gwen pinned her with a stare. "I'm sure he'd be happy to go with you."

"He won't stick around until midsummer," Ursula said.

"Why don't you ask him to stay?" Gwen tapped her temple mimicking a famous meme.

Ursula bit her lip. She'd wanted to ask him to stay for the ball, but she held back. What if he said yes? How long could she expect a whole fae prince to stay around the Grove?

"Midnight's almost here, Cindy-rella," Gwen reminded kindly.

Ursula gave her major side-eye. "You sound like Sirena."

Gwen brightened. "You're talking to Sirena again?"

Ursula gave a small grin. "We're texting back and forth, but yes. She sent me a recipe for a come-hither oil. I don't need any more attention."

As a Smitten nominee and an object of public affection, she'd been visited at the shop by many supernatural beings seeking to court her. They were all perfectly nice, but there wasn't the spark that she had with Xavier. The spark she was trying to ignore but wouldn't go away. She'd practically jumped him in Grove Garden. Forget that she'd been tempted at the traffic light to just keep driving and go someplace so they could be alone. Alone and naked.

Ursula came across the book page she needed and stopped. It was a tea blend she scribbled down from Lucy when she couldn't get a good night's sleep due to those late-night fantasies.

Her fingers ran over the title. *How to Banish Thoughts and Dreams of Certain Persons.*

The word "banish" gave her pause. That choice seemed a little extreme. She didn't want to completely rid him from her mind. One thought kept aggravating her like a popcorn shell stuck on the roof of her mouth.

I lie awake at night thinking that not kissing him is a mistake.

There was that intimate moment in the garden when she could've claimed him, but she waited too long and the moment was lost. Good. The man had a date waiting for him. He'd texted her a little while ago on his way to meet Paige for their date. She wished him luck and then put her phone on mute. There was only so much anguish she could put herself through. She didn't want to get real-time updates about whether he was successful or not. He was going to get his kiss today. She felt it in her bones.

She tried to imagine them in the garden, but for some reason she couldn't.

However, she had no issue remembering her and Xavier standing in the sunshine in each other's arms.

Ursula held the book to her chest, weighing consequences of using the brew. Dream magic was potent and extremely effective. If she drank it, then she would probably stop dreaming about Xavier. Her stomach lurched. She'd never dreamed about any man like this before and knew that she'd never dream about anyone else like this again.

Ursula knew how this story ended. Princes did not end up with witches in fairy tales or in real life. She wanted him badly, but she wasn't meant for Xavier.

Maybe another drink would help her make a choice. Ursula closed her spell book on the table. The bistro door opened. Gwen stood up stiffly from the booth. She straightened and lifted her chin.

"Welcome to Night Sky, Mr. Walker. What can I get you?"

Lincoln approached their booth wearing his usual polo shirt, jeans, and fresh sneakers outfit. His forehead wrinkled when he glanced down at her and the book. Ursula merely blinked. The once familiar urge to hide her magic from Lincoln was gone, replaced with indifference. If he didn't like it, then she didn't have to care.

"I'm just dropping off the last payment for the party." Lincoln held up a check and handed it to Gwen.

She took it. "Thank you. I'll be right back with your receipt."

Gwen hovered for a second, giving Ursula a secret *Are you good?* look.

She gave her sister a small nod of confidence. Gwen left Ursula alone with Lincoln.

He stuffed his hands into his pockets. "So, you're here alone."

"I'm not eating lunch with an invisible man," Ursula joked.

He glanced around the bistro as if becoming aware of the awkwardness of this encounter. "Maybe this is too weird."

"Linc, we passed weird several months ago," Ursula said. "We're internet legends."

He bobbed his head. "You're not wrong about that. Zoe told Mom you're coming to the party."

Ursula tilted her head back, surprised. "I haven't seen Mayor Walker in months. How is she doing?"

The sheer panic Ursula felt whenever she thought about talking to Mayor Des'ree Walker didn't appear. Instead, she was fine. Was this personal growth? She liked it.

Ursula considered Lincoln.

Worry crossed his face. "She's doing all right, but all the work at city hall is stressing her out. I told her she needs to hire more people to help, but she doesn't listen. Mom says she can only rely on herself."

"It's the burden of the superwoman," Ursula said sympathetically. "Tell her you can't keep a star from shining, but stars can burn out. She needs to delegate responsibility to the deputy mayor and take time to rest. The Grove will be fine if she takes a vacation."

Lincoln grimaced. "But will she be fine without the Grove?"

Ursula recalled what Lincoln just said a few minutes ago. "Wait. If Zoe spoke to your mom about me, does that mean she knows about us?"

A pained groan escaped his mouth. Lincoln scratched the back of his neck. "Yeah. She searched your name and... knows everything about us. I mean, Zoe even read the comments on the *Press* article. People were not kind."

Ursula winced. "How did that talk go?"

She knew how nervous she was sharing the truth with Xavier, and they weren't dating. Goddess, she couldn't even imagine what Zoe thought about the situation.

"We're working it out," Xavier said simply.

On that note, Ursula decided to change the subject. "Is Marcus coming? I mean, it's his birthday too."

Marcus was Lincoln's twin and Ursula's former best friend. She'd last seen him at the wedding standing in his tux with a faraway look in his eyes.

"No, he's overseas handling business." Lincoln's eyes dropped down to his sneakers. "We haven't spoken since the whole thing went down. After what happened, people didn't want to do business with us. They said I wasn't trustworthy. Marcus wasn't too happy about me...you know, for doing what I did."

This conversation was getting weirder by the second. If he wasn't going to say it, she was going to do it for him. For better or for worse, this story was theirs and was going to be a chapter in their lives.

"I know what you did. You jilted me," she said. There was no heat or anger in her voice. Nothing remained but the truth.

He glanced around nervously as if the punishment faery would jump out and dole out a judgment. "Don't be like that, Ursula."

"Be like what?" Ursula shrugged. She was over being embarrassed about that day. "You left and I've had to deal with the fallout. I dealt with all the pity, the stares, and the comments for months. The least you can do is acknowledge it so that we can move on and try to act normal around each other. I'm not walking on eggshells to spare your feelings."

He blinked hard and something defensive flared in his face. His questions came out rapid-fire and hot like floating fireballs from a wizard's staff. "Are you mad? Do you want me to cancel the party? Will that make you feel better?"

"Will it help you?" she shot back.

His face fell for a moment. "I don't want you to be mad."

Ursula looked at him through her lashes. "I'm not mad, but I'm not going to pretend that everything's cool. You were wrong for walking out on me."

"I left you a text," he joked weakly.

"I deserved a conversation. Point blank. Period."

What else was there to say? Lincoln worked his jaw and stared at her. Discomfort flickered in his eyes, but she said

CELESTINE MARTIN

nothing else to him. He'd take her truth because it would help them both move on. To claim their own separate happy endings. She didn't need this much drama on a Saturday morning. She was going to dab a whole lotta frankincense to clear out the energy from this interaction. Did Gwen go to Red Bank to get Lincoln's receipt?

Ursula glanced around for her sister.

She noticed Gwen was helping a barista fulfill a massive coffee and drink order.

Ursula met Lincoln's quiet, intense stare.

"I didn't want to hurt you," he said slowly. "I thought the best thing I could do for us—for me—was to walk away. I loved you but knew it wasn't enough."

Damn. That truth was so heavy, it sat on her chest and stole her voice for an instant. But she understood. Love was a good place to start for a relationship, but there had to be room for trust, connection, and laughter. She couldn't remember if she ever laughed with Lincoln or if she genuinely trusted him with her magic. To show him all the messy parts of herself.

It was just easier to hide that part of her rather than share with him.

So, Ursula the witch pretended to be the princess.

"My magic didn't scare you away, did it?" she said, trying lift to heaviness of this moment.

His expression grew serious. "No, but I shouldn't have dismissed it."

Lincoln had treated her like a princess, and she'd felt immense pressure to be perfect. So, she put away her magic to focus on embodying perfection. He'd put an engagement

222

ring on her finger and then barely touched her as if she were a valuable artifact he'd just acquired. A kiss there. A caress here. A random side hug. At first she'd felt treasured that he'd treat her so delicately, but then loneliness settled in and remained. She didn't want to be treated like she was on a pedestal anymore. It was terrible when you were knocked down to the ground from such a dazzling height. She'd fallen hard, but she survived.

"I wish we'd talked to each other sooner," he said.

"Well, we're talking now," she said.

A quiet realization came over Ursula. She had loved Lincoln, but not as much as she craved the security of being a Walker. It was a security that she wanted since her Ellis family quietly ignored her and Mama. The security she yearned for when she reread and remembered her fairy tales and folklore. Ursula, while under the spell, believed that having the last name Caraway had been a curse, but it was a blessing.

Lincoln lingered for a moment, his body tense. "I've been meaning to talk to you about...everything. I'm sorry."

Ursula placed a light hand to his shoulder. "I wish you nothing but the best."

She meant it. Since she decided to fully embrace her magic and commit herself to her list, she released any hurt she had over Lincoln. Any lingering shame over their relationship washed away like leftover beach sand being rinsed off her body. She had to let go if she was going to try to love another man. And she wanted—so desperately—to love. Besides, Lincoln was back in the Grove, and she'd have to get used to seeing him around with Zoe picking up underwear or buying groceries. She let the peace she felt flow from her hand and ease into Lincoln. The tension left his body. He leaned into her touch for an instant, then stepped away.

Gwen came over with the receipt in hand. "I apologize for the wait. Apparently we've got a film crew nearby in need of a huge coffee fix."

Lincoln took it from Gwen, a small smile playing on his face. "That's okay. Ursula and I were just catching up."

Gwen looked between them. "Is everything cool?"

"We're getting there." Lincoln looked to Ursula expectantly. "So, I'll see you and Xavier at the party."

"I don't have to get you a gift, do I?" Ursula asked with a grin.

Lincoln made a face. "No, after everything I did, Mom says I owe you a gift and a spa vacation."

Ursula laughed. "I'll take a job interview if you have it."

His face turned thoughtful. "I got you. I'll let Mom know in case there's a job opening at city hall."

"I was kidding, Lincoln."

"I'm not. She could use a person like you by her side. You're welcome to come to the party either way. We'd like to have you and Xavier there to celebrate."

There was no bitterness or anger in his words, only a sincere invitation.

She stood up from the booth to properly see him off. "I'll let Xavier know."

Lincoln waved goodbye to Gwen and Ursula and left.

"I'm going to need another drink," she said.

Gwen pointed to the treat case. "You didn't hex him on the spot. I'm getting you a cupcake with sprinkles."

Ursula picked up her spell book and flipped around for another solution. The answer had to be here. She couldn't keep fantasizing about Xavier when he could be halfway to wooing Ms. Paige at this moment. Then what would happen? She'd have to pine over Xavier while he waxed on about his lady love. No way. Her brain rejoiced at this scenario. The sooner he found his perfect kiss, the sooner he could go back to the Realm and Ursula could stop dreaming of him.

Her heart called her out of her obvious bs. *Who are you kidding? That fae man could be orbiting Neptune and he'd still be on your mind.* Ursula snapped the book shut. No matter how many times she thought about leaning in and kissing him, she couldn't allow herself to forget the truth. His kisses weren't meant for her. Princes didn't make out with witches.

Xavier glared at his warped reflection in the drinking glass and frowned. The beige liquor sloshed against the rim, spilling on his hand. His eyeglasses were slightly askew on his nose and his hair still had a few stray leaves. He didn't want to deal with his contacts, so he wore his backup pair he had packed in his luggage. Glasses or no glasses, it made no difference to him. He was a hopeless mess.

"You embarrassed me today," he hissed.

The words came out slurred and muddled, but his reflection shrank back from him. Xavier glanced around the bar. Patrons lined the bar top, nursing their drinks and watching the muted movie on the TV screen propped up in the corner. The bar back displayed high-end spirits and empty drinking glasses.

The bartender, a wide-shouldered vampire with inky-blue hair, approached Xavier. Her voice was tender, almost like a murmur. "Who is she?"

Ursula's lovely face flashed in his mind. He tried to sit up, but he couldn't quite get the hang of it. "Oh. She's...so beautiful, like...like the waxing moon in the middle of the night. Like even if the clouds are covering her splendor, she's still there shining."

Vamp crossed her tattooed arms and eyed him for a beat. "Is she the reason for your current state?"

He straightened, and his witch vanished from his mind's eye. "I...No...it's not her. I did this to me. She's a sweetheart. Literally. Everyone loves her."

"Everyone?" Vamp asked. She raised her brow in silent expectation.

Xavier rubbed his face.

He couldn't go home. Whitney would take one glance at him and know that he had failed again. But this time, it was his own fault. Paige was nice. She was the ideal fae lady with her glitter wings and attractive dress. They'd strolled in the Grove Garden path, discussed Faerie Realm politics, and chatted about the lovely weather. There was eye contact. They shared a good laugh. The date was going well. Paige stepped up, offered her lips eagerly, but Xavier froze, his mind pulling him into two opposite directions.

If you kiss her, you can go home. The Realm waits for you.

If you kiss her, Ursula's gone for good. She doesn't deserve to be a second choice.

As he was begging the universe to guide him on the right path, something caught his attention and made his ears turn cold. The old lamppost he studied the other day glowed red, yellow, then green. It cycled through the colors again. He blinked.

As the colors flashed, one word repeated in his brain: Ursula.

Xavier looked down at Paige's waiting lips. He wheeled backward as if his ears had been yanked. Stunned at the lamppost's flashing light, Xavier stumbled back and landed head over ass right into a huge bush.

"Are you all right, Your Highness?" she had asked.

No. He didn't know if he was ever going to be okay. He was a fool for believing he could want Ursula for a little while. Xavier let her warmth in, and it wasn't going away.

He ordered a ride for Paige and made sure that she made it home safely. Mortification rippled through him at today's actions. Alder princes never behaved in such a goofy way. Dismay burned in the space right underneath his heart. Only Ursula's kiss would do for him, but she wanted love. She deserved more than he could ever give. He had walked the Grove, the streets occupied with nocturnal ghosts hovering over the pavement and gargoyles patrolling high buildings.

Xavier found solace in the dark of the night with every buzzing neon sign he passed. The world was asleep, but every part of him was awake. Eventually he found his way into this dimly lit bar located in West Grove. The lights were turned down low and patrons minded their business.

Xavier pushed his empty glass over to the waiting bartender. "Do you have any fries?"

Vamp slid a menu over to him. Xavier wasn't leaving this bar until he rid himself of this feeling of complete failure.

In the meantime, there was one action he could do successfully. He took out his phone, opened his EnChant account, and clicked on the Profile Status section. Xavier scrolled down until he found the right link titled To permanently delete your profile, click here.

He clicked it and a pop-up warning appeared. This action can't be undone. Are you sure you want to delete? Make your choice. Yes or No.

This time, Xavier didn't hesitate to make the best choice for him and his aching soul.

Chapter Seventeen

Rumor has it that all the fun magic happened before and after midnight in Freya Grove.

Ursula spent the better part of the day comforting a young man who was terrified about saying the wrong thing during Mercury retrograde. The celestial event caused an increase in sales in the shop and emotions in their customers. Mama, on her annual Journaling and Gems retreat in upstate New York, asked Ursula to keep the shop open until eleven once a month whenever Mercury decided to start trouble for everyone. That planet, with its fickleness, affected personal communication for humans and magical beings. That was why Ursula waited until her shift was over to check her phone, which she had put on silent.

When she saw the message notifications, her stomach dropped.

There were a lot of messages from Xavier, each one a little zanier than the last. Ursula read the last five texts.

How do you feel about vamps? 👻 🤔

They don't have soft pretzels, but they have stuff. Good stuff.

Walls feel nice like velvet

Can you have Vim and not Vigor??

Would I look good with a rainbow wig?

She let out a groan. There was only one place where she could find vampires, good snacks, and one possibly super drunk fae prince.

While the Two Princes Tavern had a carefully curated whimsy to appeal to the many citizens, Vim and Vigor was made for the West Grove set. Vampires draped in yards of crushed velvet sipped crimson drinks from goblets. Werefolk, close to transformation, dined on shreds of curated meats at their table. Everything from the bronze and mosaic lampshades to the bar top had a sheen of antiquity about it. The bottles lined up against the bar back were decades old and filled with various-colored liquids. The wood floor was made from driftwood and the tables had been made from barrels found in an old waterfront building. They served drinks ice cold from the tap and simple snacks that could be eaten with one hand or paw.

Last year's Ursula would have been scandalized to walk into this bar at night, but no longer. Now she enjoyed clinging in the shadows and hiding away from the light. She breathed easier away from the spotlight that she had been forced into when she was going to be a Walker.

Ursula slid into the dimly lit booth, cradling her tumbler,

the scent of sweet and tangy liquor tickling her nose. Xavier had his own drink in hand, swirling the liquid with the ice cubes. His eyes were glassy, and he leaned against the booth.

"How are you? Have you eaten yet?" His voice had a degree of tenderness and care.

"Yes, I had dinner before work." She held up her glass. "I only ordered this drink because of the name."

His brow lifted in interest. "What's it called? It looks interesting."

"Sorcerer's Cherry." She held out the glass to him. "Want to taste?"

He looked at the liquor; then his eyes flicked to her face. "Maybe later."

She lit up like a tree wrapped in twinkle lights at the promise in his voice, but she tamped down her excitement. Her friend needed her. Ursula drank from the glass deeply. The cocktail was indulgent and rich, and tasted like a ripened cherry that had been sprinkled with pepper.

She moved closer to him. "Talk to me, Xavier."

He took a long sip from his drink, spilling a few drops on his hands. Okay, maybe Paige didn't like the park. He dropped his half-empty glass onto the table with a clatter.

"It all went wrong." He ducked his head. "We had a nice conversation about our families and titles, and then we went for a walk. We were about to leave when she tried to kiss me."

"What do you mean she tried?" Ursula didn't fail to catch the note of utter dismay in his voice. Oh no. She swirled her drink, letting the ice clink against the sides.

He shook his head, regretfully. "I moved—actually, I jerked away from her."

"Did you have garlic for lunch?" Ursula said in a teasing tone.

"It didn't feel right," he said. His voice was pained. "I didn't want her kiss."

"How are you going to get another one?" she asked, half dreading and half anticipating his answer. "You can always go back to EnChant and—"

Her words stopped died on her tongue when Xavier touched the back of her hand. His touch was soft, yet firm.

"I don't want another kiss." He spat into the word another as if it disgusted him. He pulled back from her. Xavier focused on his hand for a tense second, then looked at her silently. Oh. The sheer determination that glittered in his eyes spoke for him. *I want yours.*

He bowed his head. "Why do most fairy tales end with a kiss?"

Good question. Blood hummed in her veins.

"Kisses are powerful," Ursula said, trying to inject her voice with a calmness she didn't feel. "The act of kissing has been around since people were using stone tools. It's mentioned in the earliest poems, papers, and books in the world. A single kiss can express so much. When it comes to family and friends, kisses represent acceptance and forgiveness. With a lover, it symbolizes a promise and the possibility of passion."

Xavier watched her for a suspended moment. He blew out an impressed breath. "I won't ask that question again."

She took another sip of her drink and let it burn a trail down into her gut. He appeared in the dim bar light to be more ethereal than when they first met. Before on the boardwalk, he had looked like a playful daydream, but now he had desire and frustration burning in his eyes and want ringing in his voice.

"What now, Your Highness?"

"We toast the night." He tapped her glass to his, causing a pleasing *clink*. "Have you ever had a bad kiss?"

She gave a little snort. Oh yeah. "I've smooched my share of frogs."

He raised a brow. "Have you ever kissed any princes?"

She almost did. Ursula made a sound. "Not yet."

The night's still young. He stretched his arm across the back of her seat. She felt the warmth of his hand near her shoulder. Ursula leaned back into his touch. His fingers made slow, deliberate movements, sending fiery sparkles through her veins. Need constricted about her heart. They'd known each other only a few weeks, but they'd clicked automatically. The meet-cute on the boardwalk. The shared laughs. The lingering looks. How many times had she considered claiming him for herself in the most desperate, late-night moments?

Ursula clutched the glass to her chest, rattling the ice cubes. She knew how to bind souls together. Honey could work as a binding agent, but fresh sweat would be better if you wanted this certain spell to take hold. Ursula had never attempted to bind Lincoln because he didn't believe in her power. The man who didn't kiss her on New Year's Eve because he didn't entertain superstition. He wouldn't allow himself to be seduced. Oh no. He was too elevated for that supposed nonsense.

Not Xavier.

From the way he regarded her with complete awe, this

prince believed in every inch of her. She could make him sweat and bring him crawling to her bed without question. Without shame. Without mercy. To bind his blood and bone so that they became one for the remainder of their time on Earth. Goddess, she'd treat him so good that he'd want nothing else but to be with her for all his days. She'd demolish him with her affections, and he'd want to drink her bathwater by the mouthful. In turn, she'd take him into every part of her body, mind, and soul. Her wanton thoughts mortified the stars above, but she had held back from telling him how much she yearned for him. Ursula willed herself to be strong.

Let him have his happy ending without you.

Xavier spoke up again, sending her dark thoughts scattered back into the corners of her mind.

"I have one job. Show up. Kiss the beauty. Ride off into the sunset."

She shook her head hard. "There's more to the story than that, but let's start there. Spend a little time getting comfortable with your date; then you'll get the whole kissing thing."

Xavier tilted his head. "I'm comfortable with you."

"I'm not your date," she reminded.

Two words slipped out of his mouth so softly she almost missed them. "Why not?"

He put his hand under her chin, turning her face toward him. The question remained between them. *Why not?*

Her heart answered. *Because I would go wild with you.*

"I've read enough fairy tales to know how much trouble a kiss can cause," she finally said.

He gave a low chuckle that made her head spin.

Xavier didn't respond but tapped his glass with hers. *Clink.*

They had another drink. She shifted in her seat. They stayed until it was a quarter to midnight. He helped her out of the booth, paid the bill, and left the bar. Xavier, being the gentleman that he was, walked her to her building and waited while she fished her keys from her pocket. His nearness made her clumsy and her palms sweaty. Ursula tried to put her key in the lock, missed two times, and then finally managed to find it.

The lock clicked and the door opened. "Kablam," Ursula said.

He chuckled. "Is that an official magic word?"

"Yes," she said. They shared a smile. He was so striking, so princely. Everything around her felt like it was moving in slow motion. The sidewalk felt crooked under her feet. They stepped onto the landing. Tonight, she was grateful that she was the only resident in this building, and she wasn't waking up any neighbors with her magical mayhem.

Ursula motioned up the stairs to her apartment. "Do you want to come up for some tea?"

He shook his head. She tamped down her disappointment and gave him a small smile. The night was over.

"Thank you for the company. Good night, Xavier."

"Ursula?" His voice was tentative.

She paused. "Yes."

He tweaked his glasses. "I was waiting until midnight to kiss you."

"I think it's time," she whispered. Even if it wasn't midnight yet, Ursula was done waiting to taste him.

Xavier moved in close enough that he could have stolen a kiss, but he hesitated a hair's breadth away. She nodded quietly, not wanting to startle him with a single sound. Her body felt heavy and warm as his hand cupped her cheek. It smelled of caramel and vanilla flowers, leftover from his drink on his breath. His other arm was firmly on her waist; she felt the weight of his hand through her dress. He pressed his lips to hers, testing more than kissing. He was as stiff as a two-day-old bagel.

Ursula smothered a groan. It was as if he were taking sips of a hot drink that he was worried would burn him. She leaned back and met his questioning stare. *Well, that happened.*

She sighed roughly. "I mean—"

"That was a disaster." Xavier rubbed his forehead. He sounded miserable. "It was like an asteroid hitting the Earth and wiping out all the dinosaurs."

"Your Highness," she said. "It's just nerves."

He continued as if he didn't hear her, clearly caught up in his own head. "It was so bad you probably could see it from space," he bemoaned.

"Xavier." Ursula gripped him by the shoulders. He quieted and looked at her, embarrassment shining in those eyes she'd dreamed about for days. For weeks. For too long. Her mind flashed back to the garden. A rush of anticipation filled her from the inside out. She'd been, like now, eager for him to touch her. To caress. To hold.

"I wish you'd kiss me again," Ursula demanded. Sheer need bled into her voice, and frightening awareness filled her. She meant it. She wanted this wish more than she desired her next breath. Something clicked in his eyes. The shyness went away and was replaced with resolve.

"As you wish," he said.

He moved in slowly; she felt his soft hand brush the nape of her neck. She raised her face to meet his, her body trembling with impatience.

Their lips touched and...that's when it got surreal. *This* kiss was heartbreakingly gentle, as if he were a locksmith trying to carefully find the right moves and combination to unlock her. A desperate sigh escaped her lips, and he took her breath. Bliss burst from underneath the surface like wildflower seeds and bloomed all over her body. His beard scratched her skin deliciously, setting her ablaze. He tasted and savored her, unhurriedly. This kiss broke curses and saved princesses from towers. Kissing him felt hot and expectant, like volcanic lightning hitting the ground before her and electrifying everything.

This. Was. It.

Ursula clutched him for dear life, her legs went wobbly, and she couldn't collect her thoughts. What the what? That kiss came from space. It was out of this world.

He lifted his lips, lingering inches away from her mouth. "So?"

"I—" Her body arched forward, closing the space between them. Excitement swelled in her body. Something amazing just happened after midnight in Freya Grove.

She wrapped her arms around his neck and stared up at him.

"I wasn't paying attention. Do that again."

Chapter Eighteen

I wasn't paying attention. Do that again."

Xavier did what the lady requested and reclaimed her mouth. He kissed her harder this time, with an edge of want that bordered on obsession. Her mouth tasted of scorched cherries and whiskey that took over his senses. She wound herself around him, so tightly that nothing on Earth could get between them. Ursula caressed his ears, sending a burst of fire through his body and setting him ablaze. He licked her lips and nipped at the corner of her mouth, and she let out a soft moan. *Make that noise again, sweet angel.*

His hands traveled down the small of her back, squeezing her round ass and holding her close. She squealed at his playful, roaming touch. His head told him to break off the kiss, but everything else from his hands to his heart refused to obey.

This kiss was not just perfect, it also felt like it was his last. A voice in his head ruthlessly mocked him. *You'll never seek another woman's kiss after tonight.*

Those words rattled his nerve and yanked him out this precious moment. Xavier wrenched away from her and leaned against the wall to catch his breath. Ursula pressed a trembling hand to her lips. They were deliciously wet and raw. Half of him wanted to keep going until she was boneless in his arms; the other half wanted to flee and hide from his aching desire. His thoughts spun. He felt jubilant standing there with her, as if he'd discovered another world and tasted the wonders that lay before him. This feeling was short-lived when Ursula stumbled backward. A strange sound like a whine left her mouth and her skin paled.

Her face went blank, and it seemed like the light in her eyes dimmed as if she was in a trance. He called her name twice. No response. Panic threw his heartbeat into high speed. *It was your kiss. You did this to her.* If he'd accidentally hurt her with his magic, then he'd never forgive himself. His mind raced. How fast could Whitney get here? No, he needed to see what he could do for Ursula right now.

Xavier placed a gentle hand on her shoulder. "Sula, are you okay?"

She jerked once he touched her. Her eyes fluttered rapidly, as if she had been roused from a nap.

Ursula pressed a shaky hand to her cheek. The rosy blush slowly returned to her face. "I completely zoned out. I'm sorry."

His gut told him she was hiding something, but he didn't want to push. He wasn't leaving until he was certain she was safe. "Don't be sorry. You tranced out. I was worried."

Ursula placed a calming hand to his chest. The worry within him eased a fraction. "I'm fine. I think—it was just a magical headache. I probably investigated too many crystals today."

"Are you sure?" he asked. It was a little odd that this head-ache happened right after they kissed. Ursula nodded.

Her voice was shaky, but she looked much better than she did a moment ago. "I need to rest. It's been a long day."

"I'll fix you a cup of tea," he offered.

"You're not playing fair, Your Highness. Don't tempt me with tea," she whispered. "Go home. I'll call you tomorrow."

Xavier gave in for now. He'd call on her in the morning and ask after her health.

He brought her hand to his lips and pressed a kiss to her palm. "Sweet dreams, Sula."

"Good night, Xavier." She smiled brightly and it was as if the night sky appeared to him in all its radiant glory. Ursula. The constellation. Little bear. His witch. And with a strength he didn't know he possessed, Xavier gave her one last longing glance, opened the door, and left.

Cool night air touched his skin. He patted his sides, trying to feel if anything shifted.

His attention went to the sky, looking for fireworks or fall-ing stars. He listened for soaring music, but all he heard was growling gargoyles and singing crickets. His heart hammered foolishly for thinking that it would be this easy. He should feel something other than affection and desire racing through his bloodstream, making every inch of him feel alive.

He'd had his perfect kiss, but something was missing.

The moon caught his attention. It was a slice of light in the darkness of the night sky. He gave it a side smile. Something resilient was waning inside of him, but he couldn't name it. Couldn't identify it. One thing was certain: One kiss wasn't enough. He wasn't done.

He wanted to kiss her again. He wanted to court her.

But did she want the same thing as him?

Eventually Xavier found his way to a twenty-four-hour diner where there were more cups of coffee than customers inside. Xavier took a booth in the back. He studied the menu, trying to find a late-night snack, but his lips tingled at the memory of her touch. Absentmindedly, he licked his lower lip and caught a hint of that cherry liquor and fierceness. Her own liquor.

Nothing made sense anymore. Was this experience what the Queen intended for him? Did she truly intend to torment him for his arrogance with the promise of such a sweet kiss?

He let his mind drift back to that moment.

It takes half a fool to insult the Faerie Queen, and Prince Xavier had been a whole fool that one eventful dance. The House of Alder had been invited to dance and dine personally with the Faerie Queen, in honor of their active mediation of land disputes between local neighbors to the west. He hated going to those glittering parties where people watched his every move and reported his every misstep to the gossips. Xavier especially dreaded talking to the Faerie Queen, adorned in her crystal-encrusted gown and speaking judgment from her gilded chair. With her ebony skin and spider-silk hair, Her Majesty was believed to be over five hundred years old but didn't look a day over seventy. Every time she glanced at him during the dinner, a shiver went through his body, leaving him icy. It was like she could see into his heart and was bothered by what she saw there.

He'd been so nervous to speak to her that he didn't eat a bite of food during dinner. He'd drunk half a bottle of lilac wine and chased it with a glass of dandelion liquor. The world swam before his eyes as he approached the Queen. They chatted briefly about flowers and the royal gardens, then spoke about Prim's upcoming marriage.

Xavier's entire body felt loose, including his mouth.

That was the very instant he said that stupid thing that he said.

He knew he screwed up when she laughed full and long at his words. Fear ran wild in his body. There was a secret saying in the Realm: *When the Queen laughs, you'll cry soon after.*

The Queen reached into her bell sleeve and pulled out a wand.

The gilded rod caught the overhead light and twinkled with unspooled magic. It reminded him of a scorpion's tail dripping with venom. He took in a deep breath to keep from passing out at her feet. A collective gasp went through the crowd, but no one moved. She lifted herself from the throne, swishing her wand around his body.

He didn't dare flee. If he did, then his family's reputation and status in the Fae Kingdom would be decimated. He paused. *Stay still. Take the punishment. Show no pain.*

She swung her wand and tapped him on the shoulder. A blast of neon-green energy traveled from her wand and landed on him. His skin burned as if he'd accidentally splashed hot water all over his body. It knocked him back and stole his breath. Even now, months later, he still couldn't get enough air in his body.

Until tonight. Until Ursula touched him. Held him. Kissed him.

Now he breathed easier. He was free to leave this world,

but he didn't want to go. The truth rattled in his bones and scared him.

A soft voice interrupted his musings. "Do you know what you want, hon?" she asked.

He peered at the tired-eyed but welcoming waitress who stood by his table, holding a pad, and read the shell-shaped nametag pinned to her T-shirt. "Could you give me more time to think, Ms. Mimi?"

Mimi watched him for a beat, then nodded. "I'll get you a slice of cheesecake while you think."

Another day, another dollar to be made by Ursula at Light as a Feather. The early afternoon light streamed in the window, giving the mystic space a light glow. There were no customers waiting for the table reading, so Ursula focused on the sales floor and made sure that everything was clear. By lunchtime, the entire place sparkled. No matter how much she cleaned, she couldn't stop thinking about last night. Ursula arranged and rearranged the pop-up candle display to give her nervous energy an outlet. She was taking a picture of the finished stand for their social media page when an email notification popped on her screen.

He Hasn't Texted Yet: What to Do After That First Kiss.

Her phone just read her for filth.

She'd kissed Xavier. He'd kissed her back. It felt so newsworthy that she almost checked the front page of the *Freya*

Grove Press website to see if there was an article about it. Her mind kept replaying that moment in 3D. She could still taste the caramel and vanilla on his lips and feel his beard brushing against her face and the possessive squeeze of his hands on her body. She texted Xavier first thing in the morning to tell him that she was okay. Physically, she was fine. Emotionally, she felt out of control like a tap-dancing octopus.

It was all because of his earth-shattering kiss.

What made this kiss particularly special and ridiculous was that...she'd had a leap.

Ursula held her face in her hands. The kiss was so freaking good that it literally made her leap through time and space. *Quantum Leap* had nothing on her skills.

His kiss and touch had somehow activated her magic and launched her consciousness into the future. Right after their smooch, everything blended into a twisting kaleidoscope of green light. Then she was being pulled out of her body by an invisible hand. When she finally returned to herself and Xavier, she could barely stand. She leapt. Ursula couldn't recall what she had seen. Not a single second. All she remembered was the green light, the pull, and then she was back in front of her door. Her brain just drew a huge blank.

It didn't help that she was tipsy from the whiskey and light-headed from his touch.

Ursula chewed her thumbnail. Mama couldn't know about the leap. She'd start asking very invasive questions and insist that Xavier come over for dinner for more information. Mama once starred in a short-lived but well-loved psychic detective show called *Catch You Later*, and she wasn't afraid to "grill a few folks for answers."

She wasn't going to hear about the leap until Ursula figured out what she saw.

Ursula opened her phone's contacts and pulled up Sirena's info. Whenever she couldn't recall a dream or a vision in the past, Sirena always made the legendary lavender and chamomile cookies for her. Nicknamed the Cookie Jar Dreams, this treat was used to help Caraways recall lost visions and dreams in vivid detail. They were also excellent warmed up with a scoop of vanilla bean ice cream. The recipe was solely shared among Caraway kitchen witches to limit overuse. It was a closely guarded secret for generations, but Ursula didn't have time to play around. With every passing hour, it would get harder to recall the leap, but those cookies would aid her and conjure forth the missing vision.

No more stalling. It was time to bring in the Caraway cousins.

She pressed the call button. Sirena picked up on the third ring.

"This call isn't a butt dial, is it?" Sirena kidded.

Ursula let out a nervous sigh. "I meant to call you. How are you?"

There was a tentative tone in Sirena's voice. "I'm all right. What's good?"

Ursula decided to get straight to the point. "I'm fine. I had a leap."

Her news was greeted with absolute silence. Ursula checked her phone to see if the call dropped or if Sirena hung up on her. Instead, there was a burst of sound, shuffling, and Sirena's voice sounded sightly far away.

"You're on speaker. Callie's here too."

Callie's cheerful voice chimed in. "Hey, cuz! Long time, no see. I saw an ad for the Founders' Day Festival the other day and thought of you. Are you going?"

"We'll talk about that later! Tell her, Sula," Sirena insisted.

"I had a leap."

Callie's gasp echoed over the phone. "Did you see me? How did my hair look?!"

Unease chewed at Ursula's nerves. "Don't get too excited. I can't remember it."

Was her brain protecting her from her fate? Had she forgotten the leap on purpose?

"I can hear you overthinking from over here. Talk to us," Sirena said.

"I know I don't deserve it—but I need your help." Ursula scrubbed a hand over her face. Here came the big ask. "Can you give me the recipe for the Cookie Jar Dreams?"

There was a tense pause. "No, but I can bake them. When do you need them by?"

Appreciation and love for her cousin welled up inside her chest. Ursula bit her cheek to keep from bawling. How could she have forgotten how awesome Sirena was?

Ursula shook her head, even though she was alone. "You're busy with the restaurant and your wish. I don't want to bother you with my cookie order."

"I'll still be busy tomorrow," Sirena said matter of fact. "My wish is...fine. You haven't asked for a favor in months, so I know it must be important if you're calling."

Callie jumped in on the line. "What sparked the leap? Was it something big?"

Oh, he was big, all right, and sturdy. She shivered under the recollection of his touch and his searching kiss. Heat pulsated between her thighs, leaving her speechless.

"Yo! Are you still there?" Sirena's voice boomed from the phone, bringing her back.

Ursula paused too long to tell a believable lie. "Well, what had happened was... there's a fae prince and we might have... kissed."

Callie squealed. "You met a prince?! Did he spark you off?!"

Sirena laughed. "Ask her later. We only have a short window before that leap is lost for good. We've got to bake while the oven is hot."

Ursula grinned at Nana's familiar saying.

"Those cookies take so looong to make," Callie said. "We'll break open the family spell book, get out the crystals, and figure out what the universe is trying to tell you. Come over tomorrow night. We'll make it a party! Two words: slumber party."

"How old are we?" Sirena asked.

"Old enough that we can stay up all night," Callie said. "I'm logging into Empty Fridge right now. I'm pre-ordering pizzas from Rapunzel's! All this spell work is going to make us hungry. Tell me your favorite toppings again."

Ursula hesitated. "I don't want to make it awkward."

She wasn't ready to see Lucy just yet, unable to communicate how truly sorry she was for pushing her away. Neither Sirena nor Callie spoke for a second. Finally, Sirena's voice came over the phone loud and clear.

"Don't worry, Lucy's still in DC," Sirena said smoothly.

"Um—" Callie started, but Sirena cut her off.

"If you're not ready to see her yet, then you don't have to see her now. Come over. We miss you."

"All right. I'll see you tomorrow night," Ursula said.

"I'm adding garlic knots to the pre-order!" Callie shouted.

Chapter Nineteen

Ursula didn't want to hide behind the balloons by the front door but it seemed to be the best place right now. The ghosts of Ursula's recent past walked around in the Night Sky Bistro holding cups of lemonade and plates of finger food while talking to each other. Every time another Walker friend or family member arrived at the birthday party, Ursula's mouth dried up. The familiar sense of insecurity she always felt around the Walkers hovered around her head like a fine mist. It wasn't strong, but it still lingered. They, with their designer purses and weekend vacations, seemed so perfect and on point in every way. She was still a work in progress, and she wasn't going to go back to how she felt. Ursula reached into her dress pocket and rubbed the flat bloodstone between her thumb and forefinger.

Give me confidence.

She slid behind the tart orange and ocean blue balloon display and scrolled the web. Her phone beeped. Sirena texted her an update. The cookie dough was resting, and she'd have a batch ready shortly before bedtime. The magic took at least twenty-four hours to take effect, so Sirena invited Ursula to stay over for a few days in case she needed help.

Soon, the leap would be revealed.

Doubt filled Ursula once she saw Sirena's update text. All her earlier confidence ebbed away, and she was left feeling super scared and nervous. Ursula couldn't stop asking herself questions.

What if the leap was terrible?

What if your subconscious is trying to protect you from a disappointing future?

Do you really want to see what the future holds?

It wasn't long before Ursula was joined by Gwen. She wore a floral dress that showed off her curvy shape and her trademark ballet flats. Her hair was twisted up into a high bun.

Gwen carried a tray of mini quiches and spinach-filled triangles. "Where's your cutie?"

Ursula grimaced and held up her phone. "Xavier's running late."

Gwen pouted. "I hope he doesn't miss the appetizers. We're running low."

"I'm sure he'll be here soon," Ursula said a little too sharply. She had a lot going on. In between talking to her cousins again, thinking about the slumber party, and of course the Kiss that Made Her Leap through Time, Ursula felt like her head was spinning.

Gwen stopped and studied her. "You're vibing. What's going on?"

"Um...I made out with Xavier."

Gwen handed her tray off to a server. Her eyebrows jumped to her hairline. "Why aren't you making out with him right now?"

Good question. She didn't want to kiss him again until she figured out what she saw and experienced in the leap.

"Shouldn't you get back to the party?" Ursula asked.

Gwen looked over her shoulder and then swiveled back to Ursula. "We can take a break. The birthday boy's having a great time; everyone's fed and having fun."

Ursula searched the bistro and spotted Lincoln and Zoe. They were busy talking to guests and eating off each other's plates. Without a doubt, she knew that they were the goofy couple who wore matching pajamas and took family photos. Ursula watched them for a long moment, a vision of their future holiday card and a possible elopement within the next two years appeared in her mind's eye. She smiled to herself, sincerely excited for the path ahead of them.

Gwen made air quotes around a few words. "If anyone asks, I'm addressing a guest's complaint. So, start complaining, guest."

"Well, after I kissed him, I leapt," Ursula said.

Gwen stepped closer. "What did you see? Did I look good? Am I super rich?"

Ursula winced. "I don't remember anything. It's super hazy."

"Does Xavier know?"

"I was freaked out about the leap; I didn't say anything." Ursula made a face. "Should he know?"

"Tell him," Gwen said. "It might help you decide what you want from each other."

She had a point. Ursula didn't even know if their kiss was perfect enough to break the enchantment. Not that she minded making out with Xavier, but she wanted to know what he wanted. She'd already told him she wasn't looking for anything serious, but that was before the leap. Doubt bubbled up within her once again. *He told you he didn't believe in love. You won't settle for less. Do you really want to see a future without him?*

Maybe she should leave the leap alone.

Ursula wrinkled her face. "Sirena and Callie are helping me figure it out. I'm seeing them soon, I think. I might reschedule—I don't know. I said I'd go but—"

Gwen held out her hand. "Give me your phone."

Ursula gripped it. "What are you going to do?"

"You're overthinking. I'm not going to let you chicken out of seeing them," Gwen said firmly. She made a grabby hands motion for Ursula's cell. "Give it or I'll make a scene."

Ursula handed it over.

Gwen set a timer for ninety minutes, turned up the sound, then handed it back. "I need to know what the future holds for you and for me. You've got an hour and a half to shake hands, kiss babies, and make good with the Walkers. If you don't leave when the timer goes off, I'll play your slam poetry performance from college on my phone."

"You wouldn't dare." Ursula laughed with disbelief.

The bistro door opened, and more guests arrived, letting in a gust of air. The balloons swayed and popped Ursula in the back. She moved to the side so that they stood by the front window and away from any future balloon attacks.

"Try me," Gwen warned impishly. "I'll have these people discovering the glory of Poetess Ursula."

Ursula cleared her throat in awkwardness once she heard her stage name. She didn't want Lincoln's grandma to hear her very vivid description of her college boyfriend and how they warmed each other up with their hands when the dorm room heater didn't work.

Gwen won this round of sibling blackmail.

"Okay, I'll go," Ursula said. "What's got you so interested in my visions?"

Gwen gave her a sly look. "Let's just say I have a huge investment opportunity and I want to know if I make the right decision."

Ursula nodded, impressed. It seemed with her business on the rise and possible future deals that her little sister was a baby financial shark in the making. Ursula was thrilled for Gwen for making her own choices.

She did have one worry.

"You didn't apply for *Millionaire Madness*?" Ursula asked.

It was one of Dad's favorite reality shows, and during their monthly dinners he was always dropping hints that Gwen should nominate the bistro. Ursula didn't want to watch Gwen get yelled at by a hedge fund manager dressed in a dollar-bill-covered suit.

Gwen frowned. "No way, but...I can't talk about it yet. That's my reason why I need you to see your cousins." Gwen lowered her voice. "It's time you forgave yourself. Go back home."

Ursula shifted her weight, not trusting herself to talk. Love welled in her throat. The Caraway House had been home for many years, and the last nine months was the longest she'd ever stayed away from it. It was time to go back.

Ursula let out a rough breath. "It's hard. I made a fool of myself."

"We're all foolish. I'm sure they understand. They're your sisters too," Gwen insisted. "I mean, you asked them to be your bridesmaids. I get why you did it—you grew up with them and spend so much time with them. I've always envied how close you were to your Caraway cousins." Gwen made a little growl of annoyance. "My customers treat me better than some of our Ellis cousins."

"Really?" This was news to Ursula. She assumed that because Gwen wasn't a Caraway, and her mother was more in line with the Ellises' expectations for a wife, that she'd be readily accepted into the fold. It seemed that no one was going to be good enough for the Ellises.

"Yes, but that's a story for another day. Do you know why I opened the bistro in the Grove?" Gwen asked in a hushed voice.

"You have a massive crush on the gargoyles," Ursula joked.

Gwen grinned. "Yes, and I wanted to know my big sister better. You've never treated me like less than because of what happened between our parents. You shared your magic and your stories with me without question. I've always loved you for that."

Ursula merely stared at her, tongue-tied. Whatever future she saw when she eventually recovered her leap, she knew beyond a shadow of a doubt that Gwen was going to be a part of it. If Gwen had the courage to claim her future, then Ursula had the strength to see her leap.

"I hate it when you get all squishy on me," Ursula said gently. "I love you too, kid."

"So, you forgive me for lightly blackmailing you?" Gwen asked.

"No, not yet," Ursula said, more annoyed than angry.

Gwen glanced over Ursula's shoulder, outside the front window, then looked back at Ursula. It seemed like she spotted an arriving guest.

She smirked. "You're adorable when you're annoyed. I hope your man sees that."

Ursula spun around, and there Xavier was, standing outside the bistro looking at her from the sidewalk. Even though they were separated by the glass, Ursula swore she could sense his energy. Her breath caught in her throat as she felt her heart pounding against her ribs. Their eyes connected. Her skin burned with the memory of his hands wandering over her and trying to find a way inside. *Let him in.*

"He's not my man," she corrected.

"Then why is he staring at you like you're the perfect bite of food? Like he just wants to nibble you up like an éclair? Like—"

"Gwen," Ursula warned, her attention staying on Xavier. He did look ravenous.

"I don't even look at my cupcakes that way," Gwen said over her shoulder. "You've got eighty minutes left. Have fun."

Xavier entered the bistro. He was dressed in his usual waistcoat, button-down shirt, and dress pants. A honeysuckle flower was tucked into his breast pocket. This charming fae man was just as fine as he wanted to be. He held out a slightly budding yellow rose to her. Its scent was delicate and soothing, easing her party nerves.

"My apologies for being late," he said gently. "I figured this would go nicely with your outfit."

She murmured a thank-you and took the rose from him.

Yellow roses meant friendship and joy. A warm glow filled her from the inside out, making her feel a sense of excitement.

She tucked it behind her ear automatically. It felt right to wear flowers in her hair.

Xavier offered his arm to her. "Shall we?"

Ursula took it. She was going to party hard for the next seventy-nine minutes.

Downtown Grove was alive with activity. Eateries set out tables for customers to dine outside. Twilight allowed them to be anonymous, to blend in with the springtime crowd. She brushed her pinky against Xavier's hand. The desire to touch her burbled in his chest like molten rock flowing from the ground. Ursula spread her fingers and laced them between his.

Contentment eased inside his chest.

Xavier reflected on tonight's event. He watched while Ursula had nothing but kind smiles and welcoming hugs at Lincoln's birthday party. This woman, covered in flowers and magic, carried herself with grace in what could've been an uncomfortable situation. She helped Gwen keep the food platters full and spoke to every person who saw her. People kept promising to vote for her for Smitten Sweetheart, but she insisted that they consider all the nominees. The mayor gave her a card and insisted that she call her to schedule a lunch one day. Lincoln and Zoe even hugged them goodbye when they left the party. All night he wanted to pull her to his side and cover her face with kisses.

They walked hand in hand down the street.

Xavier gestured back to the bistro. "We didn't have to go. We could've stayed longer."

"No," Ursula drawled out. "It's fine."

"Okay, if you have to go home—"

Ursula held his hand tighter. "We have time."

Of all the places in the world he could've found his perfect kiss, he never expected it to be in New Jersey. The mere thought of kissing another woman appealed to him as much as drinking a milkweed smoothie. He gave a full-body shudder. Milkweed was nasty. Xavier glanced over to Ursula. She was pure honeysuckle; he wanted to taste her on his lips.

"I want to kiss you again," he blurted out.

Her left eyebrow lifted as if inviting him. "Where? Here?"

Everywhere.

He cleared his throat. "I'd like to make my intentions known, Madame," Xavier said. "I want to court you. Woo you."

Ursula regarded him for a long second. "You're still enchanted."

Xavier stopped walking. "I don't have to worry about it anymore. I'm free to leave."

Ursula opened and closed her mouth, then spoke in a soft voice. "How do you know it's broken? Are you sure?"

He broke into a wide, open smile. "I'm sure. I was late tonight because I saw a faery door."

Ursula gasped. "Was it made of stone or glass?"

"It was glass," he said.

Faery doors are exactly what the name suggests, passageways

that connected the Realm to the human world. Some doors were made of stone, others were etched into trees, but a few were made of handblown glass. Tonight, Xavier had seen the door, pressed his palms to the frame, and relished the glow of fae magic. He gripped the cool doorknob, but he didn't turn it open. Xavier stepped away. He knew she was waiting for him, so he left the door alone.

"I'd like to court you too but...you belong to the Realm," Ursula said slowly. "You'll walk through that door eventually."

Panic crackled through him like a lightning bolt across a stormy sky. He schooled his face into a calm expression. "Yes, but not right now. We don't know what the future holds."

Suddenly her face went grim. "I have to be real with you, Your Highness."

Ursula's use of his formal title caused his heart to jump nervously. Did the news of the door upset her? She toyed with the flower behind her ear with her free hand. "Our kiss sparked something in me."

He listened as she explained what a leap was and her plans to recall it. From what Xavier understood, Ursula had no way of knowing if a positive or negative experience waited for her. He felt her hand tremble in his as she spoke.

Once she finished talking, Xavier squeezed her hand. "No matter what you see in the future, call me. Day or night. I'm here for you."

She didn't have to face this task alone.

Her voice sounded as fragile and thin as fine crystal. "Thank you, Xavier."

Right then, Xavier knew that there was nowhere else in

the known universe he wanted to be. The longer he stayed in the Grove, the less he wanted to go back to the Realm.

In the Grove, everything changed. Flowers bloomed and died. Days were unpredictable and filled with surprises. However, back home, nothing changed. Everything was beautiful all the time. It became cold and stagnant. He didn't notice this issue because the Realm was all that he knew.

As they strolled into the Grove Square past the ghouls that scampered to their dwellings, Ursula stopped and sighed. "The goddess is back."

She led Xavier over to the lit-up fountain bubbling and burbling water. The three-tiered fountain in the middle of Grove Square depicted a stone goddess extending her arms into the sky, her face directed toward the ocean.

Xavier beheld the statue. "Which goddess is this?"

Ursula tapped her chin. "It's been debated. Some local historians think she's Freya, the Norse goddess of many things, including love and magic. Other folks say she's a lesser but important goddess. I have another theory."

He squeezed her hand, enjoying her touch. "Enlighten me, Madame."

Her voice took on an engaging tone, drawing him into her tale. "Legend has it, our town was founded by a wealthy man who fell in love with an ocean goddess. He could have anything in the world, but he couldn't keep the woman he loved. He couldn't live in the water; she couldn't live on land. They searched the world for years looking for the perfect space to call home when they arrived here. It was blessed by the sand and sea, so they founded this town for all the mystical beings. I think this statue is a tribute to their love."

He let the story wash over him. The urge to do something special drove him on. Xavier let go of her hand and gestured to the fountain. "Let's make a wish."

Ursula grinned at him. "Right now?"

"Right now," he echoed.

Xavier studied Ursula by the fountain light. She was ethereal. Kissable. Lovable. He mentally stepped away from that word. Not yet.

Ursula reached into her purse and pulled out her wallet. She scooped up loose change from the change pocket and handed him half, keeping the rest. She put her wallet on the fountain's edge, then turned to Xavier.

"Show me how you wish," Xavier said.

Ursula picked a dime and flipped it between her fingers. "Turn around, face away from the water, and hold the coin in your hand. Close your eyes. Make your wish. Toss the coin over your left shoulder."

She completed the steps, letting her wish drop into the water with an easy *kerplunk.* The coin glittered on the painted blue base.

Ursula stood by and watched him. "Your turn."

Xavier flipped a coin between his fingers. He turned his back on the fountain, closed his eyes, and tossed the coin. The wish came straight from the heart. A soft *plunk* followed as it landed and caused ripples in the water. The entire fountain took on a bright green hue that made the goddess otherworldly, as if she came from another planet.

Ursula gulped, impressed at the display. "What did you wish for?"

He took a step toward her, basking in her heat. "I thought it was rude to ask," he teased.

Ursula gave him a quiet laugh. "You didn't forget my rule."

"You're pretty unforgettable, Madame."

Xavier remembered it all. He committed her to his memory as if she were his favorite piece of artwork he'd visit at the museum and admire. *I could spend hours studying your soul.* Ursula leaned in and pressed her cheek to his. He lingered in close for a moment, his nose brushing against her temple. She smelled of fresh rose, honeysuckle, and a hint of spice. Harmony filled every inch of him. Xavier pressed his hand against the small of her back, holding her against him. They remained there standing by the fountain, listening to the water burbling. This space was where he wanted to stay for as long as time would let him remain here.

His wish lingered in his mind. *I wished that you get everything you desire.*

She patted his chest and stepped out of his arms.

He yearned to have her back with him. "Can I convince you to stay?"

Regret shimmered in her eyes. "I can't tonight, but I'll call you."

Xavier stayed close to Ursula so that she could feel the heat from his skin, to convince himself that she was real.

Only a month ago, Xavier had been ready to let her go. To let Ursula find her true love. To let him find his real happy ending. Now, his plans had changed. Whitney was right. What was the rush to get back to the Realm? Father humored Xavier by letting him stay in the human world because he was enchanted. Now that the spell was broken, Father could call him back at a moment's notice and rip him from Ursula's arms. Xavier couldn't tell Whitney that he'd broken the enchantment and then ask her to lie to Father on his behalf. He was still her king. If Father found out he broke his promise, then he'd come to the Grove and—Xavier shut that thought down.

Father wasn't going to find out. Who was going to miss the spare heir? Father told Xavier to break the enchantment. He completed his task and now he was extending his stay in the Grove. It was time to make memories now that he'd found his perfect kiss.

"Kiss me good night," Ursula said. Her breathy giggle turned him on and set his blood flowing.

There was something a little wonderfully wicked about the way she looked at him. He leaned down, so near to her mouth that his beard tickled her skin. "With pleasure, Madame."

He growled deeply and gathered her to him. Xavier captured his mouth with hers. He swung her up into his arms and lifted her off the ground. She squealed gleefully, making his soul soar. The prince had swept her off her feet.

Chapter Twenty

It wasn't a Caraway slumber party until someone ended up with cucumber slices on their eyes and shea body butter on their arms. The three Caraways were gathered in the living room, surrounded by enchanted items, stuffed garlic knots, and scented lotions. The space was covered in the usual slumber party items—open pizza boxes on the coffee table, homemade beauty products laid out on the floor, and of course an open spell book or two on the mantel. Ursula flipped through the spell book, taking in and enjoying the familiar magic that emanated from its pages. She looked around the living room, relishing in this moment. Callie lay on the couch in her silk pajamas, arms folded over her chest and eyes covered with thick cucumber slices. Shadow, the house cat, hid under the couch, those moon-bright eyes peering at Ursula. Sirena in her nightgown came out of the kitchen carrying a tray of sparkling fruity drinks that seemed to fizz with kitchen magic. Ursula sighed happily. Her soul rejoiced.

It felt good to be back home.

"The cookies are cooling," Sirena said. She put the tray down in an empty space on the table. "I put on the egg timer. They'll be ready soon, so have a taste of this punch."

Ursula snatched up a drink and took a sip. Her mouth puckered in appreciation at the tart lime-lemonade taste. "Delicious."

Sirena graced her with a thankful smile. "It's not a Bathwater Brew, but I improvised."

Bathwater Brew was Ursula's signature drink that she used to make for them. She didn't mind Sirena putting her own spin on the cocktail.

"When I make it next time, I'll add pineapple," Sirena said.

"A kitchen witch who doesn't follow the recipe," Callie said in a teasing tone. "You're a trailblazer, sis."

Sirena rolled her eyes at Callie. "Hush up. You look like a bougie mummy."

"Don't be mad when I get up looking refreshed and hydrated," Callie said, not moving an inch. She sighed deeply. "Why does it feel like this month lasted a year? I'm ready for it to be May."

Sirena waved her hand. "I'm not ready. May's going to be a mess. In between the Founders' Day Festival and Smitten bringing in all these hungry tourists, I'm going to be slammed at work. How many fish and chips baskets can I cook without wanting to jump into the ocean?"

Ursula made a noise of sympathy. "I get it. I won't have a day off until after July fourth."

Light as a Feather did brisk business during the late spring and summer months, and Ursula worked ten- to twelve-hour shifts for weeks. She made a lot of money, but then she was too exhausted to spend it.

"Imagine all the money you'll make because of those

tourists," Callie pointed out. "Put all that extra cash into your Dream Restaurant Fund. Make your money work for you. Invest in your dreams until they're your reality."

Sirena shot Ursula a silent look of exasperation. "Thanks for the advice, sis." She lowered her voice to a whisper. "Cal's been in hashtag Boss Mode for months. It's like I'm living with a Pinterest board of business and hustle quotes."

Callie coughed loudly. Ursula laughed.

Sirena stood next to Ursula by the mantel. "Is there anything in the book that can help you with *your* Boss Witch List?"

She shook her head. Ursula ran her hand over Nana's spidery, elegant handwriting. "Being here with you and Callie is number one on my list."

Ursula had shared the list with Sirena and Callie while they ate their pepperoni slices and mixed salad. They'd offered their support, made suggestions on how to finish her list, and demanded all the details about Xavier. It almost felt like old times again, but Lucy's calming influence was missing from the table.

"You have to bring him to the May party!" Callie said. "We're getting together for the Founders' Day Festival."

Ursula scratched her neck. "I thought you were making moon tea."

Callie shrugged. "A party's a party!"

Ursula looked to Sirena who flashed her a smile. "Do you see any fun spells?"

"There's a rose bath recipe I'd like to try. I forgot how much Nana loved her baths."

"Dad always joked that she was part mermaid," Sirena said

with a laugh. She grew quiet and still. "Speaking of merfolk, why haven't you called Lucy?" she asked. "It's almost been a year."

Sirena didn't come to play with her questions. Ursula made a face and downed the rest of her drink. She put it back on the tray and moved from the mantel to sit in the wingback chair.

"I messed up, and saying I'm sorry doesn't seem to be enough to make up for how I acted."

"It was the wish that made you act strange," Callie insisted. "It wasn't your fault."

It was time to be real with herself and her cousins. Maybe holding on to that old wish was blocking her from remembering her leap.

"It was my fault because I knew I made the wrong wish," she said.

"No." Callie sat up suddenly, the cucumber slices sliding from her face and falling on her lap.

"I wished to live happily ever after," Ursula admitted. "The day after we completed the spell, everything went wrong. All the preparations went wacky. My dream wedding became a horror show. It was like the universe was waving a thousand red flags in my face, but I kept on going."

Sirena lowered her head, staring down at her nails. "Sula, don't be like that. It wasn't the wrong wish. It might have been the wrong guy."

Ursula stilled in the chair, hearing the mix of anguish and distress in her cousin's voice. Sirena looked up at Ursula, and the question was clearly written on her face. "Do you think Xavier's the right guy?"

Ursula smiled at her question. They'd broken the enchantment; he didn't seem eager to leave the Grove. He was nothing like the princes in the fairy-tale books she read and reread in her bedroom. He hadn't rescued her from her messy life but helped her enjoy the life she had made after Lincoln. Where had Xavier been all these years? Her Prince Charming was late, but he was here. When he asked her to court him, she made a split decision. No matter what the leap showed her, she was going to keep him for as long as fate would allow. She looked to her cousins.

"What do you want?" Callie asked.

Ursula's eyebrows drew together. "As silly as it sounds, I still want that wish. I've been looking at stars and ladybugs, hoping that maybe fate will put me back on track and get me to that happy ending someday."

Callie slid to the edge of the couch. Her next words were straightforward. "But how does that look? When you think about living happily ever after, tell me what you see."

"I see a stainless-steel kitchen with an island layout," Sirena said with a half-grin. "I also want unlimited ride tickets to the Founders' Day Festival."

They shared a quick chuckle over her joke, but then they became quiet and reflective.

What did her new happily-ever-after look like?

Ursula was drawing a blank. Just like the crystal ball in the shop. Open. There were endless possibilities before her. Nothing was set in stone, but rather sand. She thought that the phrase "HEA" meant getting married, living in a monotone condo, and planning perfect vacations with her polo-clad husband. That might have been someone else's HEA, but it wasn't hers, not anymore. She could create a happily-ever-after of her own making and not be beholden to a certain idea or vision.

"Everything's blank like a piece of paper," Ursula said. She heard the note of wonder in her voice. It was the same wonder she felt whenever she gathered sand to make her castles all those years ago.

Sirena gave a shudder. "That sounds scary."

It used to scare her too, but now she readily accepted the feeling of uncertainty and openness. Everything about the wedding—from her hairstyle, the dress, the cake—kept messing up. Kept going wrong. Fate had been trying to open her eyes, but she pushed forward. She ignored her intuition, the very gift she'd been given by her family. For months, she'd fought to renew that gift. Now, sitting in the Caraway living room, across from her cousins, who made her feel like she had the power to make all her wishes come true, she listened to that intuition. A sense of calm flowed through her. The timer dinged. They all turned to the kitchen. Ursula stood, eager to have the leap revealed to her once and for all. It was time to see what the future held for her and her family.

"Who knew there were so many uses for painter's tape?" Xavier muttered.

He flipped through the book *The Wonderful Woodworking Guide*, which he'd purchased from the Rain or Shine Bookstore. He'd finished the first eight chapters in a single day, completely enraptured by the photos of sanding curves and stain indexes. When he was young, Xavier strolled through the royal woods, collecting broken branches and logs. He had loved the idea of taking something that was forgotten and turning it into a precious new thing. Father told him rather coldly that woodworking was a hobby for a bored peasant, not a future king.

Xavier had abandoned his new interest as quickly as he found it.

Now, in the Grove, he was rediscovering that hidden part of himself. No one told him that his interests and hobbies were odd or strange. In this world, he had permission to be his true self.

He was hanging out in bed reading about the best wood for certain workpieces when he heard his ringer. It was after midnight. Only one person would call him this late. Xavier closed the book and leaned over to the nightstand. He answered his phone immediately.

"Good evening, my lady," he said.

"Hey." Her soft sigh came over on the line. "I...wanted to hear your voice."

Something warm, like heated honey, oozed within his chest. Xavier lay back against the pillows.

"How's your slumber party going?"

"Everyone's slumbering but me. I'm having a wonderful time." From her shaky tone, it sounded like the opposite.

"Talk to me, Sula." The nickname slipped easily and comfortably from his lips.

"I remembered the leap."

His heart lurched. He steeled himself for whatever else she had to say. "Was it bad?"

"No," Ursula said breathlessly. "It was—"

His mind filled in the blank. Words came to him, but he didn't say anything, not wanting to speak for her. He waited, rapt, to hear that word come from her mouth. He held his breath.

"Perfect. It was absolutely perfect. I want it so much, but I don't know how to get it."

Her voice broke, snapping something within him.

Xavier clutched the phone. "I wish I was there with you."

For the first time in years, he longed to have wings so he could fly to her.

"Hold on," Ursula said. "Close your eyes."

He did as she requested and shut his eyes. He heard her whisper a few words and the cool touch of her magic flowed through him. His body went slack, and he shivered all over as if he'd gulped a whole glass of ice water.

"Okay. You're here," she sang.

Xavier blinked and glanced around. He was lying next to Ursula in a bedroom that he didn't recognize. Her hair was artfully wrapped in a headscarf, and she wore a tank top and pajama bottoms. There was a dewy glow to her skin as if she had just bathed in a secret spring.

"This is the best dream ever." He moved in to kiss her.

Ursula held up a hand to stop him. "We can't touch, or you'll wake up. It's just a little lucid dreaming spell. It's been a while since I've done one of these conjurings, so we have to be careful."

Xavier snuggled in close enough to feel Ursula's warmth. His voice went into a husky whisper. "So, you have me here. What are you going to do with me?"

"I have no idea." The glow of her smile heated him in the space of the bed.

He hovered his hand inches away from her cheek. "Was I there in the leap?"

A shadow of distress swept over her face. "Of course you were there. Why do you think I want it so much?"

Then why did she look so sad? "Tell me what's wrong. How far did you see ahead?"

Ursula cast her eyes downward. "I don't know how far I leapt. I saw us together, but I didn't know how long we stayed together. It might have been a month, or a year."

Grief and disappointment tore at his chest. He thought that once he handled the enchantment, he'd regain control of his fate. Xavier didn't know how long he could stay here in the Grove without drawing Father's ire.

"I'll stay until midsummer," he said.

There was a long pause. "Can I keep you until then?" she asked.

His heartbeat skyrocketed. He would easily grant her this request. When the time was right, he'd ask to her the ball. He'd court her and be the storybook prince. He wouldn't simply be charming; he was going to be legendary.

"I'm yours." Xavier rested his head on the pillow next to hers. "I'm yours until then."

She sighed deeply, seemingly weary from this exchange. Ursula closed her eyes and nestled in the bed.

"I'm just resting my eyes," she mumbled. Soon, her body went slack and her breathing took on a steady rhythm. Xavier lay in the drowsy warmth of the bed, letting his thoughts drift as he watched her surrender to sleep. It felt like his head and heart were in a tug-of-war between this world and the realm.

His conscience hissed in his head.

You promised Father you'd return once you broke the enchantment. You're a liar. You gave your word. Is her kiss worth your honor?

Xavier watched Ursula. He'd tell a thousand lies just to stay by her side. He'd laid down his honor just to hold her. Not only had he found his perfect kiss, but he also found something much more spellbinding and dangerous.

He found his fairy tale.

Ways to Get a Wish
~~Throw a coin in a fountain~~
~~Wish on the first star in the sky~~
Wish on a new pair of shoes before you wear
them [Grandpa James]

Things that You Can Wish On
~~Eyelashes~~
~~Ladybugs~~
Double numbers

May

THIS MONTH'S BIRTHSTONE: EMERALD

*Legends state emeralds have calming effects and
truth-telling energy. Wear emeralds if
you want to tell the truth.*

Chapter Twenty-One

How did one court a witch?

Xavier considered taking Ursula to a teahouse but decided that he wanted to do something a bit more personal. He bought her warmed chocolate croissants from Night Sky Bistro for breakfast. They shared them on the bench outside of Light as a Feather, talking about their plans for the week. He spoke to her about his upcoming classes and woodworking books. He listened to her about convincing Mama Caraway to expand the candle business and offer personalized scents to customers. Xavier adored hearing about her plans and goals for the shop.

Ursula brushed crumbs from his body, causing ripples of want to roll through him. He kissed her, then moved to nibble her at her earlobe. He feasted on her breathy sighs until she was trembling on his lap. Then, during her lunch break, he gave her an aquamarine-shaded notebook in case she wanted to write down her to-do lists. She'd rewarded him with a kiss so toe-curling that he almost passed out in front of the shop. He fought the urge to pull her upstairs, strip her bare, and smother himself inside of her body. Being a gentleman was testing his resolve.

"Let me spoil you for once," Ursula had insisted. She

invited him over for a home-cooked dinner at her apartment. He'd changed his clothes three times before he settled on a comfortable outfit.

Now, Xavier stood outside of the Bloom On flower shop, studying the plastic cones filled with half-open roses, huge gerbera daisies, and leaning tulips. He glanced around. The air crackled with new magic. Of course. It was Beltane. Sidewalks and lampposts were covered with cones of fabric and real flowers. Couples and friends strolled arm in arm down the streets wearing daisy and grass crowns. One of them— a fae with a perky smile and sharp eyes—stared at him and gave him a nod of respect. Xavier returned the gesture.

The veil between this world and the Realm was tissue-paper thin. The desire to find the glass fairy door and go over to the Realm for an instant was strong, but not strong enough. Mother loved Beltane and always had the chef cook Faery Sprinkle Cake for the entire Court. His siblings went out with their friends and left him to celebrate the holiday on his own. What was he truly missing over there? Another party that lasted for days or weeks. Being mocked by the Court for his lack of social life.

Ursula was waiting. She'd invited him over tonight for dinner, and he wasn't going to be late.

Xavier entered the florist shop, breathing in the blooms. The florist behind the counter had bluish white hair, a wide build, and gold eyes that shimmered like liquid.

"Hello," Xavier said. "Which flowers say 'I adore you beyond words and thoughts'?"

The florist quirked his lips into a secret smile. "Let's start with roses and work our way up."

Twenty minutes later, Xavier left the shop with a large bouquet of pale-yellow roses and big-faced sunflowers. He cradled it gingerly in his arms, making sure not to crush them.

Ursula had texted him that the downstairs door was unlocked, so he came up into the building. He knocked on her apartment door and waited. There was a sound of approaching footsteps and then the door swung open. The scent of fresh lemon and peppered sautéed herbs greeted him along with his date. His date. That thought pleased him to no end.

"Hi," she breathed.

Ursula wore an apron over her outfit that said KISS THE COOK. Her hair was twisted up into a bun that made her look like a happy pineapple. The smooth skin of her neck was exposed. His brain faltered. Everything about her looked kissable. Edible. Words failed him, so he turned to flowers.

"Hi. These are for you." Xavier handed her the bouquet.

She let out a squeal and took them from him. "Please, come on in."

Xavier watched as she got a vase from underneath the sink. He glanced over at the plants that lined the windowsill. "I should've gotten you another plant."

She filled the vase from the kitchen's faucet and arranged the flowers. "No, these are lovely."

He studied her. She wore the dress. *That* dress. The aquamarine dress she'd shimmied and danced into his life in that fateful spring evening. It looked even better now in the late afternoon night. He couldn't stop staring. She sparkled like a gem in a glass jewelry case. He pressed his fingers into his palm to keep from reaching for her. Last week he acted—too eager, too free.

Ursula glanced over her shoulder at him. He stilled. *You're still staring.*

"Whitney had it cleaned for me," Ursula said by way of explanation. She did a little spin, showing off the dress and flashing a bit of her juicy thigh. Xavier bit his lip. How in the world did the glimpse of a thigh make him weak?

"Gwen let me keep it, so I figured it would be perfect for tonight."

"It is. Thank you for cooking for me. It's very sweet of you."

Ursula held up a hand. "Don't thank me yet. I've never made this meal before, so this might be an experience for both of us."

She winked at him. He'd gladly eat sea glass if she served it to him on a silver platter. Ursula set up the table while he kept an eye on the simmering food. She lit the long candles and arranged the plates and glasses on the tablecloth. He opened the bottle of sparkling cider and poured their drinks. She served them plates filled with sautéed mushrooms and cheese polenta with a side of spinach.

"I read somewhere that fae like mushrooms," she said.

"That's correct," Xavier said. He leaned over and inhaled the savory scents. Lovely. As he scooped a huge bite into his mouth, he became instantly wide awake; he tasted the absolute love she'd put into this meal. He'd been served literal nectar and the leftovers of gods, but nothing had been made with such detail as this meal. As their eyes met over the table, he felt a shock run through him.

I want you to know all of me. I want you to have my name.
He stared, speechless, at her.

"Is it good?" she asked.

He pushed through his shock. "It's great."

She poured Xavier another glass of sparkling cider. He took a long sip from his drink. The fruity bubbles tickled his tongue and the sweetness rushed through his veins. She tilted her head to the side. "How are you?"

Ursula deserved honesty, so he told her. "I'm missing my family today."

"You can always talk to me about it," Ursula offered. "Have you seen any other fae from the Realm here?"

"Yes, Beltane's a huge day for fae to come and visit."

Ursula winced. "I forgot. The veil's thin enough to pass between worlds. You could've gone home today for a quick visit, but—" She shook her head. "You should be with your family or with Whitney."

"I could say the same for you, Madame," he said gently.

A knowing gleam entered her eyes. "You've made your point," Ursula said. "I'm enjoying your company. Besides, I'm going to see them at this month's moon gathering. We get together to cleanse our crystals and make moonlight tea."

"That sounds like fun."

"It's a good time. You're invited to come with me," Ursula said warmly.

Xavier nodded. He placed his empty glass on the table. "I have a gift for you."

Ursula finished her drink and sat up. "I thought the flowers were my gift."

"I want to give you something else." His words came out

with quiet assurance. He knew what he wanted her to have and keep safe.

Ursula held a hand against her cheek, a teasing smile on her face. "Please tell me you brought dessert."

"I want you to know my true name," Xavier said. His voice was firm, final. Ursula let her hand fall from her face, then peered at Xavier. Her lips were pressed shut so no sound would burst out.

He'd never told anyone—human or fae—his true name. The gravity of this moment wasn't lost on him. Xavier might as well be cutting off a piece of his soul for her to keep. She let out a sharp breath and stood, not bothering to look at Xavier. She gathered up the dishes, cleaned them off in the garbage, and placed them in the sink, averting her eyes from him. *You really messed up; she won't even look at you.*

Xavier stood and went over to the sink by her.

Ursula picked up the soap bottle and drizzled it all over the plates. Her hand turned on the faucet, filling the sink with hot water and turning the soap into bubbly suds.

"Sula, beloved."

"No, Xavier." Ursula held up her hand. "You're not telling me. I'm not listening to you."

"What if I want you to know it?" he whispered.

She slowly closed, then opened, her eyes. He was met with sheer defiance and hesitation.

Xavier wanted to give her something that would be hers and hers alone. Something that she could keep. He couldn't promise her a future. Now that he was fully disenchanted, he was destined to return to the Realm, marry a princess, and live out the rest of his life in a castle. That was how his story ended. It was how his father's story ended and so on.

The sink was half full. Ursula snapped off the faucet but didn't reach for the plates.

"Let me." Xavier eased her out of the way. He rolled up his sleeves and went about washing the dishes. Ursula stood by his side while he scrubbed and cleaned.

This was a dangerous game. If Ursula knew his true name, then she with her magic and powers could call him whenever she wanted. He'd be bound to her across time and space. He knew it was too much for her, but at the same time not enough.

"Your Highness," she sighed.

Xavier let out a low whistle. "Every time you call me by my title, I...almost come undone. I don't deserve civility. Don't call me Your Highness when you don't know all the indecent things I'd do if we were alone together."

He stopped, too stunned by his confession. Xavier reached for the dish towel by the sink.

"We are alone," Ursula said roughly. Her voice turned hoarse. "Are you scared to be alone with me?"

He swallowed. "I'm scared at how much I like to be alone with you."

That's why he courted her publicly out in the sunshine. If they were alone, truly alone, then he might be tempted to offer her more than he could give her.

"Are you really giving me your true name?" she asked.

"It's the most valuable thing I have." He couldn't give her anything more than that.

"No," she said. "It isn't."

She turned to him, with eager eyes and skin waiting for him. Xavier brushed his lips over her face, then to her neck. He moved away from the sink so he could touch more of Ursula. The earth within Xavier shook. He licked the delectable salt of her skin and sighed roughly. He eased her into his arms and fit her between his thighs. Xavier stilled, but then she snuggled into his embrace. All his blood pooled south, and he grew excited. Hard. Xavier trailed open-mouthed kisses on her neck until he captured her lips. No other soul would do.

He deepened the kiss with careful savagery, and she seemed to go boneless. Ursula, with her soft curves and sweet moans, tasted of tart lemon and temptation. Her perfume filled his nostrils and invaded his senses. Longing throbbed and made him aware of their closeness.

They weren't close enough. He wanted to be underneath her.

This was too much. He leaned back and studied Ursula to steady his thoughts. Her smooth skin glowed with pale pink undertones. Bestow her with a crown and make her yours. His soul demanded. Kisses wouldn't be enough for him tonight.

He'd want everything.

"Give me something else," she said. "Something else that won't—" She cut herself off and silently looked at the walls. He filled in the rest. *Give me something else that won't hurt you. Keep you here against your will. Bind you to me.*

"If you're going to give me something, give me tonight."

"I came over to court you, to woo you, but all I can think about—" He took a steadying breath. "I want you. I want to worship every inch of you. I...yearn to possess you in every way possible, if you would allow me that honor."

Tonight, there was no trace of the prim prince who gave her a rose that smelled of pumpkin and fae magic. Instead, it was the man of her fantasies. It had been over a year since she'd been with a man, let alone a man as enchanting as Xavier. She needed to take a moment to collect herself. Ursula moved into the bedroom area to catch her breath and get herself together.

He was leaving at midsummer, but he was hers.

For the last two weeks, they'd been kissing and touching each other into overwhelming levels of sexual frustration. It was like she was standing in line for a roller coaster and every step she took forward with Xavier just increased the antici-pation. Now, tonight, it was her time to get on and ride him hard. Her imagination and the frantic motions of her hand weren't enough to keep her satisfied; she wanted Xavier. She breathed in his alluring scent—crushed wildflowers and wild grass—allowing it to ease her nerves.

Ursula turned back to Xavier. He'd stayed where she left him, by the sink, waiting for her. Their eyes met. Fire hissed beneath her skin. After tonight, he'd haunt her dreams for months, maybe years after he returned to the Realm. Ursula knew in her heart she'd rather be haunted by Xavier than return to her dreamless sleep. The longer she stared at him, the more she realized a single truth. He'd ruin her for any other man, but no other man would do for her. Ever.

So be it. Let her be ruined.

"Remember at the party when you asked me about my underwear?" Ursula asked softly.

He said nothing but slowly nodded.

"Well, you were right."

Ursula whipped the dress over her head and threw it on the floor. He rocked back on his heels, his eyes widening in astonishment. She put her hands on her hips and posed like the models on the plus-size lingerie site she loved to browse. It wasn't every day you showed a fae prince your underwear set. Silently she gave herself directions. *Chest up. Chin out. Take a breath and hold it.* Mercy. Xavier crossed the entire space in four strides until he stood before her. She kept repeating in her head in a pep talk.

You're a badass chick. You're a badass chick in matching lace underwear.

She could only imagine what she looked like. Big boobs. Moderate waist. Mermaid thighs that touched and over-lapped. Xavier was looking at her as if she were the last bite of birthday cake. Perfection. That pure desire on his face nearly made her want to look away, but she stared back. How long had it been since she'd been wanted like this? Too long. Far too long. He blinked, drawing in a deep, shuddering breath. All the tension in his body drained away.

The formality drained out of him, too.

"I need to see all of you, please," he said in a strained voice.

Ursula felt a surge of power at his plea. She unhooked her bra and rolled her panties off her hips, down her legs, and kicked them away.

Xavier went over to the vase on the table and plucked a single rose from the arrangement. A gasp escaped her as her mind raced with possibilities of what was about to happen.

With a snap of his fingers, he carefully de-thorned the stem. He got close enough that she could see herself in his glasses' reflection. She saw herself flush, ready for his touch. His head tilted to the side and his tongue played on his bottom lip.

His eyes flashed with promise and a hint of restraint. He held up the rose before her. "May I?"

She nodded. "Do what you will, Your Highness."

He traced the rosebud against the side of her face. "Close your eyes. Be still."

She did as he requested, plunging herself into near darkness. All she felt was the tight petals brush her skin. The rosebud eased down her cheek to her neck, her shoulders, and down the valley between her breasts. Blood rushed from her fingertips to her toes, leaving her giddy. The slow trail he made over her bare body filled her with delightful eagerness. Her breath came out in slow, needy pants. It brushed against her slowly, sending wide ripples of desire that bounced throughout her body. Every part of her was conscious of where the cool flower touched her. The air heated. If he didn't hurry, she was going to pass out from sheer want.

He leaned in, his uneven breathing feeling enjoyably hot on her ear. "Pretend I'm exploring you now."

Ursula let her mind play. He traveled the rounded curve of her breast. It was his hand that caressed her sensitive nipple, which was increasingly getting hard with every passing second. It was his hand that slid down her belly and to the swell of her hips. It was his hand that was spreading and teasing her—

Wait, that *was* him. Her eyes snapped open. She looked down to see him stroking her slick flesh. The rosebud had been discarded to the table, replaced with his steady hand. *Finally.* She moaned softly as his fingers made slow circles that made everything whirl. The scent of her arousal perfumed the air.

Each gentle move was a single command. *Get ready for me.*

He didn't need to tell her twice. She'd been waiting for him for longer than she wanted to admit. For days. For weeks. Forever. Pleasant jolts went through Ursula as he increased his motions. More. She needed more. She went to touch him on his cheek, but he stopped her with a quick kiss to her wrist.

"You'll have your time soon, Madame," he said with a roguish smile. "Let me have my fun."

With that, he got on his knees and went to work destroying her with the swirl of his tongue. A shudder went through her body as Xavier licked and teased her. His beard tickled her inner thighs as he stroked her with his mouth. Her hands gripped his ears and held him right there where the heat grew and built into an inferno that was getting out of control. She breathed in his natural cologne of free wildflowers, musk, and sweet heat. His hands dug into her as he held her still. Ursula was getting closer...closer and—then she let out a strangled cry as she came, fierce and quick. His hands slowed and he whispered against her skin, pressing soft kisses to the inside of her thigh. She shivered in the aftermath, but the desire wasn't done with her.

It had been appeased but was still there, greedy for more from her, from him.

Ursula lingered in the space between pleasure and loss, between yearning and fulfillment. She could get there again if he was willing to just keep going and keep licking and keep teasing her. If he just kept touching. Desire that she'd let famish for so long was close to being fed and it was demanding to feast.

"Don't stop, please, don't stop," she pleaded. She'd been satiated, but not satisfied.

"Let's get you there." He returned his mouth and tongue back to the apex of her thighs.

Her second release came in long, surrendering moans. Heart hammering in her ears, Ursula's legs buckled underneath her, but Xavier held her up.

"I've got you," he murmured. "I won't let you fall."

She looked down at Xavier on his knees before her. *I need to see you as you were made.* "My turn," Ursula said. "Clothes. Off. Now."

Ursula lay on the edge of the bed. Xavier rose, unbuttoned his waistcoat, and discarded it on the floor. She toyed around with the idea of asking him to keep it on. *Next time.* He'd keep it on next time. He didn't merely undress. He stripped off his clothing, removing every piece deliberately slow, as if unwrapping a piece of gourmet candy. All he wore was his necklace and a wild smile.

She crooked a finger. He went to the bed and moved before her. She motioned for him to turn around. He gave her a grin as he turned in an unhurried circle, showing off every inch on his splendor. Quickly, Ursula leaned over to her nightstand and yanked open the first drawer. Always be prepared to have a good time. She crawled back over to Xavier with a foil packet, her focus on the length of him. With a deft hand, he opened it, sheathed himself, and met her.

He cocked a brow.

"Is Madame satisfied with what she sees?"

She nodded. "I eat with my eyes first, then with my mouth."

"Is that a promise?" Xavier moved forward over the bed, brushing his mouth over hers. Ursula pulled him down on top of her, and they tumbled together on the bed in a giggling heap. The weight of him felt like a thick comforter—warm and soothing. He nestled right between her legs, and the giggles gave way to stunned gasps. His erection brushed against her center, making her see stars. Xavier braced his arms on either side of Ursula and hovered about her.

She whimpered. Only a few inches separated her from everything she anticipated.

"I can't think." He let out a sharp breath.

The tenderness etched all over his face made her glow from within. She looked up into his eyes and held back a sigh.

"Don't think, just move," she whispered. Ursula brushed her mouth against his.

He kissed her quickly, then asked, "Are you ready for me?"

She lifted her hips and rubbed herself against him. All he had to do was guide himself inside of her and . . . everything would change. Sex. The final frontier. She nodded and he lowered himself down. He sank into her until they were joined together hip to hip. She didn't just see stars; she saw every single constellation in the Northern Hemisphere. Her skin felt covered in crushed starlight, like little sparks of light warmed her all over.

He closed his eyes and moaned. "I hope this isn't a dream."

"Trust me," she said, nearly breathless. "I'm real."

His eyes snapped open. Xavier's whole face broke into a dazzling smile, as if he'd uncovered a precious gem that belonged only to him.

"Yes, you are." His hips thrust in a steady rhythm, his words punctuating every stroke. "And you are mine."

Her heart squeezed. Passion flooded through every part of her as he increased his tempo. Her hands went to his hips, dug her fingers into his flesh and she held on for dear life. Xavier moved without haste, as if time was no issue or of no concern. He pumped harder, and the delectable friction of them moving together fed the growing wave of rising pleasure within her. Ursula felt her desire building up to a crescendo. She moaned and writhed beneath him, twisting her hips, matching Xavier move for move. His actions became more demanding, his groans encouraging Ursula to take him deeper. Their bodies collided, and shifted again and again, as the passion grew hotter and faster. They moved together like tectonic plates, a force as ancient as the Earth itself compelled them to shift away and toward each other, building something dangerous and powerful between them. As Xavier drove into her, his body slick with sweat and his face taut with a singular focus—to wreck her—the truth struck her.

This is how worlds are made—through heat and movement.

We are creating something new and real. This world belongs to us.

She broke apart.

Soon Xavier trembled. He came with a rasping groan, and

he took him a minute to collect himself. The ground beneath them shifted and they relished in the afterglow. Xavier lay next to Ursula, pressing his face against her neck. Ursula held him against her, her body fully charged.

Between each word, Xavier planted kisses on her neck, shoulders, and face. "You felt like paradise."

He lifted his head and looked her over. "I'm not done with you yet, Madame."

The sun left the sky and she fell apart in his arms. The moon rose, the stars appeared when he eventually lay next to her, his chest slightly heaving. Their bodies were naked and moist from their latest bout of sex.

The air smelled heady, of sweat and bliss.

"What planet are we on?" he asked shakily.

"I think we're on one of the nice ones." Ursula let out a trembling breath. "The one with water and air."

"Good," Xavier mumbled happily. Her hands moved over the length of him, relishing in nearness.

Ursula tucked herself neatly against his side. "That was—" Her mind went blank. Did he love her down so good that he knocked the words from her brain?

Xavier framed her face in his hands. He pressed a kiss to her lips.

"I agree," he murmured. "You should be laid out on a bed of roses."

There was a note of regret.

Ursula leaned over and kissed his chin. "All I want is right here in this bed."

He gave her a smile that sent her hands down his thighs

and around the base of him. She pumped and stroked him until he was left panting and yelling her name.

Much later, when Xavier was fast asleep, Ursula lay next to him, wide awake.

She buried her face into the pillow in disbelief. Xavier was here. She held back a wicked cackle. It felt like she went into the Met Museum, yanked a priceless panting from the wall, and walked out the front door. He was hers. She'd fantasized this very moment for weeks, but the reality was much, much better than her dreams.

Ursula wasn't looking for Xavier, but she found him anyway.

She gave in to a light slumber, satisfied in the knowledge that he was with her. As the minutes ticked by, that sense of satisfaction slowly morphed into worry, rousing her from sleep. Ursula tossed and turned, trying to get comfortable, but it felt like she was sleeping on thorns. She stared at the ceiling, listening to the street sounds, and her heartbeat telegraphed a message to her brain. *He was here for now. What about after? What about the leap?*

Dread prickled at her bare skin. Midsummer was coming and he'd soon depart. She wasn't going to give him up sooner than she had to. Ursula looked at the oven clock in the corner and let out a sigh: 4:44 a.m. How did it get so late? It was time to wish. She closed her eyes, nestled her head against his chest, and held on.

Let him find a way to stay for a little while longer. Please.

Ursula heard him rouse from his sleep. She opened her eyes.

Xavier blinked and gave her a wickedly handsome grin. "So, I didn't dream you."

Under his attention, her dread ebbed away. He eased his arms around her body, bringing her skin to skin.

"I'm really hungry for some reason," Xavier said.

She laughed against his chest. "Your Highness, get ready for the wonders of a buttered roll."

Chapter Twenty-Two

Before Ursula could write her full name, she knew the language of flowers and herbs. In Nana Ruth's garden, she learned the art of communicating with a well-placed rose, fern, or sunflower. Nana taught her how they spoke to people even if people were too dense or distracted to notice their messages.

"Why do you talk to flowers?" Ursula once asked her.

"I trust flowers because they've always kept my secrets," Nana answered as she watered the massive collection of blooms and plants. Flowers spoke when people had to hold their tongue. Sunflowers hinted at adoration. Daisies spoke about first love.

Ursula stared at the massive bouquet of cherry-red tulips that had just been delivered to the shop. Sweet passion. Declaration of affection. The flowers arrived with a handwritten card, which she immediately read.

Stars wished they shined like you. Until next time. Your humble prince, Xavier.

Ursula pressed a hand to her chest and dropped the card on the counter. Cue the swooning.

She had spent the night with Xavier. It was a wonderfully

reckless choice, but it was hers to make. What made it reckless was that he was everything she wanted in a relationship, but he couldn't commit to staying in the Grove. They'd come back from the deli with their breakfast, and she had been ready to stream a movie and hang out for a while. His Highness had other plans. Xavier cocked his brow, pulled her to him, and promptly lowered her to the floor, where he pleasured her until she saw the stars of the neighboring galaxy. Currently, she was sore and tired, and couldn't stop looking off into her crystal ball. Was she seriously sprung over a man—or rather fae man—after one night? *Cinderella fell in love after one night.* Ursula had woken up alone this morning, but he left her a note.

He'd let her sleep in, but he'd be back later.

Ursula sniffed the flowers, then took her seat at the reading table. She studied the crystal ball, finding the urge to look into the future. The leap had already shown her what wonderful future waited if she made the right steps in her present. Her chest expanded. It was a vision of complete domestic bliss. Ursula sat at a sunny breakfast nook smearing cream cheese on toasted bagels with her dull knives while Xavier tended to her plants in the window. They chatted about having dinner with Lucy and Alex at Sirena's restaurant.

Longing echoed through her. She wanted this vision to be real but didn't know how to give it life. He promised he'd stay until midsummer. Ursula didn't know how to ask him if he wanted to stay with her for good. She didn't tell him any details because she didn't want to influence his decision in any way.

The shop bell jingled as the door opened but she didn't look up from the ball.

"Welcome to Light as a Feather. How can I help you?" she said automatically.

"You already have," Xavier said. "You're here."

Ursula looked up from the crystal. Pleasure hummed within her the closer she got to him. She gave him a peck on the lips. "As much as I'd love to chat with you, I have a client."

"Who do you have an appointment with?" he asked.

"I have to double-check the name." Ursula went over to the counter and took out a paper planner where Mama sometimes wrote down call-in appointments. It was old school, but the system kept them organized. She turned to the today's date. "One p.m., P. Charming—" She snapped her head up and glared at him. "Sir, no, you didn't."

Xavier stroked his beard like a sexy Bond villain. "I booked your entire afternoon."

Ursula waggled her eyebrows in a come-here-lover-boy motion. "So, what do you have in mind?"

He looked at her with a naughty, delicious smile. She'd seen that same smile when he lowered to the floor and made her squeal this morning. Heat sizzled through Ursula and hit her right in her core. "I have plenty of plans for you, but business before pleasure."

"Come, Your Highness," Ursula said, inviting him forward to the reading table in the window. She recalled whispering those words while rocking on top of him, naked, while he surrendered underneath her. Everything tingled. Ursula cleared her throat and refocused herself. Work hard now, play hard later. The chair squeaked underneath Xavier as he sat.

"What can Madame do for you, Mr. Charming?" she asked.

He straightened. "I'd like to know my future."

"Pick your tool." She gestured to the crystal ball, the deck of tarot cards, and the palmistry sign on the table between them.

"I've always been fond of crystals," he said.

"Follow my lead." Ursula modeled every step for Xavier. Breathe in. Let your thoughts drift away. Hold a steady gaze on the crystal. Let incoming images and signs from the universe fill your mind. Close the gaze. Thank the tool. Breathe in. Even after all those steps, the crystal ball remained blank for Ursula. Clear. Open. Maybe that was the message. Her path was open in the best way.

Ursula faced Xavier.

"Popcorn. Twinkle lights. Letters. Teacups. Red roses," he said robotically. She sat up. Whoa. Who knew that the universe had so many messages for him? He blinked, which effectively broke his gaze. "I have no idea what most of that means."

"Life has a way of revealing things if you're paying attention," she said.

"I didn't see you there." He sounded annoyed as if the crystal played a trick on him.

She understood his aggravation, having looked into countless crystals and wishing to get a straight answer. "The universe isn't direct. It tends to be vague; you have to find meaning in those images. For example, I love popcorn. I consider it to be a food group."

He chuckled lightly. "Seriously, Sula."

"Yes, have you ever had kettle corn? Salty and sweet at the same time." She put her fingers to her mouth and kissed them. "Delicious."

"Okay, that probably explains the popcorn, but what about the rest..." His words trailed off and his gaze went distant. There was a note of confusion in his voice. Ursula took his hand and held it.

"The signs will make sense when you see them," she assured him. "Keep your eyes open."

He gave her a hand squeeze. "I'll do that, Madame."

Ursula nodded and took her hand back. "So, what else can I help you with?"

Xavier tilted his head back. "Well, I had an amazing night with this sexy witch. She has a gorgeous smile and a banging body, and she completely rocked my world. You might know her," he joked.

Ursula held back a laugh. Maybe Xavier was getting too good at using slang. "Are you bragging?"

His eyes twinkled. "No. I'm celebrating. I was hoping to keep courting her."

"I don't remember that fairy tale. I thought princes didn't court witches," she teased.

"I do," he said, leaning over the table. Something intense flared in those eyes of his. Ursula felt a pulsating current of energy moving through her at those two words. The crystal ball between them glowed and shimmered. She stared at it, more surprised than frightened.

Inanimate objects coming to life. *Didn't see that happening.*

Xavier leaned back in his chair. "I think the universe is on my side," he said smugly.

Ursula stood from the table. "So, what are our plans for the afternoon?"

"I'm taking you out for a long lunch," Xavier said. "The crystal has spoken."

There was nothing like the tempting scent of fresh, buttery popcorn being made right before watching a movie. Ursula managed to snag the last Ultimate Movie Basket from the Jewel Box Theater and had it delivered to her apartment. The massive basket included a popcorn maker, bags of concession-stand candy, and a gift card for four movie rentals. It also included tickets to a future showing at the theater, a limited-edition T-shirt, and a few other wrapped goodies she hadn't opened yet.

Unwrapping this basket seemed like a perfect time to invite Xavier over for a friendly movie night. Since their session at the shop, they'd gone out for lunch and dinner, and he'd been an absolute gentleman—opening the door, pulling out her seat, and extending his arm to her when they walked the Grove. Apparently, Xavier wanted to court her as a prince would. That idea touched her heart and turned her on at the same time.

Yes, he was being a gentleman, but she wanted to do unladylike things to him.

She wanted to be indecent with Xavier all night long and twice in the morning.

He arrived for movie night on time, of course, and brought drinks—a glass bottle of pomegranate iced tea. The plant knowledge part of her brain reminded her that pomegranates are aphrodisiacs and good for getting blood flowing everywhere. Great. Even her brain wanted her to get laid.

Ursula watched the last kernels pop on the stove.

"I feel guilty," she said. "We don't get out to Smitten events anymore. I don't want to keep you tied up in the bedroom."

Xavier licked his bottom lip. "Tie me up as much you want, Madame," he said with a sly smile. "I don't mind it."

Her face grew hot. "You know what I mean."

He tilted his head. "I know. Everything I want is right here in this room."

She smiled at him. Ursula filled the wide bowl up to the brim with popcorn, walked over to the couch, and placed it right on Xavier's lap. He deserved to have some fun before he went back to the Realm.

"I'd like you to meet my cousins," she said. "They're hosting a house party and they've invited us."

"I'd be honored," he said. "Should I bring something?"

She settled next to him. "Just bring your charming self."

Ursula adjusted her laptop on the coffee table so that they could both see the screen.

"So, what are we watching?" he asked.

She reached into her purse by her side and set her phone to vibrate. "It's a surprise."

"I thought you didn't like surprises," he said.

"I'm trying something new." She studied him, noticing the deep bags under his eyes and small yawn. A shred of guilt went through her. "We can do this another time."

Xavier sat up. "No, I wanted to see you."

Ursula queued up the movie on the computer. She picked

something light and fun—a screwball romantic comedy Callie had made her watch for her college film class.

"You hold the snacks; I control the movie."

Xavier glanced down at the popcorn, which glistened. "How much butter is enough?"

"There's no answer to that question," Ursula said. She snatched a handful from the bowl and munched. A fine layer of butter coated her fingers, which she quickly lapped up with her tongue. *Clarified butter, take me away.* She caught Xavier staring, his eyes growing big as he clutched the bowl to his chest.

"If you keep licking your fingers like that, we're not going to even start the movie," he warned seriously.

"We can watch this movie later."

Ursula held back a scream. If he didn't act right, she was going to pour the topping on him and see where the night took them. But behind the flirtation, she saw the exhaustion in his eyes. What was keeping him up at night? He needed a break from being charming.

"Resist me until the end credits," she said instead.

He flashed her a grin.

Ursula clicked the button and started the film. They laughed at the adventures of a down-on-her-luck showgirl pretending to be a wealthy woman and falling in love with a kindhearted cabdriver, but the evening carried an undercurrent of anticipation. Their fingers brushed up against each other over the snack bowl. Her legging-clad legs accidentally bumped into his when she turned up the volume button. His arm draped over the back of the couch and his hand touched her neck. Shivers of delight filled her at his light stroke. Oh yes. She nestled next to him and kept watching the movie.

By the time the credits rolled, Xavier had drifted asleep with the half-empty bowl on his lap. Ursula put the bowl on the table. She watched him for a long moment. He looked like he belonged on her couch and in her space. Ursula found herself suddenly yawning. It was getting late. Get a quick nap, then send him home to get some real sleep.

She curled up next to Xavier and closed her eyes for just a moment. Fifteen minutes.

When Ursula opened them again, it was morning. The screen saver displayed collegiate words and their definitions across her laptop screen. She rubbed her eyes and let out a small yawn. Birds chirped outside her window. Ursula reached out to touch him but paused. *Let him rest.*

Xavier let out a soft sigh and bent his body toward her, as if he was trying to warm himself with her heat. Here she was, a witch who had stumbled upon a sleeping prince. This moment right here was what the stories had promised her if she believed enough.

If she loved enough. How many times had she dreamed of finding a man like Xavier?

A smile flashed over his slumbering face, then disappeared. What dream left him untroubled? Maybe he dreamed of his castle, of his family and glittering court. Maybe he dreamed of the royal gardens he mentioned over their many conversations.

What if you just held on to him? Her heart dropped to her knees at the thought.

He wasn't staying. He was going home at midsummer. She

hovered over him. Xavier drew in a deep breath and awoke, blinking rapidly. He looked at Ursula, and his hand cupped her face. She gasped at the gentle contact.

His brows drew together in an amazed expression. "You were in my dreams."

Slowly, yearning took possession of her senses and eased her into his arms.

Ursula captured his mouth in a silent, tender kiss. Xavier kissed her back and pulled her flush against him. He tasted of tart pomegranate and raw sugar. Ursula felt his hands move up her body and slid underneath her shirt. His fingers dug into her flesh and held her close.

"Why are we still dressed?" he asked.

"Working on it." Ursula yanked her shirt off and tossed it away. She slid out of her leggings and underwear. Xavier undressed and tossed his clothes in a heap. The air felt cool as Xavier nipped at her bare skin. She straddled Xavier, pinning him to the couch. A moan escaped her as he pressed a trail of kisses over her chest and licked her budding nipple.

"Tell me what you want," he whispered against her breast.

"I want you," Ursula said. She reached down between them and stroked him. He shuddered and throbbed. The feel of his skin was smooth against the palm of her hand. Ursula then clutched his shoulders and brushed herself against his growing bulge. A strained sigh left his lips as she moved her hips and ground for what seemed forever. By the time they took a break, she was dizzy with need.

"I'm not going to last," he said. "We need protection. Now."

Ursula agreed with a quick nod. She was aroused, but she needed to keep her head on through the haze of pleasure. The nightstand felt so far away but there had to be something else. Ursula knocked over her purse on the floor, jumped off Xavier, and searched the pile.

"Yes." She found the electric-blue foil and joined him back on the couch. She carefully tore it open.

"Allow me," she said.

She took Xavier into her hand again, stroked him a few times, and then covered him. He let out a sharp breath. Ursula straddled him; he was practically pulsating. She desired every inch.

"This is all for you," he said gravely. He placed a hand on her waist and eased himself inside of her. Ursula gasped as he rocked back and forth, until they joined together.

"Do you know that?" he asked. He thrust with a gentle, urgent rhythm that stole her words. He reached between and fondled her sex, eliciting a peal of satisfaction from her. Sparks shot off within her like small exploding galaxies. She shook dazedly as he kept speaking, kept tasting her lips. He rocked his hips until she came in a long, trembling whimper.

"All my kisses belong to you now," he said.

Ursula, overcome with ecstasy, couldn't speak. She leaned forward and embraced Xavier. His words didn't sound like a simple promise; they sounded like a pledge of fidelity. Ursula pressed her face into his shoulder so he wouldn't see the tears. She found his heartbeat with her hand and felt its steady rhythm.

Resolution hammered in her bones.

If his kisses were hers, then hers would be his from now on.

Chapter Twenty-Three

☾

Xavier didn't have much experience sneaking into a house at dawn, but he was going to try his best not to get caught. At the Alder Castle, he could come and go as he pleased, but at Whitney's house he always had to check in with her and have breakfast. But over the last two weeks, he had avoided his godmother. Whitney would know that he'd broken his enchantment once she took a single glance at him, and he didn't want to put her in the awkward position of lying for him to Father. So Xavier used whatever spells and magic he had on hand to avoid a conversation with her. He borrowed an invisibility stone from a goblin and slipped in and out of the mansion. He slipped off his shoes by the door and tiptoed through the foyer.

The instant his foot hit the first stair, though, he heard her crystalline voice ring out. "Hello, stranger. You're up early."

He was, as the humans said, busted. Xavier stiffened, then faced Whitney. She was dressed in her housecoat, her gossamer wings fluttering behind her back. His stomach clenched. The last time her wings fluttered like that, Royce almost got turned into a field mouse for lying about stealing a slice of tea cake. His brother spent a week with mouse ears sticking out of his hair.

"Good morning," he said.

Whitney narrowed her eyes. "How was your evening or—rather your morning?"

He forced an easy smile. "It was nice."

That was a lie. It wasn't nice. It was wonderful. It was... perfect.

He lowered his head. It had been difficult to leave Ursula once again.

Since their intimate movie viewing, Xavier spent his nights at Ursula's apartment.

Yesterday, they'd come back from a late dinner, sat down on her couch, and discussed their lives. He enjoyed listening about her misadventures with beauty spells and how she ended up with butterscotch-blond hair for an entire year. She asked him about the Realm, so he'd told her stories about fae dancing on morning dew and an endless summer where no one grew cold or tired. She nestled in his arms and fell asleep. He watched her slumber for a long time and finally understood the phrase "sleeping beauty." Xavier pressed a kiss against her forehead and held her close.

He pulled himself back to the present.

Whitney folded her arms over her chest. "Should I even ask where you were?"

Guilt rolled through him. "I'm fine. I was safe."

Concern creased her brow. "I know that you're grown, but you've... got to be careful. You're my responsibility. I promised your parents I'd protect you. This isn't home. This town might be filled by magic, but you've got to watch who you cross here."

"I'm okay. I'm not a kid."

Whitney's wings lowered. "I don't care how old you are. You're my godson and you're my family. You can always be honest with me."

He should've told her the truth weeks ago, but he didn't know what to say. The weight of his lies and his deception hit Xavier in the chest. Whitney deserved to know the truth. He needed to come clean and hope that she would understand why he kept this secret from her.

"I broke the enchantment."

Whitney threw up her hands. Her voice echoed in the stairwell. "I knew you were hiding something. So, how is Ms. Paige? I hope she didn't gloat to all the Realm about being your perfect kiss."

Xavier shook his head. "I never kissed Lady Paige."

She narrowed her eyes. "Then, beloved, how did you break the spell?"

Blood pounded in his pointed ears. "I kissed Ursula."

Whitney's wings froze. She gently nudged him toward the kitchen. "Come on. I'm putting on the teapot. You're telling me the whole story."

Four cups of tea and three slices of buttered faery bread later, Xavier had told Whitney his entire tale. Well, he didn't tell her all the intimate details. Whitney didn't need to know about how Ursula sang to her plants or how he loved to trace the birthmark on her stomach with his fingers. He lifted his teacup to hide his grin. There were some memories of her that he wanted to keep in his heart for himself.

Whitney gave him a guarded look. "I received a letter from your father yesterday."

Father didn't believe in using modern technology and steadfastly used ink and a quill pen to communicate. Half of his letters could have been an email or a well-worded text.

Xavier let out a sigh and put down his teacup.

"Was he wishing me a blessed Beltane two weeks too late?" he joked.

She didn't smile. "The Faerie Queen is touring the kingdom and your father wants to show that you were successful in completing your task. He wants to know if you've found your perfect kiss and broken the spell. If you have, then I'm supposed to send you home immediately."

The tips of his ears ached, and he drew in a deep breath. He wasn't ready to go back yet. Maybe not ever.

"I can't go now. I have a woodworking class," he announced. "We're making a tea caddy."

Whitney furrowed her brow. "Xavier."

"I don't want to go back," he whispered.

How could he tell Father that he was happier here? He had his woodworking classes and signed up to volunteer to care for the community garden. Xavier had found a local fae group who got together once a month to talk about Realm politics and trade vegetarian recipes at the local coffeehouse. He had Ursula with her bright smiles, jokes, and her spellbinding kisses that made him feel like they were the only two lovers left in the Grove. Here he could make his own choices rather than being given options by Father.

He had existed in the Realm, but he had a life in Freya Grove. Now, he had to let it go and go home because he had to keep his promise. His heart felt crushed under a boulder.

Xavier looked to Whitney.

"Have you told her how you feel?" Whitney asked quietly.

He shook his head. "I...I can't."

Whitney placed a gentle hand on his forearm. "I can shield you from your father's magic as long you hold on to those words. Once you say them out loud, you'll give them life and he'll come and collect you."

He hung his head. Father wouldn't approve of him being with a human, no matter how wonderful she was. When they were alone together, Xavier didn't care if their kisses were perfect because they were magical.

He'd gotten his perfect kiss, but how would he be able to keep it?

Chapter Twenty-Four

The Caraway House twinkled and shined as if they were caught up inside of a huge crystal ball. The sitting room was decorated with sparkling tea lights and blooming flower garlands on the mantel. Another garland decorated the front desk and staircase leading upstairs. Heady rose and lavender incense gave the space a homey feel. A crowd of family members, casters, and magical beings lingered in the living room and the foyer. Ursula and Xavier walked in unnoticed, blending in with the rest of the guests.

Ursula let out a low whistle and looked around at the decorations. "Callie outdid herself for this meeting. It looks like someone's getting married."

She took Xavier over the mantel next to the collection of mystic items hanging on the wall.

"This place looks..." His words trailed off as he noticed the framed pictures of botanical flowers and drawings.

"Charming? Enchanting?" Ursula suggested. He nodded and studied the artful hand drawings of Caraway plants. She glanced around the living room, hoping to discreetly let her cousins know she was here.

Callie, in a baby blue swing dress, stood up from the couch. "You're here!" she yelled in glee. "Ursula's here!"

Numerous uncles, aunts, and cousins turned around and spotted Ursula. She braced herself for mixed or indifferent reactions. Ursula wouldn't blame them for being dismissive of her; she hadn't spoken to anyone besides Sirena and Callie for months. Instead, cheers and greetings erupted from the family. Uncle Leo came over and gave her one of his wonderful crushing hugs. Mama clapped her hands joyfully and embraced both her and Xavier. Being around them made her remember how carelessly she'd left them in her quest for perfection. Shame washed through her body. Who would be so foolish to forfeit this love?

She promised herself she wouldn't be a fool again and would hold fast to this family.

Sirena came out of the kitchen wielding a wooden spoon. "Welcome to the fun."

"Is Lucy back yet?" Callie asked, bouncing on her feet. Her cousin was more sunshiny than usual.

"I thought she was still in DC," Ursula said, cutting a sharp look to Sirena.

Xavier silently watched this exchange.

"No, she's back! I got my days mixed up. The program ended last month, and she's been staying with Alex since she got back right after the sleepover," Sirena said with a big, cat-like grin. Ursula's stomach clenched. She turned to Callie. "To answer your question, she should still be at the Founders' Day Festival with Alex." Sirena made a face. "I swear the two of them can finish each other's sentences."

"Um, Callie?" Another woman covered in a moss-covered

caftan approached them. Her face was pinched in displea-sure. "What's going on here? Why did you invite the Dwyers to the full moon gathering? They don't do the sky-clad thing with us. Also, did you really invite the gnomes? You know how they get around pizza."

Callie made a face. "It's not a full moon gathering—it's a surprise party."

Sirena licked her lips. "You know how we feel about that phrase!"

Ursula felt the blood drain from her face. Callie shook her head. "Don't worry. It's not for you..."

She paused, reached into her bra, and pulled out her phone. "It's go time. They're coming down the street! Places, people!" Callie raised her voice so the whole room could hear her. "Everyone hide! Shut off the lights."

Party guests scurried around the living room and some people hid in the kitchen. Ursula ducked down behind a couch with Xavier. The room plunged into darkness and there was hushed conversation. "Is it someone's birthday?" he asked.

"I don't think so," Ursula said.

Five minutes passed, then she heard the jingle of keys in the front door lock. There was a squeak of a door opening, the lights snapped on, and everyone yelled "Surprise!" at various volumes. Xavier jumped up, but Ursula peeked her head around the couch. Alex and Lucy stood in the doorway with shocked expressions, which turned into wide smiles. She pressed her hands to her cheeks.

Ursula spied the twinkling emerald and diamond ring on her finger. She let out a strangled gasp.

Xavier crouched down next to her side. "Sula, what's wrong?"

"It's a surprise party," she said with a croak. "It's Lucy's party."

She couldn't catch her breath and the room seemed so small around her. She needed air.

While everyone was distracted by Lucy and Alex, Ursula slipped out the back door and bounded down the stairs into Nana's backyard garden. She took a calming breath, letting the cool evening air enter her lungs. Twinkle lights dangled from the tree, giving the space a whimsical glow. Those lights hadn't been up there the last time Ursula visited, so she assumed Callie must have put them up for the party. Lucy was going to love it.

She wasn't supposed to see Lucy until she completed the Boss Witch List. Until she made good with her magic. Even though Ursula made wishes and used her magic without fear, she hadn't found the courage to ask for forgiveness.

Ursula didn't expect to see Lucy for a long time. She especially didn't want to see her at her engagement party. *It's too soon. I don't want to mess up her night.*

The back door opened and closed. Xavier descended the stairs and came over to her.

"I saw you step out," Xavier said. "Are you okay?"

Ursula shook her head. "I should leave."

"You were invited," Xavier said.

"It was a mistake," she insisted. This party was a complete surprise. If Lucy had had a final say over the guest list, then she probably wouldn't have invited Ursula. She didn't deserve to celebrate the good times when she had acted so badly. "I don't think she wants to see me," Ursula said. "I don't want her to see me."

"Too late, I caught you," a familiar voice said fiercely. Ursula turned and saw Lucy standing on the top step. She walked down the stairs with a measured grace reserved for royalty. Ursula's heart sped up and her breath came out in rapid pants. Xavier placed a light hand on her shoulder. Her heart slowed a fraction.

The months had been kind to Lucy, and she glowed with magic. Her short, kinky hair had grown out, and the tight curls looked like stretched ballpoint pen springs. She wore a typical late-spring outfit of a floral top with fluttery sleeves, fitted pants, and flats, and the new engagement ring on her finger sparkled under the lights.

Lucy approached Ursula; her eyes narrowed. "Caraways stick together," she said. "Always. We don't just toss away the people we love after a disagreement. You hold them close, and you work with them. If necessary, you let them go to work on themselves. To heal themselves." Lucy moved in close to Ursula. "I bet you made a boss lady list to fix everything."

Ursula let out a sob and nodded at her. Xavier caught her attention. He pointed to the house and stepped back inside to give them privacy. Oh, she adored him for that. Ursula looked at Lucy through her tears. Her cousin stared at her expectantly. All the regret she had held on to from all these months bubbled up as she looked at Lucy.

"I'm...so, so sorry," Ursula said.

Lucy reached over and wiped away her tears with her thumbs. "It's okay. I forgive you."

Sisterly love radiated from Lucy's face, making Ursula

feel truly forgiven and accepted. This moment of forgiveness was what she'd worked so hard for, for so many months. To return as a person who deserved to be called a Caraway. The regret dissolved away like morning mist being burned away by the sun.

"So, what's new with you?" Lucy asked lightly.

Ursula gave a watery laugh. "Do you have time to talk? I have a story for you."

"Give me the short version."

Underneath the twinkle lights, Ursula told Lucy the major highlights of her adventures from meeting Xavier to being named a Smitten Sweetheart. When she was finished with her tale, Lucy let out a low whistle of amazement. "You've been busy."

"That's one word for it."

Lucy took Ursula's hands and held them. Her touch was kind, welcoming. "Seriously, how are you?"

She thought for a second, then answered. "I'm wishing for better things now."

"Good," Lucy said quietly. "We've been waiting until you were ready to come home."

Ursula opened and closed her mouth. She glanced over at the garden wall. The sight brought overwhelming joy to her heart. White and yellow honeysuckle flowers bloomed and covered the back wall. The honeysuckles grew back. They just needed time. She was done. Enough was enough and she was missing all their love.

"I'm ready." Ursula embraced Lucy. The two hugged for a long moment before finally letting go.

"I have another question to ask you," Lucy said. Her eyes sparkled. "Will you be my bridesmaid?"

Ursula nodded. "I'll be your bridesmaid only if I get to make your bouquet."

It was Caraway tradition that their wedding bouquets were made by their family.

"I'd be overjoyed." Lucy nodded. "I wish—" She cut herself off and waved her hands. "No more wishing. We're going to do instead of only wishing."

Ursula couldn't agree more. "Can I see your ring?"

Lucy grinned and held out her hand for Ursula's inspection. The platinum emerald ring glittered underneath the fairy lights of the garden. Joy bloomed in her chest for her cousin. Alex had stepped up and delivered. "This ring is all you."

Lucy wiggled her fingers. "I know right? Soon, you'll be next. I can feel it."

Ursula chuckled under her breath. She wasn't looking to rush into another commitment anytime soon. The very thought of putting on an engagement ring made her queasy. "I'm done with all that nonsense. I had my turn."

Lucy pinned Ursula with a tender gaze. It shook Ursula clear to her marrow.

"How long have you been in love with Xavier?"

Her queasiness increased and she wrapped her arms around her stomach. Her brain sputtered to give a response. "I'm not...We're not...I can't..." Ursula sniffed. "I have no right to bother you with my problems."

"I'm asking about your problems," Lucy said. "Someone once told me spells end."

Shame coursed through Ursula. "I never should have said that."

Lucy held her hands and squeezed them. "It's not wrong. What will you do when this spell ends? Would you ever ask him to stay?"

Ursula felt the tears coming, but she blinked them back. "I don't want to keep him where he doesn't want to belong. I learned my lesson with Lincoln."

She didn't want to wake up one morning and have him gone.

Understanding flickered in Lucy's eyes. "I get it. I thought I was holding Alex back by asking him to stay, but I was asking him to share a life together. Do you want to do that with him?"

Ursula's face sank into a frown. "He's a whole prince, and I'm a witch. He's lived in castles and seen places I've only dreamed about. What can I offer him?"

Lucy extended her hands to Ursula. "You can offer him whatever you can build with these hands. A home. A life. A love. Offer it to him before you decide for him."

Ursula cocked her head to the side. "What made you so brave?"

"Love," Lucy said with a bright laugh. "Love and a strong cup of tea will make you feel like you can solve anything. Besides, I know what you really wished for."

Ursula blinked. "You looked at my paper."

"I've known you since we had matching onesies," Lucy said. She grew serious. "I came to the engagement party to remind you of that wish. You, my dear, deserve to live happily on your own terms. I have a feeling he's the wish you've been waiting for."

An ache moved down Ursula's throat. "How do you know?"

Lucy smirked. "Remember the chocolate spell we did as kids? I saw the letter X in the glass."

Ursula laughed and hugged Lucy again.

Callie poked her head out of the door. "I'm so sorry to interrupt. The gnomes are here and there's a grumpy merman asking for his soon-to-be wifey."

"I guess that's me," Lucy said. She hugged Ursula one more time and went back to the house.

Ursula stood there, thoughts turning over in her mind. How could you live happily ever after when you weren't your true self?

Chapter Twenty-Five

*F*reya Grove Beach was crowded with folks enjoying the Bonfire Celebration. It was the culminating event of the Beltane season, the last night before all visiting creatures and beings were slated to return to their home realms. A night for stolen kisses and confessions before the veil closed until midsummer. The crackling bonfire was surrounded by driftwood logs, beach chairs, and brown paper goody bags. A few people and magical beings meandered around, clutching their red plastic cups and making conversation. Quentin stood by the fire, poking it with a stick as if trying to force it to be hotter. Another person fiddled with a phone hooked up to two portable speakers.

The cool May wind whipped Ursula's hair into her face and yanked at her thin windbreaker. She shivered and pulled her hands into her sleeves. Dusk was approaching and the heat of the day was rapidly giving way to the evening chill. Xavier wrapped an arm around her and held her close. "I didn't know you like the beach."

Ursula settled into his side, letting herself soak in his closeness. "I'm learning to like it again."

She caught Quentin's eye. He raised a brow, dropped the stick, and approached them.

He greeted Ursula and Xavier with a proud matchmaking grin. "I was wondering where you were hiding. We've missed you at a few nominee events."

"I've been...busy."

Quentin glanced between them. "I see that Smitten Season's been good to you both."

"Hey, Quentin. Please meet Prince Xavier Alder."

Quentin playfully sized him up. "So, Your Highness. Will you be escorting our Sweetheart to the ball?"

Xavier pressed a hand to his chest. "If she'll have me, I'd be honored to join her."

Ursula rolled her eyes at Quentin. "I haven't asked Xavier because I don't even have a dress."

Xavier gave a mock gasp of shock. "We'll have to remedy that immediately. I'll call Whitney. She'll have you in a dress faster than you can say 'glass slipper.'"

Quentin clapped his hands. "Great. I'll deliver your tickets to the shop and buy more sandalwood." He extended a fist to Xavier who bumped it. "I love it when plans come together. We'll finalize all the details with the Berkeley Hotel, but we're confirmed for the ball."

"The ball is being held at the Berkeley?" Ursula asked. A cold sweat ran down her back. She hadn't been back to the hotel since the reception and avoided going anywhere near it.

Quentin's eyes widened in realization. "I didn't even think about it."

"I'll be fine," Ursula said. She glanced at Xavier. "I had my non-wedding reception at the Berkeley."

Awareness lit up his eyes. "I see."

"I don't have the greatest memories of that space," she admitted. She lowered her chin to her chest, hating that her past was being haunted by her future.

Xavier lifted her chin with his finger and met her eyes. "We'll make new memories."

Her knees went weak.

The person with the speaker frantically waved Quentin over to them. He let out an exhausted sigh. "Well, duty calls. If you need anything from me, please don't hesitate to ask. Xavier. Ursula. Help yourself to the treats. Get smitten."

Once they were alone, Xavier turned to Ursula. "So, Madame. Shall we make it official?"

Ursula straightened. She put on her best historical drama fancy British accent. "Will you do me the honor of escorting me to the Smitten Ball?"

Xavier kissed the back of her hand. "It would be my pleasure."

They went by the bonfire and sat on the sand, crackling of the wood filling the silence between them. It was nice not feeling the urge to make conversation.

Her eyes went to the sky and found a star twinkling on the distance. No, that was the planet Venus.

It shined so brightly that she didn't correct Xavier when he said, "Make a wish." She'd never wished on a planet before, but there was a first time for everything.

"I'd wish you tell me a story," she replied.

Xavier regarded her closely for a moment, then said, "In

a realm far, far away, the fair folk danced under the moon and the swaying trees in the night wind. In the shade of the Alder tree sat a prince who loved to watch the folk frolic. It was a time of temporary peace, and the fae were grabbing what joy they could before it was broken. He caught the eye of one fae maiden named Helia. She asked him to dance, and he eagerly agreed. It is said that she was as lovely as a winter rose, but she wasn't a princess. The prince didn't care, and he courted Helia."

"Of course," Ursula said. Love often found a way.

"He brought her nectar in lily cups, danced with her on dewy leaves, and feasted on the finest ambrosia. The prince, madly in love with Helia, proudly told his father the Old King he wanted to marry her. The Old King said it wasn't possible."

"Oh no," she said.

"Oh yes," Xavier responded with a steely edge. "His hand was promised to a princess in the East. Without this marriage, they'd would lose a vital ally and be left vulnerable. He had no choice but to let Helia go. Duty-bound and heartbroken, the prince left his first love and went to claim the princess's hand. Their union would bring a long-awaited peace. The kingdom rejoiced in such a match being made."

Her gut tightened. There was something else about this story that felt suspiciously too perfect. Xavier rubbed his hands together.

"The Faerie Queen married the fae prince to the princess and when they ascended to the throne, they took the Alder tree as their namesake. Their marriage mended relations and a peace treaty was signed. The Alder King and Queen lived happily ever after—they had three children, two sons and a daughter."

Understanding dawned. Ursula pressed her lips together to keep the gasp from escaping. Xavier looked to the fire; his voice took on a foreboding tone.

"They lived happily ever after for a while, but the King grew restless of the castle. One day he left his kingdom and searched for Helia. She'd married a marquess and had a family of her own, but she never forgot about the prince."

Ursula sensed his body tense next to her. He let out a harsh breath. All she could do was listen and lend him her support.

"They rekindled their relationship. It was discreet at first, but then letters turned to secret meetings. Meetings turned to secret homes. The Queen found out and…all she asked was for the King to be discreet. The Queen herself had been in love with another and denied her heart's desire. So, the King had his Queen and his lady."

Ursula pressed a hand to her throat. Somehow she found her voice. "How did you find out?"

"Lady Helia told me," Xavier said in a chilly voice. "I caught her and Father talking to each other in the gardens and…it didn't sound innocent." He shut his eyes and let out a rough exhale. "I asked her about it, so she told me everything. All the details—like it was a grand love. I'd just turned thirteen."

"That's so…" *Wrong. Cruel. Heartless.* Ursula settled on one word. "That was mean."

His eyes snapped open. He gave a grateful smile. "Indeed, Madame."

"How does this story end?"

His eyes grew forlorn. "I wish I knew. I should've told you a happy story, but I don't have any."

Ursula scooted close to Xavier, close enough that their legs were touching. She wrapped his arms around her waist and held him tightly. He hugged her back.

"Then, let's make a new story," she whispered. He said nothing but held her tighter.

That familiar feeling to steal him away from the world filled her chest. This time, however, she wanted to show the Realm what they'd missed in Prince Xavier.

Would Ursula be bold enough to steal this prince for herself? Only time would tell.

At least she could steal a kiss. Ursula leaned over and captured his lips with hers.

Click. She pulled back but stayed close enough that their lips brushed against each other. *Click.* "Is that your phone?"

"Hmm?" He pressed a light kiss to her lips. "I didn't hear anything."

Click. Where was that sound coming from? She stilled. It was the Caraway click. The family legend was real. This man was the one her soul had been waiting for for years. A small hope, as fragile as a seedling, took root.

She gave him one last peck on the cheek and looked to the fire.

He wrapped his arms around her and held her close.

Xavier might change his mind and stay here with her. All she had to do was give him a reason to stay.

She didn't even know if she wanted to get married or engaged anytime soon. Princes needed to do that. No one had ever heard of a prince living almost happily ever after in an apartment above a psychic shop with their witchy girl-friend. But she could almost see it—him tending to their plants on the windowsill while she called down a dinner order to Rapunzel's Pizza. She could see him kissing her good-bye before heading off to take care of business in the Grove. But then how long would it be before he missed the eternal beauty of the Realm? And what would she do when he did? When people got tired of the magic, they moved on and left her to pick up the pieces. Ursula didn't want to encourage too much hope in her heart. Hope had no place in the heart of a witch, but it was there. She was going to hold to it for now.

And for tonight, Ursula was going to take her prince home and keep his heart safe.

Chapter Twenty-Six

The first thing Xavier did when they got back to the apartment was check on the plants. He went over to Sir Duke and checked the soil. The Swiss plant wiggled its leaves in greeting. Xavier turned to the hyacinth flower. "Hello, Raspberry Beret."

It emitted the familiar scent that comforted him. It felt good to be home.

He joined Ursula in the bedroom.

"I think I got sand everywhere!" Ursula cried out. She brushed a few grains of sand from her jeans. "I'm definitely going to need a shower."

She slid out of her jeans, giving Xavier a view of her shapely butt. He came over and caressed her, giving her a teasing squeeze.

"Do you want any company?" he asked.

"Next time." She flashed him a promising grin, wiggled her fingers, and went into the bathroom. Once he heard the shower turn on, Xavier slipped off his shoes and undid his waistcoat. Her singing carried out from the shower and into the bedroom. He hummed along with her, picking up the melody. He'd bared his soul tonight. Xavier barely felt the heat from the fire, but he felt the warmth of Ursula's touch. Why in the world did he tell her? He'd never told anyone, not even Prim and Royce, about Father's arrangement with Lady Helia. But looking at Ursula and hearing about how she was willing to take a risk, he wanted to take one too.

He'd trusted her with kisses. Why not trust her with his secrets?

Ursula came out of the bathroom wearing nothing but her robe. She gave her hair a quick fluff.

"That water pressure will change your life," she cooed.

Xavier got up from the bed and joined her. Water glistened on her rosy skin. She stood in front of the full mirror that hung on her bedroom door and ran her hands over her shiny curls. The scent of fresh honeysuckle and rich pomegranate flooded the room and his nostrils.

How did she smell like nectar from the most precious flower on Earth?

He nuzzled her neck. "You smell nice."

She giggled and leaned back into his arms. "It's my leave-in conditioner."

Xavier eased the robe off her shoulders and let it fall to the floor. It pooled around her feet, leaving her bare and flushed. She looked at him in the reflection, at his half-lidded eyes, desire sparking in their depths. He trailed a finger down her cheek, down the length of her neck, and underneath her chin. Xavier lifted her face to his and kissed her deeply. She hummed a pleased tune against his mouth, making him vibrate with joy.

I love her little sounds. I love how she feels. I love her—

Shock hit him right behind his eyelids. His head swam.

He broke off the kiss, as his breathing went ragged, and he shut his eyes to gather these thoughts. He waited several heartbeats and then forced them open. It was too soon. He couldn't possibly tell her now. It was less than a month until midsummer.

Ursula stood nearer, the robe back on her body and belted. "Xav, are you okay?"

"I...I feel strange," Xavier said, his tongue thick in his mouth. "I probably had too much sugar today. I'll drink more water next time."

"No," Ursula said. She clutched the robe to her chest. "This thing feels different."

He placed his hands on her shoulders.

Her body trembled. "We should call Whitney. It might have to do with the enchantment."

Resolve steeled his nerves. If he stuck to Whitney's rule to keep his love to himself, then he'd be safe for now. He didn't want to spend this night with Ursula talking about spells, magic, and enchantments. All he wanted to do was listen to her fall asleep. All he wanted was to wake up and spend the rest of his time with her. He'd deal with it in the morning.

"I'm fine," he said. "I just need to go to sleep."

"Xavier," she warned sharply.

He loved that bossy tone of hers. Panic raced through him, and he willed himself to be strong. He fought from showing it on his face and flashed her a smile. Xavier brought her hands to his mouth and kissed them. "If I don't feel better in the morning, then we'll call her, okay?"

Ursula opened her mouth to protest, her body seeming to go into fight mode.

"Please, I just want to rest." He was shocked at how weak his voice sounded.

"Okay." Ursula pressed a kiss to his forehead. "I love you."

His heart nudged him forward. *She said it. Now you say it.* He hesitated. *Coward.* His brain hissed. Xavier didn't know what would happen once he said it out loud. Would he disappear or would she vanish when he was spirited away back to the Realm? He went to respond, but she put a finger to his lips. "Say it when you're ready. I wanted you to know."

Ursula got ready for bed, slipping into her top and pajamas. Xavier watched as she quietly tucked her hair under a purple satin cap, not meeting his eyes.

You can't live up to the fairy tale. You'll always end up disappointing whoever loves you.

He undressed, trying to find the right way to tell her how much she meant to him. Anything but love. Nothing seemed enough. If love required acts of courage, then currently he was a coward. But he didn't know what would happen after he said those three words.

Would the world fall down on his head, or would he feel unburdened?

She took his hand, love clear and pure in her eyes. "Let's go to bed."

He lay in bed awake next to her for hours. What was the bravest thing he could do right now? He leaned and whispered in her ear, gentle at first, but then he said it two more times. He gave her the only thing he could at this moment. His one true name. She whimpered softly and turned away from him. *Did she hear me?*

Xavier nestled himself against her. He'd try again in the morning.

Tomorrow was another day to be brave with Ursula.

He blinked his eyes rapidly. The early morning light filtered in underneath the curtain, blocking the sun. Gulls cawed outside and the sounds of the Grove waking greeted him. Relief flooded through him. He was still here. It was just a twinge. He felt her stir against his back, but it didn't feel like she was awake. He turned to her. His Sleeping Beauty still slumbered. She lay supine, her top sliding up, showing off a smooth line of tempting flesh. He'd love to awake her with a deft touch of his hand, but instead he kissed her brow.

After last night, he wanted to go slow. She stirred, not opening her eyes.

"Stay. I'll get breakfast," he said.

"Be safe," she said sleepily. He kissed her forehead. Xavier dressed and grabbed her keys from the kitchen table. He walked down to Night Sky, where Gwen stood behind the counter. She shot him a grin.

"Good morning, Your Excellence."

"Most people call me Xavier."

"I'm not most people. I'm goofy." Gwen winked. Xavier laughed. He enjoyed how friendly humans were to each other in the Grove.

She slid a menu over to him, but he kindly waved it off.

"I'll take two pain au chocolat, a ham and cheese croissant, a large iced coffee, and a lemon ginger iced tea."

She entered in his order and a barista went about assembling it at rapid speed.

"Somebody's worked up an appetite," Gwen said jokingly. "Long night?"

He blushed. "I don't need to have this conversation with my girlfriend's sister."

Xavier blinked. *Did I just say that out loud?* His whole face went numb.

Gwen's eyes went wide like an owl. "Does Ursula know she's your girlfriend?"

Xavier gave his head a little shake.

"Your secret's safe with me," she whispered loudly.

He quickly paid Gwen and dropped the change in the tip jar. The barista handed him his items. Ursula didn't know how he truly felt. He'd given her flowers, but he hadn't said the words yet. A sense of urgency filled him. He had to tell her what was in his heart even if it meant facing Father a little sooner than expected.

Xavier gave Gwen a thankful look. "She's waiting for me. I'll see you later."

He returned to the apartment. When he went into the bedroom, he was greeted with an empty bed and discarded robe. Xavier put the food and keys on the nightstand, then checked the time. Good. He needed a moment to get his thoughts together. Be brave. He'd tell Whitney after he told Ursula. Once she knew, then Xavier would come up with a plan to speak to Father about him remaining in the Grove. He made his choice, and he was staying with Ursula.

"Sula?" he called out.

"I'll be out soon," she yelled from the bathroom over the shower spray. "Go and eat."

If he needed to, he'd hop in the shower just to tell her how she made him feel.

He bounced on his heels.

"Just say it," he whispered. Maybe if he practiced a few times, then he wouldn't be so nervous. Rip it off like a bandage. "I love you. I love you. I love you."

The shower turned off, and there was a stunned squeak from behind the door. He waited for a long moment, but the door didn't open. He didn't hear the gulls cawing outside the window. Xavier glanced at the clock. Wait, time hadn't changed at all. Cold fright struck his heart. A frozen clock signaled that a powerful fae was nearby, and the only fae he knew who had that ability was back in the Realm...Xavier froze. Those familiar deep-set eyes like two pieces of steel glared down at him from his nearly seven-foot height. His bald head only made his bushy eyebrows stand out on his sharp, angular face. He wore his usual wardrobe of three-piece suit with lots of red accents. His wings, like a moth's, were ash gray and peeked from behind his back.

"Greetings, son," he said in a deep baritone.

Xavier bowed before his father. "My lord."

"I told Whitney I wanted to know the second you broke this...curse. Apparently, it slipped her mind. Thank goodness I charmed that necklace to keep tabs on you."

Xavier rolled his shoulders back and stood to his full height. "It's not a curse. It's an enchantment."

"Please," Father snapped. "Don't explain the difference

to me. I'm too old, wealthy, and bored to care. Gather your things."

"Wait." Xavier glanced at the bathroom door. "I have a few things to finish up."

Father's eyebrows lifted. "What things do you have to—"

He cut himself off suddenly, realizing where he was, and peered around the room with a critical scan. "Oh dear."

Xavier wanted to shield this space he'd come to love from his sight, but he couldn't move. Father noted the robe and Ursula's items laid out in the room.

He let out what sounded like a disappointed exhale. "Oh, my dear child."

Xavier clenched his fists but kept his mouth shut.

Father clicked his teeth together. "I thought you were smarter than that. I thought you'd see through Whitney's true love nonsense and figure out what was going on. It wasn't real. It was a setup."

Xavier gave his head a slow shake. *No, it couldn't be true.*

"I chose to come to the Grove," he said. "I picked this place."

"Did you?" Father said drolly. "Or did I simply remind you that I'd only let you leave if you stayed with your god-mother. I told you where you could visit, do you not recall?"

Xavier shut his mouth.

Father continued speaking, slowly, as if explaining a story to a sleepy child. "Listen, son. I knew that one of these Freya Grove locals would find it oh so romantic to help a cursed fae prince find love. Springtime is made for lovers. Freya Grove is the best place for romantic fools and idiots. Hormones and red wine would take care of the rest. All I needed was the right ingredients and anyone would fall in love with you. A little moonlight, flowers, and music and voilà, you got your perfect kiss and the enchantment was broken. I have to admit, it worked sooner than I thought. I owe your uncle a hundred coins."

Father's amused laugh assailed his ears. Xavier ground his teeth.

"You're lying," he said.

This whole experience was real. It had to be—this was the story he'd written. No one else. He chose Ursula and her kiss. Right? That doubt he'd pushed away earlier came back in full force, nearly knocking him to his knees. He was in control. He'd chosen to fall in love with Ursula, right? Or was everything from their meeting to their wonderful dalliance manipulated by outside forces? He could always ask Whitney, find out if she'd known about Father's accusations but no, he couldn't bring himself to believe that she'd deceive him in that way.

Father rolled his hand as if to hurry him along. Xavier took a step forward, then back. What would Ursula do? She'd fight. He straightened his shoulders and met his father's stare.

"I want to stay," he said.

Father's eyes grew frigid. Dangerous. "Come now, child. You've had your fun. Now it's time to return home. Besides, what do you have to offer anyone here? A prince without a castle, without riches, or without a title? Do not push me, because if you stay here, I'll strip you of everything," Father said in a tone that didn't leave room for argument.

Xavier blinked rapidly.

Father's eyes softened for a fraction. "Do you think she'll

still love you if you aren't a prince? Or worse, a penniless prince?"

It was the question he'd avoided asking all these months. How long was he going to be able to stay without her growing tired of him? How soon would she tire of the royal gentleman act? What could he offer her besides fun nights and lavish gifts?

Right at that moment, love didn't seem to be a good enough reason to stay in the Grove.

It was the stuff that only existed in fairy tales.

Father stood to his full height. "Let us depart. I grow weary of this place."

Xavier glanced around, looking for a scrap of paper, a receipt, anything to let her know what happened. Ursula's aquamarine notebook lay on her dresser. He should leave a note so she wouldn't worry about him. Xavier went for it, then stopped. What could he say to her that would be enough? If he wasn't a prince anymore, then how could he give her the happily-ever-after she wished for?

What would it say? *I don't trust myself to love you. Good-bye.* No, he couldn't be so heartless. Xavier didn't have the right words to tell her that he couldn't stay. He'd leave her a reminder of their time together. He dropped his necklace on the bed. She deserved more, but it was all that he had to give her. Xavier had no use for it at home. Father snapped his fingers, and they disappeared in an instant.

June

THIS MONTH'S BIRTHSTONE: ALEXANDRITE

Alexandrite is worn to invite good luck and increase wisdom to the wearer.

Chapter Twenty-Seven

Ursula let the crystal dangle over the foldout map on the Caraway kitchen table. She hadn't scryed for a lost item in a while, but she figured she'd give it a shot. Her heart put out a call. *Where can I find my fae?* Sirena, who stood by the cutting board making lunch, made a sympathetic sound.

"I don't think he's on the East Coast anymore, Sula," she said. "He's not even in this world."

Ursula let the crystal ease over the map. It kept landing on Grove Park. She swung it again, but it landed on Grove Park once more. It was probably useless to scry for a fae who wasn't lost, but she had to do something.

"This crystal is broken," Ursula said, letting a little whine bleed into her voice.

Sirena glared at the map. "No, you need to take a break. Get something to eat."

Ursula put the crystal down with a loud thud. The table rattled. "He didn't leave a note!"

Sirena grunted. "Not this again. Not everyone leaves handwritten notes like a Masterpiece Theatre drama."

Ursula exhaled deeply. "No, they don't." But Xavier did leave her notes or texted her. Always.

With every passing day, the truth was becoming clear. Xavier wasn't coming back. Or maybe he didn't want to come back. That truth didn't sit well with her.

How could everything change in an instant? One moment she'd been in the shower flirting with Xavier through the door, and the next, time seemed to freeze and she didn't hear him outside. She came out of the bathroom dripping wet only to find the food on the table and their items exactly where they left them. Once she spied his necklace on the bed, her brain went into overdrive.

Her Caraway family had gathered around Ursula when news of Xavier's sudden departure spread through the town. Mama gave her afternoons off from the psychic shop. Lucy sent over soothing tea blends to calm her nerves. Sirena cooked meals whenever Ursula came over for dinner, which was every other day. She took sanctuary in the family garden among the honeysuckle and roses. It was nice to be around family again.

"Sula." Sirena placed the turkey sandwich and kettle chips in front of Ursula.

"Thanks." She didn't move to eat it, but instead reached up and stroked his necklace. "He always left a note, but this time he didn't. Something's wrong." Ursula shook her head.

"It's been almost two weeks," Sirena said lightly. "Whitney promised she'd tell you if she heard anything else. Lucy's reading the tea leaves. Callie's calling in every favor around town. Everyone's doing what they can, so you've got to take care of yourself."

Sirena slid the plate closer to her.

Ursula stared at the sandwich. Her stomach grumbled, and

she took a few bites. Sirena poured her a cup of sweet tea and placed it on the table. Before she knew it, she'd eaten half the sandwich and most of the chips. Ursula gulped down the tea easily. Her stress melted away and she felt much better now that it felt like her body and soul were fed. Bless Sirena's hands, because every meal she made was filled with love and compassion.

"Let's talk about something fun," Sirena said. "Have you gotten your gown yet? The ball's next week."

Ursula sighed. "I haven't found anything special. I've been distracted."

She pressed her hands against her eyes. When she slept, she dreamed of Xavier, dressed in his regal finery in the middle of the crystal-green ballroom, so she didn't. She'd stayed up so late last night that it hurt just to blink. When she was awake, she kept thinking about what went wrong with Xavier.

She hadn't felt this way even when Lincoln left her at the altar. Back then, she hadn't invested her whole self into their relationship. Now with Xavier she'd given in to the fairy tale and she'd fallen head over butt for him. Her heart felt as if it were dangling off a cliff's edge, waiting to drop and break into a thousand pieces. Her mind went over their last night together in painstaking detail. The kiss. Him suddenly falling ill. They fell asleep holding each other. He'd whispered something in her ear—but she couldn't quite remember it. Was it a location? A place? No . . . it was something else.

A name. His true name. If only she could write it down.

Ursula opened her eyes. "Do you have something I can write on?"

Sirena went to the kitchen junk drawer and searched

through it. "Lucy always has an extra notebook floating around here."

Sirena rummaged through a few cabinets, until she found a spiral-bound notebook and pencil, then handed it to Ursula. She opened it to a fresh page, then scribbled down all the possible names he could have whispered. Was it Islefair? Thistleglen? Could it be Hazelspark?

With each line she filled, her heart tottered away from the edge of despair. Two full pages later she hadn't figured out his name. Ursula rolled the crystal against her palm. A silent plea repeated in her mind. *Clear my way so I can see the path behind me and before me.* She willed it. She wasn't scared to see what the crystal held, but she wanted to see a way forward.

Suddenly, a swirl of purple and gray smoke filled the crystal. The smoke thickened and sparked as if a small fire grew before her eyes. The fire burst and then extinguished. A fire without air. His name struck her like a thunderbolt.

She wrote it down and circled it. *Say it. Say it and he'll come to you. The magic will compel him to come back.* Ursula hesitated. Did he want to come back? Even now, she wondered what kept him from reaching out to her. Maybe she overwhelmed him with her sudden declaration of love. But when she was standing there, seeing the clear distress in Xavier's eyes, the words slipped easily from her. It was her love to give him.

Her phone buzzed with notification. She checked it and her jaw dropped. It was an email from Lincoln. They saw each other in passing around the Grove but hadn't spoken since his birthday party. Ursula read it carefully.

The subject line was Job Posting—Special Assistant to the Mayor—Freya Grove.

Interested, she opened the email and saw a one-line message above the hyperlink.

I think this job is perfect for you. I still owe you a spa day.

She clicked on the link and read over the job description and qualifications. Ursula let out a quiet laugh of excitement as she went over the bullet points. This job was everything that she could wish for. She bookmarked the website so she could apply for the position later.

Ursula opened her note app and looked at the Boss Witch List.

One by one, she mentally addressed each numbered point. She had no need for wishes when the one person she wanted and loved had willfully left without an explanation. No wishing could bring Xavier back to the Grove if he made the choice to leave. As for the magic, she'd grow back into the craft with time, but she relished rediscovering crystals and flowers. She'd forgotten how much she learned, kneeling in the fresh dirt by Nana's side. The other evening when she couldn't sleep, she wrote down everything she remembered about herbs and flowers Nana had told her. The last numbered point gave her pause. All the things she thought needed fixing—her job, her career, her social status—were fine. She wasn't any richer or more successful since she made the list, but this morning after she got out of the shower, she'd stopped and looked at her reflection in the mirror and smiled. Pride had bloomed inside her chest the longer she stared.

To Ursula, there was nothing in the mirror that needed fixing.

But she missed the fae man who saw her as she was and cherished her.

Xavier paced around the castle, trying and failing to find a space to hide from everyone. He kept being found and followed by a nosy lord or lady who wanted to discuss his trip. No, thank you. The memories of Freya Grove belonged to him and no one else. All he wanted was a quiet second alone. Was that so much to ask?

Since Father had spirited him back home two weeks ago, Xavier had been the flavor of the month. The realm was still buzzing with news of the returned prince from the human world. Before the enchantment, Xavier was invisible to the court. He was the spare, not the heir to the Alder throne, and that was okay by him. He had distractions—his gardens, his personal hobbies, and his mediation job—to keep him from truly feeling the gaping loneliness.

But now that he'd felt the welcoming and warm community of Freya Grove, he noticed how emotionless the Faerie Realm could be. Here, gossip wasn't harmless chatter, but a weapon used to cut down an ally or an enemy. Love was a liability, not a gift. No wonder Whitney left this glittering but sharp world that could leave a fae dazzled, yet dismayed.

Mother and Father held a lavish dance in his honor in the ballroom, but he'd been too distracted to enjoy it.

Lack of sleep and a broken heart were weighing on him.

Lords and ladies gave him lingering looks that made him feel like a rare plant on display. Servants rushed from rooms like birds being chased away by a running child whenever he entered in their space. Maybe there was a special guest coming to the house, but then again there were always comings and goings. He'd spent most of his formative years hiding out in the greenhouse or library, but currently there seemed to be fae lurking in all corners of the castle. Eligible ladies from all over the Realm were invited over to the estate for drinks in the salon to see the spare in his natural setting. He'd already received three invitations to dinner from a handful of local royals eager to reacquaint themselves with the Tin Prince. Prim and Royce celebrated his return, but Xavier couldn't muster up a smile for them.

Over dinner, Father rambled on about his hopes for getting Xavier married off within a year. Mother slid a concerned look over at Xavier. Prim and Royce traded glances. Xavier gritted his teeth. There was no use in fighting; he was going to go along to get along.

He was home, back where he belonged in the court with the fae.

Misery was his constant companion.

That evening, Father called an impromptu after-dinner meeting in the salon. It was probably another princess or lady who wanted to talk about his romantic escape into the human world. Xavier arrived first in the rose and turquoise room. His gut twisted as he stared at the fresh turquoise color that had escaped his attention all the previous times before. A witch he knew once wore turquoise like an empress. That color only added to his unsettled mood.

Someone had turned on the fireplace in advance of their arrival. The fire crackled, and Xavier remembered Ursula aglow by the bonfire, her lovely hands covered in sand. It was the same dream he had of her, by the fire at the beach. Waves crashed in the near distance as the stars twinkled in the sky above her. No more.

He banished that fantasy from his mind. His sudden departure from Freya Grove left Xavier with a yawning feeling of emptiness that had only grown now that he was back in the Realm. He hadn't even reached out to Whitney, too scared to learn how much he hurt Ursula. He couldn't tell the love of his life that it all might have been a complete and utter illusion. Father had created the perfect conditions to aid him in finding his perfect kiss, and Xavier accidentally fell in love. He'd literally vanished on Ursula without a word. He acted without honor, and for that he couldn't bring himself to write down a single word. She was free to forget him now. To move on. To find someone worthy of her love and trust. The salon door opened, and another guest arrived.

It was the second to last fae royal he wanted to see.

"The prince returns," the Faerie Queen said in an unreadable tone.

Xavier looked over to the door. Father would be here soon. Maybe Mother would join them. Prim was too busy to attend, but Xavier even hoped Royce might join them. As if sensing his uneasiness, the Faerie Queen left the door open a crack.

"I asked your father if I could see you privately, away from everyone else."

Xavier bowed in greeting. He straightened and faced her. Looking into those eyes, he felt a little angry and bit bold. "You haven't come to enchant me again."

The Queen barked out a laugh. She waved her hand. "No, I've come to arrange a tea."

No thanks to you. He bit his tongue. He didn't want to be rude, but he was tired. Tired of missing the Grove. Of missing Whitney and her unwavering support. But most of all he was tired of missing Ursula. It was better if he got this meeting over with Her Majesty so he could be left alone with his misery.

"We can have our tea now," Xavier said. "I'll call the kitchen to make arrangements."

The Queen shook her head. "No, I insist you come to my castle. We'll have a private tea and conversation. I want to know all about your visit."

Xavier smiled bitterly. "I was only gone for a short time. Nothing much happened."

The lie slipped from his mouth easily. It hurt too much to remember.

The Queen just stared at him. Xavier didn't look away. And this time he noticed rather than only ice, there was an undercurrent of heartache. Pain. Loss. He took in a sharp breath once he recognized that emotion. She knew how he felt.

"I never like to rush a good cup of tea," the Queen murmured. "You'll visit me tomorrow afternoon."

He was too tired to refuse her order. He bowed again. "I'll be there."

The Queen nodded, pleased with his response. "I figured you'd want to be alone, so I told them to not disturb us for the rest of the night. You have the room. I'll leave you to your thoughts."

He bowed. She wished him a good night, then departed, leaving him alone. Xavier studied the flame flickering in the fireplace. His future was being written without his permission. He'd once thought it was a relief not to have that responsibility, but now he mourned the life he could have created with Ursula. It was time he told her what was happening and how he couldn't return to the Grove. The Tin Prince had finally found his heart, but it was back thriving in the Grove. If he was going to learn how to readapt to this Realm, he had to let his heart go and truly reclaim his mocking title.

Chapter Twenty-Eight

What did one wear to afternoon tea with a Faery Godmother?

Ursula decided on a business-casual outfit, a cute moon-and-stars-covered blouse with a pencil skirt and heels. She was trying to give off a head-witch-in-charge vibe. She needed to show Whitney that she was meeting not only to catch up over a cup of tea, but to also get answers about a certain fae prince. Enough was enough. It wasn't until Ursula was asked out on a date by a strikingly handsome man that she considered her relationship with Xavier. Their status was more than complicated, and she assumed they'd have that "exclusive or not" conversation later, but later never arrived. Where did she stand with him? She didn't want to move on, but she wanted answers from Xavier.

It was getting busy around Freya Grove with the ball quickly approaching and Ursula working full-time at the psychic shop. She put in her application for the special assistant job and less than forty-eight hours later she had a scheduled interview with human resources and Mayor Walker. Even if she didn't get the job, she was making a step toward building the life she wished for.

So, when Whitney called Ursula over for tea, she made a point to block out the rest of her afternoon. She drove over to the mansion immediately after the city hall meeting and parked in the driveway. Ursula was welcomed into the home by a stately doorman, who showed her to the reception room. She clutched her notebook to her chest as she stood waiting. Whitney appeared in a cloud of Red Door perfume, dressed to thrill in a cute business pantsuit that showed off her lithe shape.

"Welcome, my darling." Whitney leaned in and gave Ursula a big hug. Her wings lightly brushed her face. "You're early!"

"I figured I'd rather be early than late," Ursula mused.

"I like that about you," Whitney said, stepping back from their hug. "How are you doing this afternoon?"

Her lip shook. Ursula didn't have it in her to pretend to be okay. "I've been better."

Whitney pressed a hand to her chest in a sign of understanding. Ursula might have missed her lover, but Whitney was missing her closest family.

She clapped her hands together. "Are you ready for the ball?"

Ursula shook her head. "I have the shoes, but I don't have the gown. I don't know if... I want to go."

Whitney pressed a hand to her throat. Her eyes widened. "Child, give yourself permission to have some fun. Come along. Let's have some tea and handle our business."

Whitney showed Ursula into the garden room. There were flowers on everything from walls to the carved roses on the chair backs, to the delicate bluebell design on the teacups.

They sat down at the table; Ursula placed the notebook within reach.

"He told me you liked flowers."

Ursula looked to the roses. Her body hummed. "I do."

Whitney pulled her wand out of her sleeve. She tapped it in the air and a teapot appeared, filled with hot steaming tea. Ursula noticed there was an envelope tucked between the teacups.

Whitney slid the letter over to Ursula. "It arrived yesterday."

Her name was written on the front in his elegant script. She snatched up the letter and opened it, half expecting him to jump out. Xavier told her fae were crafty. Instead, his ball ticket fluttered to the table. Her heart dropped at the sight of it. They had planned to go together.

He's not coming back.

She read the first line. *My dearest Madame Caraway,*

The body of the letter was formal. Polite. Cold. He even had the nerve to thank her for their lovely time together but that he regretfully did not see himself returning to the Grove. It was as if another person wrote the letter, and Ursula almost believed it, but then she got to the last paragraph.

Now, I know that there are no walls or rules that can hold your fearless spirit and elemental magic. You could easily adapt to my world, but I could not dare step into yours. I'll always remember the story you spun for me and how much I yearned for it to be true. It was my pleasure to be with you for the brief time we had. Do not waste your time or wishes on me.

She placed the letter on the table, letting out a shaky breath. "Did you read it?"

Whitney sighed heavily. "I don't need to. I changed his diapers. I know my beloved godson. He's chivalrous to the point of misery. The prince would deny himself any joy if it made you happy or if he thought that it wasn't meant for him."

Ursula wrinkled her brow. "What do you mean?"

"I shouldn't say anything, but I can't get banished twice."

Her chest tightened at this news. "You're banished from the Realm?"

"From the Alder Court," Whitney said. "I got into a huge fight with Xavier's father a while back. I told him my god-son's soul mate lived in the human world. He flew into a rage, told me to not come back and never tell Xavier. Well, fate stepped in, and he ended up in the Grove.

"Just like Cinderella knew her prince and Beast knew his Beauty, I knew that you were destined to meet. I needed to step back and let love find a way."

"But he's still not coming back," Ursula said. She needed to know why.

Whitney frowned. "His father probably threatened to strip him of everything, including his title and his wealth."

Ursula seethed. She hated to think that the King would be so cruel to his son, but it wouldn't surprise her.

"He has to be brave and walk away," Whitney said softly. "I don't think he knows how to return yet. That's a door only he can walk through; you can't make him. No one can."

Determination flared through her. *I could. I can. I'm a*

Caraway witch. Ursula tapped the notebook. "He gave me a way to make him."

Whitney pressed a trembling hand to her mouth. Ursula still felt his lips against her ear whispering to her in the dark. His true name. He'd given her the one thing that solely belonged to him, that no other soul possessed. He'd given it to her to keep it safe.

"It's lovely. It suits him," Ursula said.

The name that would snatch Xavier from the Faerie Realm and bring him here by her side in an instant. All she had to do was say it. Whisper it. Scream it. He'd granted her the ability. It was within her power to do so.

She slid the notebook over to Whitney. "Keep it safe. I'm not using it."

Whitney touched the cover. Her eyes bored into Ursula. "Tell me why."

Ursula stared down at her teacup. *I've tried for too long to bend fate to my will. I've tried to bend people. I love him enough that I won't do that. If he wants us, then he'll decide on his own.* Whitney watched her expectantly, waiting for an answer. Ursula decided on the best and most diplomatic one she had.

"I can make sure the door's unlocked for him, but that's it."

Whitney nodded. "A wise witch once told me some people are in our lives for a season, a reason, or lifetime. You must decide which one he is."

"He's my lifetime," Ursula said. "I told him I love him, before—he returned." Ursula let out a breath. "He's rooted in me deep. I can't—I won't—shake him easily."

Whitney took Ursula's hands in hers and squeezed. "Then you're blessed to have given him the gift of your love. Too many times we wait too long to tell people we love them."

He knows I love him, but what was he going to do with it?

"I have a plan," Ursula said slowly. She ran her tongue over her lips in thought. What if she went to the ball and waited for the prince? What if she made her own happy ending instead of wishing for it? Cinderella wasn't guaranteed a happy ending, but she still went to the ball.

Whitney let out an excited yelp. "Is it a heist? I've always wanted to do an *Ocean's Eleven* type of heist, but I don't know what I'd steal."

Ursula giggled. She was going to like hanging out with Whitney. "Maybe next time, but I'm going to need three favors from you."

Whitney gave a curt nod of agreement. "Talk to me."

Ursula held up three fingers. She counted off her favors. "One, I need you to deliver a letter back to Xavier today."

"Done. Write it in my study now. I'll get it to him."

"Two, do you know anyone who can make me a quick flower crown?"

"I do. What's the last favor?"

"I'm going to need a dress. Do you know any good stores?"

Whitney took Ursula by the hand and pulled her out of the tearoom. "Let's get my purse and my feather wand. We're going to the outlet mall."

My Dearest Xavier,

I hope this letter finds you in good health. Whitney gave me your letter. For someone who claims to be a tin prince and says he doesn't have a heart, you've got so much love to give away. Stories can change. Witches borrow wings and frolic with the fae. Princes can live happily ever after without their castle and crowns. All you have to do is decide which story you want to tell and then make it a reality.

I've enclosed your ticket to the ball. I'll be there with flowers in my hair.

If you don't show, then I'll have my answer and I'll leave you to your realm.

Always,
Ursula

He'd read her letter a dozen times. He'd studied every *i* and every *t*, trying to figure out if there was something he was missing between the lines. She was letting him choose his path. She had his name, but she was letting him decide. He held the ball ticket in his hand.

"You've got mail, Prince Xavier?"

The Faerie Queen poured them each a cup of tea and set them up with snacks in the salon. She didn't rush, making sure to fill the teacup all the way to the top, humming to herself. Xavier held back a troubled sigh. Midsummer was in less than seventy-two hours. Royals openly discussed their plans to go to the Grove and have a passionate fling. He'd locked himself in his study until it was time for him to have tea with the Faerie Queen.

"I do love a good tea in the afternoon." She handed Xavier his cup, then made herself comfortable on the plush seat with her own drink. "Shall we start?" The Queen glanced at him. "Tell me who's got you sighing so sadly like that."

The teacup rattled in his hands as he placed it on his lap. He had a serious case of butter hands; everything seemed to be so slippery. He focused on trying not to break this cup into a dozen pieces.

"She's just a friend," he said.

The Queen gave him a side-eye. "Oh, she must be a very special friend if you won't say her name."

Indeed, she was special. He downed his tea in one gulp, trying not to think of the letter burning in his pocket. The brew filled him with a warmth he needed after the coldness of the day.

"Would you like another cup?" she offered.

"I'm afraid tea won't help my situation."

"I think your situation would change if you went home," the Queen said.

"I *am* home," he said a little more sharply than he intended. He'd come back. He'd kept his promise.

Her eyes brimmed with tenderness. "Are you certain about that? This place is where you started, but is it where you want to end up?"

"I can't stay," Xavier said. For the second time in a month, his heart broke. He placed the teacup on the table with a clatter. He yearned for Ursula, body and soul. He missed his new home.

The Queen took his hand and squeezed. "You think I enchanted you for fun?"

Bile rose in his throat, making his neck hot. "I don't know."

Her wings fluttered. "It was to rescue that heart of yours."

Xavier blinked. His brain tried to make sense of what he was being told.

"Your mother wrote me. She told me about her beautiful son who buried his heart in the center of Earth to keep it safe. I was begged to help you experience the love that she missed out on. I gave you a friendly, enchanted shove in the right direction."

Shock wedged in his throat. *Mother* asked the Faerie Queen for help.

His face creased. "But Father said he tricked me into going to Freya Grove. He said all I needed was the right ingredients and anyone would fall in love with me."

The Queen waved a dismissive hand. "Poppycock! You can have the right ingredients and make a mess. I can toss a tomato, vegetable stock, and spinach into a pot and it doesn't magically create a soup. It's the love and care you put into those ingredients that turn them into a meal, into something that will feed your soul."

He bowed his head. The Queen had a point. Father couldn't have known how he'd respond to being in Freya Grove. He had no way of controlling how he'd react to Ursula and to her magic. Father said whatever he needed to say to get

Xavier to return to the Realm with him. He pressed his fingers to his head and growled. Father played him like a fiddle, and he danced right into his trap.

He had to know what went wrong with Mother and Father. Was he destined to fall short of a storybook ending?

He met the Queen's eyes.

"What about my parents?" he pleaded. "Their happily-ever-after went wrong."

Her expression turned sad, but thoughtful. "My son, they were barely twenty when they stood before me to say their vows. Hardly old enough to know how their hearts might change. Their union might not have been a love match, but they love you. They loved their people, and they loved their kingdom, enough to give up their own desires and wed."

Xavier absorbed her words. His parents may have been denied their happy ending due to circumstances, but he didn't have to give up his. He still had the freedom to choose his ending, but the cost seemed too high. How could he give Ursula a happily-ever-after if he didn't have his crown?

Xavier cleared his throat. "So, my Queen, what happens now?"

She clucked her tongue. "That depends on you. I just invited you over for tea."

The Queen snapped her free hand and a piece of paper appeared between her fingers. She read it out loud to him. "'All I want is to live happily ever after.' Does this wish sound familiar?"

He took the paper from her with a shaky hand. His fingers traced the simple request. His chest felt as if it were being rubbed raw. He knew her sweet handwriting from watching her scribble and jot down notes. It was Ursula's wish.

"I thought you'd be the one to make this special request come true," she said.

His fingers went over the last three words. But Father's words, cold and harsh, summoned the old doubts. What if all he could offer her was a penniless prince at her doorstep?

"She loves a prince, so what if I can't be a prince anymore?" he said in a small voice.

A devilish look came into her eyes. "Well, if anyone threatens to take away your royal title, I'll just bestow you with another." The Queen tapped her chin. "I'll knight you. Sir Xavier Henrie George Alder. I like the way that sounds. It has a nice ring to it."

"I can't promise her a happily-ever-after," Xavier admitted. "I'm a second son, a spare. A fae who can't even fly. Father will take away my title and . . . she deserves more. She deserves better."

"Hush," the Queen said. She placed a light hand on his shoulder. "Tell me what's better than love? You're more than just your title."

It came to him with blinding clarity. There was nothing more than love. He once thought it wasn't enough to stay in the Grove, that it wouldn't be enough to bind him to that world. But now, love was bringing him back to Freya Grove and making him strong enough to walk away from this gilded realm. He loved the Grove, the citizens who embraced him as their own and his beloved godmother.

Most of all, Xavier loved Ursula. She was giving him a

choice, and he was choosing her. Forever. For always. He wasn't compelled to break an enchantment. Attend the ball or remain in the Realm. Love her or leave her alone.

If you can't promise her a title, promise her what you can.

His mind went wild with possibilities. A smile played on his lips. He'd care for their plants. They'd talk over breakfast, meet for lunch, and make love at midnight. He'd brush away her tears and give her reasons to dance and laugh. Promise the breath in his body. Promise all his kisses. Promise her everlasting love. He'd show up at her door with flowers in his hand. Hope lifted his heart; he had done all those things already, but she didn't know he meant to do them forever. He hadn't even told Ursula that he loved her. It wasn't too late for him to show her and tell her how much he completely, wholeheartedly cherished her.

"I have to go back to the castle." There was so much that he needed to get done within the next twenty-four hours. He needed to talk to Prim and Royce. He needed to talk to Mother and Father. He needed to pack a bag, immediately. Hopefully, he could make it through the glass door and be back in the Grove before midnight.

The Queen smirked at him. "You can borrow my carriage."

Chapter Twenty-Nine

☾

Caraways stuck together, and they loved any reason to stay in a hotel room.

Once Whitney, with Mama's assistance, helped Ursula find her gown, it only made sense to rent a room in the Berkeley Hotel, where the Smitten Ball was taking place. Quentin managed to get Ursula a luxurious suite on the seventh floor at the last minute. She owed him a big bear hug and a jumbo-sized bottle of sandalwood oil.

Sirena and Lucy insisted on staying with Ursula and aiding what was being dubbed Operation HEA or Bust. Sirena had packed them a feast in their portable cooler, and they'd been, in her own words, "princess pregaming with Ursula" for the last two hours. Lucy had styled her hair into a braided updo and helped adjust the white peony and daisy crown. Sirena kept feeding her cheese and crackers with seltzer water, so she didn't pass out from hunger. Ursula managed to do her makeup and captured the ethereal mood with her lipstick and her eyeshadow. Gwen texted her messages of love and encouragement.

Ursula fiddled with her flower crown, deciding whether to scream or cry. She jiggled her knee attempting to shake the nerves out and fight the urge to run back to her car.

Lucy, wearing a loose sunflower dress, showed no signs of nerves. She looked Ursula over with a wide smile. "I'm loving the whole faerie witch princess vibe. It's very romantic."

Ursula glanced down at the outfit. Her stomach clenched. "Is it too much?"

Sirena made a face. "You're meeting a fae prince at a ball to declare your love for him. It's just enough."

Ursula grumbled quietly. Did she have to pick the most bridal-looking outfit?

When she walked out of the dressing room at Betty's Boutique, Whitney and Mama had clapped and cooed over her. And when she looked in the store's mirror, she'd felt everything—the excitement, the joy, the love—she wished she had felt on her canceled wedding day. The empire-waist cream gown with woven crystals and ribbon made her feel as if she was going to dance the night away with a prince. Her prince.

She hoped that he joined her tonight.

Ursula opened her phone, scrolled back to Diane's old text, and read it. *The course of true love never did run smooth.*

She laughed to herself. True love waited for her at the end of this rough road, but she was ready to receive Xavier. Her heart was eager to hold him close.

"What time is it?" Ursula focused on the digital clock on the nightstand. Her stomach clenched again. Did time decide to take an energy drink? Because it was racing by too fast.

"Don't focus on that. Worry about your crown being crooked." Lucy straightened her crown. She gave her a hopeful grin. "Lovely."

Ursula looked to her other cousin. "Sirena? Can I have the time?"

Sirena held up her phone and the time appeared on the screen. It was almost time to head down to the ballroom.

"This is just like *Ever After* with Drew Barrymore waiting for her prince to arrive," Sirena said with a wistful, almost romantic sigh.

Ursula frowned. "Wasn't he late?"

"The hero still showed up," Lucy said. "He also kissed her."

"Listen, Drew got her prince. You'll get yours," Sirena said. She touched her long-chained pendant, twirling it between her fingers. Ursula narrowed her eyes. Sirena, a stickler for not wearing dangling jewelry in the kitchen, didn't do necklaces. She'd ask about it later when she wasn't feeling like a jitterbug.

Ursula needed her eternally optimistic cousin to throw some confetti on her or give her a Boss Lady pep talk. "Where's Callie?"

Sirena mumbled something under her breath about down payments and roommates.

Lucy turned to Ursula. "She's apartment hunting. Her commute's too much, so she's moving to Meadowdale for the next year."

Ursula slid a look over to Lucy. "And you're moving out with Alex."

Lucy smiled but didn't say anything.

"The cheese stands alone," Sirena said. Her eyes were filled with a deep longing.

She thrust a half-filled plastic cup into Ursula's hand.

Ursula was hit with a cloying tropical scent and winced. "What's that?"

"It's for courage," Sirena said with a wink.

"No, she's not meeting her Prince Charming smelling like a drunk coconut." Lucy took the cup from Ursula and drank it in one gulp. She hissed and patted her chest. "Ugh, sis. You always had a heavy pour." Lucy cleared her throat. She glanced over to the clock and nodded. "It's time. If you're on time, that means you're late."

Nerves got the best of Ursula. Words tumbled out of her mouth. "What if he doesn't—"

Lucy held up a hand. "No. We're not inviting that negativity right now."

"But I have to consider it." Ursula played with the ribbon dangling from her dress sleeve. *What if he doesn't show up?*

Lucy held her by the shoulders and met her eyes. "If he's foolish enough to pass up on a boss witch like you, then we're going to take you home, feed you cookie dough ice cream, and tell you how much we love you."

Ursula blinked back her tears. Those words were exactly what she needed to hear. She was ready to go to the ball.

"It's time." Ursula picked up her clutch. "Let's do it."

Sirena gave Ursula a fist bump. "You got this, cuz. We're here for you."

Ursula gave them a thumbs-up and sashayed out of the room. She'd have to walk the next part of this path alone. Her expectant heart knocked against her ribs as she went down the hallway and boarded the elevator. As it descended to the first floor, her stomach rose into her throat, and she worked her bottom lip with her teeth. The elevator dinged, the doors opened, and she exited and made her way to the ballroom. All her wishes had led her to this moment, crowned in flowers and filled with hope. She didn't know what was happening next and couldn't see the proverbial forest for the trees.

The sight before her left her breathless. This was a vision of midsummer. The huge ballroom was decorated with gauzy lights and flower garlands that hung from faux tall trees. Glass pots of wild thyme, violet, and sweet musk roses with tall candles made up the table centerpieces. A chamber quartet played a classical take on a popular song while guests danced on the floor. The laughter and chatter pulled her into the room.

Every doubt told her to stop, to flee, but her heart repeated one clear command: *Claim your wish.* A witch didn't fear the forest; she made the woods into her home and thrived. Ursula scanned the ballroom floor, trying to spot that one familiar face she yearned to see.

"My enchantress," his voice said behind her.

Ursula pivoted and faced him. Xavier stood a few feet away in a midnight-black tuxedo, holding a bouquet of luscious dark red roses. Her heart leapt. Dark red roses symbolized love and complete devotion. She stilled, afraid if she moved that he'd dissolve away. He closed the gap between them, his gaze focused solely on Ursula. The ballroom around them faded away.

"My prince," she whispered.

"I didn't want to be late," he said. "I'm not too late, am I?"

"No," she choked out. "You're never too late."

Ursula flew into his arms, almost knocking the flowers onto the ground. He held her tightly. His familiar wildflower scent comforted her. *He's here and he's real.* She pressed kisses all over his lips, eyes, cheeks, and chin. He laughed and held her so close that she thought their souls would fuse together into one beautiful thing. Xavier leaned back and studied her with love in his eyes.

"My dear Madame," he said. "I've missed you."

She melted against his chest. "I missed you too. So much. How long can I keep you?"

Ursula didn't want to waste any time, so she got straight to the point. Midsummer would be over soon, and they had so many plans to make. They needed to figure out how they were going to make this very long-distance relationship work. Hopefully there was a realm-friendly data plan that she could sign up for. She pressed her lips together, waiting for him to respond. No matter what, they'd make it work out.

His face grew solemn, and he tensed. "Well, how long will you have me?"

A joyous laugh parted her lips. Excitement warmed her from top to bottom. "I'll have you every day if you grant me that honor."

His shoulder sagged in relief. He let out a breath and smiled. "I can't promise you that everything's going to be a fairy tale, but I'm going to work to give you magic in our lives."

"Does that mean—" Ursula wrapped her hands around his middle. Her mouth dried up. "You're moving to the Grove. You're here for good. What about…everything?" *Your castle. Your family. Your life.*

"We're still working on the details, but I'm here for good. I'm staying with Whitney until I can afford my own place,"

Xavier said. "I don't have any leads on a job, but I'm sure someone will be interested in hiring a former fae royal."

Regret lapped at her skin. "I...I didn't want that to happen."

Hurt shadowed his handsome features. "Father will come around eventually, but I'm not rewriting our story for anyone else." There was a note of finality in his voice. "I walked away from you once. I'm not doing it again."

"But it's your title." Her chest ached for everything he was forfeiting at this moment.

"What was the point of having a crown if I couldn't lift my head?" Xavier said. "I'm done with just existing. I want to live. I love you."

It was too much, but it was just enough.

Ursula responded with a watery laugh. "I love you too."

They embraced underneath the makeshift midsummer twilight sky of the ballroom. Xavier presented her with the roses and escorted her to their table. They enjoyed their evening, danced all night, and celebrated when Ursula won second runner-up at the Sweetheart awards.

They went back to her apartment, popped kettle corn, and settled on the couch still dressed in their finery.

"Tell me a story," Ursula said.

Xavier hummed to himself for a moment. "Once upon a time, there was a witch who loved iced tea and plants. She was gorgeous and had the biggest heart, but it had been a bit bruised. This witch was on a quest to find a wish, and nothing was going to get in her way."

Ursula said, "So far, so good."

Xavier twirled her dress ribbons around his fingers. He

waggled his brows. "You look like a present I'm going to love unwrapping."

"Keep going with the story," Ursula encouraged. "I'll unwrap myself."

"Good idea." Xavier nodded. "One day she met an enchanted fae prince who had an awful sense of direction. He couldn't find his way home. He was under a spell that kept him from seeing beyond his own nose. She agreed to help this prince if he joined her on her quest. The two of them went on many travels."

Ursula pulled at a ribbon, loosening her sleeve from her shoulder.

"What type of travels?" she asked. "Please tell me there's room service in your story."

Xavier pressed a kiss to her now bare skin. "No, but we faced our fears, dined by a roaring fire, and made love under the honeysuckle flowers."

She blushed. "I've never done that."

"I guess that's just my imagination," he said with a saucy smile. He tucked her close to his side. Xavier's voice took on a grateful, more humble tone.

"Over time, the prince noticed how amazing the witch was. Even if she didn't need him, he wanted to be by her side. When they finally reached his castle, the prince was happy for a moment, but he realized that he didn't belong there anymore. He'd grown into the person he was meant to be. He wanted to be with his beloved witch. He wanted to make all their wishes come true together."

"What a brave prince," Ursula said.

"What a lovely witch." Xavier reached up and stroked her

cheek. His touch made her soul sing. "The witch kissed the prince and rescued him. They rode off into the sunset and loved each other for all their days. And they lived happily ever after."

Ursula took his face into her hands. "Happily ever after sounds like a great place to start."

She kissed Xavier until she felt light-headed with joy. She leaned back and saw the future in his eyes. The leap had only been a preview of the life they'd share together. There was going to be veggie pizza. Plenty of crystals. Popcorn-filled movie nights that ended with long bouts of lovemaking. Growing big plants and snaking herbs in the windowsill and in a garden. Possibly marriage and growing a family. Gray hairs and wrinkles. But they were always together making all their wishes come true.

"Make a wish, Xavier," she said.

"I did." He leaned in and pressed his nose to her forehead. "You're already here."

About the Author

A native of New Jersey, **Celestine Martin** writes whimsical romance that celebrates the beauty of everyday magic. She's inspired to write happily-ever-afters and happy-for-now endings starring the people and places close to her heart. When she's not drinking herbal tea and researching her next project, Celestine, with her husband, spoils their daughter in New York on a daily basis.

You can learn more at:

Website: CelestineMartin.com
Twitter @JellybeanRae
Instagram @CelestineMartinAuthor